UNDER *the* MIDNIGHT *Sky*

ANNA ROMER

UNDER THE MIDNIGHT SKY

PLEASE NOTE: This is the revised, shorter Second Edition, and is different in places from the original First Edition and Bolinda audiobook versions.

ISBN: 9781923019126 (paperback)
ISBN: 9781923019003 (ebook)

Second Edition: April 2023
First Edition published by Simon & Schuster Australia: May 2019

Visit the author's website: annaromer.com

For my friend Selwa,
with   love

1

ABBY

THE SKY GREW LIGHTER as I ran along the deserted highway, my breath puffing clouds in the cool air, my trainers pounding the bitumen. Despite the chill, my skin was hot and damp. By the time I reached the edge of the forest reserve on the outskirts of town, my heart was racing.

I should stop. Turn back. Go home.

You're nearly there.

I pressed on, despite the churning in my stomach. Keep going, one foot after another. That was the mantra, right? I'd been running away since I was twelve. Running from my family. From my hometown. Running from my husband and the secure life he could have offered me. It was easy to run away from something. Running to face it was a heck of a lot trickier.

Almost there.

As the sun crested the horizon, silvery light flooded over the mountains and turned the world to gold. But down here under the roadside trees, the shadows seemed to get darker. Like my mood. When I returned to Gundara a few years ago, my therapist suggested I do something every day to face my fears. Stir them up a little so I could release them in easy-to-manage chunks. She probably meant for me to journal or say affirmations in the mirror, but that all seemed too tame for my particular demons.

Better to face them head-on, here along this deserted road to the place that still haunted my dreams.

I veered off the old highway and ran downhill along an overgrown dirt road, breathing deep and savouring air that was heavy with the scent of gum leaves and vegetation. Magpies flitted through the treetops, their shadows swooping and soaring around me, their melodic calls echoing eerily.

Twenty minutes later, I stood at Pilliga's Lookout.

A mossy concrete viewing platform overlooked the gorge, famous for its wild vistas. Tall ribbon gums towered like giants along the lip of the gorge. Boulders emerged from the ground like monster skulls. Water rushed far below, babbling over rocks and hissing past the shady gorge walls.

Leaving the platform, I wandered down into the trees, pushing through thickets of blackthorn and tea tree and joined an old trail that ran along the embankment. Skinny saplings huddled together along the embankment as if seeking safety in numbers. Bugs hummed and birdsong rang around me, lorikeets and king parrots, their hungry shrieks sounding like the cries of a stolen child.

I ducked beneath the trees into deeper shadows, and a shiver flew over my skin.

The Deepwater Gorge Reserve had once drawn campers and hikers from all over the country for its wild beauty and extensive walking trails. I used to hike to Pilliga's Lookout with my family as a kid. It was a steep walk, but the views over the river made our sweaty pilgrimage worthwhile.

I was ten when I last came here with my father. We had stood together on the bluff, gazing across the endless trees and rock formations that stretched forever, clutching our hats against the wind. Dad had grinned at me and winked, and in that moment my world seemed perfect. I felt safe and loved and brave–

"And never would again."

The bush went still at the sound of my voice. Goosebumps rushed up my arms. I should get back. The sky was fully light now, shadows scuttling deeper into the bush away from the sun. I took a sip from my water flask, then zipped it back into my pocket and retraced my steps to the lookout.

From there I chose a different path and looped around to the old campground. Years of neglect had plunged the picnic area into disrepair. A burnt-out barbecue shelter cowered behind some gutted fire pits and a concrete picnic table. Desolation hung over the place. Even the surrounding bushland seemed to catch its breath.

Or maybe that was me.

A branch cracked and I whipped around, my pulse flying as I searched the open area, the dampness on my skin turning to ice.

Breathe, Abby. Breathe.

On the other side of the campground, under a tall ironbark tree, I caught a flash of bright red. Was someone there? Kids used to hang out here after school, but not anymore. A hiker, then? Lost their way and set up camp for the night? But there was no makeshift camp.

I went closer.

It was a teenage girl.

She lay at the base of the trunk, curled up like a foetus, her face tilted into the ground. Blood oozed from a wound over her ear, gleaming wetly in her dark hair. Her red sequined jacket glittered fiercely against the dull green shadows of the bush.

"Hey, are you all right?" I knelt and patted her arm.

She didn't stir. Her clothes were filthy, her feet bare. Her knees skinned through the torn fabric of her leggings. Had she slept here all night? I couldn't smell alcohol or pot, just the sourness of blood and sweat.

I patted her again. "Gotta wake up, okay? You can't stay here."

I checked her breathing and pulse and then shone my phone light into her eyes. The pupils constricted normally, but her skin felt cold and clammy. As I placed her in the recovery position, I noticed her hands.

Scratches covered the knuckles. Dry blood crusted a thumbnail. All her nails were filthy and broken as if she'd been trying to claw her way out of something.

Ice poured through my veins.

Was it happening again?

I staggered to my feet and searched the trees. Prickles skated up my arms. Was someone watching, or was fear getting the better of me? I ran back to the barbecue area. Leaping onto the picnic table, I thrust my phone about. No signal. If I wanted to call an ambulance, I'd have to return to the highway.

I went back to the girl.

I hated leaving her alone out here where she was vulnerable. But what if she had a concussion or neck injury? Trying to carry her back to the road could make things worse. My only option was to go alone to call for help and then return to her as quickly as possible. I took off my denim jacket and tucked it around her, propping my water flask by her side.

"I'll be quick, sweetie. I promise. Just hang on, okay?"

I got up and walked backwards. Leaving her ripped me

apart. She looked so small lying there. So young and alone. Defenceless. My stomach clenched. Was that how I'd looked the day they found me cowering in the tree shadows, my little fists bruised and bloody, my clothes torn?

Breathe, Abby.

"You'll be okay," I whispered to the girl's motionless form. "I'll be back before you know it." Wrenching around, my breath catching in my throat, I sprinted in the direction of the road.

FIFTEEN MINUTES LATER, I had almost reached the highway. The overgrown track climbed uphill, a brighter place now that morning sunbeams had chased the shadows. Even the magpies were gone, their eerie calls replaced by the bright twitter of lorikeets and wrens.

I pushed up the last stretch. Usually I went easy on my homeward run. Not now. I ran hard, forcing one foot in front of the other, my skin hot and pulse flying. As I approached the road, I tripped and fell, barely registering the skinned palms, cursing the few moments lost as I picked myself up.

On the highway, I jogged along the verge back toward Gundara, my lungs raw and a stitch gnawing under my ribcage. My phone had grown sweaty in my hand and it wasn't picking up a signal. Had I killed it when I fell back there on the track? But then it pinged with new messages and I slumped to a stop.

I dialled triple zero and gave a detailed description of the girl and where to find her. Then I started back along the overgrown road. By the time I reached the campground, forty minutes had passed.

I came to the ironbark tree and stopped in my tracks.

The girl was gone. My drink bottle lay in the dirt, but she'd taken the jacket. A solitary red sequin sat nearby. I picked it up, and it clung to my finger like a drop of blood. I slipped it into my pocket and looked around.

She couldn't be far. That head wound would slow her down. She must be confused, probably scared. Maybe she wandered off in a daze.

I searched the shadowy corners of the barbecue area and even ran a lap around the campground, scanning the trees, calling out to her. Back at the ironbark tree, I gazed around, bewildered.

"Where the hell did you go?"

2

ABBY

A FIST THUMPED on my front door, shattering the morning stillness. "Abby, open up!"

Groaning, I stumbled out of the shower. I only knew one person who hammered like a cop instead of knocking politely—and he was the last person I wanted to see right now. Wrapping my hair in a towel, I dragged on my terry robe. My limbs tingled after my morning run, but there was no endorphin glow, no pleasure rush. The hot water hadn't chased away the images in my head of the campground girl and her bleeding hands. And the weird feeling that somehow the past was coming back to haunt me.

The fist banged again. "Abby, come on. Open up!"

I stumbled down the hallway, rubbing my eyes. Unlocking the deadbolt, I ushered my brother inside. "Jeez, Duncan. You trying to wake the whole neighbourhood?"

Duncan stood a head taller than me, his sandy hair raked into spikes, his cheeks flushed pink after riding his bike across town to get here. His nurse's scrubs were covered in cheerful

Halloween cartoon characters even though it was only April. He swayed towards me, and I braced myself for one of his sweaty bearhugs, but instead he thrust a thin, bookish parcel into my hands.

"This is for you."

"Um, thanks. What is it?"

"Something from Dad's."

My heart sank. I wanted to give it back, but Duncan bounded away along the hall. I followed him into the kitchen. The kettle was already boiling, and he was ransacking my pantry for chocolate biscuits. He held up a packet of seaweed crackers and shook them at me accusingly. "Seaweed? You're kidding, right? What happened to the girl who loved Tim Tams?"

I elbowed him out of the way and put the crackers back on the shelf. "Is there a reason you're here, Dunc? If so, please tell me it's a good one."

"I heard about your adventure at the campground."

My shoulders sagged. "Oh."

He peered into my face. "You okay, sis?"

"Yeah." I leaned against the counter. "I guess."

The kettle shrieked. Duncan splashed boiling water into the teapot and gave it a swirl. His gaze skated around a bit, then he lifted his eyes and narrowed them at me.

"You look rattled."

"I'm not. Well, maybe a bit. I'm worried about the girl."

He filled two mugs with tea and added milk, then claimed one and tossed the scalding liquid down his throat like a whiskey shot.

He winced. "She's probably at home by now. Sleeping off a raging hangover."

"I hope you're right. I stayed after the ambos went. Walked down to the gorge, then doubled back along the hill. Calling out to her. I don't understand how someone can just disappear like that."

"You seem a bit freaked out. Maybe it triggered something?"

A tendon in my jaw spasmed. "I'm fine."

Duncan seemed suddenly fascinated by his empty mug. "I can't believe you still run out there. That place gives me the creeps."

I shrugged, working a hole into the paper parcel with my thumb. "I'm used to it."

"Be careful, okay? It's not safe going out there alone every morning."

"Safe?" I glared at him, my anger prickling up. "Really? Because I'm a woman and it's universally accepted that I'm a victim? Why is it always our fault when something happens to us? Men and boys should learn to respect us, instead of everyone dumping all the responsibility on our heads."

"Jeez, Abby. You're right, of course. I get it. But people are talking."

I hugged the parcel. "What have you heard?"

"That there was no girl. That you just imagined her and wigged out. You know, after what happened to you as a kid."

"I didn't wig out."

"Yeah, sis. I'm sure you were fine. But—"

"I know what I saw." I hadn't meant to sound so snappy. Duncan was only trying to help, but the thought of not being believed raised my hackles. I had worked too hard dealing with my past to let it phase me now. Besides, I didn't want my brother—or anyone—knowing how deeply finding the campground girl had shaken me. I groped around for something else to say to break the sudden silence, but Duncan beat me to it.

He pointed to the parcel. "You gonna open that, or what?"

I tore off the paper. Inside was a framed photo of us as kids. We were standing with our parents at one of Deepwater's lesser-known lookouts, high above the river. Mum had her arm around Duncan. Dad's hand rested on my shoulder. Our battered picnic basket sat on the ground at our feet like a faithful old dog.

My heart slowed. "Where'd you find it?"

"On Dad's lounge room wall."

Since our father's funeral five months ago, Duncan had been clearing out the old house and taking his sweet time about it. I didn't offer to help, and he didn't ask, but he'd been bringing me little gifts every week. Things Dad had hoarded that my brother, God love him, thought I might like. Dad's compass, a battered copy of *Great Expectations*. Even a bunch of love letters Mum had sent in the early days.

Duncan nudged my shoulder. "Cool picture, isn't it?"

I studied it more closely.

Me, Duncan and Dad were all smiling. But it was Mum who stole the show. Her eyes alight, her plump face ruddy from the hike. The breeze catching her dark hair. And the megawatt smile that even now made my heart clench. So many memories of her. The way she would giggle uncontrollably when my father tickled her, throwing back her head and going limp in his arms. The way she cooed our names in a funny voice when we hugged her. But my clearest memory was her empty chair at the table, and Dad's silence in the years after she left.

I thrust the photo at my brother. "I dunno, Dunc. Why don't you keep it?"

He stepped out of reach. "I've got others. That one's special. Check out your big grin. You used to live for our camping trips."

It was true. I had loved those trips. The picnics, the long

sunny hikes. The four of us laughing and cracking jokes as we trekked into the wilderness. As if it was another world and all the tension at home, the fights, Dad's drinking—were all forgotten out there.

I tucked the frame behind the tea canister and hugged myself.

"Thanks, Dunc. It's special."

"Dad would have wanted you to have it."

I bit my lips together and busied myself at the sink. Rinsing our mugs, emptying tea leaves in the compost pail. Trying to loosen the knots in my shoulders. The last thing I needed right now was a row with my brother, but I sensed one brewing.

Duncan slid the photo out from behind the canister and propped it in open view.

"The four of us were happy together. Before Mum left."

"You mean, before Dad drove her away."

"That's harsh."

"It's true, though. If he wasn't such a pisshead ..."

"She drove him to drink with her nagging."

"Dad's brothers were all drinkers, Dunc. He had booze in his blood. All Mum ever did was try to help him, and that's how he repaid her."

Duncan sighed. "Mum ran off and left us, but Dad's the one you blame for what happened to you at the reserve. That's pretty messed up, sis. You know what I think? After all this time, after all the therapy, you're still running away. From anyone who tries to get close. From your family. Seriously, Abby. What has to happen for you to finally stand still long enough and face up to it?"

I unclenched my jaw, wanting to argue. Wanting to tell him he was wrong about me, about all of it. But the fight had gone out of me. I dried my hands on a tea towel, ignoring the tremor in my fingers. Reaching over, I slid the picture back behind the canister and then steered my brother out of the kitchen. In the hallway, I opened the front door and ushered him out onto the porch, shading my eyes against the sun.

"Dunc, I need a favour."

"What's that?"

"Ask around at the hospital. See if anyone admitted a teenage girl with head injuries."

"If you promise me something."

"What?"

"Stay away from that horrible place."

"I can't. It's part of my—"

"Therapy?" Duncan shook his head. "You need to move on, sis. Stop living in the past and start enjoying the now. Life's too short to spend every moment obsessing over ancient history. It's just making you miserable."

"You make it sound easy."

He leaned in and kissed my cheek. "Just be careful, okay?"

We hugged, and he climbed astride his bike and coasted down the hill toward town. I lingered by the steps, his words echoing in my mind.

After all this time, you're still running away.

Other houses in the street huddled behind hedges, their chimneys trailing wisps of smoke. The sky was a cloudless blue and the day promised warmth, but I couldn't stop shivering. Back inside, I shut the door and wilted against it. My legs were too rubbery to stand, so I slid to the floor and rested my head on my knees, squeezing my eyes shut.

Stay away from that horrible place.

I rubbed my face with trembling hands, and then let my fingers climb up through my hair, behind my ear to the crown of my head. To the scar. The hard lump under my fingers that always sent me reeling back into the past.

To that day at the reserve twenty years ago when I was twelve, and oh so determined to join my classmates on the excursion my father had forbidden me to go on. I hurried along the track towards the gorge, my clothes sodden and my shoes squelching. Rain had turned the track to mud, and the further along it I went, the more lost I became. So stubborn, why hadn't I turned back? Admitted defeat and gone home? So much for proving my navigation skills to the kids at school. But on I walked, shivering in my wet clothes, my shoes slapping through muddy puddles as I peered through the haze of rain for something familiar.

Instead, I saw *him*.

Standing up ahead on the track.

As though he'd been waiting.

Maybe even waiting for me ...

Breathe, Abby. Four counts in, four counts out. I blinked away the past and got to my feet. Hadn't I already let go of all this stuff and moved on? Maybe my brother was right. If finding the girl had triggered my old fears, it probably meant I hadn't healed at all. The old wounds were still festering. I needed to flush them out and deal with this for once and for all.

Which meant finally telling the story I'd been running from for most of my life.

3
ABBY

"Ah, Abby." Kendra Nixon-Jones smiled tightly from the other side of her desk. She patted a fair strand back into her topknot and regarded me with vague disapproval. "If you're here to beg an extension for your festival piece, then I'm afraid you're out of luck. I need that story by Monday as agreed."

I tossed my flash drive onto the desk. "When have I ever needed an extension? There's my story. Including new photos of the region's best attractions."

Kendra stared down her nose at my flash drive, shaking her head. "It always makes me laugh when you deliver something in person, including all your research notes and photos. These days we have this thing called email?"

"You mean the emails you ignore and then complain I don't deliver? No thanks. Besides, there's something else."

She trailed her gaze over my casual attire, frowning at the Moulin Rouge tank top, the threadbare Levi's, the cherry Doc Martins. My hair in a wild dark tangle that wasn't quite a ponytail. She grabbed a pencil and drummed it on the desk. "Well?"

"I want to write a feature on Deepwater Gorge. About what really happened there. Not just local hearsay, but the truth. So that people remember. There's so much hype about the old campground being haunted. Did you know there's a company hosting torchlight ghost tours? They're taking groups out at night, visiting sites where the victims were found. No council permits. No consideration for the victims' families. It's not only illegal, it's in poor taste. With the festival coming up, the community needs to understand the dangers."

"Abby—"

"School kids still go out there, daring each other to stay overnight. I was at the campground this morning. Guess what I found? An unconscious teenage girl with a head wound. She looked as if she'd been attacked or chased through the bush—her hands and arms all scratched, her clothes torn—but we'll never know because when I got back after ringing the ambos, she was gone. The police said she probably argued with her boyfriend, that it happens all the time and isn't worth the fuss—"

"Abby!"

"A feature in the *Express* will bring back people's aware-ness." I pulled a sheet of paper from my back pocket and placed it on her desk. "I've sketched an outline, and could have the final copy on your desk by Monday."

Kendra scrunched it into a ball and tossed it in the bin. "No."

"But—"

"There's no story. Those murders happened twenty years ago. The man responsible jailed. You don't seriously think the girl you found this morning was another victim, do you? If so, you're more paranoid than I thought."

"You didn't see her, Kendra."

"Listen to me, Abby. I like your work. Our readers adore you. You give the *Express* some class. But I call the shots around here. And if I tell you to leave this Deepwater business alone, then that's what I expect you to do. Understand?"

I pressed my lips together. Nodded.

Back in high school, Kendra was one of the cool girls, sporty and popular. Her shoes mirror-polished, her tunic pressed. Her hair pulled back in a ponytail that swished and gleamed as she laughed with her besties. *Hey Shabby Abby, can't your dad afford to buy you decent shoes? Don't worry, you can have these old things when I'm done with them.*

I shuffled uncomfortably. Writing for the *Express* kept me in touch with the community. Most people opened up when they learned I wrote for the local paper. They were more willing to talk, happy to provide personal anecdotes and insights. If one of my stories helped an isolated farmer or a frazzled single mum to feel more connected to their fellow humans, then I had done my job. I couldn't risk all that, not even for my dream article.

Kendra opened her bulging organiser and flipped through. "Since you're here, I have the perfect assignment for you. A big-shot Sydney writer has recently moved to the area. He bought a derelict property in the hills northwest of Gundara. Local estate agents are wetting themselves. They think it's confirmation of the coming bull market."

I slumped, already bored. "Anyone I know?"

"His name's Tom Gabriel." She slid a printout across the desk. "This is the last interview he did. It appeared in the *Sydney Morning Herald* all the way back in 2008. Tom is notoriously hard to pin down. He's very antisocial."

I jammed the printout in my pocket. I'd heard of Tom Gabriel. The Stephen King of fictionalised true crime. His novels were mega-bestsellers across the globe. Made into films or miniseries. I'd always avoided them. Crime wasn't my cup of tea. Too much death and darkness.

"What makes you think he'll talk to me?"

Kendra rubbed her hands together, giving me a smug, cat-who-got-the-cream smile. "You'll have your work cut out for you. He hates journalists. Hates them. Eight years ago they sued him for smashing a TV camera that some pushy news broadcaster shoved in his face."

"Nice guy."

"Word is he's a real arsehole." She leaned back in her chair. "Get me his story, Abby. All the dirt, all the scandal. Why his marriage bombed so spectacularly. Apparently he's a womaniser, so there's a clue. And a drunk. I want to know who he's currently dating. How much he earns. Why he's taking so long with his new book. Everything. This man is big news. Big. News. If we bag an interview with him in time for the Autumn Fest, we'll put Gundara on the map. I want photos, too. Lots of photos."

"What if he won't talk?"

"Oh, you'll work something out."

"What makes you so sure?"

She regarded me from beneath lowered lids. "Because if you pull it off, I'll let you write your Deepwater story. I'll even give you the front-page headline."

"You're on." I loped to the door, already planning my outline.

"Wait, Abby. That girl you found this morning, who was she?"

I turned back. "No idea."

"Let's keep it that way, shall we?"

"What do you mean?"

"Don't go shooting your mouth off, is all I'm saying. At

least not until after the festival."

"The festival?"

"Has it slipped your attention how many tourists it brings to the area every year? Tourists with bulging pockets."

"You're worried about money?"

Kendra sat back and peered along her nose. "Everyone's worried about money, Abby. All of Gundara relies on the tourist dollar. We can't go printing stories of doom and gloom about one of our biggest tourist attractions. Lord knows, we don't want to scare people off with horror stories before they've even arrived."

"I thought warning people was the whole point."

"You just worry about getting that Tom Gabriel interview. Leave the thinking to me."

ON THE WAY back to my car, I studied the people passing by. A couple of people were familiar and nodded greetings, but most were strangers to me.

I'd spent more than a decade away from Gundara. In that time, it grew from a backwater village to a town of eight thousand. Families and self-starters flocked here from Sydney, attracted by the cheap real estate. The town had prospered. Quirky little cafes popped up like cheerful weeds between the corner pubs and solid stone buildings that dated back to the gold rush. Antique shops opened, and weekend markets filled the streets with people. But several years ago, the economy had nosedived. The torrent of people from the city slowed to a trickle.

As I strode through the open mall, I noticed how quiet everything was. The bright autumn sun beat down on streets that were mostly deserted. The wind skated empty wrappers past the vacant shopfronts and boarded-over doorways of failed businesses that had sold up and gone.

Kendra's words chimed hollowly in my head. *We don't want to scare people off before they've even arrived.* The Autumn Fest was a big deal for Gundara. The town relied on the tourist dollars it generated. Without funding, the council couldn't pay for road repairs. They would cut back essential community services like the Rural Fire Service. Kendra was right, the town needed to thrive. But at what cost? Overlooking a possible attack on a teenage girl?

As I unlocked my Fiesta, the back of my neck prickled and I glanced up.

A man sat in a battered Hilux on the other side of the carpark, watching me. He was about seventy, with black horn-rims and a thatch of stringy grey hair that fell past his collar. A black-and-white border collie with long matted fur pricked up its ears in the passenger seat beside him. The man caught my eye and didn't look away.

A band of muscle tightened around my ribs. Did he recognise me?

I slid into the driver's seat and buckled up, revving the engine in my haste to get away. Out on the street, I turned too quickly, cutting off another motorist as I sped towards home. But there was no escaping him. Once seen, I couldn't unsee him. His craggy cheeks, his down-turned mouth. The lank grey hair that framed his face and hung too close to his collar. Mostly though, it was his eyes. They were blue as the wings of a kingfisher. Blue as an autumn sky. The same cold, steely blue I still saw every night in my nightmares.

4

ABBY

My stomach rumbled as I pushed through my front door. I just wanted to devour a toastie and a bowl of custard flavoured ice-cream, then collapse on the lounge and spend the afternoon escaping into one of my dog-eared Mills and Boons.

"Not gonna happen."

I threw my bag on a chair and went into the kitchen, marvelling over the shittiness of my day despite it barely being noon. First the girl at the campground, and then Kendra's dismissal of my gorge story. And the rotten cherry on the cake —seeing *him* in the carpark. Roy Horton.

I brewed tea and grilled a sandwich and took it over to the table, taking out Kendra's printout. I didn't want to research a dusty old author. He might be a mega-seller, but honestly, smashing a TV camera? Talk about overreacting. How was he going to respond when a small-town reporter like me turned up requesting an interview?

I scanned the article. It was a behind-the-scenes story that painted Tom Gabriel as a drunkard and womaniser. A black and white author shot accompanied it.

Hmm. Not so old and dusty, after all. He wore a baseball cap and snug T-shirt and was frowning at the camera. Arms crossed tightly over his chest, shoulders rigid. Jaw clamped beneath a prickly shadow of stubble. He was twenty-nine, according to the article. By now, he'd be approaching forty.

I bent closer, taking in the arrogant jut of his jaw, the hostility in his intense eyes. He was the type of man I usually avoided. Full of his own importance, set in his ways. The sort of man who shook hands with a woman just so he could grind her knuckles a little and show her who was boss.

"We'll see about that, won't we, Mr Bigshot?"

I hurried along the hallway to my tiny spare room. Afternoon sun streamed through the window, lighting up my collection of framed moths and insects, my birds' nests under bell jars, a tuft of boobook feathers, and my miniature skull collection—mice, silvereyes, even a snake.

I moved aside a tower of rare vintage gardening books and booted my laptop.

A ton of links came up when I typed in Tom's name, including a bio on his publisher's site. He had attracted the interest of a publisher while still at university, and his first novel had won industry awards and garnered huge press. As his career advanced, he became notoriously reclusive and hard to pin down for interviews or photo shoots. From Goodreads, I pulled up his back-cover blurbs. There was a chilling sameness to his themes. Kidnappings, abductions, murder. Lots of murder.

I squirmed in my chair. "No wonder I've avoided you. This interview better be worth it."

It will be. You'll get to tell your story, remember?

I peeled a red sticker from the roll in my desk drawer and

went over to the topographical map tacked to my wall. It showed Gundara from a bird's-eye view, and the vast expanse of wilderness that surrounded it. In the past two years I had kept a detailed record of my daily runs, circling the terrain I covered. All the trails I'd followed, the rocky overhangs and toppled trees I'd climbed, the deep gullies I navigated. I told myself my runs were therapy. But really, I was searching. Searching for the place that still—even after twenty years—featured in all my nightmares.

"I don't know what it was," I told the lady police officer, my breath hitching. "It was a cave or something." The officer crouched in front of me, her face gentle. "Can you describe this cave, Abby?" My head hurt. The doctor was coming to stitch it, but I wanted to go home. "It was dark inside. Very dirty. I mean, there was dirt on the floor, but underneath the dirt was metal."

I smoothed my hand over the map and placed the sticker on the campground area where I had found the girl. I wrote the date next to it, and stood back. If my Deepwater article alerted other girls to the dangers of the reserve, then maybe I could stop searching for the cave. Stop obsessing over something that belonged in the past.

Needing fresh air, I shut down my laptop and went out to the back verandah. An icy wind rattled the leafless grapevine, and I breathed the sweet cold air deep into my lungs.

Purple storm clouds, dark as bruises, moved over the distant hills. Somewhere below them, the Deepwater River carved a ravine through dense eucalypt forests. Locals called this vast expanse of wilderness the reserve. Twenty years ago, campers in a remote part of the park had discovered the remains of a teenage girl. The body had lain in its shallow grave for at least a decade. Weeks later, police searchers found more remains buried nearby, another teenage girl. No one could identify the girls, and nobody came forward to claim them. The uproar died down. Life settled back to normal. Until twelve-year-old local girl Alice Noonan went missing the following year.

I gnawed my lip.

A month after she disappeared, her body turned up. She hadn't been dead that long. One or two days at most. She was grubby and malnourished. Bruises covered her hands. Dry blood crusted under her torn fingernails. She had starved to death. People were saying someone had kept her a prisoner. Police searched the reserve and went door-to-door, finally arresting a young local man. When they locked him up, Gundara breathed a sigh of relief and did its best to forget.

If I shut my eyes, I could picture Alice so clearly, as if she was standing right here beside me. My beautiful friend, the girl who'd been like a sister. Her big cinnamon-brown eyes, her pixie face. Her thin, inky hair scraped into a ponytail. Hair not yet tangled with leaves and crumbs of earth. Hands and fingers not yet scratched. The way she used to be before she started haunting my dreams.

I stared at the distant hills, the autumn breeze murmuring around me. *I want to write a feature on Deepwater Gorge,* I'd told Kendra. *About what really happened there, the truth. So that people remember.* It wasn't entirely true, though, was it? I didn't want to write about the gorge so others would remember.

But so that I could forget.

5
LIL

"JOE?" Lil froze before the mirror in her bedroom, ears pricked. That loud bang had definitely come from further along the hallway. Strange. Joe was in the kitchen, filleting a snapper. "Joe, was that you?"

She frowned. Of course it was Joe. Who else would it be? They lived miles from town, surrounded by farms and rolling green hills to the horizon. Barely another soul within cooee. Nice and quiet, just the way she liked it. Sometimes though, it was *too* quiet.

"Joe?"

Joe said they were too old to live out here, especially since his angina diagnosis last year. He could no longer help with the physical work, the mowing and gardening, the thousand-and-one daily tasks their small holding required. Lil refused to sell. She'd always done the lion's share of the yard work. She took great pride in keeping the garden tended and the wood basket full. Besides, she cherished the privacy and freedom. The beautiful birds that visited their garden. The peace.

Most of all, the farmhouse symbolised her happiest years with Joe. Typical of her, she supposed. Unable to let go. Clinging to the past, craving the familiar. Joe called her a hoarder. Of knickknacks, useful scraps of fabric, old letters. Hair and toenail clippings for the compost. Balls of string and rubber bands. Extra food for the pantry. Chocolate bars in her bedside drawer.

"If it wasn't for me," Joe was always saying, "you'd be on that show, *Australia's Worst Hoarders*." He was right about the hoarding. He just didn't understand how it pained her to let things go. Actually physically pained her.

She studied her reflection. She had pinned her thick hair into submission, the grey strands tucked out of sight, her face powdered, a hint of lippy applied. There was still an hour before her Saturday drama group, but she needed to leave soon. Town was forty minutes away.

More clattering came from down the hall. Lil hurried out to her sewing room and froze in the doorway.

"Joe, what in heaven's name?"

He jerked around. "Lil! I thought you'd gone to drama group?"

"Without saying goodbye?"

He shrugged sheepishly, holding up his hand. Blood welled from a gash on his thumb, trailing a bright thread down his arm.

"The kitchen box is out of Band-Aids. Thought you might have spares in here."

She glanced at her old Singer sewing machine cabinet. There was no sign of disturbance. Joe hadn't rummaged in the drawers, thank goodness. Just upended a needle box and scraped aside her chair.

"There's nothing in here," she scolded. Her heart beat

harder at the lie. She hated the person she became at times like this, a grouchy old bear protecting her den. But inside that den was a secret with the power to destroy them both. "I wish you wouldn't come in here. It's my private area, the way the shed is yours."

"Sorry, love. I wasn't thinking straight." He held up his injured hand. "Think I'll survive?"

She pulled a hanky from her pocket and wrapped it around his bleeding thumb. "What've you done to yourself now?"

"Dang filleting knife. I'd just sharpened it to prep that snapper I caught yesterday, and it came to life and bit me. The knife, I mean. Not the snapper."

His attempt to make her smile fell flat. What was going on with him? His shaky voice, his pale face. It might have been the blood. Joe had never coped with medical emergencies. Not since the war. But there was something else. They'd been married fifty-four years come November, and she could sense when he was plotting something. She glanced again at the Singer cabinet.

Joe hated mess. One look inside should have sent him scurrying out to his shed in a tidying frenzy. The sewing room was Lil's territory, and she kept it chaotic for two reasons. One, the disorder comforted her. She knew where everything was. Mostly. And two, the mess kept Joe out.

At least it had until now.

She led him back along the hall to the kitchen. Settling him on a chair, she unwound her hanky and inspected his bleeding thumb.

"I wish you wouldn't go poking around in my room."

Joe smiled. "I knew it. You've hidden a body in there, haven't you?"

She scoffed at this and turned away, but her legs wobbled. She wasn't hiding a body, but sometimes it felt that way to her. "What on earth made you think I'd have Band-Aids in my sewing room, of all places?"

Joe shrugged. "Dunno, love. You know me, I'm an idiot sometimes. Rush about without thinking."

She sighed. "Oh, Joe."

How could he still melt her like that? Over five decades of marriage and years of friendship, and he could still soften her cranky heart with a glance. She'd never tell him that, of course. No point giving him the advantage. But in moments like this, she loved him so much she ached.

She bent and kissed his wrinkled cheek. "Silly old fool."

He gave her a grateful look. "Forgiven?"

She turned away. Best not encourage him. She had her reasons for keeping the sewing room door shut.

She rummaged in the first-aid box. Well, look at that. Band-Aids, just as she'd thought. The blood must have distracted him. A senior moment, he always called it. She filled a bowl with warm water and washed and dressed Joe's hand. His eyes shone as he watched her, that same grateful, admiring look in his eyes.

"You always fix me up, Lil."

"Hmm."

"What'd I do without you?"

"I'm not planning to depart anytime soon."

"You know what I mean."

She gave a soft, dismissive snort. Inside, though, a chill was creeping. They were in their twilight time. Living day to day, thankful for each sunrise they saw together. There were no secrets between them. Not anymore. She had told Joe the truth about her childhood—at least, a heavily edited version of events —and then promised him it was all behind her. All forgotten.

And it was. Except for what she'd hidden in her sewing-machine drawer.

The diary.

Heaven help her, that bloody diary. She had tried to burn it years ago. One winter, with Joe away at a Forestry Commission event in Sydney, she'd even brought it out and stood with it in her hands in front of the fireplace. Willing herself to throw it in the flames. Thirty minutes. Forty. An hour might have passed. Her back grew cold and stiff, her face and hands roasted hot. The fire died down. In the end, she had returned the book to the sewing room, defeated. Its hold over her was too great, its poison too deep in her blood. As long as she lived, she'd never be free of it.

She rubbed her forehead, blinking away the shadows.

Joe gave her a questioning look. "All right, old girl?"

"Why wouldn't I be?"

He smiled fondly and nodded in his usual way, then levered himself up from the table to boil the kettle for a cuppa.

Lil scratched the back of her neck. Her scalp grew tighter. The blood drained out of her face. She could actually feel it retreating like a warm tide, leaving just a pasty mask behind. Inside her skull, a bubble of darkness dislodged and began to expand. When the kettle boiled, she made herself a strong coffee. She was a tea drinker, the weaker the better, but sometimes the extra caffeine helped her fight off the shadows. She drank it scalding black, washing down a Xanax for good measure. For a moment she stood in the stillness, listening to the quiet clang of Joe's spoon in his cup, the creak of his chair.

When she felt more herself again, she retreated to her

sewing room and shut the door behind her. She settled on the chair in front of the cabinet and slid open the bottom drawer, taking out a small thick book with a tattered red cover. Rubbing her damp hands on her skirt, she turned to the first page.

6

FRANKIE'S DIARY

He's given me this book to write in. Why couldn't it be a novel, or a storybook with pictures? Anything but blank pages staring back at me. He says it'll be good for me. That writing my thoughts every day will keep me out of trouble.

But we're already in trouble, aren't we?

Lilly won't stop crying. She pulls all the tangles out of her hair and leaves them laying on the floor, fuzzy little injured things, limp as dead spiders. The pillow has left a thick knot on the back of her head which she keeps tugging. I'm worried she'll rip it out and pull off a chunk of scalp. I tried untangling it this morning, but she whined and fidgeted and finally shoved my hands away.

We got lunch. Bread and dripping with fatty ham. He told us proudly that he baked the bread himself as if we should congratulate him.

"When are we going home?" Lilly screamed.

He answered with a glare, and took away our empty plates, locking the door behind him.

Heavy wooden planks line the walls and ceiling of our room. He has reinforced them all with bolts. I tried unscrewing one, but tore my fingernails and now they're clogged with blood. This afternoon I stomped across the room, searching for a loose floorboard. When I couldn't find one, I hammered my palms against the walls and kicked them.

Lilly's saucer eyes fixed on me as tears dribbled down her cheeks. Mum used to say I was the brave one in the family, but I don't feel brave now. I know what he's planning. We have to escape, before it's too late.

There's no electric light. We have to rely on whatever daylight can find its way through our little window. At night, the moon peeps through our window bars. The wind comes too and clangs the wooden shutters. The air brings the smell of gum trees and dust. We hear the leaves in the wind and the drone of insects, and sometimes the distant mumble of a river, but nothing else. I guess we're a long way from Sydney.

The door is heavy too. There's no handle. At least, not on our side.

We dragged the mattress onto the floor and examined the cast-iron bedframe. It's welded together and too heavy to budge.

Lilly flopped. "Oh Frankie, he's thought of everything. We're going to die here!"

"Hush, Lilly."

She's right. He planned this from the start. Enchanting us

back at the hospital with stories of how brave he was in the war, or with fairytales about his home in the bush. Luring us with wonders. A wrought-iron aviary full of colourful birds. An apple orchard and magnolias that bloomed bigger than dinner plates. While we marvelled, he was making his plans to trap us here in this room.

There's a curtain strung across one corner, making a small cubicle. A kind of bathroom, I suppose. It's got a steel bucket with a wooden rim for us to sit on. A container of ash, and a wad of newspaper squares. When we use the bucket, we have to scoop on some ash to kill the smell. There's a tiny basin with a towel and soap where we can wash ourselves and get water to drink. In the mornings we take turns hauling the full bucket to the door and he collects it, replacing it with an empty one.

It's been two weeks. He won't answer our questions. We don't know why he's keeping us here. Or how long we'll stay. Or even if Mum knows we're all right. Lilly nagged him all last night about letting us go. When he ignored her, she threw her shoe, and it struck his face. He left in a rage and stomped downstairs into the yard.

We climbed onto the wooden trunk to spy on him. He disappeared into the shed, then came and sat directly below us on a log seat. Bent over something, a kerosene lamp burning yellow beside him. His arm slid back and forth in a long stroking motion. Then he shifted, and we saw the axe across his knees. The sharpening stone rasped as he drew it slowly along the gleaming blade.

Half the night we lay awake. Huddled under the sheets, our faces sticky with tears. We tried to cry quietly as we strained to hear. Listening for his footsteps. Waiting. But he never came.

"Look, Lilly." Through the window, an enormous golden

moon had drifted into view. "The moon's saying goodnight. She's telling us to shut our eyes and go to sleep."

"Frankie, I'm scared."

"Here, hold my hand. Now take one last look at the moon, Lilly-bird, and kiss the stars goodnight. Then shut your eyes and sleep will come."

"Goodnight, moon," she snuffled, then placed a kiss on her fingers and blew it towards the window. Snuggling in beside me, she was soon asleep.

I lay awake. The rasping noise had stopped, but I could still hear it in my head. Could still see his arm moving back and forth as he sharpened the blade. Was it a warning? Was he trying to scare us? If so, he succeeded. I'm scared, but it's only made me more determined.

We're going to escape, me and Lilly. We're going to go home. Before he uses that axe.

7
TOM

Tom cracked his knuckles and rested his fingertips on the keys. He hammered out a gush of words on the old Remington —no annoying buzzing computer for him—and then frowned at the mess he'd made. Hell, what was wrong with him? Wooden dialogue, stilted action. And a heroine whose motivation eluded him.

Ripping the paper from the drum, he balled it up and flung it at the window. "Useless crap!"

An itch took up residence on his ankle. He slid his wooden ruler down inside the plaster cast, probing for the right spot. Ugh. He hated this.

Outside, the sky was brewing a storm, but the lush green shadows beneath the trees were calling to him. How he'd love to wriggle his sweaty toes in that cool grass. He had bought the house back in January, and finally moved in three weeks ago. Rotten timing, his publisher said—with a book deadline looming, his tree change was madness. But Tom needed the isolation to think, to let his creativity unravel. To get away from people, from distraction. From the past.

Besides, Ravensong was his dream house.

He had walked through the initial inspection with his mouth hanging open. The soaring ceilings and giant picture windows looking out onto a rambling wilderness garden had taken his breath away. The cavernous library had a crystal chandelier that belonged in a palace. Upstairs he found a warren of rooms, all fully furnished. In one he even found a bunch of personal items—eyeglasses and a manicure set. A rack of clothing that included a moth-eaten army uniform from the Second World War—apparently abandoned by whoever had lived here before.

The garden had wide brick pathways meandering between established trees and flowerbeds. A sprawling veggie patch, and pumpkins invading a pair of galvanised tanks full of pristine rainwater. In a grassy orchard he discovered a quaint vintage caravan, home to a nest of swallows. Even more intriguing was a massive wrought-iron aviary buried beneath a rampaging mountain of ivy. The icing on the cake was the half-feral black tomcat living in the shed.

But it was the views from the upper-floor windows that won him in the end. Ten minutes' walk from the house, the land sloped down into a deep, forested gully, which he suspected was the start of Deepwater Gorge. Years ago, he'd been obsessed by the murders committed there, and haunted by the young victims. He had always dreamed of writing a novel about their story, and finding Ravensong seemed like a good omen.

Until the accident.

Soon after moving in he'd discovered another window, up

under the roofline at the back of the house half-hidden by the eaves. No glass pane that he could see, just a row of bars. He hadn't been able to locate it from inside the house, so he had grabbed a ladder from the shed to investigate. Too caught up to notice the cracked rungs. He had lain there half the night until he mustered the strength to crawl back inside and call an ambulance—

The phone shrilled.

"Whoever you are, you can bugger off! I'm trying to write a bloody book here."

Trying—and failing dismally.

The clock was ticking. After ten days in hospital, and now a week at home, he still had written nothing decent. The painkillers fogged his brain, but without them his broken bones complained so loudly he couldn't concentrate. His ribs were knitting well, hip hip hooray, but his lower half was still a mess. Broken ankle, smashed tibia, and what felt like half a ton of plaster encasing his lower leg. The other knee with a grade-three ligament tear. The steel brace he wore to keep it still turned walking into a nightmare. He was three months away from his book deadline and fast approaching certain catastrophic failure.

Writing is easy, American journalist Gene Fowler once quipped. All you do is stare at a blank sheet of paper until drops of blood form on your forehead. Tom sank his face into his hands. It wasn't just the meds. He'd been sweating blood for months—hell, for over a year—and had still failed to produce anything worthwhile. He'd lied to his agent and publisher. Sixty thousand words, he'd told them. All going well. Should have some chapters ready in about . . .

Never.

He was screwed. His career was over. When the truth got out, they'd wipe their hands of him. Never let him publish another word. He couldn't even give back the advance. He'd written a big fat cheque for Ravensong, and renovations had chewed up the rest.

The phone stopped shrilling. Peace at last. Until his stomach took up the chorus with a series of gurgles. Breakfast had been a non-event. Some days, the ordeal of dragging himself to the kitchen and assembling a bowl of cereal seemed Herculean.

He pictured them finding him here, months in the future. Or rather, finding his remains. Hunched over his typewriter, his finger bones still poised hopefully on the keys. The black tomcat, who he'd christened Poe after his childhood idol, would pick clean his bones, leaving just a sad old carcass—

The phone started again. He groaned.

Probably his agent checking up on him. She kept nagging him to get a housekeeper. A glorified babysitter, more like. He was already paying a mint for a guy to deliver his groceries, not to mention shelling out big bucks for a physiotherapist to home visit, but still his agent nagged.

What if you fell again, Tom? Couldn't get to the phone? Had to spend another night hurt, unable to call for help? What if, heaven forbid, you perished out there? Your fans are expecting your next book, you can't let them down.

Of course not. Yet how could he make his agent understand? He liked the solitude of living in the bush. Craved the fresh air and the wide-open spaces. Needed the quiet. He'd never get his book written with a housekeeper poking about the place.

The phone stopped, but his stomach was now gurgling like a drainpipe. He needed to eat. Grappling with his crutches, he hobbled out to the kitchen. It was a bombsite. Empty beer cartons, the remains of last night's dinner in the sink, a mountain of unwashed dishes. How had he sunk so low?

Years ago, he had lived in the desert for months to research a historical story. Digging for water and baking yams on a campfire with only a mad dog and an albino kangaroo for company. Yes, it had pushed his boundaries, but he'd survived. And a couple of broken bones would not hold him back.

He'd show his agent. His publisher. The whole damn lot of them. He didn't need a housekeeper. He could get the place shining again without one. His boxes unpacked, his gear sorted, his meals made. Hell, he'd even get the damn novel written. Even if it killed him.

He collected the beer bottles he'd left strewn around the place and stacked them on the bench to recycle. Found a rubbish bag under the sink and stuffed it with the worst of the mess. He dragged it through the back door, along the verandah and into the bin. Exhausted, he headed back inside.

As he opened the screen door, thunder boomed in the distance. Poe streaked along the verandah and then shot between his legs and into the house, knocking him off balance. As he grabbed the door handle, one of his crutches slid out from under him and walloped his damaged knee on the way down. With a howl, he pitched backwards, slamming the door in his own face and coming down hard on his bad ankle.

His vision greyed. When he surfaced through the fog of pain, he was clinging to the doorknob. Both legs threatening to buckle under him. If someone had tried to wrench off his kneecap with a screwdriver, it couldn't have hurt more. And the shattered ankle ... well, best not think about that. Just get yourself inside, man, and numb it with your meds. He tried the handle. The damn door wouldn't budge. He rattled the knob and shoved, but it stayed shut. Remembering the dicky latch, he groaned.

"You're kidding, right?"

He looked back along the verandah. The open kitchen window was tempting, but he'd never make the climb. This door was his only way inside. Good thing it had a glass panel. Turning his face away, he struck the armrest of his crutch hard against the pane. It shattered inwards, leaving an outline of jagged shards. He reached in and felt around. The deadlock had engaged. He'd need a key. The same key sitting right where he'd left it on the kitchen table.

He withdrew his arm too quickly, catching it on the glass. Blood welled from the cut. It inscribed a perfect red line around his forearm and then began to drip.

Was this a cosmic joke?

He swayed forward, gripping his remaining crutch for balance. They would find his skeleton curled against the back door in the foetal position. Desiccated by wind and rain, his bones gnawed clean by Poe, those blasted swallows nesting in his rib cage.

Lightning flickered in the distance. He glanced back along the verandah. The kitchen window was his only hope. He took a shuffling step, then stopped. A distant sound rumbled, and he held his breath. A car motor?

"The delivery guy, thank God."

As the sound droned closer, he remembered the grocery van had been two days ago. He pressed his bleeding arm against his side, trying to staunch the flow. Was it Monday? Was he expecting anyone else? Lord, his brain was a fog. He shut his eyes, hoping to clear it, but the greyness was back and he was sinking into it like a stone into murky pond water.

"Hello?"

He jerked back into himself, blinking to his senses. A woman was hurrying down the path that ran beside the house. She had to be his new housekeeper. His agent must have hired someone, after all.

She had scraped back her glossy dark hair into a schoolmarm ponytail, displaying a perfectly oval face that caught Tom's interest. He took a mental snapshot, filing it away for future contemplation. Prominent forehead wrinkled in a frown. Wide-spaced intelligent eyes, lush mouth. Perfect fodder for one of his trademark sassy detectives. She was wearing a blue Indian-style tunic that skimmed her curves, teamed with navy pants and a moss-coloured cardigan.

Tom shook his head. Who wore cardigans anymore?

Her long legs covered considerable ground as she clomped along the pathway in high, impractical shoes. She paused at the foot of the verandah steps to peel off her cardigan, exposing pale slender arms. When she saw him, her eyes widened.

"Oh, heck. Are you all right?"

"Just dandy," Tom told her sourly. "Who are you?"

She climbed the steps and hurried over. "I'm Abby Bardot. I tried to call earlier. Looks like you could use some help."

Tom pointed along the verandah to the kitchen window. "Don't suppose you could climb through and unbolt the deadlock? The key's on the table inside."

She didn't bother looking at the window. Instead, her cool gaze shifted from his face to his arm, then his ruined shirt, before lingering perhaps a little too long on his track pants. Probably taking in the knee splint and plastered leg, but a rush of heat prickled through him all the same. She was way too easy on the eye. Way too distracting. He was almost sorry she wasn't the prying busybody he'd imagined.

Almost.

She retrieved his fallen crutch and handed it to him, then dug in her shoulder bag and pulled out a battered iPhone. "I'm calling an ambulance."

He tucked the crutch under his arm, wincing as he resettled his weight. "Good luck getting reception. Anyway, the ambulance is an hour away. By the time they arrive, I'll have bled to death."

She made a scoffing sound, then gave up on her phone. "Yeah well, whatever. If you don't staunch that flow, you *will* bleed to death." Pulling an enormous hanky from her pocket, she flapped it open and stepped up to him.

He blinked. The greyness was sliding back. Spots clouded his vision. He wasn't aware that he'd swayed forward until she was there in front of him, her hands firm on his shoulders.

"All right there, Tom?"

He blinked away the dizziness and glared at her, intending to bite out a few choice words—*I'm not a freaking geriatric*—but the words died on his tongue. Close up, she was something else. The creamy skin dusted with freckles. The full, determined mouth. Her grey eyes fringed with long, dark lashes. And a wariness in them that made him think of a vixen he'd once seen at the mouth of her den, fangs bared as she safeguarded what lay within.

He drew a breath, then wished he hadn't.

Her scent. Damp skin and talcum powder, and something sweetly floral. For a moment he floated. He forgot the ache in his legs, forgot his throbbing arm. Forgot the deadline for his non-existent novel. He even forgot the nagging loneliness that had dogged him these past few years. All he could think about was the perfume of summer wildflowers and honey, and how the world seemed to be tilting over and sweeping him sideways—

8

ABBY

HE STARED AT ME BLEARY-EYED, his face blank. He was going to fall, wasn't he? Slither onto the decking boards in a dead faint, and if I tried to stop him I'd be dragged down too. I leaned in and pressed my palm against the side of his unshaven face.

"Tom?"

He blinked, pulling himself upright and gripping the doorframe. "Wha—oh. I'm fine."

I folded my hanky into a makeshift bandage. "Hold out your arm."

"Can't you just climb through the window and unlock the door?"

"You've a bit of weight on you, Tom. If you pass out from blood loss, I don't fancy breaking my back trying to drag you inside. Now hold out your arm."

He glared a moment longer, then obeyed.

I bound the hanky around the wound and knotted it.

Blood quickly saturated the thin fabric, but it would do for now.

He frowned. "You're here for the job, right?"

"Job?"

"You're my new housekeeper. My agent sent you. Didn't she?"

"I'm with the *Gundara Express*. I was hoping you might agree to a story."

He jerked to attention. "Oh wait. You're a *journalist*?"

"I've been trying to ring you. I want to interview you for the paper and—"

"I don't do interviews."

"It's for a community newspaper and you're pretty big news. I'll give you final say in what gets printed. Anything you don't like, we won't publish. You'll have full control."

Heat rushed to his cheeks. "That's what you say now. But in the end, you'll print whatever you like."

"I wouldn't do that."

"You're all the same, you journos. Twisting the truth to suit yourselves. Not giving a damn how many lives you ruin, as long as you get your precious bloody story."

"Won't you think about it? It'd be great morale for the town—"

"Just leave, okay? Get off my property. Go back to whatever devious little corner of Hicksville you climbed out of and leave me the hell alone."

We glared at each other. Finally, I spun away. *Loser*. No interview was worth this amount of grief. I'd find another way to get my Deepwater feature in the paper. My heels thudded on the decking as I made for the steps.

Tom cursed softly. "Wait."

I looked over my shoulder.

"While you're here—" He gestured towards the window.

I lifted a brow, feigning puzzlement.

He huffed. "Can't you at least help me get back inside?"

"So sorry," I said. "I'm in a bit of a rush. Hicksville's calling." I clomped down the steps. Thunder grumbled in the distance and the first spots of rain fell on my arms. Probably for the best. I'd hate to get caught in a downpour.

I was halfway along the path when he called out.

"All right. I'll think about it, okay?"

I looked back. "Plus photos?"

"Absolutely freaking not."

I turned away.

He growled. "Okay, okay. I'll think about that too."

"Great!" Worth getting caught in the rain for. I skipped back along the path and up the steps. Dumping my bag and cardi on a wooden chair, I clomped along to the window. My brother would call this the stars aligning. Blind luck, my dad would have said. I didn't care what it was. The interview was in the bag, I could feel it. I just had to convince Tom Gabriel he needed it as much as I did.

I rattled up the window, frowning at the combat zone of unwashed plates and mugs on the sink inside. On the nearby counter, a battalion of empty beer bottles stood in rows beside an overflowing compost pail. What a slob. I glanced back at Tom, who was leaning on the door, eyes half-closed. He had sagged onto his crutches and his T-shirt was riding up, revealing a glimpse of hairy abs above the waistband of his track pants. He looked exhausted, his face greyish and unshaven, a lock of gingery-fair hair falling into his eyes.

He noticed me looking and waved his good hand at the window. "I leave it open for the cat. He likes to come and go as he pleases."

"Right."

I turned back to the window. Good thing I'd favoured trousers over a mini-dress and leggings. I hoisted myself up onto the ledge and jumped onto the floor inside. Then gaped around. *Wow.* Despite the chaos, the house was dazzling. Soaring ceilings. A black slate floor like a glossy river of molten glass under my feet. Double doors opened into a vast lounge room. The floorboards needed a sweep, and a mountain of packing cartons leaned against one wall. A tower of books sat gathering dust on a blackwood sideboard, and under the window was the most gorgeous big leather sofa I'd ever seen.

"All right in there?" Tom called from outside.

I unlocked the back door and swung it open for him. "Where's your first-aid kit?"

He pointed to a cupboard by the sink and I retrieved the box and followed him into the lounge room. He sank onto the sofa with a moan. I offered painkillers, but he shook his head and eyed the first-aid kit.

"I thought you said Hicksville was calling."

"It's taking all my willpower to ignore it right now."

In the kitchen, I filled a clean container with Dettol and hot water and returned to the lounge room. Tom had taken off his blood-soaked T-shirt and was using it to mop himself down. He was heavyset, probably after too much time behind a desk, but there was a muscular definition in his arms and under the soft gingery fuzz of his chest hair, and lower down even a hint of abs—

He chose that moment to glance over. His gaze lingered, curious rather than hostile, and then the corner of his mouth twitched and something about the not-quite-there smile sent scorching heat rushing to my cheeks. Heck, had I been checking him out? *Focus, Abby. Remember why you're here.*

I dragged over a chair and sat beside him. The cut on his arm was ragged, though not deep. I dipped a wad of cotton wool in the Dettol water, and mopped the wound, sponging away the blood.

Tom watched my every move. "Done this before, have you?"

"Hmm. My dad drank like a fish. Had his share of falls."

"He live in Hicksville too?"

"Not anymore. He's dead."

Tom looked at me sharply. "God, I'm sorry. What a dickhead thing to say."

I glanced up, a witty comeback already on my lips—*wouldn't be the first time, would it, Mr Bigshot?* But Tom seemed genuinely mortified, his face rumpled and his green gaze fixed on mine.

I shrugged. "You weren't to know."

"You must miss him?"

"I guess."

Tom made a sound in the back of his throat, a clearing. "I cried for months when I lost my dad. We were really close. He was my big hero guy. I still miss having him around." He must have noticed my bug-eyes, because he added hastily, "And no, you can't use that in your damn interview."

I tore off another piece of wadding. "So there'll be an interview?"

He rotated his arm, inspecting the cut. "We'll see."

I rummaged in the tin for sticking plaster and scissors, hiding my smile as I snipped plaster off the roll. Inside I was high-fiving myself. Already I could see my byline on the front page of the *Express*. My Deepwater feature circulating all over town. My message reaching those who most needed to hear it, young women and girls like the one I found at the campground.

A thunderclap exploded overhead. I jerked to attention and dropped the scissors. Tom collected them and passed them back, his brows drawn.

"Jumpy, are you?"

"Just hate the rain."

Right on cue, the sky split open. A deluge started pouring down. The day had darkened though it was barely ten o'clock, and the wind had picked up, thrashing through the camellia bushes outside the window.

I doused Tom's cut with Betadine and dressed it with gauze and a bandage. Out of habit, I patted it gently to smooth the creases, the way I had done a thousand times with my father.

"Good news is you won't need stitches."

"The bad news?"

"You'll have a nasty scar."

Tom settled back into the sofa, the age-worn leather creaking under his weight. "That I can live with."

I took the bundle of bloodied gauze to the kitchen and threw it in the bin, along with my ruined hanky. I swept up the broken glass and collected my things from the verandah. Back in the lounge room with Tom, I pulled on my cardigan. There was no hope of an interview today, and anyway, my stomach was lurching. The drive home would take an hour or more in the rain. Might as well get it over with.

As I got to my feet, the storm went into overdrive. Thunder boomed, and the rain started roaring down in a massive deluge. My shoulders jerked up, and a button popped off my cardigan and clacked onto the floor.

Tom frowned at the button. "Heck of a drive back to town. That bridge washes out in heavy rain, not sure I like your chances."

Impossibly, the rain grew louder. Outside, the camellias had vanished behind a grey haze. The ghostly white arms of a naked birch tree swayed as if in anguish. I wiped a damp palm on my trousers and took out a roll of mints, offered him one.

"They're sugar free."

He peeled one off and handed it back. We chewed for a while, listening to the rain. The pulse in my throat slowed. The knots in my shoulders loosened. I wandered over to the window and squinted through the haze. The ground around my car in the driveway looked like a miniature ocean.

"Your driveway's flooding," I said, my voice strangely robotic.

Tom frowned over. "That bridge will be under water by the time you reach it."

"Jeez."

"You know, there are rooms upstairs. You're welcome to pick one."

"You mean stay here?"

"It's the least I can do. You really helped me out today, climbing through that window. Playing Florence Nightingale. I dread to think what would've happened if you hadn't arrived when you did. There's lots of food, plenty of DVDs. Don't worry about me. I'll keep out of your way."

I retrieved my button and tucked it into my pocket. "It's really pissing down, isn't it?"

"Yeah, not a good sign. If the bridge goes under, you could be stuck for a couple of days."

I blinked. Days? Marooned in the middle of nowhere? With a guy I met all of five minutes ago? I should take my chances on the flooded road, after all—but my skin turned damp at the thought of all that water. All that rain. Staying here suddenly seemed the lesser of two evils. Besides, it would give me a chance to convince Tom to give me that interview.

"You get internet out here?"

"I've got a satellite connection, but it's limited to sunny days."

"You're isolated, aren't you?"

Tom picked at the dressing on his arm. "No one else around for miles."

"You don't get lonely?" I hadn't meant to ask such a personal question, but Tom didn't seem fazed by it. He settled back against the cushions.

"I'm too busy to feel lonely."

Was it my imagination, or did his voice hold a twinge of regret? Intrigued, I took a step nearer.

"One of the upstairs rooms, you said?"

He nodded. "Take your pick. The upper wing has its own outside entrance, but it's got inside access too. It's private. There's even a bathroom, although I suspect the plumbing's dodgy. Just a shower. The bath, should you want one, is in the washhouse outside."

He lifted a brow as if expecting me to baulk at this, but I just nodded as if bathing outside was an everyday occurrence.

"Mind if I check it out?"

"Be my guest." He pointed to an oak sideboard. "Keys are in the top drawer. The hallway's through those double doors. At the end, you'll find the stairwell."

The three upstairs bedrooms had soaring ceilings and windows that overlooked the garden. All had double beds and vast wardrobes full of jangling coat hangers. Halfway along a tight hallway, I found a fourth room. It felt like an attic and was oddly shaped. A single cast-iron bed huddled under a dusty patchwork quilt. Opposite the bed sat a small wardrobe and a wicker chair under the window. I pushed aside the curtains and squinted through the rain. Beyond the garden was dense bushland that must form the northernmost tip of Deepwater Gorge Reserve. The landscape here lacked the wow-factor of the parklands closer to town, so hikers and campers rarely bothered making the trip. Yet its wild beauty hummed in my veins. Rolling mountains slept beneath their dark blanket of trees, oblivious to the rain. Steep gullies dipped down to the river, where the water boomed along craggy banks.

Below me in the garden, wide brick pathways meandered between overgrown trees and disappeared into the shadows. In places, a muddy skim of water had already submerged the red bricks.

I returned to the lounge room.

"Well?" Tom said.

"It's a lovely room. And to be honest, I hate driving in the rain."

Tom's face relaxed. "Right then, Abby. Welcome to Ravensong."

I blew out a breath. "I'd kill for a cuppa right now. Want one?"

While the kettle boiled, I stood at the kitchen window. Curse the rain. It flowed along the pathways and made rivers through the grass. I didn't fancy being cooped up all day twiddling my thumbs, but what other choice did I have? Keeping busy was my only hope of staying sane. I looked around at the piles of bottles and unwashed dishes, the towers of cardboard packing boxes—and smiled.

Back in the lounge room, I passed Tom his mug, and then sank into a big, comfortable chair opposite, blowing on my tea. "Your place is a bit chaotic," I said casually. "Would you be open to an exchange?"

Tom took a gulp of tea and winced. "What do you mean?"

"Seems like you could use some help unpacking. Tidying up."

"In exchange for—?"

"That interview you said you'd think about."

I waited for him to explode again, the way he'd done on the verandah.

He blinked at me, then scratched the stubble on his cheek and sighed.

"You're right, the place is chaos. It bugs the hell out of me. Since the accident, I've been useless. I thought I was coping, but I'm under pressure to finish my new book. I guess it all got away from me." He frowned down at his knee brace for a moment, then fixed his cat-green gaze on me. "You make a decent cup of Darjeeling, by the way."

"Wait till you try my toasted sandwiches."

His lips curved, not quite a smile. "You've no idea how good that sounds."

"Then we've got a deal?"

"Sure, why not."

9
SHAYLA

SHE WAS COLD. Couldn't stop the shivers. And her head hurt. God, it hurt. She tried to blink, but her eyes were full of grit and she couldn't open them, not even a crack. She ran her tongue around her mouth, tasting blood.

Jeez, her head.

If she focused hard, she could move her hand. She slid it towards her face and probed her fingers against her eyes, rubbing away the gumminess. She was lying on something soft. A mattress? The rough blanket under her was stiff and smelly.

This wasn't her bed.

She rubbed her eyes, trying to remember what happened. The argument with her dickhead step-father. Her mum screaming at her to piss off and go. She had waited on the road-side. Hours and hours in the sun, her bag heavy. So thirsty. Mrs Bilby growing restless. Just when she was giving up hope, a car pulled over. She got in. Drank something, water maybe. After that was a blur. She had a glimmer of lashing out and stumbling through the trees. Falling and getting up again, blinded by the blood pouring out of her hair, but she didn't stop, didn't dare. Someone was crashing through the trees behind her in the dark, calling her back.

Her breath hitched on a sob. "Mum?"

She rolled sideways off the mattress and got to her feet. She raised her hands in front of her and shuffled forward until her fingers bumped something flat and metallic. A wall. She moved along it, feeling along its icy surface, eyes blinking wide, but there was nothing to see, just black. No door that she could find. No window. Where was she? She tried to remember what happened to Mrs Bilby, but couldn't. That was a blur, too.

She hammered the wall with her fist. "Let me out of here!"

The darkness gobbled her words into its dull, dead silence. Her legs buckled, and she slumped back onto the ground. What was the point calling out? She was trapped. Alone in some forgotten hole. Lost in the blackness.

And no one knew she was here.

10

ABBY

That afternoon, I made my bed with fresh linen from Tom's cupboard downstairs and then got started on the kitchen, clattering happily away at the sink and dragging out several loads of empty bottles to recycle.

Despite the house's remoteness, I could see why Tom loved it. With its lofty walls and lovely old landscape paintings, and back bedrooms full of relics from another time, it was a writer's paradise. The library was now my favourite place on earth. It kept luring me back, and each time I saw it fell a little more in love with the tall bookshelves, and the vast picture windows, and the chandelier that blazed overhead like my personal galaxy of stars. I ran my fingers along the wall-to-wall shelves, browsing children's books from the early 1900s, peering into crumbling, leather-bound volumes of poetry, and beautiful old atlases and dictionaries. After dinner, I chose a couple of novels and tucked myself into an old leather chair in a cosy corner, blissing away the hours until I started to yawn.

The following day, I vacuumed the entire lower floor,

dusted and mopped, and unpacked half-a-dozen boxes—mostly books. With the chaos under control, the house really blossomed. The floorboards gleamed like dark honey, and the beautiful old bones showed off Tom's rugged-chic furniture and huge colourful paintings to perfection.

Tom holed up in his office for most of the time, pecking at his typewriter and creating a mountain of waste paper, which I later shredded and set aside to recycle. When I delivered toasted sandwiches and tea, I attempted some small talk, but it mostly fizzled. He seemed preoccupied. No doubt filled with remorse over having promised me an interview, but fair was fair. We'd made a deal.

After dinner, I retired upstairs with an armload of Tom's novels. I showered and washed the dust out of my hair, then flopped into bed. I wrote in my notebook, jotting down interview questions to ask Tom, and then I sewed the button back on my cardigan with borrowed needle and thread. When I started yawning, I reached for the novel on my bedside table.

It was the story of two young brothers, survivors of a plane crash lost in the bush, on the run from their uncle, who planned to kill them and claim their inheritance. I read past midnight, then sat staring into the darkness beyond the window.

The story was brilliant. Nothing like the graphic violence I'd expected. Tom had handled the distressing material with deep sensitivity, and I'd even shed a tear in places. He deserved all the awards and movie deals. The glowing reviews. But why did he live so far from town, all alone out here—when in town he'd be getting the royal treatment, being wined and dined and fussed over? He was interesting, I'd grant him that. I pictured him somewhere below me, warm in his bed asleep. Or perhaps he was lying awake, thinking about me. Resenting my presence here, despite our agreement. Feeling intruded upon, counting the days until the weather cleared and I was gone.

I switched off the light and flopped onto the pillow.

The rain's eerie song on the roof got louder. It hissed against the windowpane and splashed below in the garden, lulling me into a dream.

I was a twelve again, trudging along the forest trail.

Only now, someone was walking with me. It was Alice. My heart crumpled like a poppy petal. She had started at my school that year, and latched onto me at once, taking me under her motherly little wing. For five months, we were inseparable. Siamese twins, joined at the hip. Sisters. Our dark heads always together, whispering secrets, me and her against the world. Our friendship surprised everyone, me most of all. I had finally done the impossible—found someone who loved me. And now here she was walking beside me. Exactly as she'd been back then. A pixie-faced girl with black hair and large intelligent brown eyes. Only now those eyes were accusing.

Tears flooded out of me. "Oh, Alice. I'm so—"

Sorry, are you, Abby? You should be. Why did you run away? You made him mad and then he came after me. He kept his guard up after that. Never gave me a chance to run. Not like he did with you.

My dream-heart broke. "Go away, Alice."

Obediently, she faded into the past. I lay motionless. Rain battered the roof, and the sound kept me trapped in my dream. When would I stop blaming myself for what happened? Stop wasting the life I had stolen from her?

11

ABBY

The morning rose silently, as if the universe was holding its breath. I ventured outside and looked at the patchy sky. The rain had stopped. A bank of storm clouds parted and the first few watery rays of sunshine broke through. I checked the front driveway, but it still lay under a mud lake. Tom suggested we head to the back garden for the interview because the ground was higher and less boggy.

He manoeuvred down the back steps. "I'm going nuts inside."

"Just don't get that plaster wet." I held his crutches, an ache forming between my eyebrows as I watched him. "We don't want you sliding over and breaking anything else."

"Yeah, thanks for your concern, Florence. I'll be fine."

He took back his crutches and refitted them under his arms, breathing the damp air into his lungs. Then he swung off along one of the wide pathways, avoiding the puddles. When we reached the edge of the garden where it met bushland, he stopped again and drank in another breath.

"Ah, the air. So fresh after the rain, isn't it?"

"Don't you want to sit somewhere?" I flipped through my notebook to the jottings I'd made last night. "You might be more comfortable."

"It's good to stretch my legs." He narrowed his eyes at me. "Unless you need to sit? A townie like you must feel utterly wrecked after trekking so far from the house."

I scoffed. "Shall we start?"

"You'll give me a final say before this thing goes to print?"

"You have my word."

"Great! Let's get it over with." He took a sheet of paper from his pocket and placed it on top of my notes. "There you go."

"What's this?"

"A list of topics I'm willing to discuss."

I scanned his messy scrawl. "Where do you get your ideas? Seriously, Tom? I'm not asking that."

"It's a classic interview question."

"You're not the one conducting this interview. I am. Besides, it's boring."

His brow shot up. "You think my ideas are boring?"

I groaned. "Okay. So where *do* you get your ideas, Tom?"

"Newspapers, mostly."

"And?"

He frowned at me a moment, then looked away. "That's about it."

"Fascinating."

"You're not writing it down."

I scrunched his sheet of paper and hurled it into the garden.

"You write fiction based on true crimes. We get the gist, Tom. My readers want to know the juicy stuff. Why your marriage failed, for instance."

"Why would anyone care about my marriage?"

"You're famous. When us townies read about your divorce, we don't feel so bad about our own dysfunctional lives. It's comforting."

"And will knowing I'm an emotionally stunted arsehole comfort you too?"

"Really, Tom. You're not that bad."

He grunted and continued down the path. "Legions would beg to differ."

I caught up to him, squelching through the sodden grass. "Okay, what about this. How did you get published?"

"Fair question." He gave me a sideways glance. "Okay, let's see. After my dad died, I would have been twenty. Since he didn't make it to retirement, I decided to live his bucket list for him. I deferred uni and bought a motorbike. Rode it wherever the mood took me. Camping along deserted roads under the stars. Following rivers into the forest and then the deserts beyond. I learned to trap rabbits and find bush tucker and raid abandoned orchards."

"I can picture you doing all that, despite—" I gestured at his legs. "It must drive you crazy being cooped up."

"It does."

"You grew up in Sydney. Didn't you miss the city?"

"Yeah, at first. Until I realised my restlessness came from something else. A dream of my own that I'd been avoiding."

"Writing?"

He nodded.

"Why were you avoiding it?"

"Failure terrified me. But the more I tried to suppress my dream, the louder it shouted. So I started small. Began my first novel in a school exercise book. Pretty soon my backpack was bulging with slim, dog-eared volumes. When I finished that novel, I started another."

"Were they any good?"

"First novels—are you kidding? They were rubbish. Until I started writing about things that mattered to me. Dad was a cop and loved nothing more than speculating over unsolved cases. We used to argue for hours trying to unravel them. Those were my happiest memories. Once I realised that, my stories took off."

"A publisher discovered you at uni, didn't they?"

"That's media hype." He stopped walking and regarded me. "Truth is, my savings ran out. I returned to Sydney, intending to work for a few months before I hit the road again. I mentioned my story to an old university mate, who described it to his chum at a publishing house. It took me twelve months to marshal the courage to hand over my manuscript. When I did, a surprising thing happened."

"They loved it and the rest was history?"

He laughed softly. "I got lucky, that's all."

The garden fell silent. The breeze held its breath, and the trees stood motionless. Raindrops glittered in the grass. Even Tom was still, and I feasted on the sight of him, his wind-blown hair and rugged unshaven face. The directness of his gaze as he studied me in return. I didn't mind him looking. After only a few days I felt comfortable with him, and in the silent garden he seemed almost like an unsolved case himself and I was the one unravelling *him*. I swayed towards him, other questions burning on my lips. *Why are you alone out here? Are you still living your father's bucket list, or are you running away from something? Have you, like me, been running away all along?* But then the wind picked up and rattled the branches and the spell broke. Shadows shifted across Tom's face, gathering in his eyes.

I tried to smile. "I'm sorry your dad never got to see you achieve all that. He would have been proud."

Tom straightened. "I reckon he would. He was one of the good guys."

"What about your mum? Is she still alive?"

He nodded. "She remarried a few years after Dad died and moved to Melbourne. She's a radiologist. Planning to retire soon. I don't think she and Dad were all that suited, because she seems a lot happier these days." He looked over at me. "What about your family? You said you lost your dad."

"Yeah, there's just me and my brother Duncan now. Mum ran off when we were kids. We're not in touch with her."

"That's tough. Must have been hell for your dad. I bet he found it a comfort to have you around."

"Dad and I weren't—" I'd been about to trot out my old line about us not being close, but considering Tom's admiration for his own father, it seemed a callous thing to say. Besides, Dad and I *were* close once. "He did his best with us. In the early days, he took us camping all the time. He was a survivalist and taught me and Duncan to fend for ourselves in the event of major catastrophe—zombie or alien invasion, that sort of thing. But after Mum left, he withdrew into himself. Hit the grog . . ."

Tom stood near, his gaze intent on my face. When I didn't say anymore, he nodded. "It must have been tough on him. Having to cope alone with two kids, meanwhile trying to swallow his heartbreak."

"Sounds like you're speaking from experience."

"I guess I am. At least about the heartbreak."

"You were married once. What happened?"

He narrowed his eyes. "Nice try."

"I'm curious, though. Why would someone like you choose

to be alone? You're pretty famous. You could probably be with anyone you liked."

A soft growl came from his throat and he set off along the path. "My ex-wife was just like you. Smart, ambitious. An independent woman with an enquiring mind. Do anything for a story."

"She was a journo?"

"Yeah, one of your mob. I liked all those things about her. That's what drew me to her in the beginning. We used to have these crazy conversations that went on for days. We were married for seven years, and we were good together. Or so I thought. One day I discovered her fooling around with another journalist."

"Ouch."

"When I confronted her, she lashed back by writing a bunch of lies about me. That I was a womaniser, a drunk. That I plagiarised to my heart's content, and badmouthed other writers. Okay, I might have gone heavy on the booze. But the rest was lies. To be honest, the whole thing broke my heart. I could handle the media storm that followed. The one-star reviews, the dip in sales. Her betrayal, though . . ." He shook his head, wincing. "Maybe you're right about the fame thing, but once your trust in someone is broken, it's damn hard to repair."

"Not all journos are like that."

He grumbled under his breath and kept walking.

We came to a clearing. Around us, eucalypt saplings glimmered with raindrops, and a tall, rough-barked angophora raised its crooked arms into the sky. The roar of water drifted up from the gully, the river unseen behind the trees.

Spots of rain fell, and Tom squinted up at the sky. "Those clouds look pretty bleak. We might as well stop for the day." He turned and headed back towards the house, sagging on his crutches.

I trailed behind, flipping through my notebook. "One last question, Tom. What's your latest novel about?"

Tom spoke over his shoulder. "It's set right here in Gundara. You're probably too young to remember, but I'm sure you've heard all about it. Those young girls who were killed at the reserve back in the nineties?"

I stopped walking. The sky seemed suddenly dark, and the air so cold it was almost unbreathable. My lips parted, but words failed me. A crime writer buys a remote house on the edge of national parkland that has a history of murder. How had I not seen this coming?

Tom noticed I wasn't following and looked back. "Something wrong?"

"You're writing a novel about the Deepwater murders?"

"Trying to. Just not getting very far."

"Why?"

"Writer's block, I guess."

"No, I mean why write about Deepwater?"

He sent me a curious look. "It's a fascinating case."

I dragged in a breath and tasted the rain. Tasted dampness and wet leaves and earth. Deepwater was mine. I knew the story backwards and understood events the way only a local could. I ran those bushy trails every day. Heck, I'd almost been a victim. Tom was an outsider. To him, it was just a fascinating case. To me, it was ... personal.

"You can't."

Tom huffed. "If you're worried about the victims' families getting hurt, you needn't. When I'm done with a story, most readers won't even recognise the original case. That's how I roll."

"What's the point of no one knowing?"

He shuffled into a patch of sunlight, squinting for a moment, then he shaded his eyes. "I write fiction, Abby. I'm not trying to solve a crime or bring anyone to justice. Not usually. When I fictionalise these stories, the crime is only a vehicle. My goal is to explore the darker places of the human heart. What makes a good person do bad things, or what makes a bad person go beyond normal human experience and commit the unthinkable."

"You said not usually. Are you trying to solve this one?"

He frowned at me as if unsure he'd heard right. "Isn't it already solved?"

I inhaled deeply and tore my attention away from him. Behind us, the roof of the house was visible between the trees, its terracotta tiles almost blood-red in the stormy light. A shiver flew over my skin, and I hugged my cardigan tighter. Alice drifted up beside me, tilting her pixie face and peering at me with her sorrowful eyes. *Already solved? Oh Abby, are you sure?* Then she morphed into another girl, older and taller, with hair as dark as a crow feather.

A girl in a red sequined jacket.

Of course the Deepwater case was solved. The killer in jail, and no more bodies unearthed since. So why did my heart quiver erratically, as though it secretly believed the opposite was true?

I gulped a breath. "Tom, did you ever discover why someone commits the unthinkable?"

He looked at me for a long time, then shrugged and turned back to the path, making his way towards the house. "Like pretty much everything else in my life, Abby, it's still eluding me."

12

TOM

He sat at the redwood table on the verandah, bathed in the yellow glow of a citronella lantern. It was only five o'clock, but oppressive black storm clouds mottled the sky, making it seem like night.

He glanced at the doorway. Abby was taking her time. He uncorked the brandy bottle, savouring the syrupy sharpness in his nostrils as he poured a glass and tossed the contents down his throat.

How had it come to this? Sitting outside on such a dreary day, feeling weirdly alive, despite having just exposed bits of his fiercely guarded past to a woman he'd only just met. A woman who was, God help him, a bloody journalist.

He filled his glass again. She wasn't like any of the journos he'd met before. Not like his wife, despite what he had said. Not like anyone. The hopeful way her brows shot up when she asked a question, her chin tilting to the side. Her husky voice, her wary grey eyes. The cosmos of tiny freckles that dotted her skin. He liked how she listened when he spoke. Actually listened, her attention focused on him as if what he said mattered to her. She was always aware of him, and that made him want to open up to her even more. To share parts of himself that he'd closed off for years.

She appeared in the doorway, lit from behind by the kitchen light. "The rain seems to have eased."

Tom stared. He had lent her some clean clothes while her own were drying after the sudden downpour that caught them earlier. A favourite pair of threadbare old jeans he'd hoarded since his university days, and a thin cashmere jersey he'd recently shrunk in the wash. She had belted the jeans and rolled up the legs, tucking the jersey into the waistband and pinning her dark hair in twin bunches. Far from the shapeless figure he'd hoped the clothes would bring her, he found she was just as distracting as ever.

He backtracked to what she'd said. "Yeah, the rain. I guess you'll be heading off in the morning, then? If the road's clear."

She joined him at the table and eyed the brandy, toyed with her glass. "I've still got a few questions, Tom. That was our deal, wasn't it?"

Tom gulped more brandy. "Nothing too personal, I hope?"

She fiddled with a spike of hair that had escaped its bunch. "How would you feel about me staying longer so I can write the article here? Then you can read over it and change anything you're not comfortable with while I'm still around. Sound fair?"

"How long will it take to write?"

Her shoulders slumped. "In other words, how long will I continue cramping your style? Couple more days, at most."

Tom reached for the bottle, but Abby hadn't touched her

glass, so he re-corked the brandy and pushed it aside. He didn't want a top-up. His head already swam. Partly from the liquor. Mostly, he blamed her for his whirling, unsettled thoughts. He got to his feet and collected his crutches.

"Stay as long as you like and make yourself at home. I've got work to do." Without giving her a chance to reply, he hauled himself up from the table and escaped inside. He shut his office door and switched on the desk lamp, settling into the familiar cocoon of light.

He wound a fresh sheet of paper into the Remington. Typed a sentence, then drifted again. He shouldn't have been so gruff with her. She was being fair. Making an effort. Being funny ... not to mention totally adorable with her hopeful eyebrows and husky laugh. He had opened up to her so easily that it stole his breath away. Why was that?

"Yeah, probably those big soulful grey eyes."

Part of him resented her for gate-crashing his solitude, distracting him. Since she'd been here, he caught himself seeking her out, observing her with increasing interest. Her slim body bent over one of his boxes. Her bare arms as she rolled her shoulders and stretched. She wasn't what he'd expected. Nothing fazed her. His criticisms fell on deaf ears. His harsh words rolled off her. Last night, for instance, when he got snappy over her rough handling of his valuable old dictionaries, she just smiled to herself and gave him that look—*yeah right, loser*—then continued unpacking.

Was she still on the verandah? He reached for his crutches. Be good to hang out with her again, make up for his gruffness. Hear that husky laugh again.

"You idiot." He sagged back into his chair. "Don't even go there."

No point getting ideas. He'd already messed up his

marriage. Alienated his wife and made mortal enemies of his in-laws. Not to mention pissing off an army of ex-girlfriends. He had no right getting hot and bothered over another woman. Especially not a journo. And especially not one with the beauty and brains to do a lot better than a cynical bastard like him.

13

ABBY

"ANY LUCK AT THE HOSPITAL?" I had to jog to keep up with my brother's long strides. "Did anyone admit a teenage girl?"

It was nearly lunchtime. We were walking along the foreshore of Lake Winsey, a ten-minute hike from our childhood house on the north side of town. As kids, we had spent all our spare time here, searching the shoreline for flat stones to skim across the grey water, or playing hide-and-seek in the maze of tea-tree thickets. These days, it was still our favourite meeting place to catch up on one another's lives.

"Only the usual dramas." Duncan swiped a wind-blown lock of sandy hair out of his eyes. Today his scrubs had little blue aliens. "A guy smashed his knuckles when he punched a friend's car. A middle-aged woman skewered her thumb with a sewing machine needle. Otherwise, it's been a quiet week. No head wounds. No teenage girls admitted."

My shoulders slumped. "I can't stop thinking about her. How she just vanished."

Duncan gave me a sideways look. "Maybe her injuries weren't as bad as you thought."

"Hmm."

"So who's this dude you've shacked up with? Anyone I know?"

I jabbed him with my elbow. "I'm not shacking up with him. Okay, I am. But not like you think. I drove out to interview him. There was a storm, it flooded the road, I got stranded. Tom offered me a room. End of story."

"Stranded for three days?"

"The bridge only cleared this morning. It's been under water since Monday. Drive out and see for yourself, if you're so concerned. The road is a mud bog, and there's smelly creek weed all over the bridge. Anyway, I'm helping Tom with a few things. In exchange for the interview."

Duncan snorted. "Things?"

"He's on crutches, so I've been unpacking his books and making him lunch—"

"Lunch? Careful you don't poison the poor guy."

"Ha ha, you bloody comedian."

"Keen on him, are you?"

I rolled my eyes. "Really, Dunc. *You* might go around shagging anything with a pulse but I'm more discerning. Tom's nice enough, in a rugged librarian sort of way, but to be perfectly honest he's not my type."

Duncan made a guttural sound. "Yeah, you're keen."

"I'm there for the interview. Nothing else."

"So what is he, some bigwig?"

"Kendra called him the Stephen King of true crime."

"Heck!"

"Yeah. He's the real deal, too. On all the big bestseller lists, his books made into films. He's reclusive, though. A bit of a hermit, so I'm super chuffed about getting the interview." I winced. That last bit I had practically yelled. I snuck a look at my brother, hoping he hadn't noticed.

Duncan's brows were up near his hairline. "That sounded totally fake. Come on, sis. Tell me why you're *really* there."

I wilted into my cardigan. "In exchange for the interview, Kendra promised me a front-page feature."

"About?"

Water spray misted across the surface of the lake, kissing my face with its icy breath and making me shiver.

"The gorge murders."

"Jeez, Abby." Duncan shook his head and picked up pace.

I ran to catch up, skipping across the shingles so I wouldn't fall behind. My legs were long, but Duncan was a beanstalk.

"I want to tell the truth, Dunc. People need to know what really happened."

"They already know what happened."

"Not from my perspective."

He sighed up at the sky. "That's a terrible idea. It's only going to open up old wounds."

I knew he was only being protective. After our mother left, my eight-year-old brother had discovered his maternal streak. While Dad and I floundered hopelessly around in our misery, my brother started cooking breakfast for us, and then packing our lunches. He even started cutting recipes from old *Women's Weekly* magazines that Mum had left behind. As his confidence grew in the kitchen, he branched out to other duties. Laundry, making the beds, even ironing Dad's work shirts. Now, as he loped along beside me, I glimpsed the little mother hen who had tried so hard to keep our father and me fed and loved.

I patted his bony shoulder. "I know you worry about me, baby bro. But I'm okay."

"You're not, though, are you? What's this really about?"

I dragged in a breath. "Remember when I gave evidence at Jasper's trial?"

"Yeah."

"What if I got it wrong?"

"Got it wrong *how*?"

"What if it wasn't Jasper who attacked me in the forest that day? I remember running away from him, and I'm pretty sure I fell. After that, it's a blur." I leaned nearer. "Dunc, do you ever think that because of me, they convicted the wrong guy?"

"I never doubted you. You were such a wreck afterwards. You saw the bastard up close and personal. He tried to—Jeez, Abby, it was twenty years ago, for crying out loud. Why are you questioning yourself now?"

"I keep thinking about that girl at the campground. I'm sure something bad happened to her. Yet no one knows anything. And the whole scenario felt so familiar—the girl lying there with blood in her hair. The scratches on her hands and arms. She reminded me of . . . well, of me. Back then." I swallowed. Voicing my fears made them seem overblown and childish, as if I'd shone a torch into the murkiest corner of my nightmares and found only cobwebs. But knowing my fears were unlikely didn't make them any less real. "Dunc, what if it's happening again?"

He grabbed my shoulders. "It's not."

"But—"

"Jasper Horton is in jail, Abby. It's over, okay?"

I pulled away from him and continued walking.

"It's not over for the campground girl." The wind snatched my words, dragging them away into the casuarinas that grew on the shore. We were almost at the carpark. I took out my keys.

"It's not over till I know she got home okay. I mean, why isn't someone worried about her?"

Duncan grabbed his bike from where he'd propped it against my bumper bar. He squinted in the wind, his sandy brows creased as he gazed across the lake. "This is probably nothing."

"What?"

"You know I'm still doing Meals on Wheels?"

"Yep."

"One of my oldies was a bit out of sorts last night."

"Oh?"

He looked back at me. "About her granddaughter. The girl had an awful row with her mum the other week. On her birthday. She ran off to stay with her dad on the coast."

I pricked up. "And?"

"It annoyed old Mrs Pitney that the kid hadn't phoned. At least to let everyone know she'd arrived safe with her dad. Her mum isn't worried because the girl has a history of running off, but it's been a week and no one's heard from her."

14
ABBY

As I drove along the rutted bitumen road that led out of town, a feeling of desolation settled over me. The streets flanking the western edge of Gundara grew shabbier. Nearby was the local landfill, and the wind had deposited scraps of tin and plastic bags and paper along the road. I came to a row of poky housing commission houses and parked on the rubbly verge. Halfway along sat a fibro house in need of a lick of paint. I'd driven past it before, glaring at the snotty-nosed brats who always swung off the garden gate throwing stones at cars. Today, the yard was empty. Grass grew up around mower carcasses and abandoned toys, and in the driveway an old Torana was succumbing to rust.

I knocked on the front door. Yelling erupted from the back of the house, and a child screamed. A moment later, the scuff of feet approached. The door cracked open and a pair of red-rimmed brown eyes glared out at me.

"Whatever you're selling, I'm not interested."

She went to shut the door, but I stopped it with my hand. "I'm here about your daughter."

The door jerked open. A thirty-something woman tugged her dressing gown closed over her pregnant belly. She dragged on a cigarette and blew smoke in my face. "You a teacher?"

"No, but I'm concerned about—"

"A cop?"

I shook my head. "Is she here?"

She glanced over my shoulder into the street. "You're kidding me, right? Shayla hasn't been here all week. She pissed off again, didn't she?"

"Any idea where Shayla is now?"

The woman blushed, an unflattering crimson that spread up into the dark roots of her bleached yellow hair. "You're with DOCS, are you? Shit, you shoulda said. Look, I already told you people—"

"I'm not from DOCS. My brother knows Shayla's grandmother. She's worried about the girl."

"Tell the old bat to mind her own bloody business."

"I found an injured girl at the reserve last week, but she ran off before I could help. The girl was brunette and slim build, and she was wearing a red jacket. Does that sound like Shayla?"

The woman swore under her breath. She ducked back inside and slammed the door in my face.

I waited, hoping she'd gone to retrieve a photo. The minutes ticked away. I knocked again. When she didn't reappear, I turned and pushed through the gate onto the street. At least I had a name. Shayla Pitney. As Duncan said, it was probably nothing. Like all country towns, Gundara had its share of families doing it rough. Drugs, grog, poverty. Kids ran away all the time. Hitched or caught trains, and after running out of cash or getting turfed out by whatever friend they'd lobbed on —they usually returned home.

"Hey!"

I twisted around. The woman was leaning in her doorway, flapping a piece of paper at me. I ran back along the path.

It wasn't a photo. It was a note scrawled in green texta.

Up yours, Mum. I've had enough of your crap. I've gone to live with my dad on the coast. Love, Shay.

"Love Shay my arse, can you believe the little bitch?" The woman shook her head, her mouth down-turned. "She was always trouble. From the minute I got up the duff with her she gave me grief."

I passed back the note. "Have you heard from her?"

The woman pulled an incredulous face. "Yeah, right. Not likely to, neither. This isn't the first fricken time she's racked off. And I'm pretty sure it won't be the last."

"What about her father on the coast? Do you have his number?"

"I haven't seen the prick for ten years. Why would I have his number?"

"I don't suppose you could call me when Shayla gets back?"

She scoffed. "The only thing I'll be doing when she gets back is giving her a swift kick up the arse. You know she went through my wallet before she left? Cleaned me out. Ripped off my new jacket, too."

"Was your jacket red?"

"What of it?"

"The girl at the reserve was wearing a red jacket."

The brown eyes narrowed. Here was her chance to drop the

uncaring mum act and show some concern. Instead, she scowled and tugged her robe more tightly over her breasts.

"Those jackets were on sale at Kmart. Everyone's got em."

"But—"

"But nothing. Stay out of my face, you hear? Or I'll tell the cops you're stalking me. Now piss off before I do me block."

"Why aren't you worried?"

She screwed up the note and jammed it into her pocket. "Because Shayla's a bloody troublemaker. She does this all the time. The cops are sick to death of dragging her back here, and I'm sick of dealing with all her shit. The little slag is more trouble than she's worth."

Back in the car, I drove aimlessly, first heading out past farmland and then looping back via a different road. I coasted along Gundara's poorer backstreets, passing the run-down houses and neglected gardens without really seeing them. Shayla had to be the campground girl. The girl had long dark lashes and olive skin—exactly like the woman I'd just spoken to. But what could I do? It was up to the girl's mother to report her missing, not me.

I drove to the town centre and parked outside the police station. At the front counter, a middle-aged officer straightened her glasses.

"How can I help?"

"Last week I reported an injured girl out at Deepwater campground? Well, I'm pretty sure her name is Shayla Pitney."

The officer grabbed a notepad. Word must have got around, or she'd seen the ambulance report, because she didn't seem surprised by my account. She made some notes, then studied me through the bulletproof glass.

"You're a relative?"

"No, I don't know her personally."

"You spoke to her mother, Coral Pitney, is that correct? And Coral said the girl was with her dad?"

"Shayla left a note for her mum, yeah."

"So what makes you think she's missing?"

"My brother told me that Shayla's grandma is worried. She hasn't heard from Shayla all week. And Shayla's mother mentioned a red jacket like the one the injured girl was wearing."

The officer checked her notes. "You said the girl had a serious head wound. So you called an ambulance, but when they arrived the girl was gone." She looked up and her face softened. "Kids go out to the reserve sometimes to drink and party. You realise there's a chance she just recovered and continued to her dad's."

I shuffled closer. "After talking to her mum, I'm not so sure."

The officer rocked back on her heels and frowned. "Are you certain it was Shayla you found? Did her mother show you a photo?"

"I've never seen a photo. It's just a hunch."

"Look, I can see you're concerned." The officer smiled kindly. "We take reports of this nature seriously. But we see this a lot. Kids unhappy at home, running off." She glanced over her shoulder into the corridor, then leaned closer. "I know this family. They have a ton of issues. Coral's got five kids, another on the way. Quite a handful on a limited income. Young Shayla's disappeared more times than I care to count, but she always comes home when she runs out of money."

"I hope you're right."

"The good news is that in ninety-eight per cent of cases we find the person safe and well within a week."

"What about the other two percent?"

She tapped her pen on the notepad. "If she doesn't show up by next weekend, we'll start making enquiries. Like I said, she's most likely okay."

Climbing into my Fiesta, I drove east to another section of town. It was Gundara's oldest suburb, its wide streets sheltered by leafy evergreens, and the occasional red-gold autumn blaze of an elm or maple. Worker's cottages huddled neatly along the street, their compact gardens colourful and well cared for.

Except for one.

I pulled onto the kerb opposite. The little place looked abandoned. Paint peeled off its pink weatherboards, its windows tightly shuttered. Knee-high grass choked the yard, and bundles of newspaper sat in piles on the verandah. Sandwiched between the other well-tended houses, the little pink cottage was a shabby guest at an elegant dinner party. Had it always been so neglected? Or had Roy Horton let it crumble around him only after his son went to prison?

I imagined Roy inside, moving from room to room, sweating over his memories. For two decades he had kept insisting to anyone who'd listen that his son was innocent. Why was he so certain? Did he truly believe the investigation had overlooked something, or was he clutching at straws, a father unable to cope with the horrifying truth of his son's actions?

The front door opened. A man stepped out, his black trousers hanging low off his hips and a brown cardigan buttoned over a flannelette shirt. He walked along the verandah, puffing a trail of cigarette smoke as he bent over and picked up a newspaper. When he saw me, his back stiffened.

I tried to raise my hand and wave, but my fingers were gripping the wheel so tightly I couldn't unclench them.

He was going to march over here, wasn't he? Ask what the hell I was doing, idling at the kerb, staring daggers at his house.

He didn't, though, just frowned back as if hoping to ward me away with the power of his glare. Over the years Roy had probably suffered more than his fair share of people ogling the cottage where the convicted Deepwater killer once lived with his parents. After a moment, he hunched his shoulders against my scrutiny and plodded back inside.

<h1 style="text-align:center">15</h1>

JOE

HE STOOD in the sewing room doorway, gazing around at the chaos. Whatever Lil was hiding in here, he would find—but where to start? Pincushions and baskets of fabric scattered willy-nilly. Lil's good sewing scissors gathering dust on the windowsill. The overlocker draped with a tea towel, loose threads escaping their bobbins like a tangle of multi-coloured hairs.

How Lil navigated the mess was a constant bewilderment to him. With the drama group starting up again, she'd soon be bustling around in here, sewing costumes and scrims and goodness knew what else.

She'd gone off in a huff this morning. Not wanting to leave him alone. *Stay out of my room, Joe. You hear me?* He had sighed with relief when she finally left. And now here he was again, smack bang in the forbidden zone.

He crept over to the sewing machine cabinet and slid open the top drawer. Pushing aside the tangled bias binding, he exposed a box of press studs. Hmm. Nothing too incriminating.

The next drawer held a million bobbins, their cotton threads tangled in a mess that made his head spin. What about the bottom drawer? He dug around but found only a jumble of tape measures and knots of yarn, pincushions bristling with pins. He bent lower to reach right to the back, then gasped.

Thumped his chest, then clutched at it.

Lurching upright, he gripped both hands on the back of Lil's sewing chair and tried to breathe through the spasms. Curse his rotten ticker. This was the third angina attack in a fortnight.

He groped in his pocket for the spray. Thumbed off the cap and pumped the mist under his tongue. Serve him right for snooping. Once, a long time ago, he'd barged in looking for a needle and thread—an old army habit, darning his own socks— and found Lil hunched in her sewing chair. Her face raw, her eyes glistening and red rimmed as she stared down at something in her lap.

His first instinct was to comfort her, but as he went over to give her shoulder a reassuring pat, she turned on him.

Get out . . . get out, you stupid man!

Lord, her eyes. He shuddered. Once, in New Guinea during the war, he'd stumbled upon a man's body at the edge of the jungle. Poor bastard had been there for weeks, judging by the state of him. Mostly bone, his uniform in tattered fragments. Joe was just a kid, barely eighteen. He'd joined the AIF three years earlier in 1942 after getting a friend's dad to sign his enlistment form. In that time, he'd seen his share of bodies. Why did this one draw him over? His brain was half-addled by not enough sleep and too much gunfire. He had nudged the corpse, but then staggered back when an enormous snake reared up out of the ribcage, its fangs bared as it hissed at him, its tiny oil-drop eyes ablaze with warning.

Joe shook off the memory. He should be ashamed, thinking of Lil that way. Like a snake, of all things. Especially when the opposite was true. Lil had given him a decent life, a full life. She was sensible and solid. Inside her protective shell of crankiness beat a warm heart. He loved that about her. It grounded him.

He'd never forget his first glimpse of her. A girl of sixteen, all long limbs and a mane of thick blonde hair. Quietly spoken and wary, she always was a bundle of contradictions. Mostly they were best of friends, open with each other about just about everything. But sometimes—during tougher times, he'd noticed, such as after one of her many miscarriages—she'd withdraw. Her face would harden and her voice turn abrasive. Even the way she stood, square-shouldered and stiff, as if daring him to cross her. And her eyes. The eyes of a stranger. Lil's shadow-self who sometimes slipped out through a breach in her soul and took charge until the real Lil found her way back to him.

Joe shut the cabinet. Lil had been so troubled lately. If only she'd confide in him. But whenever he asked, she'd clam up and withdraw into her shell. How could he help if she kept shutting him out?

He plodded over to the doorway, rubbing his chest.

Time was running out. He needed to know she'd be alright without him. Needed to know her secrets so he could put her mind at ease. Not be forced to leave her with a heavy heart.

He looked back at the cabinet.

"Whatever you're hiding, Lil, I'll figure it out. If it's the last thing I do."

16

LIL

THE CAR RATTLED along the road as it sped her closer to town. She tried to focus on driving, but the small book on the passenger seat kept creeping into her peripheral vision. Tempting her to pull over and steal a glance inside. Lose a little more of herself to the secrets it contained.

Ever since Joe's snooping on Saturday, she'd been taking the cursed thing along wherever she went. Hoping to pass a dam or a river where she could sink it deep into the mud. Yet knowing that when crunch time came, she'd chicken out. She always did. The siren call of the past was just too strong.

Slowing the car, she pulled onto the roadside. Monday's storm had left behind a trail of tattered clouds. The sky looked forlorn, a grey dishrag with everything wrung out of it.

She knotted her fingers in her lap and gazed down at them. Why was she trembling? She frowned. They weren't *her* hands, surely? Big-knuckled and solid, just as they'd always been, only now the skin bulged over wiggly blue veins, darkened by age spots. It seemed only yesterday that her hands had been smooth and plump with youth. An eye-blink ago that she'd been a girl of nine, mapping out her life with confident anticipation. She had dreamed of being a singer. A great opera dame like Nellie Melba, or a queen of the Australian theatre like Gladys Moncrieff. She believed her music would save her. Transport her from her shabby home in the suburbs to the high society of Paris, London, New York.

She exhaled shakily. Her plans, her dreams. "How did they all go so dreadfully wrong?"

17

FRANKIE'S DIARY

MONDAY, 13TH JUNE 1949

This morning he sat opposite me at the table with his back to the window, a dark blob against the light. His brows furrowed as he watched me.

"How long have you girls been here?"

"You know exactly how long."

"I want to hear you say it."

"Why?"

"I just do."

We'd eaten breakfast, just the two of us in the bright room. Lilly was sulking. I could see her through the doorway, a lump of shadow on the bed. She should be at the table with us, but she'd gotten cross again with Ennis over burning our toast, and had huffed off to cry alone.

Ennis rewards us for being good by letting us sit in the bright room. The bright room is long and narrow. At one end is the doorway that leads into our bedroom. There's a second door, but he keeps it locked. We love the bright room. Showers of sunlight pour through the stained-glass windowpanes and paint the walls and floor in rainbows. When we stand in the light, it paints us, too. After our cramped room, it's heaven.

"How long?" Ennis prompted.

"One year and three months."

His brows shot up. "Oh, that long? It's sped by, hasn't it?"

I glared at him. "For you, maybe. Anyway, why do you ask?"

He studied his hands, squinting in that guilty way he has. I prodded him and finally he admitted he'd read a story about us in the newspaper.

I begged and begged to see it.

He shook his head. "You won't like it."

"Why not?"

A long silence. His hair is down to his shoulders now. He ties it back with a shoelace but strands always escape and cling to his whiskers. After cutting off his beard a few months ago, he looks handsome again, the way he was when we met him. Like a film star with his dark eyes and sharp cheeks. The stubble growing on his chin spoils the effect, makes him look like a vagrant. He doesn't shave every day, says it brings a rash.

Like I care.

"Please, can I see the story?"

He fell silent, knotting his fingers under his chin. I'd pushed too hard. Soon, he would mumble his excuses and leave like he always did.

"I best be getting to work."

"No, wait."

The days have turned cold. He'll spend more time away from us now, trudging into the bush with his axe. Cutting firewood, loading it in his truck, delivering it to one far-off town or another. We hate seeing him drive away.

"What if you don't come back?"

"Of course I'll come back."

"What if something happens to you?"

He took my hand and smiled kindly. "Nothing will happen. I'll never leave you, Frankie. Never."

I sat still. I used to cringe from his touch. Not that he was ever cruel. At least, not anymore. I couldn't forget when he brought us here, the rough way he knotted the rope around our wrists. Pushing and shoving to get us up the stairs to our room.

I dragged my hand away.

Our room was in darkness. Lilly was still sulking. She sings to herself sometimes, but mostly she just blubs quietly. She's too thin, her eyes too big for her face, her hair long and lank, matted with knots. He bought us a hairbrush each, but Lilly won't use hers. The day he presented it to her, she threw it at him and the next day he had a bruise on his cheek. I felt scared for her, but he didn't even get cross.

"She misses her mum," he said.

"Then why won't you let us go—"

He had glared at me so hard I couldn't finish. Sometimes I forget he's the enemy.

"Please let me read the newspaper story."

"No."

"Will you read it to me, then?"

He reached across the table again for my fingers, but I slid them out of reach. He sighed. "It's not just one story."

"What?"

"I've made a scrapbook. All the articles they used to print about you two in the papers. Pictures and everything."

I started blinking, trying to understand. Me and Lilly in the news? What if the papers talked about Mum, mentioned that she missed us? What if they said how close the police were to finding us? My lips trembled. I grabbed his wrist.

"I want to see your scrapbook."

"It would be too upsetting."

I frowned, finally realising what he'd said. Everything they used to print. In the past. I slumped back. A whooshing noise roared in my ears.

"Why would it be upsetting?"

He wrinkled his brow, worked his lips into a frown. "Because they've given up hope. The cops and everyone. They're not looking anymore, Frankie. They think you're—"

They think we are dead.

The walls shrank around me, my skin flushed hot. I couldn't breathe. I wanted to ask more, to press him for details. Did the paper mention our mum? Had she given up hope too? Did she think we were dead? But I couldn't ask anything because my throat closed up and numbness settled on me.

"Come on." Ennis stood up. "I've got another book for you. I think you'll like it."

He took my hand and led me back to our tiny room. I stumbled after him, my legs like wood, my body knotted. Only my brain must have been functioning normally, because everything was suddenly clear. If the police and all the experts think we are dead, it means we probably soon will be.

18

TOM

WHEN THE ALARM under his pillow shrilled at five o'clock, Tom dragged himself out of bed. Pulled on his track pants and jumper, slid his good foot into his shoe, and moved as quietly as his crutches would allow along the hall to the kitchen. Made himself a pot of Darjeeling and spilled only half of it on the way to his office.

Usually the graveyard shift got his brain working. He loved being awake while the rest of the world slept. It triggered his muse. But since Abby's arrival, his muse had taken flight. Now in the early mornings, all he thought about was her. She was proving to be his greatest distraction. Or rather, her absence was the distraction. He had grown accustomed to her clattering about in the kitchen, or padding past his office door. The house seemed lonely without it. Why couldn't she be an early riser like him?

He lumbered to the middle of the room. She was right above him. Probably snoring peacefully, her face obscured by that mane of shadowy hair. He slid his weight off one crutch and hoisted it upside down so its rubber foot pointed at the ceiling. Good thing he was tall. Those ceilings were lofty ten footers. He tapped the rubber base against the plaster. It echoed nicely, a faint *boom-boom*.

He shuffled sideways and repeated the motion, this time a little more loudly, imagining her up there stirring in her cocoon of blankets, frowning into the dark, her dreams interrupted. Little wrinkles forming on her freckly forehead.

Whoa. That final rap had been too robust. He staggered sideways, wincing as his knee took the brunt. He lost his balance and flung out his arm, making a wild grab for the book-case. Stupid. His fingers snatched at thin air, but somehow he stayed on his feet. The extended crutch wasn't so lucky. It arced across the room and struck his desk. As it fell it clipped the teapot, which upended onto the floor and shattered in a bomb of glazed ceramic.

Tom glared at the puddles of tea gleaming on his polished boards. "What a bloody mess."

Footsteps thundered down the stairs and then along the hall. The door burst open. Abby stuck her head in, her face flushed. She wore jeans and a pink T-shirt teamed with her favourite moss cardigan, and was barefoot. Her hair swam around her like a cloud of chocolate silk.

"Everything okay?"

"Hunky dory," he growled. "You mind letting me get on with it?"

She eyed the fallen crutch, thinned her lips at the broken teapot and its puddle of tea leaves, and then retreated into the hall.

Good. Though without her, the room felt emptier. That'd teach him to be a dickhead and play childish pranks when he was supposed to be writing. He nudged the fallen crutch out of the way with his cast. No more distractions. He'd already wasted enough time obsessing over someone who'd be gone in a few days.

The clock was ticking. His deadline inching closer. It was time to get busy. Ignore the distractions and write his damn novel.

He started back across the room, navigating the tea-leaf puddles, and was almost at the desk when his solo crutch slithered from under him. He grabbed his chair, which overturned, and he hit the floor with a grunt. A grey cloud descended. He swam around in the haze, unwilling to surface, then his senses came roaring back into focus.

She was by his side, her hands on his ribs as she gazed worriedly into his face, a lock of her hair fallen forward, tickling his jaw. "What have you hurt?"

Only his manly pride. What little remained of it.

"I'm fine. Help me up, would you?"

She extended her hand. He grasped it, easing himself into a sitting position and then back onto his feet. Abby's fingers lingered on his arms, her touch butterfly-soft, her brow creased by tiny lines.

"Thank God you didn't land on a piece of the teapot."

He ignored this comment. His indignity quota for the day —hell, for a bloody lifetime—had already been well and truly exceeded.

Abby leaned near, a breath away as she peered into his eyes. What was she doing now, checking for a concussion? He opened his mouth to insist he was fine, but then stopped. She was so close. Navy rings circled her grey irises. Delicate crow's feet fanned from the corners of her eyes. Tiny freckles danced across the bridge of her nose, and her worried pout made him want to lean in and smother it with his lips—

She touched his shoulder. "Feeling okay, Tom?"

No, he wasn't. He was further from okay than he'd ever been in his life. "Yeah, I'm good."

"You're pale and you've broken out in a sweat. Where are your painkillers? Let me get them for you."

"Nah, they mess with my head. I can't think straight. Can't write. Thanks, though."

She gazed about the room, her brow wrinkling, then she brightened. "Hey, why don't I set you up on the verandah? It's nice out there, the sun rising, a view over the garden. The perfect place to write. It might inspire you. Go on, I'll bring out the Remington."

He stared at her. His fingers twitched and something uncurled in his chest. It felt a little like awe. Write on the verandah. Why hadn't he thought of that? He wanted to kiss her. He wanted to . . . well, best not go there. Instead, he settled for a half-smile. "You realise that's an absolutely brilliant idea?"

"Off you go, then." She made a shooing motion. "I'll be out in a tick."

He hauled himself to the door. He'd been a stupid jerk trying to wake her. To her credit, she'd handled it all like a champ.

He looked back. "Listen, when you're done, grab that photo album over there in the bookcase. Bring it out and we'll have a look. It might give you some background for your interview."

19

ABBY

I COLLECTED the teapot shards and then mopped up the tea. When I was done, I took Tom's photo album from the bookcase, trailing my fingers over its worn cover. What secrets lay inside this battered old book? Resting it on top of the Remington, I manhandled the big old typewriter into my arms, but then stopped again.

A neat bundle of typed papers sat in the middle of the desk.

I put down the typewriter and picked it up. Could this be Tom's Deepwater novel? I glanced over my shoulder at the door. If I had written a first draft, I'd hate for someone to read it without asking. So put it back, then. Resist temptation. Do the right thing and walk away.

I flipped through the papers, scanning the typewritten lines. I was right. It was his novel about Deepwater. Okay, maybe just a quick peek. I settled into the desk chair and quickly got drawn in. Tom told the story from the perspective of a victim's mother, describing her life before the abduction. Then afterwards how everything crumbled under the weight of her grief.

When I got to the part where she vowed to find her daughter's killer at any cost, my eyes began to leak.

I slumped back. I had met Alice's mother, of course, on those rare days she came to collect her daughter after school. All I remembered was her mousiness. The stringy hair that was neither dark nor light, the baggy clothes that swamped her slim frame, and the round pixie face so like her daughter's—except for the deep frown lines carving between her brows. But now, sitting in Tom's office with his novel on my knees, the understanding struck me. If Alice still haunted me, then she must haunt her mother a million times more. Visiting her in dreams. Inspiring bouts of panic, of dark regret. Forcing her to replay her memories over and over until they faded and blurred like snapshots in a dusty old album.

Somewhere, a clock chimed. I jumped to my feet. How long had I been sitting here? Tom must be ready to send out a search party. I placed the typewritten pages onto the Remington, balanced the photo album on top, grabbed a couple of other things Tom might need, and carried it all out to the verandah.

Tom positioned the typewriter on the redwood table, then picked up his pile of papers and flipped through them. Could he tell I'd read them? Did he have a sixth sense that someone else's eyes had violated his private writings? He made a grumbling noise and shook his head, then tossed them onto the table and looked at me.

"What did you think?"

Heat flooded my neck. I started fussing over the jar of pencils, but then sighed and met his gaze. "It was pretty good, actually. For a first draft."

"You think I got the tone right?"

"Well . . ."

"Nah, me either. I keep stalling with the mother's point of view. It needs sensitive handling, but I can't find her voice."

"She'll be a hard nut to crack," I agreed.

"To be honest, I'm not sure this is my story. I've been working on it for over a year, and it's just not happening. I'm not one to complain about writer's block, but this one's got me stumped."

I settled into the seat opposite him. "Have you been to the gorge?"

"Years ago. I was planning to return a while back, but then —" He gestured to his legs.

"When you go, wait for a rainy day."

"A rainy day?"

I nodded, rubbing my arms. "Start with Pilliga's Lookout, the views are stunning. The deeper you go into the reserve, the wilder it gets." I groped around for the right words to describe it. "On sunny days, it's magical. Sunlight fans through the trees, and waterfalls sparkle near the river. Granite cliffs shoot up taller than skyscrapers and then plunge into dark ferny gullies. The walking tracks take you into a fairyland of mossy stone outcrops and ancient beech groves. But when it rains, the whole place comes alive. The shadows come out. The scent of wildflowers bursts over you like nothing else—" I picked up the jar of pencils, suddenly fascinated by the loose shavings in the bottom. "You said you were there years ago?"

"Yeah." He watched me, frowning. "A camping trip with my dad. It's what inspired me to be a writer."

I abandoned the pencil jar and sat up straight. "Oh?"

He opened the photo album and gestured me over. I shuffled my chair till we were side by side, my arm gently bumping his. Tom flipped through until he reached some photos of a woman and a young boy. The woman wore an elegant dress and had pinned her hair in a high bun reminiscent of Audrey Hepburn.

Tom tapped the page. "That's Mum. Beautiful, isn't she? Unlike the pint-sized wretch next to her."

"Not a wretch," I murmured, leaning in. "Just a normal little boy." Normal, although perhaps cuter than most. In one picture he stood in his school uniform with a skinned knee and black eye. In another, his mother held his grubby hand—somewhat gingerly—at the gates of a posh private school. He was grinning from ear to ear, one arm in a cast, the other cradling a football.

"Accident prone, even as a kid?"

"I much prefer to say 'adventurous'. But yeah, I had my moments." He turned another page and tapped a photo. "This is my favourite."

Tom was about twenty, a fresh-faced young man with wild hair and woolly sideburns. He had his arm around an older woman who shared his striking features. She had angled her face to look up at him, smiling with warmth and admiration.

"That's my gran," Tom said. "She's still going strong. Lives in Melbourne. She's a botanical artist."

"Talented family."

"Hmm. You'd like her. She's had a fascinating life."

"Does she loathe being interviewed, like her grandson?"

Tom rasped out a laugh. "Knowing Gran, she'd give a limb to have her picture splashed all over the newspapers."

"I should interview her."

He slid the photo from the plastic sleeve and passed it to me. "Here, take it. Your readers might like it."

"Aw, Tom. That's really generous. My readers will love it. I'll make a copy and get it back to you." In my eagerness to take the prize from him, my fingers brushed against his and I fumbled. Tom picked up the photo and placed it on my palm, and when he noticed me gazing at him, he winked. Suddenly my heart was a galloping mess. I sat perfectly still trying to rein it back in, and Tom went back to turning pages.

"Look at these. Me and Dad on a camping trip."

Tom would have been about seventeen, his dad late forties. They were standing next to a tent that didn't seem to want to stay upright. Behind them, tall ribbon gums flanked a track leading down to the river.

I leaned in. "That's Deepwater?"

"Yeah, a beautiful spot. Bit remote, though."

Tom's father was a square-built man with a red face, wearing jeans and a new-looking flannelette shirt. Tom wore an identical outfit, and his usual cheeky grin. Cute. His dad was smiling too, but shadows darkened his eyes.

"Where's your mum? Did she take the photo?"

"No, we propped the camera on a branch. Mum was never a big camper. Hated it, actually. I don't blame her. Dad and I were hopeless." He shook his head and laughed. "Our tent fell down the minute we crawled inside. We spent half the night trying to wrangle it back up. Next morning, Dad suggested we trek to the other side of the gorge. By mid-afternoon, we were lost."

I was trying not to smile. "How'd you get back?"

"We eventually stumbled on our original trail and retraced our steps. I gotta say though, navigating the wilderness is not for the fainthearted. I never thought I'd be so relieved to see our saggy old tent."

"So getting lost that day inspired you to write?"

Tom shifted, and his smile fell away. "Not getting lost. It was September 1996."

"Oh."

He nodded. "A few months after we returned home, they found a girl's body near to where we camped. A local girl, wasn't she? It was all over the papers. I read everything I could get my hands on about it. Learned about the two unknown runaways they found the year before. Those girls haunted me. I saw them every night in my dreams. I couldn't stop thinking about them. Lost and alone out there. That last girl buried in a shallow grave. That's why I wanted you to ask me where I got my ideas, what inspired me. Because long after our camping trip faded to a blur, that one image stayed with me. It's what drove me all those years."

"So it's not just another story for you. It's personal."

"Yeah." He raised his palms and sighed. "The human brain is a crazy place sometimes."

We sat in silence, both of us gazing at the open album with its patchwork of childhood memories. He'd been kind to open up this way and show me his photos. Of all people, he might understand that Deepwater was personal for me too. *Tell him*, a little voice urged. *Tell him what you found. No one else seems to care, but maybe he will?*

I swallowed the knot in my throat. "Tom."

"Yeah?"

"About a week ago, I was running through the old campground. I go out there most mornings. It's a pretty trail. Anyway, I found an injured teenage girl unconscious under a tree."

Tom sat up and regarded me. "Was she okay?"

I rolled the kink out of my shoulders. "I ran to the highway and called an ambulance. By the time I got back to the campground, she'd gone. She must have recovered and gone home. That's what I hoped, anyway. But yesterday I visited a woman whose daughter ran away. I described the girl I found, but she didn't seem worried. I told the cops, but they can't do anything until a family member comes forward. Which the mother won't do because she thinks the girl is on the coast with her dad."

"You think it was her at the campground?"

I sagged, nodding. "My gut says yes."

Tom searched my eyes. "You need to trust it, then. Sometimes you just know, don't you?"

"I guess." I tugged the end of my ponytail, looking away. My legs jiggled.

"Abby, are you okay? You look pale."

"All this talk of the gorge, and . . . you know. It's given me the yips. Reckon I'll go for a run and get some air."

THE GARDEN behind the house was still boggy, so I climbed to higher ground. I found an overgrown trail that meandered into the bush and ran along it, splashing through puddles, finding my rhythm. When the trail grew too rocky, I slowed to a walk.

Below me stretched the north end of the reserve, a rolling blanket of hills and valleys and shadowy trees that stretched forever. The river snaked through its centre, carving stony beaches and deep gullies between the vegetation. The hiss of water drifted up, bringing with it the scent of damp leaves and mossy pebbles.

Sometimes you just know, don't you?

From the moment I found her in the campground, I sensed something was wrong. A girl alone and injured, her hands scratched up and her knees skinned, her bare feet bruised and torn. Like someone who had raced through wild bushland. Running after someone ... or maybe running away.

I wandered closer to the edge, feeling helpless. Other emotions were burning deep down. *You can't give up on her, Abby. Not until you know for sure she's safe.* I pushed my fingers through my hair and found the scar, massaging the lump as if it somehow contained all the answers. But as usual, all it gave me was a dull ache that sent my thoughts rushing back to that long ago rainy day.

FOR TWO WEEKS, I nagged my dad to let me go on the school orienteering excursion. At twelve, I was awkward and friendless, desperate to prove myself to my classmates. The excursion was my chance to impress them with my bushwalking skills. But my father bluntly refused.

"I need you to mind your brother."

"Please, Dad. All the other kids are going. I don't want to be left out."

Not that I wasn't already. None of the other kids turned up to school in threadbare uniforms. When their old shoes wore out, they got new ones. They had textbooks that weren't out of date, and schoolbags that weren't held together with gaffer tape.

"Sorry, Abs. I gotta work and I need you here."

Things had been tough for Dad since my mother walked out. One morning we'd come down to breakfast and found her note. She'd addressed it to my father, but he was too hungover to read it so I'd done the honours. Her last words to us had scored into my brain. *Don't bother looking for me, you bloody drunk. I'll send for the kids when I'm settled.* She never bothered. We never heard from her again.

After that, my eight-year-old brother refused to speak about her. Instead, he started shadowing Dad, who didn't appear to mind. If Dad drove to the shop, Duncan went along for the ride. If Dad sat on the back verandah to smoke, Duncan was beside him holding the ashtray.

Despite my endless letters to relatives and whoever else I could think of, I could never trace Mum. An aunt said she moved to Canada. A distant cousin later told us she'd remarried.

Everything fell apart without her. Dad withdrew. Duncan started getting into trouble. And I just faded into the worst version of myself. My one strength was navigating the bush. Hence my desperation to join the excursion. If I could show everyone at school how good I was at orienteering, then maybe they'd accept me for who I was. See past my ratty uniform and scuffed shoes. Past the broken bag and too-long hair and the sticky-taped glasses. Past the father who picked me up from school in a beat-up old Lancer, reeking of beer and stale cigarettes.

I had to go. Just had to. Duncan would be okay by himself.

The morning of the excursion, I packed my haversack and set off on foot. I figured I could walk the fifteen kilometres to Deepwater Gorge in two hours.

It took way longer. By the time I got to the campground, my school group was gone. I was sweaty and footsore, but determined to catch up. So I headed along the track into the trees, using my compass to navigate northwest towards the gorge. As I walked, thunder boomed in the distance and the first spots of rain fell. An hour later it was drizzling. My jeans stuck to my legs and my hair hung in dripping ropes. As I searched the rain-drenched trees, my heart sank into my soggy shoes. Where had the track gone?

"Hey, are you lost?"

I whirled around. A man stood there. His grubby jeans and ragged flannel shirt clung wetly to his lanky frame. He wore his hair mullet style, shorter all over the front and long down the back. When he smiled, he looked like the wolf who swallowed Red Riding Hood's grandmother. His eyes, though ...

Bluer than gems in the gloomy forest. Bluer than a kingfisher's wing-feather. So blue, they kept me transfixed like a rabbit in headlights. Frozen, as he walked towards me, smiling his wide hungry wolf's smile as if I had transfixed him, too.

BY THE TIME I got back to Tom's garden, my track pants were muddy and my runners sodden. I stopped under the lofty magnolia tree at the back of the house and began my post-run stretches. My skin was hot and damp and my lungs burned, but my head was clearer than it had been an hour ago.

I ran like the wind that day. Away from the man with blue eyes. Stumbling past trees, mud skidding and sliding under my feet, branches whipping my face. I must have fallen and hit my head, because a blackness overcame me. I woke in an airless place like a cave. My head hurt. When I touched my scalp, my fingers came away wet and sticky. The icy darkness gobbled up my cries, and unseen things invaded the corner of my mind where the nightmares lived. There were other memories too. Vague and disjointed, like flecks of blue sky through the clouds. A warm hand clasping mine. Someone wrapping me in a blanket, fussing over me. The crackle of police radios. Sipping thin black cocoa so hot it burned my tongue.

I hugged the magnolia's smooth trunk and gazed up into its branches.

Dots of early afternoon sunlight shimmered through the leaves. Nearby, a willie wagtail chirped her warning. In the bushes, Poe's black tail lashed back and forth as he slunk away into the shadows.

My stomach grumbled.

I propped my runners in a sunny patch to dry and hurried off in search of breakfast. I took my toast to the library and spent a few hours answering emails and catching up on the news. After lunch, I worked on Tom's interview, fleshing out my ideas and adding new insights and anecdotes. Usually, I wrote with my brother in mind as the audience, which stopped me waffling. This time, though, I wrote for Tom's grandmother —the white-haired woman with the kind smile and gleaming green eyes. My words flowed with a bright fresh energy that was curiously addictive and I totally lost track of time. At four o'clock, still half in the zone, I remembered my runners at the back of the house and went to retrieve them.

Late sunlight painted the garden gold.

I gazed up at the house, a little mesmerised. Light gilded the rear wall, highlighting every tiny detail. The sandy texture of the old red bricks, and the vibrant green of the rambling wanderer vine that invaded them. Tom's new solar panels gleamed against the mossy terracotta roof tiles, and directly below the eaves, in the window of my upstairs bedroom, a draft fluttered the faded curtains.

Next to it was a smaller window I hadn't noticed before. Higher than mine, almost hidden by the roofline. And were those *bars*? I shielded my eyes from the glare. Further along, the panels of a stained glass window shimmered like rainbows. Could it belong to the other half of my divided bedroom?

I raced up to my room. The brass latch and hinges on my window were stiff with age, but after some tugging and pulling, they gave way. I leaned out, inspecting the external wall. The tiny barred window was a couple of metres to my right. I leaned out as far as I dared, but could see nothing unusual. At least, not from the outside.

I followed the upstairs hallway down to a long narrow sunroom. The leadlight window reached from one end to the other and captured the afternoon sun. Light filtered through the grimy panes, painting the room with red and blue and green and deep rose red. A rustic table and three chairs sat in the centre. A firebox huddled beside a crate of cobwebby split logs.

Where was the little vent-window? From outside, it seemed closer to my bedroom than to the stained glass.

I placed my hand on the wall that abutted my bedroom. Not smooth plaster, as I'd expected, but painted plywood. The grain was rough and cool, the white paint yellowed by age and years of wood smoke. I walked along the wall, thumping it with my hand. The panels echoed dully. At the far end, the wood sounded different. I hit it again, harder. Behind the dusty panel, something metallic rattled. When I ran my fingers over the beading that joined the panels, I found a satiny patch where the join felt smooth. I gave it a push, and something clicked on the other side.

The panel slid sideways. Behind it sat a heavy iron door. The key was still in the lock, but it stood ajar.

I pushed into a small, dim room, similar in size to my bedroom. High on the wall to my right was the tiny vent window, its bars black against the afternoon sky.

In the centre of the room sat a single bed, its iron bedhead jammed against the far wall. An overturned chair stood nearby. In the far corner, someone had strung up a curtain, maybe as a privacy screen. I drew it aside. A large iron bucket sat there, its wooden seat making me wince. Really, a toilet up here inside a stuffy attic? Beside it on the floor was a tin of wood ash and a battered scoop.

"Someone lived in here?"

I turned in a slow circle. On the bed, the covers lay in disarray. An indent flattened the pillow, as if someone had recently slept there. A blackish stain covered half the pillow, with a large shadowy discolouration beneath it on the sheet. In the dim light, it looked like a bloodstain. I traced my fingertips over the blackened fabric. It was as hard and unyielding as old leather.

As I stepped back from the bed, something scraped my foot. A child's picture book. I picked it up. It was a fairy tale by Hans Christian Andersen called *The Nightingale*. Its cover was sticky with dust, dog-eared and worn. I tilted it to the light. The cover illustration showed a Chinese emperor peering at a tiny brown bird in a tree. I took it out into the stained glass room and sat down to read.

The emperor of China was walking in his garden one day when he heard beautiful birdsong. Surprised to discover that the exquisite melody came from a plain little brown bird, he captured the nightingale and imprisoned her in a cage. For many years, she was his greatest joy. Then one day the emperor received the gift of a mechanical bird made of gold and studded with gemstones. He soon forgot the real nightingale and the little brown bird escaped from her cage and flew back to her home at the edge of the garden.

After a year, the mechanical nightingale broke down. Despairing, the emperor fell ill. The court started making preparations for his death—but that night the real nightingale returned to the emperor's window and revived him with her beautiful song.

"Crazy bird. Why would she do that?"

I flipped to the end of the book. Tucked into the flyleaf were four loose pages. Not from the picture book. They were smaller and rippled with age, covered in lines of tiny handwriting. Ragged along one edge as if torn from a diary.

20

FRANKIE'S DIARY

I've been praying for a miracle for months, and maybe this is it. He gave Lilly a book for her birthday. We've been reading it over and over, but still the ending makes no sense. Why did Hans Christian Andersen make the nightingale return to the mean old emperor?

The story made Lilly cry. "It's us," she blubbed through her tears. "We're the nightingales. And him—" She flung out her arm and jabbed her finger at the door. "He's the emperor who trapped us in his cage."

She's right. Why else would he give us this book? He must think we're here to save him. Or else he thinks he's saving us. And now, despite our fury over the story, we can't stop reading it. Can't stop studying the illustrations, reading and rereading as if somewhere in the story lies our answer. The key to our escape. Our miracle.

Lilly nagged all day. "Frankie, when will he let us out? I want to go home."

"Soon," I told her with fake cheerfulness. "We're getting so big he can't afford to keep feeding us!"

Poor Lilly. She was nine when we came here. Now she's eleven. Sometimes it feels like barely a week has passed. Other times I'm Sleeping Beauty and a hundred years have sped by outside.

When I reminded him about Lilly's birthday, he insisted on a cake. Baked it himself in the wood stove downstairs, the sweet aroma drifting up. We drooled all morning, imagining double layers with pink icing and candles, maybe even fresh cream. But when he brought it up on a fancy plate and set it on the table in the bright room, it was just sultana damper glazed with honey.

"I'm afraid it's the best I could do," he said, seeing our crestfallen looks. "Everyone's low on supplies. Blame the war, if you like."

To save his feelings, we put on a show of enjoying it and washed down the dry crumbs with hot cocoa. I felt bad for Lilly. Celebrating her birthday in this stuffy cupboard of a room. She should be out in the sunlight enjoying a proper party, playing with other children her age. Going to school, doing normal things. Not worrying about when he'll finally crack and drag one of us down to the chopping block.

We've been here for a year and seven months.

Every day the same.

We climb out of bed and wash ourselves, do each other's hair. Drag the bucket beside the door for him to replace. We do our star jumps and bending, leaping on and off the wooden trunk until our blood races. If we're good, he lets us eat breakfast in the bright room and soak up the sun. We love the bright room. The sun brings rainbows through the stained-glass and makes everything seem better than it is.

After breakfast we do the mending and other odd jobs he needs. We rip up squares of newsprint for toilet paper. Sometimes he brings the soft tissue the apples come wrapped in, and we'll cut it up with scissors. We peel potatoes and such, but when I offer to help with the cooking downstairs, he says no. Upstairs is our domain. At least for now. The rest of the house and the garden belong to him.

Most days he lingers with us, telling stories about when he was a kid living with his grandad. He tells good stories, but sometimes he gets a little heated. Raising his voice, jumping up from the table and waving his arms about. Not to scare us. He just gets swept away.

Like yesterday, after the cake. He ruined everything by raving about the war. The guns that roar in his head. The moaning and screaming wounded. He started tugging his hair. It's so long now, past his shoulders, each lock black as a shadow that turns to ink in the sun. Sometimes it escapes the shoelace he ties it with and sticks out around his flushed face like the hair of a mad person.

Lilly cried herself to sleep again tonight. Before she drifted off, she clung to my arm.

"You think she's forgotten us, Frankie?"

"Who's that, love?"

"Mum."

I swallowed the lump in my throat, remembering the newspaper article about everyone giving up hope. "Mum would never forget us, Lilly-bird. How could she?"

"Will she come for us soon?"

"You know, little Lil, I think she might. She just needs to figure out where we are."

"What if she can't?"

"She will. Mum's smart."

"She's always drunk."

I kissed her head and slid my arm around her skinny shoulders. "She'll find us, Lilly. I promise."

"How do you know?"

I thought for a moment. "Remember the day we drove here in the truck?"

She nodded. "We wanted to see the birds."

"It seemed to take forever, didn't it?"

She blinked, and a tear dribbled down her cheek. "We drove for days."

I squeezed her hand. "No, Lilly. One day and half a night. That's all. Which means we're not so far from home. Eventually, Mum, or Mr Burg from school, or the police—someone—will find us."

She gave me a watery smile, but didn't seem convinced.

"Come on," I said, tucking her closer beside me and nodding at the window. "Take one last look at the moon, Lilly-bird."

Lilly remained silent as we peered through the bars at the night sky.

"Come on," I encouraged. "Say your part. Take one last look at the moon—"

She hiccupped a little sob. "And kiss the stars goodnight."

She's asleep now. The tears dried in grubby smudges on her cheeks, her pudgy fingers curled against her palm. I hate seeing her sad. My sweet baby sister, the tiny girl I once cuddled and cooed over like a doll. My brave Lilly-pilly, so clever, with our mum's quick mind and beautiful voice. But all her funny little songs are stuck somewhere down inside her, unable to get out.

My poor little nightingale.

The bird in the story escaped its cage in the end. We're not birds, though. He might trap us here forever. Unless he gets bored and kills us. I've been searching for a way out since we arrived. Now, after Lilly's crying, I feel more desperate. As if the air is getting thinner and thinner and soon we won't be able to breathe.

I lit the candle just now and read some of her book. Where the nightingale wins the emperor's heart with her song. And it came to me. Our way out. Like the nightingale in the story, I could win the heart of our emperor. Gain his trust, make him love me. And then, the minute he lets down his guard, we'll slip through the bars and fly away.

21

TOM

HE STOOD in the library doorway, frowning at the figure slumped in front of an empty bookshelf. She had arranged book piles around her on the floor, and the messy bun and big square glasses made her look like a sexy, slightly unravelled librarian. She was clearly looking for something inside the books, too caught up in her search to have heard his crutches creaking along the hall.

It was ten o'clock. Night pressed dusky fingers against the library windows, smudging the corners of the room with shadows. The chandelier burned overhead, a constellation of glittering crystal stars.

He shifted his weight. His bones had been complaining since dinner, but rather than drug himself to the gills he had gone to see if Abby wanted to watch a DVD with him. Clearly she was too busy. Judging by the mess of books, she was on the hunt.

"Lost something, have you?"

She jerked around, dropping the book she held, which thumped onto the floor in a puff of dust. "Oh, it's you."

"Expecting someone else?"

As she got to her feet, her leg knocked a book tower. She made a wild grab for it, but the books slithered onto the floorboards with an almighty crash. She brushed the dust off her jeans and walked over.

"I was after a book."

He gestured at the mess. "Do you always demolish an entire library when you need something to read?"

She pushed her glasses up onto her head, displacing a loop of hair over her ear. "Guess I got carried away."

Tom huffed. Typical journalist, couldn't help snooping. She was clearly looking for something, though he couldn't imagine what. The books weren't his. They'd come with the house. Abby was wasting her time searching among them for secrets. He should tell her, but he was too busy fighting the urge to reach out and tuck that stray lock of hair back behind her ear.

He was glad she'd be leaving soon. Once she finished her interview, she'd hightail back to town. He'd never see her again. Well, good riddance. It was what he wanted, right? He turned away and retreated along the hall. His body felt hollow. He needed to fill the sudden emptiness with something. Anything. A drink, maybe. He remembered the half-full bottle of brandy he kept for emergencies.

"Wait, Tom." She reached into her back pocket and took out some pages, which she unfolded and held out to him. "They're torn from a girl's diary. I found them upstairs in a hidden room."

He swayed back. "Hidden room?"

"It might be nothing, a hoax or a dead end. But I've got a hunch it's for real."

He took the pages and scanned the top few lines. "Praying for a miracle," he read aloud, then looked back at Abby. The prospect of reading a diary from 1949 intrigued him. Old letters and journals gave an authentic flavour to his research. What intrigued him more was the hot flush in Abby's cheeks, the brightness in her eyes.

"Why does it matter to you?"

"Just read it, Tom. You'll see why it matters."

TWO HOURS LATER, Tom sat at the big table in the library, poring over the book about the Chinese emperor and the nightingale. Abby's description of the concealed room stuck in his head. The barred window and cramped bathroom. The steel door without a handle. When she told him about the bed— with its black leathery stain that she insisted was blood—he had actually shivered.

At first, he read the diary pages with scepticism. Halfway through the second reading, he recognised it as a story that mattered. A story he could use. A story that would thrill him to write and, if handled correctly, skyrocket him straight back into the limelight. Hello again *New York Times* bestseller list. Hello another movie or miniseries. Blood drummed in his head and he had to stop himself rushing off to his desk in a wild frenzy.

"Tom?" Abby came over, holding up a black album with tattered corners. Gold writing embossed the spine, and as she settled on the chair beside him, he caught a whiff of old leather and paper dust. She opened it and began flipping through. "It's a scrapbook."

Newspaper articles filled its pages. The same faces appeared repeatedly. The younger girl was prim and sweet faced, her blonde hair cut in a chin-length bob. In contrast, her dark-haired sister scowled at the camera, arms crossed tightly over her chest, her wild locks cascading unrestrained over her shoulders. Most of the headlines were the same. WIGMORE SISTERS STILL MISSING.

"Lilly and Frankie," Tom mused aloud. "Just like the girls in the diary."

Abby watched him with bright eyes. "Their names and ages, the dates. It all matches up. Our Frankie and Lilly upstairs were the missing Wigmore sisters."

"What do you think happened to them?"

She shrugged. "All I know is that someone died up there, Tom. On that bed. And I can't bear to think which of the girls it might have been."

22

ABBY

WE SAT side by side at the table, reading through the scrapbook. Searching for anything that might tell us what had become of the girls. Someone had gone to a lot of trouble to follow the Wigmore case. They had collected three years' worth of articles and pasted them into the album. We could only hope that somewhere in these pages they had also left a clue to the girls' fate.

The Sydney Morning Herald
Wednesday, 31st March 1948
SISTERS MISSING
Police are investigating the disappearance of two girls believed missing since Good Friday. Nine-year-old Lilly Wigmore and her sister Frances, 11, were last seen outside their home on Stanley Street, Concord, on Friday morning. Their mother, Mrs L Wigmore, widowed since 1942 when her husband was killed on

active service in North Africa, is a laundress at the Repatriation General Hospital. Mrs Wigmore left home at 6 am that day for her early shift. She last saw the girls when they lingered at the fence to wave her goodbye. "They seemed chirpy that day and insisted on wearing their best frocks," Mrs Wigmore told police. "Which was unusual, as Easter is traditionally a sad time for us. It's when the girls lost their father."

Lilly is tall for her age at 5 ft. 3 in., solid build, with mousy hair cut short with a fringe, and blue eyes. Frances is slim with long brown hair and hazel eyes. She is of average height. Police urge anyone with information regarding the girls to come forward.

The Sydney Morning Herald
Thursday, 23rd September 1948
LITTLE HOPE FOR SISTERS
Six months after the disappearance of nine-year-old Lilly Wigmore and her sister Frances Wigmore, 12, police hold little hope for the girls' safe return. The sisters were last seen outside their home on Stanley Street on Good Friday. "They're sensible girls," their mother Mrs Wigmore said this morning. "They would have returned home by now. Something has happened to them."

The Sydney Morning Herald
Wednesday, 20th July 1949
MOTHER's PLEA FOR WIGMORE GIRLS
More than a year after the disappearance of Sydney sisters Frances and Lilly Wigmore, the girls' mother, war

widow Mrs L Wigmore, has offered a plea for witnesses who may know anything about the girls' whereabouts. The sisters, brunette Frances, who would now be 12, and blonde Lilly, now 10, were last seen outside their Concord home in 1948. "I'm not giving up hope," Mrs Wigmore told the Herald yesterday. "Everyone's forgotten, but I know my girls are out there. Every night I leave my porch light burning so they can find their way home."

I slumped back in the chair. "Their mother might not have given up hope, but everyone else thought they were dead. Meanwhile they were alive and well upstairs. At least, until Frankie's diary entry in October 1949."

Tom scratched his whiskery jaw. "Ravensong's a long way from Sydney. It's a good six-hour drive. Probably longer back then. Were they taken randomly, or was it planned? None of the reports mentioned a ransom. And if there wasn't one, why were they kept alive?"

"You think he killed them?"

"God, I hope not."

My heart sank. What other outcome could there have been? The dark bloodstain on the bed was bad enough, even without Frankie's fearful entry. *He could trap us here forever. Unless he gets bored and kills us.* I hugged myself, my face hot. How could I bear not knowing? Going over to the window, I wrenched it open. Cold night air rushed in. A moth fluttered drunkenly, and when I tried to shoo it outside, it zigzagged away and got lost in the shadows of the room.

I looked over at Tom. "You said there's internet?"

He reached for his crutches. "It's a cloudless night, we might get lucky. It's over here."

I followed him to a cramped alcove, where he connected his laptop to a satellite modem. He typed in the girls' names, and a long list of links came up. The first took us to a website about unsolved Australian crimes. In 1966, thirteen years after Lilly Wigmore arrived home, Professor Markham from the University of South Australia had interviewed a retired police inspector about the case.

Professor Markham: Inspector, back in 1953, you were the first to interview Lilly Wigmore about her ordeal. What were your impressions of her?

Inspector Upshaw: Lilly sat wide-eyed through our questioning and appeared not to hear half of it. Even the child psychologists we called in couldn't get anything from her. She didn't know what happened to Frankie, and could not identify her abductor.

Aside from minor cuts and scrapes and some nasty bruising, she appeared well looked after during her time in captivity. Her hair had grown to her waist, but she was healthy and acquainted with recent news events. Medical examinations confirmed that Lilly's captor had not abused her, at least not physically. Her emotional state was a different story. She had completely shut down.

Professor Markham: Could Lilly explain where she'd been for five years? Did she give a location?

Inspector Upshaw: Unfortunately not. In June 1953 a neighbour reported a young girl loitering in Stanley

Street, Concord. The girl told local police who she was, and that she wanted to see her mother, but her mother had died of pneumonia in 1951 leaving Lilly with no relatives. A social worker by the name of Mrs O'Grady took Lily under her wing and eventually fostered her. Mrs O'Grady and her husband dedicated themselves to raising Lilly as their own.

Professor Markham: What about Frankie Wigmore?

Inspector Upshaw: In the year following Lilly's return to Sydney, police issued media pleas for Frankie Wigmore to come forward, but she never did. By then, most of us believed Frankie was dead.

Professor Markham: Is that why Mrs O'Grady withdrew Lilly from the public eye?

Inspector Upshaw: When Lilly showed up in 1953, the press went into a frenzy. They bombarded the O'Grady family with requests for interviews with Lilly.

Not all the attention was positive and soon other questions started flying. Who was Lilly protecting? Was her sister dead? Had Lilly witnessed a murder? And if so, why did Lilly refuse to help police locate and catch her sister's killer? Why was she so reluctant to give evidence, or at least speak in more depth of her ordeal? Then the naysayers chipped in. Had someone really abducted Lilly and her sister as she claimed, or had the girls simply run away?

The way the media treated Lilly outraged Mrs O'Grady. Lilly had already lost her parents, and her sister's whereabouts were unknown. Now the media was publicly picking over the girl's grief. Certain reporters began throwing around accusations, suggesting that young Lilly was to blame for her sister's disappearance. One day the O'Gradys left town, taking Lilly with them. Even the federal police could not trace them, or at least that's what they claimed in ongoing press releases.

Professor Markham: But the public was keen to know the truth. Perhaps they even deserved to know?

Inspector Upshaw: I'm sure Mrs O'Grady would disagree, Professor. Young Lilly had been to hell and back, and the O'Gradys vowed to protect her at all costs.

I printed everything out, and we returned to the table.

"The articles are interesting, Tom. But we don't know what happened to Lilly. If only we could find the rest of the diary."

He scratched the stubble on his jaw, eyeing me thoughtfully. "Since we can't find Lilly, and Frankie is possibly dead—"

"You're thinking we could find the kidnapper?"

"Hmm. Lilly and Frankie lived here for five years. That's a long time."

"Could he have owned the place?"

"It makes sense, Abby. Why would he risk keeping them here if an owner might show up?"

"Then we need a list of owners between 1948 and 1953. The Land Titles registry would have them, but that might take months."

Tom dug in his pocket and threw a key on the table. "Ravensong's contract of sale is in the bottom drawer of my filing cabinet. Grab it for me, would you?"

Pompous grouch that he was, I could have hugged him. "Yeah, boss."

On my way along the corridor, I rubbed my eyes. The grandfather clock was chiming midnight. Had I really only discovered Frankie's diary pages a few hours ago? It seemed like a lifetime. Dust clung to my face and clothes. My eyes burned from fatigue, but my brain was spinning. The Wigmore sisters had taken hold of me. Frankie's words had burrowed under my skin, as if written especially for me.

Most days, I forgot how it felt to be trapped. Then the slightest thing would trigger me. Smelling something dusty or stale, or entering a closed-in space. Sometimes I'd even glimpse a little dark-haired girl in the street and my heart would stop. Of course it wasn't Alice. Just my mind playing tricks. Just the old guilt rushing back to taunt me. My past was still a prison no matter how many years or decades went by. But what if I could break free? What if finding Lilly and Frankie was the key to finally escaping my fear?

I crouched in front of Tom's filing cabinet and dragged open the bottom drawer. It creaked under the weight of documents, but I found the deed of sale easily and almost skipped back to the library.

Tom hunched over the table, shuffling absently through the album. Purplish shadows sat under his eyes and hollows carved his cheeks. He had refused his meds, insisting they clouded his head too much to write. He must be hurting, but when he saw me he brightened. I sat beside him and spread out the contract.

He scanned it quickly, then tapped the last page.

"That's him. Ravensong's previous owner."

I leaned in to read the name. "Joe Corbin. I wonder if he's local."

"You grew up here. Does the name ring a bell for you?"

I shook my head. "My brother might have heard of him. Duncan makes it his business to know everyone."

23
LIL

SHE WAS LATE. Only ten minutes, but she hated letting the women down.

The Kurrajong Players was an all-female drama group. Most of the members were former residents of the Northern Tablelands Women's Refuge. From humble beginnings, the Players now put on a yearly production—always musicals, dear to Lil's heart—mostly sponsored by local businesses. Two years ago their version of Gilbert and Sullivan's *Iolanthe* won rave reviews, as had last year's *Pirates of Penzance*. Best of all, their efforts garnered a tidy profit.

Lil made her apologies and got down to business.

Gundara Hospital urgently needed modernisation, and the women were keen to contribute. The building could use a full-scale renovation—way beyond an amateur drama group—but Lil could dream.

Fifteen years ago, she had retired as the women's refuge coordinator. She hadn't realised until then how much her work had meant to her. Seeing the women arrive in tears, broken and despairing, often with little ones clinging to them. And then watching so many of them recover their lives and even blossom. It had given Lil's life purpose.

At her retirement party, many of the women had returned to shower her with thanks. So much warmth and love. She'd been too emotional to confess her true feelings. That helping her girls, as she called them, was the least she could have done. That she was the one who owed thanks to them for saving *her*.

After retiring, she had returned to the refuge as a volunteer. She'd grown close to the new coordinator, Diane. Close enough to consider her a friend. Lil usually shied away from friendships. Joe was all she needed. But there was something about Diane Abernathy that brought Lil out of her shell. Maybe it was the cheerful frizz of carroty hair, or maybe Diane's friendly nature. When she boomed out a laugh at the most inopportune times, it proved infectious. Lil was often swallowing giggles at board meetings or wiping her eyes in church, all thanks to Diane. Diane's crazy cackle had lifted many of the women out of the doldrums. Helping them find joy in the ridiculous, in the mundane. In things that might otherwise depress them.

"Lil?" She blinked. All the women were looking at her. Diane, who had spoken, wore a quizzical expression. "Off with the fairies again, are you?"

She ignored the remark and took out her clipboard. "As I was saying, I think it should be another musical. Only this year, something more challenging. If we're serious about raising the money we need for the hospital, then I don't think Gilbert and Sullivan is going to cut it."

"Last year's turn-up was brilliant," Diane said. "Who doesn't love a good Gilbert and Sullivan?"

"True." Lil smiled over at her friend. "But why not challenge ourselves this year?" She nodded at another volunteer. "Claire, how would you feel about doing the lead again?"

The young Aboriginal woman had arrived at the shelter four years ago, so downtrodden and self-conscious that she'd barely been able to utter a word. Lil and Diane had worked hard to draw her out of that protective shell. She'd vanished for a while, and Diane had worried about her. Then Claire turned up again. She had found a job she loved in a tiny rural school for Aboriginal children and was on a quest to help others the way the shelter had helped her. Then she'd surprised everyone by offering to sing the lead at last year's performance. They were delighted to discover she had the voice of an angel.

Claire flushed. "Why don't you do it, Lil?"

Lil's heart skipped a beat. "I don't sing, love. But you'd be perfect."

The younger woman smiled shyly. "What've you got in mind?"

"Yes, Lil." Diane sounded impatient. "Spill the beans."

Lil took a breath. "Anyone familiar with *Les Misérables*?"

Diane let out a whistle. "You're not serious?"

"It would draw the crowds."

Claire raised a hand. "What's it about?"

"A man gets a second chance at life, but he messes up. He's a crook, you see. One day he meets this old fella who shows him there's another way. So the crook chooses a different path. A better path. And in the end finds he's created a life of meaning." Lil looked around at the women's faces. "And here's the fun part. I'm thinking we can tackle the whole thing ourselves."

Claire looked puzzled, but hopeful too. "You mean just women?"

Diane's booming laugh made them all jump. "What do I always tell you girls about blokes?"

Fiona sat taller in her seat. "Who bloody needs em!"

Suddenly everyone was laughing and chattering excitedly. Lil and Diane exchanged a look. The new woman with the bruised face—Jenny, Lil remembered—put her hand up.

"What if you can't sing?"

"We'd never ask you to do anything you're not comfortable with, Jenny. There's always lots to do. Sewing costumes, designing sets, helping others learn their lines. If you're good on computers, you can help design brochures or email local businesses about donating funds or materials."

"Whew!" Diane wiped imaginary sweat from her brow. "Lil, you've got my head spinning. I'd almost forgotten those endless to-do lists. Almost. I don't know about anyone else, but I could use a cuppa. And a big wedge of caramel slice."

A thunderclap outside made everyone sit up. Lil went to the window. In the hour she'd been here, the afternoon sky had grown overcast. An enormous cloudbank was drifting from the southeast, its underbelly smudged with the telltale haze of rain.

"I'll forego the tea this time," she told Diane. "Better hit the road before that storm sets in."

Lil hurried across the carpark, still smiling. Considering the bombshell she'd dropped on the women, they had taken it in their stride. *Les Mis.* How about that? All-female cast, the story cut back to its bones. Performed by women who had lived the life portrayed in the story. Victor Hugo would be proud.

As she unlocked the Forester, someone called out to her.

She turned, expecting to see Claire or Diane racing after her with something she'd forgotten—her reading glasses or a book or the plate from last week's morning tea. But she didn't recognise the young woman hurrying across the carpark towards her. A tall girl in her early thirties, with thick brown hair and creamy skin. She wore a jean jacket over a pretty floral dress and black lace-up boots.

"Mrs Corbin?"

"Yes?"

"My name's Abby Bardot. I'm sorry to approach you out of the blue like this. I'm trying to track down Joe Corbin, and my brother told me that a Mrs Corbin volunteers at the guide hall on Saturdays."

"Joe's my husband."

"Do you think he'd be up for a chat?"

"About what?"

"I'm doing an interview with the man who bought Ravensong from your husband a few months ago. His name's Tom Gabriel, he's an author. You might remember him?"

Lil frowned. "If there's a problem with the property, then I'm afraid we can't help you."

"There's no problem." Abby stepped closer. "Quite the opposite. The house is amazing, and I'm keen to know more about its history. I was hoping Mr Corbin might help me?"

Lil gathered her wits and tried to smile. "Joe never went to the house, dear. It was an investment. I'm afraid he won't be able to tell you anything of its history."

"Did you ever go there?"

Lil held still. "No. Never."

Abby took some creased pages from her pocket. "I found these in an upstairs room. They're from a girl's diary. I did a bit of digging and I think the girl who wrote them was Frankie

Wigmore, a girl who went missing in the 1940s. I've pulled the house apart looking for the rest of the diary, but . . ."

Lil stared at the rumpled pages, her smile withering. Her heart must have stopped beating because her brain felt starved of oxygen, her lungs as useless as dishrags.

"Where?" she whispered. "Where were they?"

Abby frowned, tucking the pages back in her pocket. "Inside an old book."

The image of a colourful children's book popped into Lil's mind. The Chinese emperor in bright silks, and the drab little bird he had trapped inside a golden cage. She had the vague flash of an argument, of Frankie snatching the diary from her fingers, and of trying to hide the pages she'd torn out to spite her sister—

"Mrs Corbin?" Abby touched Lil's arm. "Are you all right?"

Lil shut her eyes. How many times had she run her fingers along that ragged edge in the diary, wondering. What had Frankie written on the missing pages, what thoughts, what schemes? What awful truths.

All she had to do was ask. Abby had a kind face and gentle eyes. She would let Lil read them. Lil parted her lips, but the words jammed in her throat. Her legs shook. She needed to sit down.

"Help me into the car, would you?"

Once settled, she took a sip of water from the bottle in her bag, and then cleared her throat. "Come and see me tomorrow, say eleven. Bring the—" She gestured at Abby's empty hands. "We can talk more then. My husband's going fishing, so it'll just be us."

She tore a corner from her clipboard notes and wrote her address. Abby beamed and thanked her, then said her goodbyes.

Lil hoisted her legs into the footwell and shut the door. In the safe bubble of quiet, she fumbled in her bag for a Xanax. When she felt strong enough, she started the ignition and drove out of town.

Lord, how desperately she wanted those pages. The ache of yearning in her chest grew unbearable. If only she'd been faster. Snatched them from Abby's fingers, locked herself in the car. Sped away with them.

She slumped forward with a sigh. Who was she fooling? Abby would probably want something in return for the pages. An explanation, at least. Lil might even have to tell Abby some of her history at Ravensong. Not all of it, mind. Just enough to quench the girl's curiosity so she'd give the pages to Lil and let her keep them.

24

FRANKIE'S DIARY

I haven't written here for weeks. We've been in a whirlwind rehearsing for our Anzac Day concert. Working out the songs, adjusting some of our old clothes to make funny hats and collars, even cutting paper flowers from one of Lilly's press-out books.

And finally, yesterday, we were ready.

We transformed one end of the bright room into a stage, dragging aside the table and arranging the chairs at the other end for our audience of one. We fashioned a curtain from bedsheets, and Ennis brought up an old birdcage and two gilded chairs for props. At dusk, we lit candles and lamps, and began the performance.

Lilly sang like an angel.

Meanwhile I danced and acted out the story. We had turned Hans Christian Andersen's The Nightingale into a musical fable of sorts, rewording our favourite songs and carols so they told the story of the emperor and his two nightingales. To honour the brave Anzac diggers—our dad and Ennis among them—we turned the emperor into a war hero, and Ennis wore his uniform and bowed and even joined in some songs.

As our play unfolded, I watched him from the corner of my eye. Our plan was working. He nodded and smiled, and during a mournful song his eyes became wet. Afterwards, he clapped and roared for an encore. We curtsied and blushed, beaming in triumph.

After the concert, he brought a bottle of sherry from the cellar. He peeled away the wax seal and popped out the cork, glugging the ruby-red liquid into three fancy gold glasses. He swallowed his in one gulp and then poured another. Lilly and I took tiny sips. After a while, Lilly began to giggle and twirl about, her face flushed beetroot red as she re-enacted bits of our play and shrieked her songs. By the time I bundled her under the covers, she was shivering. I closed the window shutter and went back to the bright room.

"It's cold," I complained to Ennis. "The air's turned bitter."

Ennis brought up firewood and stacked it beside the Warmray. He scrunched up sheets of newsprint and built a pyramid of sticks and split logs inside the firebox. He took out a match, but then handed the box to me.

"You do the honours."

I sank to my knees beside him and struck a light. The kindling crackled and burst into flame. As I gave Ennis back the matchbox, he took my hand. Squeezing my fingers gently around the wooden box, he gazed into my eyes.

"You were lovely tonight, Frankie."

"Thank you."

"Lilly has a wonderful voice, hasn't she?"

I smiled. Yes, she does and what a shame to keep her trapped here like a bird in a cage. Of course I didn't say it aloud. Instead, I looked up into his eyes and batted my lashes.

"We did it for you, Ennis."

His face lit up. The sheen in his eyes made me sit back, and an unexpected warmth settled through my bones. Silly boy. Was he really blind to our tricks?

Later, curled beside Lilly in our bed, my head swam from the sherry. I kept thinking of his face. His handsome, brooding, whiskery face. The way his eyes shone with pride when we sang. And his wistful words. You were lovely tonight, Frankie. And then the warm, melting feeling in my bones.

We had gone to great trouble to win his trust, and tonight we'd succeeded—but I felt bad. He kept us locked up here, true. But he spent so much time with us, and everything he did centred around us. We had trapped him, too.

He never complained that we were an inconvenience, the way Mum did. He read to us, gave us lessons. Told us about his war adventures, or quizzed us about our lives before we met him. He ate his meals with us like a family and brought little gifts from town when money allowed. Back at Stanley Street, our mother never paid us much mind. Too caught up in grief over our father's death. She went to the club, leaving us to eat our dinner alone. We put ourselves to bed long before she staggered home with whichever of her boyfriends she lured back to fill our father's side of the bed. We were ghosts at Stanley Street. Sad, abandoned little ghosts. But here at Ravensong, things are different. We're the stars in the midnight sky that everything else revolves around.

That *he* revolves around.

Sometimes I daydream about not going home at all. Of living downstairs, the three of us like a normal family. Bathing in the washhouse instead of in the tin tub Ennis carries up. Eating our meals in the big dining room, sleeping in beds of our own.

I don't tell Lilly such things. She's so bent on getting out of here, returning to Stanley Street at all costs. The idea of going back to Mum obsesses her, keeps her going. And I don't have the heart to argue.

Without that purpose to anchor her, I fear she might slip away. Like a feather adrift on a swirling gust. Go nutty, like after the sherry. She's always been that way—needful and intense. Without me at her side to keep her anchored, I fear she'd burrow too far into herself and disappear.

25
LIL

THE NEARER she got to home, the darker the sky seemed to grow. It was late afternoon, but the approaching storm had turned the day almost black.

Lil shivered. Glimpsing those diary pages in a stranger's hands had set off a chain reaction. All the way home she had clutched the steering wheel, dreading what tomorrow would bring. Would Abby really give her the missing diary pages? What would she expect in return, a run-down of Lil's history, her past? Would she ask about Frankie?

Lil gulped the damp air, then eased out a breath.

"I'll think about it tomorrow," she said aloud, reciting the words Joe had encouraged her to say whenever her thoughts overwhelmed her. "All I want now is a hot cup of tea and to see Joe's face." Joe always knew how to cheer her up. He'd call her his girl and fuss over her, bring out her slippers and massage the tension from her neck. Tell her everything had a way of turning out for the best, no matter how it seemed right now.

Her headlights caught the familiar red letterbox, and she

breathed a sigh. Pulling into her driveway, she parked the car and then hurried along the path to the front door. She was halfway there—hunched under her umbrella as the rain hammered around her—when she realised the house lay in complete darkness.

Had Joe forgotten to turn on the lights? He was probably flopped in front of the telly absorbed in cricket reruns, oblivious to the time. Oblivious to how much she needed him.

"Joe—?"

She unlocked the door and went inside, trying the closest light switch. Nothing happened. The phone was out too. She huffed. Blackouts were common in this area. She collected a torch from the cupboard and went along the hallway.

"Joe, I'm home. Where are you?"

Not in front of the telly after all. The lounge room was dark like the rest of the house. She checked the bedrooms, then the sewing room. Thankfully, it was just as she left it. In the kitchen she found the pantry door agape. Strange. When she spied the overturned chair, her heart fought against her ribs.

On the floor next to the chair, was a lump of shadow.

She aimed the torchlight, and her throat closed. Joe lay on his back, one arm outstretched. He wasn't moving. Lil went to her knees beside him and pressed her palm against his face.

"Can you hear me, love? Please, Joe. Are you all right?"

He moaned and opened his eyes, blinking in the bright beam. Blood trickled from a gash on his eyebrow. One eye seemed unable to focus. Lil pressed her face against his and breathed in his familiar scent. She couldn't lose him. Not now, not ever. She was a grumpy old hen sometimes, but underneath it she was jelly. Joe was her backbone. Her strength. If something happened to him, she couldn't imagine going on alone.

"There's mobile reception at the turnoff." The matter-offactness in her voice soothed some of her panic. "I'll drive back and ring an ambulance. I hate leaving you alone, but I won't be long, I promise."

"No ambulance, Lil." Joe gripped her hand. "I'm starting to feel better. Help me up, would you?"

"Oh, love. Your poor head. Can you sit?"

"I think so."

Lil wasn't taking any chances. She drew up his swollen eyelid and shone the torch into his eye. Joe protested, tried to pull away, but she held him firm. The pupil dilated normally. She pressed her fingers to his throat until satisfied his pulse was strong, and then she dug her hands under his arms and helped him sit. He shuffled back until he was resting against the cupboard.

"I'm alright, Lil. Sorry to scare you."

"What happened?"

He patted his chest. "Not sure. I got up on the chair to look for biscuits in the pantry. Must've had a dizzy spell and toppled off. Silly old coot, eh?"

"Are you sure you're all right, Joe?"

"Thanks to you, love. You always fix me up."

He took out the little spray bottle the doctor had given him and had a couple of puffs. Then, with Lil's help, he climbed stiffly to his feet.

Lil put her arms around him and held him for a moment. Joe was eighty-nine in July, twelve years her senior. Time had dimmed his eyes, stolen the strength from his body, and replaced his once-strong limbs with frail bones and arthritic joints. Lil was as strong and able-bodied as she'd always been, thanks to her passion for gardening. Yet she'd transfer all her health to Joe in a flash if it meant buying them more time together.

"Think you can walk?"

He nodded.

She helped him along the hall. Joe held the torch now, and they moved slowly, following the beam of light to the bedroom. Lil undressed him and then got him into bed. She stripped off her damp clothes and put on a clean nightie, then climbed in after him. They lay in the dark, whispering until Joe drifted to sleep.

Lil stayed awake, listening to him breathe. Joe was her world. Her anchor. Losing him scared her more than anything. Tonight, they'd been lucky. But one day their luck would run out. All her earlier fears about the diary and being asked to expose her past seemed foolish now. Almost trivial compared to this fresh fear of losing Joe. After a few shaky breaths, she pressed her face into his bony shoulder and wept against it.

26

ABBY

On Sunday morning I drove south from Ravensong, heading toward Gundara but then turning east at the crossroads onto a wide tree-lined road. The road grew shady as the trees thickened and formed a leafy tunnel that blocked the sun. I travelled through a forest of ribbon gums and red stringybark trees, then the trees thinned and the landscape opened into scrubby farmland.

A bright red letterbox stood cheerfully beside a gravel driveway.

I checked the number and pulled in.

The pine trees flanking the drive dripped after last night's storm. The shadows beneath them were dank and black, but rays of sunlight were breaking through. I passed an old timber farmhouse and parked in the shade beside a green Forester.

Collecting my cake container, I walked along the path towards the house, breathing the sweet air. Neat grass walkways curved between flowerbeds and shady fruit trees. An enormous raised veggie patch spilled over with huge purple cabbage heads, frilly lettuces going to seed, rampaging spinach, and late tomato plants still flowering in the rich soil.

As I approached the house, the back door opened. A woman stepped onto the verandah. She still wore a nightgown and her thick, shoulder-length hair tangled around her face as if she'd just climbed out of bed.

I froze on the path. "Mrs Corbin, I'm sorry. I can come back later—"

"Abby, dear." She gripped the railing and waved me over. Dark circles shadowed her eyes, and worry lines creased her brow. "I'm afraid we had a bit of excitement here last night. Joe had a fall."

"Oh no, is he all right?"

"Seems to be. Though I don't think we can talk today."

"Has he seen a doctor?"

She glanced over her shoulder at the open door, then spoke more quietly. "He keeps saying he's all right, that he doesn't need to see anyone."

"But you're worried."

She nodded.

"Then let me drive you into town. A quick check-up will put your mind at ease."

"Oh." She glanced at the door again and adjusted her glasses. "Would you, dear? I'd feel so much better knowing he's all right."

"Of course, Mrs Corbin. I'd be glad to."

"And Abby?"

"Hmm?"

"I suppose you'd better call me Lil."

I pulled up straight. Was that Lil, as in Lilly? She retreated across the verandah before I could ask. The screen door clattered. The noise snapped me out of my daze. My fingers tingled and my limbs felt strangely light, as though I had just slipped through a wormhole in time. And I had. If Lil Corbin was who I thought she was, then she would have answers. All I had to do now was convince her to share them with me.

LIL INSISTED we have breakfast before the long drive into town. "Joe needs his strength, and I think we all could use some cheering up."

We sat on the verandah at a large table, and Lil spread a feast before us. Scrambled eggs on toast with fried tomatoes. Yoghurt, and a carafe of juice. A pot of strong tea. I carved up my lemon meringue pie, and after a refill of tea, Joe's face finally regained some colour.

I mentioned Ravensong only in passing, to explain to Joe what I was doing there, and then moved on to lighter topics. Joe's ordeal had shaken them up. They didn't need an inquisition. We chatted about the storm, how glad we all were for the rain. Lil spoke about her drama group, and Joe divulged one of his secret fishing spots. I described my job as a journalist and how I got an interview with the reclusive Tom Gabriel. Joe was a fan of his books, and had seen the news article about Tom's arrival in the area. No doubt it had amazed him to read Tom's name on Ravensong's contract of sale, although he didn't mention that.

After breakfast, I drove them into town. The emergency waiting room at Gundara Hospital was empty for a Sunday. The doctor called Joe in, and I sat in the waiting room with Lil.

She rubbed her knees, gazing along the corridor where Joe

had disappeared, her face pale. I had the crazy urge to slide my arm around her shoulders to offer comfort. Ever since she'd emerged that morning on the verandah, ruffled and anxious in her nightie, my protective instincts had kicked in. I kept seeing flashes of a little fair-haired girl, locked in the room next to mine at Ravensong, crying for her mother, and it melted my heart.

I didn't hug her. Instead, I took out a roll of mints and offered her one. "They're sugar free."

Lil took a mint with murmured thanks, but then held it between her thumb and forefinger. I chewed my way through one after another. Within minutes the roll was gone, leaving just a wad of foil in my palm. I caught Lil staring at it and sighed.

"Did you know that chewing helps ease stress? I read it somewhere. That's why dogs love gnawing bones. For them, it's like a massage. Or meditation."

Lil slipped the mint into her pocket. A faint smile touched her lips. "I've a feeling I'll need it later. The doctor will probably insist on bed rest, but keeping Joe in the house is like re-enacting the Great War. I don't know what he does in his shed, just that he spends every waking hour doing it."

I rummaged in the pocket of my jean jacket, took out another roll of mints and slipped it into Lil's hand. "Here, take it. I've got a stash in the car. I'm a nightmare to be around when I've nothing to chew."

She glanced at me with damp eyes, but then gave a raspy laugh. "You certainly have a way with words."

My cheeks caught fire. "I do?"

Lil nodded. "You remind me of someone. A girl I knew."

I barely dared to breathe. "A sister?"

Lil looked at her hands. "But you're softer, Abby. Kinder."

"What happened to her?"

A long pause, and Lil's chair creaked as she shifted her weight. "I lost her."

I pinched my lips together, biting back the torrent of questions that wanted to spill out. I had brought the diary pages with me. Eager to hand them over for any information Lil gave me about her time at Ravensong. But maybe I was being too hasty. Lilly Wigmore had guarded her secrets fiercely as a child. She wouldn't reveal them to a stranger, not now. Not unless that stranger had something valuable to give her in return.

Lil caught my eye. "You know what it's like to lose someone, don't you?"

Surprised by her question, I nodded. "My father died last year."

"You must miss him."

"We weren't that close." My fingers tightened around the wad of foil, crushing it into a ball. Lil was watching me, waiting for me to elaborate. I squirmed in my seat. If I wanted Lil to open up and trust me with her secrets, then I'd have to unwrap some secrets of my own. "Dad never coped that well after Mum walked out. He turned to booze. He was already a heavy drinker, which I suppose is why she left. But afterwards, he drank with a passion."

Lil nodded. "You must have happy memories too?"

I hugged myself, surprised how easily it came back to me. "Dad was a scientist before he retired. He travelled all over the place. Analysing water acidity in the Great Barrier Reef, pollution levels in Sydney Harbour, that sort of thing. He loved his job. Loved talking about the environment and conservation. He inspired my interest in it. After Mum left, he lost his spark. Withdrew from my brother and me. From everyone. It was—"

I broke off. I had forgotten how I used to look up to him. He had taken me to see his friend's beehive once, as my birthday present. The friend had showed us how to smoke the bees and harvest some of their honey. The jar he gave me was one of my favourite things, even after it was empty.

Lil reached over and gave my hand a gentle squeeze. "He died last year, you said?"

"Yeah."

"Still so raw to talk about, isn't it?"

I swallowed, not knowing what to say. The tips of my ears were burning. When I left Ravensong that morning, I had foreseen a polite cup of tea with Lil and Joe, perhaps a moment of intense interest as they recounted what they knew of the house's history. Maybe some intriguing clues to ponder. I hadn't expected to connect with Lil in such a personal way.

She settled back in her chair. "Grief never really goes away. It's like a pebble in your shoe, always nagging, but as time passes you just learn to live with it."

Her eyes were red rimmed, glassy with unshed tears. Was she thinking about the sister she'd lost? About Frankie?

"Lil?"

"Yes, dear?"

"If I give you the diary pages, will you tell me what happened to her?"

An invisible veil settled over Lil's face. She glanced along the corridor, checked her watch. Shifted in her chair, tucking her feet out of sight beneath her.

"Why are you so curious, Abby?"

I drew a deep breath. Since finding Shayla in the campground, my old fears had resurfaced. Then, when I discovered the hidden room and Frankie's diary pages—and the blood-stained mattress and tiny claustrophobic barred window—it seemed to be a sign. A ray of hope.

"I once lost someone I cared for," I told Lil. "A childhood

friend. After she died, I grieved for her terribly. But worse than that, I blamed myself for her death. That was twenty years ago, and I thought I'd dealt with it. But a few things lately have brought it all back. Especially finding the diary pages. I know it makes no sense, but if I can save Frankie—by understanding what happened to her—then there's a chance I can save myself too."

Lil shifted in her chair. She studied her hands, smoothing her fingertips over her knuckles, pressing the blue veins and age spots. "Perhaps I'll tell you a little. In exchange for the pages."

I sat up. "Really?"

She dug in her pocket and took out the little mint I'd given her. Examined it for a moment, then popped it in her mouth. Then she settled back in the creaky plastic chair and closed her eyes.

27
SHAYLA

T HEY'D FORGOTTEN HER, hadn't they? Left her here to die. Alone. Starving and shivering in the dark, reeking of her own sick. Someone tossed a plate in earlier, and she'd wolfed the meagre meal. Two dried bread rolls and some greasy sausages, which she vomited up. Typical her. Whenever she cried hard, nothing stayed down.

She crawled across to the door. Sometimes she waited there, planning to fly out the next time it opened. Hours might pass, days—she had no clue of time. Then without warning, the door would shriek open and a flashlight would blind her, and a noisy clatter would deafen her as the tin plate hit the floor. While she scrabbled about in the dirt gobbling her food, someone replaced the bucket.

The bucket. "Ugh. Gross."

All the fights with her mum seemed petty now. Sitting in this damp, horrible place made her see things differently. Her room at home was plain and boring but it was better than this dump. At home she had a proper bed instead of this smelly mattress and stiff, scratchy blanket. At least there'd been food and TV. And sometimes Mum was okay. Almost nice.

Mostly she missed Mrs Bilby. Where was she now, out in the bush somewhere munching wild grass? Maybe even close by?

Sometimes Shayla stirred in the night, thinking she could feel Mrs Bilby's velvet nose kissing her face. She'd wake all hopeful and teary, but then there'd be that sick jolt as she remembered where she was. Still trapped in this shithole, no one knowing she was here. Did anyone miss her yet? Were they worried? Were they even looking?

Spidery legs ran across her foot, and she jerked away.

"Someone, please," she whispered. "Please find me."

The dead quietness swallowed her words. Her voice was like a dry leaf scratching down from some forgotten tree. No one was coming to find her. They'd all probably stopped looking ages ago. She was going to die here, wasn't she? Lost and alone in the dark, and no one would even care.

Something in the back of her mind cracked.

She rolled onto her back, drummed her bare feet against the door and screamed.

28

TOM

"We've found her." Abby bustled through the kitchen door at six o'clock, her face flushed and her eyes shining. "We've found Lilly Wigmore."

Tom stared at her. One minute he'd been making salad, pondering how best to marinate the salmon he'd taken out of the freezer earlier. Was lemon and garlic the surest way to get a woman hooked, or should he try chilli and ginger? He'd gone with the lemon, and now here she was in the kitchen with him, pink cheeked and smelling like a garden, a thumbprint of dirt on her brow.

He put down the chef's knife. "She a friend of Joe Corbin's?"

"She's his wife." Abby dumped an overflowing basket of vegetables on the counter. "And her name's Lil. She sent these for you, special delivery from her garden. She grew it all herself. And get this Tom—she's promised to tell me what happened to Frankie. In exchange for the diary pages."

"Hang on." Tom was trying to process everything at once.

"The guy I bought Ravensong from is married to Lilly Wigmore?"

Abby nodded. "You can imagine she's hesitant to talk about the past. I don't want to press her too hard. But Tom, we've found her."

Tom wiped his fingers on the tea towel he'd tucked into his waistband and considered her. The rose flush in her skin, the brightness in her eyes. The thumbprint of grime on her forehead that he was longing to smooth away. He'd never seen her like this, unguarded, almost childlike in her excitement.

"Oh, Tom," she rushed on, "they're the most gorgeous couple, so devoted. Lil's the straight guy, all stern and cranky, but then she'll smile and the sun comes out. Joe's hilarious, quite the comedian. You must meet them, they're—"

Tom stared at her, but he'd stopped listening. The blood pulsed sickly in his veins. *Are you really going to whirlwind into my life and turn everything upside down, and then vanish in a few days and forget me?*

She touched his arm. "Okay there, Tom?"

"Hmm." He picked up his knife, resumed slicing the tomato. "Did Lil say much about Frankie?"

Abby's spark dimmed. "Not yet, but she will. She wants those pages."

"Anything about the kidnapper?"

"Zilch."

"What about Ravensong? Did she and Joe ever live here?"

"Lil said that in 1980 she and Joe decided on a tree change from Sydney, as neither of them had family there anymore. Lil saw the house in a rural newspaper. It was a deceased estate, owing over twenty years of rates. The council repossessed it and sold it for a song, but the Corbins never lived in it."

"Bad memories?"

"Lil didn't say, but they couldn't bring themselves to sell it either. So it just sat vacant for years. She and Joe bought the farmhouse and carried on with their lives."

"That's quite a story."

Abby smiled and started unpacking her basket of veggies. "Inspired, are you?"

"Maybe."

Inspired didn't quite describe it. Tom felt like a kid at Christmas. Since Friday night, a story kernel had taken root in his mind. The girls in the attic, the bloodstained bed, the missing sister. He would have to fictionalise the facts, disguise the truth to protect his real-life subjects, the way he always did —but his fingers itched to hit the keys. There was just one snag.

"When are you seeing Lil again?"

"Wednesday."

"You think she'll tell you what happened to her sister? This is Lilly Wigmore, remember. The girl who kept her secrets. Who never breathed a word to the detectives and media hounds who made it their business to crack her. What makes you think she'll talk to you?"

Abby wiped her hands on her jeans and slid the diary pages from her back pocket. She waggled them in the air.

"I've got this juicy carrot to dangle in front of her."

Tom took the pages from her and unfolded them. He pretended to read, even though most of it he'd already memorised. The paper was warm. Distracting. He passed it back.

"Does being here creep you out?"

She made a scoffing noise. "Because someone might have died upstairs?"

He nodded.

She smiled, inching closer, her gaze steady on his face. "It'd take more than a seventy-year-old bloodstain to rattle my cage."

Her smile slipped away. "You seem different tonight, Tom. What's happened?"

"Nothing, I'm good. It's just—" Reaching out, he cupped the side of her head and smoothed his thumb over her eyebrow. "You've been in the garden."

She stepped back, brushing at the spot.

"Lil gave me a guided tour. She's in her seventies, but she does everything—chops firewood, mows the lawn. She even built a shade house last summer. Honestly, Tom. The woman's unstoppable."

Tom blinked. Such soft skin. He wanted to touch her again, but then he recalled something from his time in the desert all those years ago—a brown snake he'd caught in order to throw it out of his hut. He had only gripped its narrow tail for a moment, yet he'd never forgotten the soft velvet nap of its skin. Or the sinewy strength beneath.

He eased out the breath he'd been holding. Abby might be rose petals and velvet on the outside, but letting down his guard with her could prove fatal. He could end up like the last time he lost his heart. Badly bitten. Even broken.

"Tom, where have you gone? I feel like I'm having a conversation with the invisible man." She was frowning at him, her head tilted like a curious bird as she waited for his response.

His chest was suddenly tight, his words choked off. His thoughts racing. Yes, he could end up broken. But wasn't that better than never taking a chance at all? Never knowing? Abby fired him up like no one else he'd ever met. Was he really going to stand by and let her walk out of his life? Did he even have a choice?

He returned to the cutting board and picked up the knife.

"The salmon's ready for the oven," he said over his shoulder. "I hope you're hungry."

29
ABBY

WE ATE at the big redwood table on the verandah. Candles fluttered in hurricane jars, and kerosene lamps burned citronella. The lemony scent mingled with the sweet perfume of jasmine that drifted from the garden.

Tom had baked the salmon to perfection, its crispy skin enclosing flesh so buttery and delicate it melted on my tongue. I couldn't get enough of the Greek salad, wolfing down most of it while he related funny anecdotes from his past. The dinner, he explained, was to thank me for all my hard work—unpacking boxes, making sandwiches, getting the dust bunnies under control.

"And for firing up my creative engines again."

"That wasn't me," I objected.

"You found Frankie's diary, and then you found Lil and Joe. You won Lil over enough to convince her to open up about her past. It's been you doing all the hard yards, Abby. I'm the one reaping the rewards. Nothing has inspired me for years. But now—"

"Tom, they're easy yards. I'm enjoying the whole cloak-and-dagger thing as much as you are. Tell me, how long will it take you to finish the book? I'm already dying to read it."

He narrowed his gaze. "Not so fast, young lady. I've been blabbing about myself all night. How about you take the stage?"

"Nothing to tell. My life story is incredibly boring."

"Come on. You managed not to yawn too much during my ramble. Let me return the favour."

I snorted, then tried to cover the sound with my serviette and knocked over my wineglass, which made me giggle. Tom spluttered, and that set us off like hysterical teenagers.

I wiped my eyes. "Someone must have spiked the pinot grigio because what you said wasn't all that funny."

He made a hurt face, and that got me going again. My giggles, punctuated by noisy hiccups, took me a good five minutes to get under control. Tom's wisecracks didn't help. My ribs ached and my face felt stretched out of shape. I hadn't laughed so hard in . . . well, in longer than I could remember.

Tom got serious. "So, off you go. And I'll do my best not to yawn."

I rolled up my serviette and dabbed it over the wine mess. "I went to university like everyone else. Attended wild parties, drank too much red wine, smoked too much pot, and graduated with far better marks than I deserved."

"What did you study?"

I hesitated. For ten years I had blocked that part of my life, hoping it would wither away and let me forget. No such luck. It had withered away, all right. But never left me completely. I took a deep breath. "Sustainable farming."

A look of wonder spread over Tom's face. "You're a farmer?"

I fought the urge to roll my eyes. "I wanted to be. Once."

"So how did you go from farmer to"—he grimaced—"journalist?"

"By an extremely meandering path."

He steepled his fingers and leaned forward, resting his elbows on the table. "Tell."

I took a fortifying sip of wine. "After uni I still wasn't sure where my real passion lay, so I started doing short courses. Permaculture, organic stock breeding, natural land management. I cast my net far and wide, exploring all possibilities."

"Did you find it?"

"Crazily enough, I'd been looking in all the wrong places. Branching out, instead of homing in on what I loved. One day I realised my thing was microcosms. Life in miniature. Tiny things had always fascinated me. Doll's houses, terrariums, ant farms. As soon as I realised that, the answer came easily. I enrolled in a beekeeping course in Western Australia and flew over to Perth where I—"

Where I met my husband. And where, in a whirlwind three weeks, we had fallen in love. Or at least, Rowan had. He was a course convener. We met over lunch one day and hit it off. He dreamed about having a family, doing the whole off-grid self-sufficiency thing, which I adored. But despite the passion of our early days—including the wedding that happened so fast it took my breath away—I kept him at arm's length. Getting close to people always seemed to end with them leaving. Or dying.

I never told Rowan about Deepwater. I never told him about Alice, or the guilt that still haunted me. That still made me fear getting close. So when I said goodbye that scorching February day nine years ago, he watched me leave with eyes that were full of confusion and disappointment. I had memorised that look and wrapped it around my heart as a silent reminder to keep my distance.

"So you flew to Perth," Tom prompted. "Beekeeping?"

I refilled our wineglasses. "Met the man of my dreams and got married. A year later, we divorced."

"What happened?"

"My brother says I push people away."

Tom's smile shifted down a gear. "Maybe you just married the wrong guy."

I shrugged. "He wasn't the problem. I never had a lot of luck settling in one place. Itchy feet, you know?"

"So what about the beekeeping?"

"After that, I quit the whole farming gig. I flew to New York to visit a friend and ended up at a Greenpeace rally. It moved me, I guess. I felt inspired to write about it, and on a whim sent my story to, of all places, the *New York Times*. They bought it. You could have knocked me over with a feather."

"It must've been one hell of a good article."

I pulled a face. "Beginner's luck."

"More like a passion for your subject."

"Hmm. I never thought of that."

Tom narrowed his eyes. "And it gave you a taste for the power of words, so you kept going."

"In a way. I ended up at the New Orleans Jazz and Heritage Festival that year, which blew me away. So I wrote about that, too. Interviewed a few of the old musos. One thing led to another, and I started writing editorials for various newspapers." I shrugged. "It was fun. I adored the US, so I travelled around. Writing about out-of-the-way places. Selling my articles freelance."

"What brought you back here?"

I found my smile, but the warm sunniness of a moment ago

flickered and died. I gazed out over the garden at the treetops, silver in the moonlight.

One night, at a guesthouse in North Carolina, I'd been kicking back watching television and had stumbled on a documentary about notorious Australian murders. Hearing the Australian accent, I'd pumped up the volume. And there he was. A thirty-something man with shaggy brown hair and scorching eyes—blue, I recalled, though the poor reception on the small TV turned his pupils blacker than spots on a rotten apple. Those eyes looked directly out from the screen and fixed their gaze on me. *I know you. You're that Radley girl, aren't you? The troublemaker who cost me everything. The one who got away.*

I had sat frozen on the couch. My legs tucked under me and a glass of champagne raised to my lips. Staring numbly at the decades-old footage while a female voiceover delivered the grim report.

The stunning Deepwater Gorge Nature Reserve, situated fifteen kilometres from the rural town Gundara in north-eastern Australia, is a popular tourist spot. But in June 1995, when bushwalkers discovered the remains of a teenage girl buried in a shallow grave, the reserve became a place of speculation and terror. Further searching led to the discovery of another body ten kilometres away. Experts say that both bodies lay forgotten in the forest for over a decade.

As I sat in front of the TV that night, champagne turning sour on my lips, everything changed. My sense of adventure withered. I was suddenly a fly in amber, trapped in time. Frozen by the memories that I'd buried along with the gawky little nobody I used to be. Memories of the sweet young friend I had sent to her death.

"Abby, are you all right?"

I pushed back my chair. "Dessert?"

Tom frowned. "I hope you like sticky date pudding?"

"Great!" I stood too quickly, knocking my chair over. As I set it back on its feet, I elbowed my plate off the table. It hit the decking side on and dropped onto its face, cracking in two.

I looked at Tom. This time, my antics hadn't made him laugh. He was watching me, his eyes thoughtful. I collected the broken plate, then the other empty dinner dishes and salad bowls, and retreated to the kitchen. By the time I brought out dessert, my hands had stopped shaking.

"Custard ice-cream on the side?"

Tom brightened, but I could tell his smile was as fake as my own. "Sounds good."

I scooped some ice-cream into my bowl, but then choked down my sticky date pudding, barely tasting it. My knee knocked against my chair leg. My cheeks flamed. All I could think about was leaving the table. Escaping to my room. Hiding under the covers.

Tom cleared his throat. "Do you drown everything in ice-cream?"

"Pretty much."

He put down his spoon. "What happened just now, Abby? One minute we were getting along famously. Now we're all weird and stilted." He tried to smile. "I feel like I'm having a conversation with the invisible woman."

I rolled my shoulders. He had heard me earlier, after all. "Running away didn't solve my problems. So I returned home to sort out my life."

"How'd you go with that?"

"Still working on it, I guess." I pushed back my chair, carefully this time, and got to my feet. Collected the last of the dishes and the empty wine bottle. "It was a lovely dinner, Tom. Thank you for cooking, it was a real treat."

I loaded the dishwasher, tossed in the detergent and set it purring. When I'd finished, I threw a last glance over my shoulder to the window.

Tom remained at the table, the citronella lanterns painting him in flickering lights. He sat motionless, glaring out at the night. As if my departure had turned him to stone.

30
TOM

HE WAITED till her light was off, then heaved himself up and lumbered over to the railing. Moonlight bathed the distant hills. Oh to be out there now. Camped beside a river somewhere, far from civilisation. Just a crackling fire for company and stars glittering overhead.

Weeks ago, the wilderness had been his happy zone, but his injuries made it impossible to escape there now. It had always been his go-to place, even as a young man trying to make sense of the world.

And I'm still trying.

They'd been getting along so well. Laughing, being stupid, guards down. Even now his mouth twitched as he thought of her, the way she'd wheezed with laughter, that wild hair lashing her shoulders, her eyes alight. If only he could go back to that moment before the mood turned. Ask a different question, change the subject. Or just take her hand, reassure her it was okay. Okay to be scared. Okay to be a mess, not have all the answers.

He doused the lanterns and returned to the table, placing his hand on the back of her chair. He'd wanted to charm her. Peel away the layers, get inside her well-guarded head. Instead, she'd charmed him. Driven him crazy with her snorts and cackles, her clumsy antics. Her talk about microcosms and doll's houses. And at the end, she'd almost broken him with her aching vulnerability.

The night air cleared his head. He didn't want to be out there under the stars. He didn't want to be lost. Not anymore. He wanted to be upstairs, tucked under that raggedy old patchwork quilt. With her.

"In your dreams, mate."

Back inside the house, he shuffled quietly along the hall. He made it as far as his bedroom door. Lord, he was wired. How would he sleep with his mind racing? He should use the brain activity to get to work.

In his office, he settled into the big leather chair and switched on the desk lamp. Peeled the cover off his typewriter.

Behind him, the pad of soft feet.

He glanced around, half-hopeful, but it was only Poe. The cat bounded to the top of the bookcase and stared down, his shaggy black hackles raised and his ragged ears flat against his skull. The wild green eyes glowed with contempt as he hissed at Tom.

"Yeah," Tom murmured. "Same to you."

Since Abby's arrival, the kitchen window stayed shut at night, trapping Poe inside. *Tom, do you realise the damage a normal domestic cat can do to wildlife? And Poe is hardly a paragon of normalcy. He makes the word 'feral' seem tame.* Poor old Poe, deprived of his hunting, had gotten it into his furry head to blame this indignity on Tom.

Tom flinched as Poe let out a yowl resembling the cry of a

bird. One particular bird took up roost in Tom's mind—Edgar Allan's raven. The blackbird who'd perched above the door and recited its tale of woe, slowly turning the writer mad.

Something to look forward to.

Tom stared at his typewriter. Ideas were already flowing for his recent novel based on the Wigmore kidnapping. He could block in a few scenes. Start with Lilly's arrival home in 1953, then cut back in time to the abduction.

He fed fresh paper into the typewriter and tapped out a few paragraphs. Paused to read what he'd written, and then sighed. The bird motif was stuck in his head. Not Poe's raven. This time it was the small brown songbird who'd bewitched an emperor.

He looked at the ceiling. Up in that room, with its barred window and bloodstained sheets, two young sisters had lived caged together for five years. Faded little songbirds forgotten by the world.

He hunched over his typewriter and pounded out a paragraph. Then stalled again. He had travelled extensively, always gravitating to the less inhabited places. The deserts and wildwoods, the isolated coastal plains and mountains. Being caged was alien to him. How did it feel to be confined to a room year after year while everyone forgot you existed? He had never needed to know.

Never wanted to.

Until now.

31
ABBY

IT WAS MIDNIGHT, so I didn't bother with shoes or dressing gown—just padded downstairs as I was and tiptoed towards the kitchen. A light shone from under Tom's office door. He was keen, I'd grant him that. Working this late. As I crept past, a board creaked under my foot.

"That you, Abby?"

I froze. Oh no. He was going to see my threadbare pyjamas and fuzzy bed socks. The door opened and Tom leaned in the doorway. He looked rumpled and sleepy, the dress shirt he'd worn at dinner replaced by a comfortable pullover, his hair raked about.

He squinted in the dimness. "You okay?"

"Couldn't sleep."

He scrubbed his hands through his hair, furthering its disarray. "There's still ice-cream in the freezer."

I hurried past. "Yeah, I know."

We perched on barstools on opposite sides of the counter. With the double doors to the verandah wide open, our only

164

light was the frail glow of the moon. Maybe it was the darkness, or the crisp night air flowing in—or our mutual state of dishevelment—but the stilted feeling was gone.

Tom's eyes gleamed softly in the dimness. "I want to see their room."

I scooped up the last of my ice-cream. "You'll never make it up the stairs."

"Which is why I need your help."

"Absolutely not. It's too risky."

"Doc Worland said I need to walk more on my ankle. Moderate exercise encourages the bones to knit faster. You'd be helping me heal."

I scraped my bowl clean, then tapped the sticky spoon against my lips. "That's possibly the worst idea I've ever heard. Even if we get you upstairs, coming back down will be trickier. You'll be taking a tremendous risk. You realise that, don't you?"

Tom grimaced. "Let's cross that bridge when we come to it, eh?"

"Why, Tom? I've described the room, and you've pored over the photos I took. What if I slipped? What if you broke something that's just mending? Why risk getting injured again?"

A shadow flickered across his face. "I need to see it for myself. Breathe the air. Get a sense of *being* in there. Try to feel what the girls were feeling. It's the only way I'll really understand what they went through."

"They went through hell, Tom. Is that so hard to imagine?"

"It's easy enough to imagine," he said in a low voice. "But I've spent a lifetime using my imagination. I want to put myself in their shoes, Abby. Get inside their heads. This is the only way."

32

LIL

Lil gazed about the kitchen. She had made jam tarts, and the sticky-sweet scent of strawberries lingered in the air, mingling with the buttery aroma of pastry. She arranged the tarts on a floral platter and then filled the kettle for tea. Joe's dahlias sat in a vase on the sunroom coffee table. He stood beside Lil in the doorway, admiring their handiwork, when Abby's car rumbled down the drive.

Lil had been looking forward to the girl's visit since Sunday—but dreading it, too. Abby had a brightness about her that Lil admired. It was just a pity she was so bent on digging up the past.

Abby climbed the steps onto the verandah and surprised Lil with a peck on the cheek. Then she shook hands with Joe.

"How are you feeling, Joe? Recovered from your ordeal?"

"Good as gold, thanks, Abby. Can I get you a cup of something?"

They sat around the coffee table, eating jam tarts and sipping hot tea. When Abby asked about the costumes Lil was making for the musical, Lil retreated to the sewing room and returned sporting Madame Valjean's tatty prison frock. She gave them a twirl, then disappeared again and came back wearing a beautiful satin ball gown she'd refashioned from an op-shop wedding dress and dyed gold.

"I'm impressed," Abby said, clapping her hands. "You're a woman of many talents, Lil. Will you sing in the musical, too?"

Lil shook her head. "Not me, I'm afraid."

"I wish she would," Joe said. "She's got a bloody marvellous voice!"

"Oh, Lil," Abby said. "Sing us a snippet now. I'd love to hear you. And what about the libretto, did you rewrite it yourself?"

Lil huffed, gathering the rustling satin skirt around her and walking to the doorway. "Hardly a rewrite, just a few alterations. You'll have to be there on opening night to hear it. I'll get you tickets, if you like. Do you think Tom would like to come too?"

"I can probably twist his arm."

Lil snorted and disappeared again. When she returned a few minutes later wearing her own skirt and blouse, she sat on the edge of her chair and looked at Abby expectantly. There was a knot in her stomach. Her nerves fizzed. Her fingers grew damp in anticipation of holding those diary pages, and of reading her sister's lost words. If the story unravelled quickly, Abby might offer them today.

She glanced at Joe. "Abby and I might have our little chat now, love."

"Righto," he said good-naturedly, getting to his feet. He hovered a moment, then he reached over and patted Lil's arm. "You know where I am if you need me, old girl." He rinsed his teacup in the sink, then hurried outside to his shed.

Lil summoned a smile, despite the butterflies dancing a jig in her stomach. "Where would you like to start?"

"I'd love to know about Frankie's diary. I've searched the house but never found it, I don't suppose you—?"

"Oh no, dear. The diary is long gone."

"Did you ever read it?"

Lil stared at the milky brew in her teacup and shook her head.

Abby made a regretful noise. "We should start with your life in Sydney."

Lil drained her tea dregs, rattling the cup back onto the saucer with shaky fingers.

"Our mother worked in the laundry at Concord General, Sydney's biggest repatriation hospital. She hated it, of course. It was endless sweaty work, boiling all the sheets and bed linen, burning blood-soaked dressings. The shifts were long and Mum had always struggled with her health, but the war had taken our father, and she had us girls to feed. She never wanted kids. Her big dream was to be a movie actress, and she had the looks. Then she met Dad and got pregnant, and—"

She caught herself rambling and inhaled a breath, blew it slowly out.

"My sister and I used to wait for Mum after school in the hospital grounds. Mum liked a tipple, and it was our way of making sure she stayed sober. At least until we got her home and fed. One summer day we were playing behind the hospital woodshed and saw a young soldier sitting alone on a bench smoking. His dark hair poked at odd angles from under his bandages, and the hospital robe hung off his thin frame. His face was gaunt and pale. And so terribly sad. At least it was until he saw us. Frankie gave him a wave, and he smiled and beckoned us over."

Lil rested her hand on her chest. She should slow down, but the story was bubbling from her depths like a suppressed volcano. She found that she no longer wanted to hold it.

WHEN THE YOUNG serviceman called them over, Lilly's shyness overcame her. She hung back, but Frankie was already marching towards him, confident and beaming.

They started chatting. He wanted to know all about them. Frankie tossed her hair and answered all his questions. Even though she was only eleven, she accepted a cigarette and blew rings into the air. She told him about their mother's new boyfriend and the terrible rows they'd started having. She bragged about how many days they missed school. While she spoke, the young soldier roamed his eyes over them. Probably taking in their worn-out shoes and hand-me-down clothes. Frankie's long, unfashionable hair and Lilly's bowl-cut bob and crooked fringe. Their chafed, dishwater hands and grubby, split fingernails.

The serviceman talked about his life before the war. Living large in his grandfather's mansion, surrounded by parklands and bush.

"The garden has an aviary in it. Do you know what that is?"

The girls shook their heads.

"It's a huge birdcage. My grandfather designed it and had it made to look like one he'd had as a kid in Norway. It's like a Chinese palace, with many levels and turned-up eaves. Wide doors where you can slip in and sit among the birds. Before the war I had finches of every colour living in it. Green and yellow, and scarlet parrots too, even a family of blue wrens."

Frankie pretended to swoon. "Divine!"

"Your grandfather must be really rich," Lilly blurted.

That made him laugh. He took her hand and winked. "Stupendously so."

Frankie nudged Lilly aside. "The birdcage sounds dreamy."

"It is spectacular," he agreed. "Though it is a long way off."

Lilly exchanged a glance with her sister. Visiting a grand house with its own little emperor's palace full of colourful birds filled her heart to bursting.

Frankie smoothed a hand over her wayward hair. "We'd love to see it."

The serviceman smiled. A long, admiring smile that lit up his face and, despite the bandages, gave him the air of a dashing Hollywood film star. He linked his fingers in theirs and made them a promise. "And so you shall."

"You wanted to go with him?" Abby asked.

Lil nodded. "Oh, yes. Things at home were always fraught. We lived in a cramped little rental house and Mum wasn't much of a housekeeper. Mostly, she left Frankie and me to our own devices. Getting ourselves ready for school, making our own sandwiches for lunch on the days she remembered to buy bread. Doing our laundry on washdays. We were resourceful and independent girls, but we missed the coddling and attention that children crave." She laughed. "It must sound as if we were very spoiled girls, to miss being coddled. We'd had a taste of affection when Dad was alive, I suppose. After he died, Mum all but ignored us. She'd never been the touchy-feely sort. If it hadn't been for Frankie, we'd have starved. She was more a mum to me in those days than my mother was. Without one another, we would have been lonely."

"Until Ravensong?"

Lil rubbed her brow, overwhelmed as that Good Friday in 1948 rushed back. Almost seventy years ago, but it seemed like yesterday. Packing their bags and leaving Stanley Street. The stream of Frankie's endless chatter as they travelled. The rough roads jolting them from side to side. Dozing intermittently, stopping for a roadside meal. Until finally, their arrival at the fairytale house—a house far gloomier and shabbier than they'd imagined. And then stumbling stiff-legged from the truck and out into the misty, tree-shadowed dawn, and inside the big old house that would become their home for the next five years.

Abby sank back into the cushions. "Your mother must have been sick with worry."

"We thought we'd be gone a few days at most. It was Easter, and Mum always drank herself into a stupor. It was the anniversary of our father's death. We assumed we'd be back in time for school the following Tuesday, with Mum none the wiser."

"But you never saw her again."

"No."

"It must have been awful, Lil."

"It was unbearable. And yet we loved being there, too." She laughed softly. "It sounds absurd, doesn't it? Living in a couple of upstairs rooms, no outside contact. Barefoot most of the time and wearing our threadbare dresses. Doing our chores, reading books, making our own fun. Yet we'd never been happier."

She took off her glasses and massaged her temples. Her story had grown legs of its own, and was running far ahead of what she intended to tell Abby. She had dreaded revisiting the past, but her heart felt surprisingly light.

Abby got to her feet. "You're tired, Lil. You've been open with me, and it must be draining. Why don't we continue another time?"

"You might be right, dear. I feel a headache coming on."

"Can I get you something for it?"

She spoke so kindly, that Lil had the sudden compulsion to grip Abby's arm and cling to her. If today's revelations had brought this much relief, then imagine how it would feel to tell the entire story? Instead, she smiled and got to her feet. "I'll be right, pet. Why don't you return on Sunday?"

Abby gave her a brief warm hug. "Will do. And thanks for the jam tarts, Lil. They were scrummy. Tom does a great shortbread. I'll ask him to make us some for next time."

"Sounds lovely, dear."

Abby collected her bag. Just as she was slipping outside, Lil called her back. "You'll bring the diary pages?"

Abby's cheeks were flushed and her eyes bright, as if with tears. "Of course, Lil. See you then."

From the window, Lil watched her run down the steps and across the yard. When her car had gone, the shed door opened and Joe poked his head out, frowning along the driveway at the dust cloud.

Lil didn't feel like talking. Her head really was aching. Shadows swarmed at the corners of her eyes. Perhaps she should have a tablet and ask Joe to make her a pot of tea? She wandered into the lounge room. Maybe a few hours of mindless TV. Then she had a better idea. The sewing room beckoned, and who was she to ignore it?

33
FRANKIE'S DIARY

FRIDAY, 11TH MAY 1951

When we finished our morning lessons in the bright room —Ennis reading from an art book and showing us the pictures —Lilly flopped on the floor beneath the window. The colourful glass window panes showered her in a sunny rainbow of pink and green, pale blue and gold. She started dressing the paper dolls Ennis had bought her.

A year ago I'd have escaped to my corner of the bright room to read or sew or practise my handwriting. But lately I've been lingering at the table, sitting up tall, tugging the long ends of my hair. Talking to Ennis.

I'm fourteen now. The same age as Juliet Capulet when she married Romeo.

I'm not sure the exact moment everything changed. I was such a kid when we first met Ennis in the hospital grounds. His poor bandaged head and his shoulders all hunched like an old man. But as we got to know him, he started getting brighter and smiling more. Telling jokes and funny stories to make us laugh. Growing younger right in front of our eyes.

Somehow he's transformed again. I can't decide exactly how, just that I enjoy sitting near him. Enjoy studying his face, discovering little freckles or scars I haven't noticed before. The way his eyes widen when he looks at me, the way his pupils turn gold in the sun.

He shut the art book. "Questions, Frankie?"

"Yes, but they're not about art."

"What then?"

"How old are you, Ennis?"

"Twenty-four."

"Oh, fancy that. Mum was twenty-four when she had me."

He didn't like us mentioning our mother. He glanced at the window and worked his mouth the way he did before one of his rants.

"Ennis," I said to distract him. "Tell me something."

He frowned. "What?"

"A story. About your life. Before the war, I mean."

"When I was a kid?"

"No, older. My age, for instance. Did you have a sweetheart?"

The poor thing blushed. He shook his head and studied his hands. "I wasn't sophisticated, like you. My grandfather was very strict. The only girl I ever knew was my sister."

I gaped. "You have a sister?"

He looked down, transfixed by his hands. "It's eight years since I saw her."

"Eight years?" I looked across the room at Lilly, still playing with her cut-out dolls. She irked me a lot, but if I couldn't see her face every day, if eight years passed without talking to her or even seeing her, or hearing one of her funny songs, my soul would shrivel up and die. "You must miss her."

"I used to. Very much. Until you and Lilly came to stay."

Without thinking, I reached for his upturned hand and tickled my fingertips on his palm. He closed his fingers over mine, gently at first, but then so hard my bones ground together. I tried to pull away, but he clung to my fingers like a lifeline.

"Ennis, you're hurting me."

He let go and withdrew. "I'm sorry."

"Never mind."

"I'm an oaf sometimes."

I rubbed my hand. "Why haven't you seen her for eight years?"

"She died in 1943. Typhoid."

"Oh no."

He shrugged, shifting in his seat. "You remind me of her. She had the same brown eyes as you."

"They're hazel."

He nodded, rushing on. "It's more than looks, though. You have her spirit. She never flinched when Grandfather gave her the strap. Wilful, he called her. A handful of trouble. Sharp-tongued and opinionated, unwilling to suffer fools. So different to quiet little Ennis who never set a foot wrong."

I glanced at Lilly. "Sounds familiar."

"My sister had a secret."

I waited, but he stayed mute. Minutes passed. He was slipping away from me, I could tell. Becoming that person who talked obsessively about the war. Transforming from a gentle boy into a frightening devil. But we hadn't been talking about the war. We were talking about him. He had given me a glimpse behind the mask he wore, a glimpse of someone I wanted to know better.

I had to bring him back. "What secret?"

Ennis shuddered and blew out a breath. When he looked back at me, he was the old Ennis. The safe Ennis. The Ennis who read to us and listened to our woes. Who baked cakes—as humble as they were—for our birthdays.

My Ennis.

He tucked a wisp of hair behind his ear. "Everyone thought my sister was a drudge, but she wasn't. She made herself seem drab so Grandfather wouldn't look at her in that ugly way he sometimes did."

"Ugly way?"

"You know. The way you said your mum's boyfriend sometimes looked at you."

"Oh, dear."

"But behind her drabness lived a bright soul. Smarter and stronger and kinder than anyone gave her credit for. Grandfather couldn't see it, but I could. I'd always seen it. My sister was the one I loved best. She was clever and beautiful. Like you, Frankie." He leaned forward and cupped my cheek with his fingers, his touch as soft as butterfly wings. "Just like you."

I barely dared to breathe. Strange feelings rushed through me. I was hot and tingly and weak, as though my bones were about to dissolve and trickle onto the floor.

Over in the corner, Lilly sat up from her dolls and looked at us. I should have reassured her, but Ennis needed me more and I couldn't look away from him. Tilting my face, I rested my cheek against the rough warmth of his palm.

"What was your sister's name?"

"Violet."

"That's a lovely name. I wish I'd known her. I want to know so much. About you. About the world outside. Sometimes it seems to whiz past, like it's leaving me behind."

Ennis withdrew his hand as if burnt. He stood so quickly that his chair fell over with a bang. Without saying more, he ushered us back into our room and locked the door.

Lilly glared at me accusingly. "So now you like him?"

Ignoring her, I flopped on the bed. She taunted me, but finally grew bored and left me alone. Later, just before dark, I heard Ennis below in the yard. I dragged the trunk over beneath the window and climbed onto it. Lilly tried to clamber up beside me. I elbowed her down, but she caught my arm.

"What's he doing?" she demanded. "Why are you spying on him?"

I shook her off and stood on tiptoe to peer through the bars. Lilly punched my leg. "Frankie, what's he doing?"

"He's got the axe." That shut her up.

Below in the yard, Ennis stalked over to the woodpile. I had watched him chop wood a thousand times. Why did this time feel different? Sinful, almost. I pressed my face against the bars.

He wore no shirt, despite the autumn cold, just work pants and boots. He carried an armload of logs to the block and positioned the first one. Whack went the axe. The log exploded, falling around him in pieces. Muscles clenched across his back and his hair gleamed black in the dying sunlight. He twisted the axe free of the block and positioned another log.

"Why are you ignoring me?" Lilly whined.

"Go to bed," I said crossly. "Leave me alone."

"So you can moon over your boyfriend?"

I rolled my eyes. "Shut up."

"You're a slag like Mum."

"Shut up!"

She stomped off to bed in a sulk, but I didn't care. The boy in the yard below mesmerised me. In the fading daylight, with his long hair and lean body and the strength rippling across his shoulders, he looked like a fairytale prince. My heart skipped and sang for him, it wanted him near. Did he feel the same about me? I remembered what he said earlier. *My sister was the one I loved best. She was clever and beautiful. Just like you, Frankie.*

TUESDAY, 22ND MAY 1951

This morning's lesson caused a roar. Ennis brought us a cutting he'd taken from the newspaper as he sometimes does. I perked up, thinking it was about me and Lilly—I still badger him about seeing his scrapbook. Only, this wasn't about us. The cutting showed a dark-haired woman with rouged lips and a sour face.

"Jean Lee carried to scaffold," I read aloud. "Apparently unconscious and with her face completely covered, Jean Lee, thirty-one, a domestic of Sydney, was carried, handcuffed, to the scaffold by the hangman."

"Who's Jean Lee?" Lilly demanded, reading over my shoulder.

"She's no one now," Ennis said flatly.

I crumpled the article and whirled to face Ennis. "Why have you brought us this?"

Lilly tried to grab the newsprint from me, so I shoved past her and threw it in the fire.

Ennis looked at Lilly. "Jean Lee killed a man, so they strung her up by the neck."

I marched across the room and shoved him. "Stop it. You'll give her nightmares. What are you playing at?"

Ennis ignored me and stalked to the door, then looked back over his shoulder. "You're always asking for news, Frankie. When I bring it, you tell me not to bother. What's it to be, then? Are you interested in the outside world or not?"

Lilly was crouching in front of the dying fire, frowning at the mound of ash. Tonight there would be tears. She would cling to me and cry. Ask the same thing she always asked. "How much longer, Frankie? When will he let us go?"

I glared at Ennis, pushing down my feelings for him. "I'd love to know about the world! But not just from reading a tatty old newspaper cutting. I want to live in it and learn these things for myself. Enough is enough, Ennis. Me and Lilly want to go home."

34
TOM

They reached the landing at the top of the stairs and took a break. Tom felt as if he'd just climbed Mount Everest. His ankle, knee and hips throbbed like nobody's business, but as he gazed along the upstairs hallway, the promise of what lay ahead of him made it worthwhile.

He caught Abby's eye and winked. "Glad that's over."

She was gripping his arm, watching him closely. "You need a longer breather?"

"Nah, I'm good."

She looked doubtful as she passed him his crutches. "You're pale. Pain level?"

"Okay."

"Can you walk?"

"Hmm."

He adjusted the crutches, still savouring the feel of her arms around him as she'd taken his weight on the way up. Her hand on his ribs, the silky tickle of her ponytail against his arm. The intoxicating press of her breast. She was stronger than he expected, and he had fought the urge to pull her against him right there on the stairs and kiss her. *Focus, man. She's doing you a big favour, here. The least you can do is control your primal urges.*

At the end of the hall they entered a long room with a beautiful stained-glass window. He remembered it from his first tour of the house, but there'd been so much else to take in that he had only given it a cursory look. Since then, he'd spent hours poring over the photos Abby had taken, but they were no substitute for being here. He sensed a weightiness in the atmosphere, as though the air was denser and colder here than in other parts of the house.

Abby went to the wall and slid open a panel, exposing the narrow steel door, which she pushed open. Tom stood on the threshold of the hidden room and looked inside. Late afternoon sun shone through the barred window, but the corners of the room were already gathering shadows.

"It's tiny. Bad enough for one teenage girl, but two?"

"You can see why Lil avoided talking about it."

"Five years in here," he murmured. "It really was hell."

He approached the bed. His injured foot dragged a little, his cast leaving a trail in the thick dust. As he breathed the stuffy air, his imagination caught alight. The two sisters sat on the bed, their heads together. One fair, the other dark. They were reading The Nightingale, their quiet murmurs mingling with the swish of pages. They seemed small and fragile in the half-light, so absorbed in their book that Tom felt afraid for them. What horrors had they experienced up here? Why had only one sister returned home?

"You poor bloody kids."

The girls on the bed whipped their heads around to look at

him. Right at him. Lilly's eyes filled with terror. Frankie's fierce gaze burned with defiance. Her back was stiff, her shoulders squared, her expression intense.

Tom inhaled and glanced behind him, catching Abby's eye. "Shut the door, would you?"

She studied him a moment, then retreated. The hinges squeaked as the door closed. The latch engaged with a metallic click. In the dim light, he noted there was no handle on his side.

He examined the window. The sun shone beyond the bars, but it barely entered the room. In the garden below, leaves whispered and birds called from the branches. Tom tugged his collar. Already he felt hemmed in. Breathless. The sisters must have been desperate to play in that garden. How trapped they must've felt. How much worse with the door locked. Their only link to the outside world a pitiful gap of sky high in the wall.

And the man who kept them here.

Tom saw a weedy guy with a haggard face and bloodshot eyes. He almost smiled. Most of the villains he'd written into his books were burly toughs. Muscle-bound bullies with tiny brains. This guy, this kidnapper of children, however, was in a league of his own. He was smart, all right, but browbeaten. Nothing to lose. Desperate. All of which made him unspeakably dangerous.

Tom looked at the bed.

Abby's photos of the room hadn't prepared him for the raw awfulness of what he was seeing. Threadbare sheets on a sagging mattress, the centre shadowed by a long black stain. The pillow still dented as if someone had only just lifted their head from it, discoloured where something dark and wet had soaked into the thin fabric.

He ran his fingers along the edge of the stain, recoiling from its stiff, leathery resistance. Blood, most definitely.

He flexed his fingers. Ideas were sparking. He was keen to be at his desk, his fingers pounding the Remington's keys. He loved sliding into the zone like this. Letting his imagination run wild. Words were banking up in his mind, threatening to overflow, bringing with them a landslide of intriguing, pulsating images.

He glanced around for a light switch, found none. The sun was sinking behind the distant hills and the gloom was suffocating. A feeling of wrongness swirled around him. It was like nausea, only outside his body, enveloping him like foetid air. And was it just him, or had it become impossible to breathe?

He squared his shoulders and tried to shrug the feeling off.

Years ago, while researching the details of a nasty murder case for one of his novels, he'd come across an article about haunted houses. It offered the theory that houses absorb energy impressions of the people who live in them. Powerful emotions got imprinted on the walls like sticky fingerprints on glass. Sometimes those emotions were so intense that other people could detect them.

Did that explain what was happening now? Was he picking up the emotional fingerprint of Frankie Wigmore's murder?

He'd never been woo-woo. The supernatural held little interest for him. He based his novels on true-crime cases for a good reason—he liked their gritty reality, the way they made him rethink what it meant to be human. What it meant to hover between right and wrong, knowing instinctively on which side he belonged. He enjoyed pushing the boundaries of everyday experience, and peeling back the layers to the truth beneath. Imagining how he would react if the same thing happened to him. The anguish he'd feel if the people he loved were in danger. The horror of being helpless to save them. As a writer, the darker end of the emotional spectrum was his domain—but usually he only got to explore it from behind the safety of his typewriter. This room, with its sticky, unpleasant residue of the past, had gotten under his skin. Left its mark on him. Changed him in ways he didn't yet understand.

Downstairs, the phone rang. The door opened behind him and Abby peered in.

"Will I get that?"

He nodded. "I can't imagine who'd call at this hour. But yeah, thanks."

Abby's footfall rang along the hallway and then more faintly on the stairs. Then silence. Eerie, all-consuming silence. Tom ran his hand over the dust on the iron bedhead and then rubbed his gritty fingers together. As a boy, he had craved the outdoors. Escaped at every opportunity into the bushland behind his parents' home in Katoomba. Explored creek beds and climbed trees and hunted frogs in muddy waterholes, soaking up the glorious freedom.

How would he have survived in here? After five minutes he was already chafing to get away—but five years? It was a lifetime for a child. An endless, mind-numbing lifetime. Since his accident, Tom had spent most of his time inside. He was no stranger to cabin fever, but the idea of living year after year trapped in this tiny room was beyond hellish. Beyond anything he could imagine. Which made him wonder. How had Frankie and Lilly managed not to go utterly and completely barking mad?

"You know," the old man wheezed, twisting from the passenger seat of Abby's car to gaze around at Tom. "I've been a fan of yours for years. Lil's not much of a reader, but I was thrilled to bits when I heard you'd moved to the area. What a shame we had to meet like this."

Tom sat propped in the back, his crutches on the floor, his bad leg stretched along the seat. He patted Joe's shoulder. "We'll find her, mate. Whatever it takes."

Joe stared through the car window. "I appreciate you not calling the cops. Lil does this sometimes. Wanders off. Usually she's back well before dark. She wouldn't want a fuss made, which is why I rang you."

Abby slowed as they approached a bend. "Where does she go, Joe?"

"Just around the place. Ever since I've known her, she's had these turns. Not surprising, after what she went through. She retreats into herself, gets lost in there somewhere. We visited doctors over the years. She baffled most of them. It's not Alzheimer's. More a sort of identity disorder they call psychogenic amnesia. Blackouts and confusion, loss of memory. You can wander away from your life and not remember it."

"It must be frightening for you both."

"It's a worry sometimes." He lifted his glasses and rubbed his eyes. "We didn't tell anyone about Lil's past. She didn't want to. Got upset every time I suggested it might help to talk to a counsellor or psychiatrist. She wouldn't hear of it. So in the end I stopped suggesting and just started managing the problem."

"Does something trigger the turns?" Tom asked, adjusting his leg.

"Stress. Upsets. A change in the weather." Joe's bony shoulders twitched. "Who knows? We have long stretches with no trouble. Then one night she'll wake up and wander through the house. Off to the bathroom, so I think. Then before I know it, she's driven away somewhere. Couple of hours later she's back with no memory of even leaving. She says it's like having a nightmare and waking in a sweat, with this hazy sense that she's in danger."

"Danger from what?" Tom asked.

"Oh, Lil's not in any danger." Joe took out a little puffer bottle and considered it, then tucked it back in his pocket. "She's just never been able to shake herself free of the past."

"I feel awful," Abby said. "It was stressful for her the other day, talking about her abduction. This is my fault, isn't it?"

"Aw, Abby." Joe peered at her. "Don't say that. Don't even think it. Lil's a strong woman, she's got her own mind. If she hadn't wanted to talk to you, she'd have sent you packing."

"It gave her a headache."

"After you left, she told me it felt good to offload. They were her exact words. Good to offload. I'll tell you now, lass. I'm the only one on the planet she's told about her past—until now. She likes you, Abby. Trusts you. She wouldn't have opened up otherwise."

Tom studied the roadside trees. "Heck of a worry for you, Joe."

"That it is, Tom. That it is."

They turned onto the New Forest Road and drove north toward Ravensong. The landscape along the eastern side of the Deepwater Gorge Reserve was rugged and thickly forested.

Loggers cut down most of the old growth a century ago. Now the trees grew close together, making it difficult to access the steep, rocky land. As dusk turned to night, yawning shadows swarmed between the boulders and turned the forest into a black morass.

Abby pointed ahead. "There."

A dark-coloured Forester stood askew on the verge, almost hidden by the bushes. As they pulled up behind it, Abby's headlights caught the open driver-side door.

"She's here," Joe said, unbuckling his seatbelt and stumbling out.

Abby was right behind him as they hurried to Lil's vehicle. Tom was slower, hating how his crutches slipped about on the rocky verge, praying that Lil was in the car, unharmed. But as he approached, Joe looked around.

"She's gone walkabout." The old man wandered down the road, calling Lil's name.

Abby pressed her hand to the bonnet. "The engine's still warm. She can't be far." She walked a little way then stopped. Joe was barely visible in the dark, his hoarse voice echoing through the night.

Abby returned to Tom. "I'm worried she's wandered off into the reserve in a daze and got lost. I only hope she's not hurt. I have to find her."

"It's pitch black out there. I'm coming with you."

"Thanks for the offer, but you'll slow me down. Even for someone who knows it, this part of the reserve is rough."

Tom cursed his useless legs. "How will you find your way back?"

Abby took a torch from her Fiesta. The cone of light turned her into a shadow. "Every ten minutes, sound the car horn. I'll stay within hearing range." Fumbling out a fresh roll of mints, she offered one to Tom, but he shook his head. She popped one in and chewed, hugging herself as she gazed into the darkness, her eyes huge and gleaming. "If she's out there, I'll find her. I promise."

35

ABBY

WHEN THE CAR horn sounded in the distance, I paused beside a vast old gum tree and glanced back towards the road.

"Right on time," I whispered.

Nearby, the bushes rustled. I shone my torch over and a wallaby bounded away, its powerful legs thumping the ground.

I continued downhill, pushing between prickly banks of tea-tree and ducking under low-hanging branches. After a while, the car horn sounded again, but it was faint. As it cut out, I listened. Leaves whispered in the damp air. Insects droned as night settled in. An owl flew past, its enormous wings eerily quiet. Then I heard the crunch of approaching footsteps.

I spun around and searched the trees. "Lil, Is that you?"

The footsteps continued to approach. A light bobbed through the trees. I shone my torch into the darkness and called to her again. Why wasn't she answering me? Between the ghostly tree trunks, I caught sight of a tall, woman-shaped shadow pushing through the undergrowth.

"Lil!"

She broke through and shone her light in my face. Her back was ramrod straight and her frown fierce.

"Why have you followed me here? What do you want?"

I lowered my torch. "Lil, it's me. Abby. Joe's waiting at the car. He was worried you might be unwell. Let's get you back there, okay?"

Lil peered into my face. Torchlight carved hollows into her cheeks and under her eyes, flaring eerily off her glasses. Her usually soft features had sharpened, and her eyes were small and hard. With one long-legged step, she closed the gap between us.

"Oh, it's you. All grown up."

I froze. Had she mistaken me for someone else? I closed my fingers around her arm and gave her a shake.

"What did you say?"

The car horn blared in the distance. Lil blinked and the ice in her gaze melted. Her eyelids fluttered, and she pulled away from me with a frown.

"Abby?" She gazed around. "Why are we here?"

"Come on, Lil. Let's get you warmed up."

I shrugged off my coat and wrapped it around her shoulders. What had Joe said? She needed warmth, quiet, hot tea. A familiar environment where she could settle back into her old self and recover.

"I was dreaming, Abby."

"It's over now, Lil."

"A terrible dream."

"Come on, Joe's waiting for you. Here, take my arm, it's not far."

She gripped me tightly. As we walked, she hung her head, muttering to herself so quietly I couldn't make out her words. Only that they were full of anguish and pain.

I led her back through the trees, navigating the rough ground as I followed the distant glow of headlights. When we reached the verge, I finally made out what she was saying.

"Oh Frankie, leave me alone. Please, leave me alone."

36
TOM

Tom stood on the grass beside the back steps, swirling the dregs of his tea as he gazed at the sunny garden. Abby had gone into town for supplies, then dropped by to visit Lil and Joe. She phoned to say that Lil had recovered from last night's escapade. Despite a couple of scratches, she had no memory of her trek through the bush.

After Lil's vanishing act, and the Glenlivet or three Tom had drunk with Joe afterwards, Tom should have been feeling fuzzy-headed and hungover. But his mind was clear and his body primed—as if he'd been drinking wheatgrass shots rather than whiskey. He should be at his typewriter working, but jeez, it was nearly the weekend.

He found a bucket in the shed and filled it at the tap, then lurched off along an overgrown path towards the old orchard. The bucket banged against his crutches and he spilled half the water down his leg, twice dropped the carryall with its soap and scrubbing brush, and tripped on a tree root—but none of that dimmed his determination.

Last night he had watched Abby go into the bush alone, and it haunted him. He kept reliving the moment when she looked at him in the torchlight, her eyes gleaming. That look had puzzled him—until now. She'd been afraid. Deeply afraid. Not that it stopped her. She had guts, he'd give her that. Meanwhile he was stuck on the roadside with Joe, honking the horn at intervals. Loathing how useless he had become.

Gripping his bucket, he reached the orchard and made a beeline for the derelict caravan.

He'd seen it the day he inspected the property and forgotten about it. But the other night at dinner, when Abby's eyes lit up as she spoke about her love of travel, he'd remembered it. And then after her act of bravery last night, he had decided that the perfect way to show his esteem for her was by giving her something she'd love. Something that might make her less inclined to forget him.

His first job was to clear the swallows' nest, which thankfully the birds had abandoned. It took until lunchtime to scrub the plywood walls clean of cobwebs, dirt and bird droppings. The teardrop shape made him think of the 1960s, but its wood construction made him wonder if they'd actually built it closer to the 1930s. A crack ran along one edge of the roof, but a couple of brass screws and a tube of silicone would fix it.

Tossing the filthy water onto a flowerbed, he made his way back to the house, planning to return that afternoon with his toolbox. He stowed the bucket and scrubbing brush in the shed, but as he approached the house, he heard Abby clattering about on the verandah.

She was sanding the kitchen windowsill, which had jammed since the damp weather. Her cheeks were pink from the sun, her peaches-and-cream complexion dotted with freckles. And that hair. Inside the house it looked chestnut, but the sun turned it to dark liquid honey threaded with gold.

She saw him and frowned. "Where did you get to?"

"The orchard."

She strode over, hands on her hips. "How did you get down the stairs?"

"With great difficulty."

"Why didn't you wait till I got back? I could have helped."

"I've got something for you."

Her eyes narrowed. "What?"

"A surprise."

"Oh."

"Let me guess. You hate surprises?"

She squared her shoulders. "Actually, Tom, I'm quite partial to anything that keeps life interesting."

"Then follow me."

37
ABBY

W E   M A D E slow progress through the garden.

Tom was filthy, his track pants wet and muddy and his leg cast smeared with grime. But his face glowed from sunlight and exertion—and maybe something else. What was he up to? He was right about me hating surprises, but how bad could this one be? Something in the garden, blossoms or a noteworthy view. Afterwards, I'd have his full attention. *Lil said something strange in the forest last night, Tom. It's been bothering the hell out of me all day. She gave me this funny look and said 'Oh, it's you. You're all grown up.' I think she mistook me for Frankie. Is that where she goes during her turns, looking for her sister?*

"How much further, Tom?"

He glanced over his shoulder and winked. "Not far. You're gonna love it."

We pushed past grevillea bushes and tromped through high grass. Bush wrens chattered in the undergrowth and, overhead, a single swallowtail cloud drifted in an otherwise empty blue sky. I could tell by the way Tom's bad leg dragged that he was tired, but his mood was positively buoyant. I smiled to myself. He'd been kind to Joe last night, chatting away and putting him at ease. Joe must have been terrified for Lil, but Tom's solid presence had reassured him. Not to mention the expensive whisky he'd plied him with.

Tom stopped walking and gestured for me to go ahead. I entered a clearing defined by a ring of fruit trees—pears weighing down the branches, and shiny red autumn apples hiding among the leaves.

Across the clearing stood a vintage caravan. Its silvery plywood walls were wet. It looked newly scrubbed except for the blooms of frilly lichen still clinging to them. The curved roof glinted in the sunlight, and bees danced around its teardrop window.

"Magical, isn't it?" Tom said.

He ushered me over and unlatched the door. I glanced about inside. It was pristine and cosy, a tiny table and booth seats, a miniature sink, all remarkably well preserved, but when I opened my mouth to agree with Tom on its adorable quaintness, a gust of cold, stale air flooded my lungs.

"It needs a few repairs," Tom was saying, "to get it roadworthy. The inside could use some vamping up. Curtains, a cushion or two. But it's tiny, light enough to tow behind your Fiesta. I thought you could—"

"No." I swallowed, shut my eyes. He'd gone to a lot of trouble to surprise me. He was being kind. I recognised the lovely gesture, but how could I explain? The way my throat closed up from the stale mustiness, the way my pulse flew at the sight of the shadow-infested corners. The way my spirit shrank inside me like a walnut withering in its shell.

Tom put his hand on my arm. "Abby, what is it?"

I shrugged him off. "I've got work to do."

I left him alone in the orchard and hurried back along the path. When the house came into view, I kept going past, veering along another track and heading deeper into the garden.

"I DON'T KNOW what it was," I told the police officer, shivering in my grubby jeans and torn blouse. "A cave or something."

I was sitting on a plastic chair in Gundara Police Station, a blanket wrapped around my shoulders. My scalp stung where someone had doused my wound with Dettol. The doctor was on his way. I needed stitches and would have to be brave.

The lady officer crouched in front of me. "Can you describe this cave, Abby?"

"It was dark inside. Very dirty. I mean, there was dirt on the floor, but underneath the dirt was metal."

The officer nodded and smiled at me, but then she glanced around at her colleagues and they exchanged worried looks. I shrank into myself, hugging my arms about me. I knew what those looks meant.

"Why won't you believe me?" I shouted.

"How did you get into this cave? Did you fall in?"

I frowned at her, trying to remember. My brother said I'd been gone for three days, but it felt longer. A year had crawled by, a lifetime. I was no longer twelve, but a hundred.

I looked down at my hands. My knuckles had raw patches. My fingernails were bleeding. Dirt stuck to the blood, making little black moons around the nails. I had skinned my knees and elbows and torn my clothes. Worst of all I was hungry, but it was a kind of sick-hungry. Soon after they found me, a man had given me hot cocoa from a thermos but it scalded my tongue and then I'd thrown up. I remembered the stale bread I had gnawed on in the cave, and the faint smell of cold bacon fat came back to me, making me gag.

"Abby, did you hear me? How did you get inside this cave?"

I started crying. "I want to go home."

"Listen to me," the officer said patiently. "I know you've been through a lot. But we need to ask you more questions. Rule out a few things."

My father loomed in the doorway. "What things?"

The officer got to her feet. "Abby said she saw someone in the bush. A man holding a weapon. She got frightened and ran away and we're just trying to—"

"We already know that," my father boomed. "What are you doing about it?"

"I assure you, Mr Radley—"

"You're gonna find this guy, right? Lock him up and throw away the key? Because if you clowns don't get off your arses and arrest this mongrel, there'll be hell to pay."

The officer's face remained calm. "I understand your concerns, Mr Radley. Your daughter's upset and you're keen to get her home. First we need to determine whether this actually was an abduction—or just a scared little girl getting lost in the bush."

38
TOM

HE FOUND her under a gum tree. Her head rested back against the trunk, and her eyes were closed. The dappled sunlight played over her face, making shadows of her eyelashes and glimmering on her damp cheeks.

His fingers tightened around the crutch grips. If it wasn't for the damn knee brace, he'd have knelt beside her and gathered her into his arms. Maybe had the courage to press a kiss against her hair. Anything to comfort her. But he just stood there, an intruder, awkward in his filthy clothes and crutches, wishing the ground would open up and swallow him.

She wiped her eyes, then got to her feet. "You must think I'm an idiot."

"Of course not. You okay?"

"I guess."

"Want to talk about it?"

She sagged back against the tree. "Not really."

"It might help."

"It was sweet of you to clean up the caravan for me. I don't know why I reacted that way. It was just—" She blinked back tears and stared up into the tree canopy.

"It's something I've said, isn't it?"

She looked up at him with wet eyes. "Don't flatter yourself, Tom. Most of what you say, I take with a grain of salt."

"Good. I think. So the caravan was a terrible idea?"

"It was a lovely idea, but it triggered something. A memory."

"Ah, Abby. I'm sorry."

Another tear leaked out. She caught it with the tip of her finger and huffed a shaky laugh. "I don't know why I'm having this reaction. I'm never teary, I feel like a stupid crybaby."

Her face crumpled again, the tears welling. It shocked him to see her like this. Vulnerable, all defences down. If only he could crush whatever was causing those tears. Chase it down, stomp it out of existence. Except he feared the thing upsetting her was him.

"Abby, I'm sorry. I never meant to rattle you. I just wanted to do something for you, after everything you've done for me. Putting up with my whingeing, my moodiness. You've been a real sport, and—" He winced. His jabbering was making it worse.

Abby slid down the tree back onto the grass, burying her face in her hands.

Tom swayed towards her. He let one crutch drop and then the other, keeping his bad knee straight as he worked his way down beside her. Broken glass speared his bones, but it was worth it. He took her in his arms and drew her close, and she melted against him, her body a warm weight. She pressed her face against his chest and fisted her fingers in his shirt.

A magpie alighted on a branch above them, sending down a rain of leaves. The bird warbled, filling the air with its sharp, sweet song. Tom rested his lips on the top of Abby's head, breathing her scent. If only he could hold her this way forever. Protect her, distract her from whatever nightmare she was trying to outrun.

The magpie ceased its song and flew away. Abby shifted to look at him.

His pulse hammered. Without really thinking, he tilted towards her and brushed his lips over hers. Briefly, she kissed him back. Her lips tasted every bit as sweet as he'd imagined.

Then her eyes widened. "What was *that*?"

He winced. Not the response he'd hoped for. "I thought it would distract you. From the caravan and whatever it made you remember." He tried to cover his embarrassment with a smile, but it felt like more a grimace. What was he, insane?

Abby gave an uncertain laugh. "I guess it worked."

Her face was close, and he felt the quickness of her breath on his lips. He leaned in to test his theory a second time, but Abby drew away and tilted her head, giving him a frowny sort of smile.

"Jeez, Tom."

"What?"

Her gaze dropped to his mouth, and she nibbled her bottom lip as if deciding something, then she laughed huskily and shook her head. "How the heck am I supposed to get you back on your feet now?"

"Guess I'll have to stay here," he muttered, his senses still reeling. "With you. For all eternity."

"Huh." Her smile widened. "Then you're doomed."

Untangling herself from his arms, she got to her feet and gazed down at him. She was inching back towards the old Abby, the one with her guard up. Tom didn't care. He was still drunk with the memory of her in his arms. Of her mouth against his. Still intoxicated by those moments she let him hold her close.

"Come on." She put out her hands to help him up. "Easy does it."

It took an excruciating, pride-destroying millennium to get back on his feet, although it was probably closer to five minutes. By the time he was standing, one thing was certain. Something had happened to his heart. It felt squashed out of shape. Bruised. Fluttering and glowing like a candle flame in a windstorm.

Abby was right. He was doomed.

39
ABBY

AFTER DINNER I slipped back into the garden. The cold air cleared the cobwebs, leaving my mind empty as I retraced my steps to the orchard. I stared across the trampled grass clearing at the caravan. No longer magical, it was just a sinister blob crouching in the shadows. I walked over and placed my hand on its teardrop-shaped flank. The plywood was rough from the weather and vaguely warm. When I shut my eyes, it shapeshifted into something resembling a cave.

Can you describe it, Abby? It was dark inside and very dirty. I mean, there was dirt on the floor, but underneath the dirt was metal.

The cave existed. I was sure of that now. It wasn't just a figment of my haunted dreams, but real and tangible. When I looked inside the caravan today and breathed its close air, a window in my mind opened and I slipped through. I was back in the cave, trapped in the dark, unable to breathe. Any lingering doubts about its existence vanished. My cave was definitely a memory and not, as everyone back then had encouraged me to believe, a panic-induced invention.

I knew one thing, though. It hadn't been a cave.

I shut my eyes and summoned it again. The panic. The dank cold. And me yelling as I hammered the walls with my fists. The walls had shuddered and boomed over my screams. But what sort of cave had a metal floor and walls?

An owl shrieked overhead in the darkness. I sprang away from the caravan, shielding my face. My heart punched against my ribs, so I buckled over, hands on my knees while I caught my breath. And there in the shadowy garden, with my pulse beating hard in my ears, another possibility revealed itself.

Someone else might know about that cave.

Someone who had known all along.

MY PULSE RACED as I climbed the steps to the front door. Grass grew up between the decking boards, and a crate of mouldy newspapers had become a feeding ground for snails. When I knocked, a dog at the back of the house started barking. I took a deep breath.

Behind me in the street, a group of kids rode past on their bikes, laughing and skylarking. A lawn mower droned in a neighbouring street, and somewhere a television blared. I counted to ten and then knocked again.

The door opened, and a wiry man frowned out. "Yeah, what do you want?"

"Hello, Mr Horton. I'm Abby Bardot from the *Express*. Have you got a minute? I was hoping to have a quick word."

Colour darkened his whiskery cheeks. "You're that Radley girl, aren't you? My word, you've got a hide coming round here. Why would I talk to you?"

"It's about Jasper."

"Haven't you done enough?"

"Please, Roy. It's really important."

His eyes narrowed behind his horn-rims, and he glanced behind me into the street, working his jaw from side to side, as if chewing something leathery and unpleasant. "You'd better come inside."

I followed him along the hallway, dodging piles of taped-up boxes, squeezing past a battered bicycle that hung from the doorknob of a shut door. The other doors along the hall were open. As I trailed Roy towards the back of the house, my nostrils flaring at the mustiness, I glimpsed rooms with chenille bedcovers and old-fashioned lamps, and more boxes. In one room, a glass-fronted cabinet held a collection of hunting knives. Some were long and curved, most had grooved blades and wooden or steel handles. High on the wall above the cabinet hung three antiquated rifles and what looked like a mummified cat. My palms grew damp again. Why hadn't I told anyone I was coming here?

"That's Jasper's stuff packed up there." Roy pointed at the boxes. "I'm keeping it here for him till he gets out. All them cartons are full of books. He's a big reader, so he is."

I followed him through to a tiny kitchen. The cupboards were tobacco-stain yellow, probably dating back to the 1960s. Everything was spotless, dusted and scrubbed. On the table sat gardening gloves and a big newspaper parcel tied with string.

"You picked a bad day." Roy grappled the parcel into his arms. "Grab them gloves for me, would you?"

I held the door open as he went outside. On the porch, a

black-and-white border collie sat to attention and started wriggling and whining, thumping its tail on the deck. Roy silenced it with a word, and the dog flopped down again.

After the chaos of the front yard, the well-tended rear garden surprised me. An expanse of manicured lawn took up most of the space, flanked by long, narrow veggie beds full of bobbing seed heads and a few large zucchinis.

Roy nodded to a spade propped against a rickety shed, so I grabbed that too. I followed him to the far edge of the garden, where he placed the parcel on the grass. He took the spade from me and started digging.

"You said you're with the *Express*. This a story you're writing?"

"No, Roy. It's personal."

He tossed a load of earth aside and plunged the spade into a fresh section of grass. "So what do you want to know?"

"Did Jasper have a caravan that he camped in?"

Roy stood to attention, sunlight flaring off his thick glasses as he glanced back at the house. "Van? Jasper never had no van. What's all this about?"

I shaded my eyes from the brightness.

"They kept Alice Noonan somewhere before she died. A vehicle, maybe. Possibly a caravan."

"It weren't my Jas." Roy put his heel on the shovel and drove it into the ground.

"Please, Roy. Will you try to remember? It was a long time ago, but it could be important."

"He had no van." A load of dirt came up and thumped onto the grass. "He had no car."

"You're absolutely sure?"

"My boy never got his licence."

I rocked backwards. "What?"

"He rode his bike, or walked. When we went cutting wood, it was always me who drove the truck. We fought over it all the time, my word we did. I even offered to help him go for the test, pay for it. It's a bloody chore running a wood business with only the one driver, especially in winter. But Jas wouldn't hear of it. Anyway, the cops know all that. How can it be important?"

I toed a clod of dirt back into the hole. "You still believe he's innocent?"

Roy stopped again, shading his eyes with a cupped hand. "I don't *believe* he's innocent, Miss Radley. I know it without a doubt. My boy never killed them girls. I'd swear it on his mother's life."

"What makes you so sure?"

"My Jas was a bit of an odd one. Uncomfortable around people, never said much. But he weren't no killer." He picked up the newspaper parcel and placed it down into the hole, then stretched the kinks out of his spine. "I bet you weren't expecting to attend a funeral today, were you? See that little body down there? Sulphur-crested cockatoo by the name of Ollie. They live for sixty years—this little old man was in his seventh decade. Died last night."

"Oh, I'm sorry."

"Belonged to my boy. Young Jas rescued him after a bushfire and brought him home. The poor bird was naked, all his feathers singed off. Ollie was already middle-aged. Might have had his own little family, but the fire burned them up. Bushfires are mongrels like that, aren't they?"

I nodded.

"Jas was always rescuing animals. Helping helpless things. When he was six or seven, he turned up with this big old tomcat. Car hit it, broke its jaw. Jas wouldn't let the vet put it down, insisted they fix it. Took me two years to pay off the damn jaw plate, but I didn't resent a penny. My boy loved that beat-up old moggy. It used to follow him around like a dog."

Roy collected the shovel and filled in the hole. "You asked me why I'm so sure Jasper is innocent. He was a good kid. Gentle as a lamb. Never hurt a fly, let alone them poor lasses they found at the reserve. My boy, he didn't have a mean bone in his body. Until—" He stopped shovelling and leaned back to blink at the sky.

"Until?" I prompted.

He knuckled one eye and then the other, then resumed filling in the hole. "I suppose you know about those girls he got in trouble over?"

The ones he'd indecently assaulted. "Yeah, I heard."

"Jasper was clueless around people. After his mum died, I probably left him too much to his own devices. Failed to teach him proper boundaries. He should never have touched that lass. If she was my daughter I'd have been outraged, too. But Jas never meant no harm."

"It didn't look good on his record."

Roy shook his head. "Jasper always loved animals. He could practically read their minds. But people? Poor young bugger had no idea, did he? He went off the rails after that trouble with the girls. Moved out of home and into a flat with some uni students. He had a few jobs, but none lasted long. That winter he started helping me with the firewood business, chopping and hauling, doing deliveries. Then he stopped coming by. I visited his flat a couple times, worried about drugs. He had black circles under his eyes, his were clothes filthy. He started talking all this rot, too. I tried to get him to see a doctor, but he refused."

"What do you think it was?"

Roy tossed the shovel aside and stomped down the earth over the bird's grave.

"Depression, maybe. It turned him into a completely different person. Before all that trouble with the girls, he was this sunny, lovable kid. Then afterwards, he was all storm clouds and rain."

The sun had dipped closer to the horizon and shadows cut knifelike across the yard. I stared at the bird's grave. Why were things always so complicated? I had hoped Roy might remember something about a caravan, that would help me make sense of my response to the one in Tom's orchard and possibly lead me to Shayla. Instead, I'd encountered a father whose fond memories of his little boy had blinded him to the dangerous man that boy had become.

"I only met him once," I breathed. "But it was . . . *after*."

Roy's mouth pinched as he studied me with damp eyes. "Pity it wasn't before, Miss Radley. You'd have liked him a whole lot better back then."

By the time I returned to Ravensong, the sun was sinking and glimmers of dying sunlight shone through the trees. Grabbing my grocery bag, I hurried around the house and up the verandah steps. Tom's typewriter sat on the redwood table. Next to it was a pile of papers weighed down by binoculars, but Tom was not there. There was just the cat, his green eyes watching me, his black tail lashing through the dry leaves that had blown up onto the decking. Below him, safe within the prickly branches of the grevillea bush, a family of willy wagtails flitted after bugs.

I put my groceries on the counter in the kitchen and just stood there, with Roy Horton's words replaying in my mind. *Jas was always rescuing animals. Helping helpless things.* Did Roy really believe that this proved his son's innocence? That being kind to animals meant Jasper would never harm a teenage girl?

But Lil had said something too. *It sounds absurd, living in a couple of upstairs rooms, no outside contact. Yet we had never been happier.*

The young serviceman had been kind to Lilly and Frankie. Fed and clothed them and created the stable environment they craved. He probably believed he was saving them from their lonely lives in Sydney, but what sort of saviour kept someone trapped against their will? He had watched the sisters, perhaps for days or weeks before he made contact. Noticing their threadbare clothes and scuffed shoes, their wide-eyed eagerness for affection. Scheming. Making his plans and preparations to steal the girls away from their mother and keep them locked up.

Had Jasper observed me the same way? A girl from a poor family. A girl no one would notice missing, at least not straightaway? What about the other Deepwater victims—the two runaways, and Alice, whose mother was struggling to raise her alone after a messy divorce. Had Jasper observed them from a distance, too? Waited for the perfect opportunity? Did he think he was helping more of his helpless things by locking them up to keep them safe? It made a warped sort of sense, but what about Shayla? Had she been running from someone the day I found her? Not Jasper because he was in jail. Unless—

Unless Jasper wasn't the one.

I stood rock still. Cold air blew under the back door and

slithered around my ankles. When I mentioned a vehicle hidden in the bush to Roy Horton, he had glanced back at the house, his glasses flaring in the sunlight, his shoulders tensing. *When we went cutting wood, it was always me who drove the truck.* But why would Roy go after Shayla? To cast doubt over Jasper's guilt and prove his son wasn't a monster—but that didn't add up, either. If Roy wanted to cast doubt on his son's conviction, why wait twenty years?

"Maybe he didn't wait." If hikers hadn't stumbled off course in 1995, they would never have found the runaway girls' remains. Same for Alice. Campers discovered her grave by accident. Were there other undiscovered bodies out there, rotting in shallow graves? Overlooked because everyone thought the killer was in jail? It was possible. But Roy? A man in his seventies who had doubtless been through one inquisition after another since his son's arrest. The police would have watched him closely. They were probably still watching him—

A guttural howl erupted behind me.

I startled and my foot shot out, kicking Poe's food bowl across the kitchen floor. The cat sprang in a sleek arc from the open window, and bounded towards me. I clutched my chest.

"Unlike you, I only have the one life. And you just about scared it out of me."

Poe yowled again and lashed his tail. I cleaned his bowl and dished out some mince, then topped his water bowl from the tap.

"You're right, Poe. Standing around theorising won't get those groceries unpacked."

"Abby, is that you?" Tom's voice echoed from the other end of the house. "You're not out there talking to the damn cat again, are you?"

I smiled, shaking off my speculations about Roy. My theory

was full of holes, anyway. I put away the groceries and then hovered, running my fingers over my hair. Lingering in the shadows, thinking of yesterday under the tree. Tom's lips on mine, the fleeting warmth of his breath against my skin. The gentle strength of his arms tightening around me as I cried into his shirt. Was the kiss his way of comforting me, an unconscious action? Was I reading too much into it—or had the elusive Tom Gabriel kissed me for real?

"No, it's Jack the Ripper," I called, unable to keep the laugh out of my voice.

I latched Poe's escape window and stalked through the house. Tom sat in the library at his laptop, the printer whirring beside him.

"I've found something." He passed me a pile of printouts. "A name, at least."

"The kidnapper?"

"Could be. Plus some history about the family who built Ravensong."

I leaned my backside against the table and read through the printed pages. They were from a memoir, *Gundara Remembered*, dating back to the 1930s, written by a local Gundara midwife, Mary Quaile. She had included sepia photos of people in family groups, a few solo portraits, and some silver gelatin landscapes fading to ghostly grey. But it was her visit to Ravensong that stood out. Especially her account of the people who owned it in 1942—Lars Gilbertsen and his wife Inge, and their two grandchildren.

I looked at Tom. "Lars died in 1943, so it can't have been him. But maybe the grandson? Mary Quaile calls him a sullen dark-haired boy of fifteen. Lil said the young serviceman she and her sister went with had dark hair."

Tom leaned back. "If the grandson was fifteen in 1942, it

would put him in his early twenties when Lilly and Frankie were abducted in 1948. Mary couldn't say what become of him. But it's a start."

"Ennis Gilbertsen." A tingle ran up my arms. "It's more than a start, Tom. It's bloody brilliant. I can't wait to show Lil. I hope it doesn't freak her out."

"You'll have to tread carefully. Fingers crossed she's more forthcoming with you than she was with poor old Inspector Upshaw back in the 50s."

We celebrated with dinner at the redwood table on the verandah, surrounded by candlelight. Our conversation gravitated around the Wigmore sisters, and we re-read parts of Mary Quaile's memoir to each other, debating whether the grandson could be the elusive kidnapper—and speculating about what became of him. But a subtext drifted beneath the surface of our discussion. *The kiss*, it seemed to say. *Shouldn't one of you at least acknowledge it?* But neither of us did. And I couldn't decide if I was relieved . . . or disappointed.

After the dishes were done, Tom returned to his Remington on the verandah.

I went back to the library and re-booted Tom's laptop.

Hi Kendra, we have lift-off. Gabriel has agreed to the interview. Will have it on your desk by Wednesday night in time for Friday's festival launch. PS: Looking forward to that front-page feature you promised.

I sent the email and sat back. I should head off to bed, but it was only ten o'clock. Reading the memoir—and then bantering about it with Tom—had switched my brain into overdrive. I was itching to see Lil again and show it to her, but that would have to wait till Sunday. So I checked a couple of social media sites and emailed Duncan. At eleven, Tom came inside and took a shower. The water pump droned, and the pipes gurgled. Did the room get a little steamy, or was that just me? I shut my eyes and pictured Tom in a stream of hot water, his skin turning pink, his shoulders glistening with droplets. The soap lathering to a delicate froth of bubbles in his chest hair—

Breathe, Abby. Don't forget to breathe.

What would he do if I snuck along the hall and crawled into his bed? *Surprise,* I'd whisper when he climbed in beside me. *You did such a stellar job of taking my mind off things yesterday afternoon. Any chance of a repeat performance?*

Ha. A girl could dream.

40

ABBY

ON SUNDAY MORNING I pulled into Lil's driveway, a tin of Tom's shortbread on the passenger seat. Lil was in the garden, pruning withered flowers from a rosebush. She waved and hastened over, beaming from beneath an enormous sun hat. She thanked me for the shortbread, placing it on a shady garden bench, then linked her arm through mine and steered me down the hill towards the edge of the garden.

"Joe and I have a surprise for you, dear. It's a bit of a hike, though. Are you up for it?"

"Sure am. Where's Joe?"

She smiled mysteriously. "He's waiting for us. Come on."

As we walked along the grassy path, Lil told me about her drama group.

"They're such a good bunch of girls. Most of them just need some kindness to bring out their best." She looked at me and smiled. "Like us all, I suppose."

"It must be heart-breaking too?"

"Oh, yes, sometimes I despaired. Sadly, there are some we

can't reach. Addicted to drugs, lifelong victims of abuse. I always believed that anyone with enough faith could overcome their baggage, but some women have lost all hope. Lost any faith in themselves and given up trying. It's something we all struggle with, isn't it? Time passes and the setbacks wear us down. It seems easier to just give up. I suppose that's why I love the drama group so much. All my girls have resilient spirits."

"No hard cases?"

Lil smiled sadly. "There are always those. We have this one girl, Jenny. She turned up with a black eye and split lip. Now, barely a month later, she's helping me with the costumes and seems to have discovered a love of fashion. She's asked me to help her fill out a form to study at Gundara TAFE."

"Good on her. She'll be one of your success stories, then?"

"I hope so. Time will tell. Most of these women grew up believing they're not worth anything. We learn so much from others, don't we? Parents, school teachers, relatives. That's how we learn to fit in and develop community spirit. But if our role models display unhealthy behaviour, how are we supposed to know what's right? Or even what's expected of us? So at the shelter, we provide new examples to follow. Kinder, more rational ones." She laughed and lifted a brow, her eyes shining. "And sometimes it works."

"You're genuinely passionate about helping women, aren't you?"

"I am, indeed."

"Have you ever told any of them about—?"

Lil shook her head. "Sometimes I wanted to open up, but never did. While I'm at the shelter, I prefer to keep the focus on my girls. Ah, look." She patted my arm and darted ahead, pulling aside the prickly boughs of a grevillea bush. "There's Joe."

I followed her down to the edge of a large shady billabong. Joe had rolled up his baggy jeans and waded into the water until he was ankle-deep in mud. He squelched over holding a bucket of riverweed.

"Good to see you, Abby love. Magnificent day, isn't it? What do you think of our visitors?" He gestured at the scene behind him.

A pair of black swans sailed majestically on the water, trailed by six fluffy cygnets who were squeaking excitedly.

"Oh, they're beautiful! Do they live here?"

"They arrive around Christmas every year," Lil said. "And stay till the end of May. Joe thinks it's because of all the trees protecting the billabong, but—" She laughed happily. "Oh, Joe, you scoundrel. Show her."

Joe laughed too. He grabbed his bucket and sloshed over to the water's edge, flinging soggy strands of riverweed into the middle of the billabong. The swans squeak-honked and rushed for the weed, their tail feathers quivering.

"They like the water beetles on the weed," Joe called over his shoulder. "Gets em in a frenzy every time."

Joe's bucket quickly emptied. The swans trumpeted at Joe in their melodic way, coasting over to see why the supply had stopped. When one of the larger swans waddled up the shore towards him, Joe headed back up the bank to join us on the grass.

"Whew!" He wiped his brow, smearing his face with mud. "That big fella had a bit of speed on him, didn't he?"

Lil started giggling, and the sound was infectious. Joe and I joined in, and soon the sound of our laughter drowned out the sound of the swans. As we headed back to the house, Joe hurried ahead to wash the mud off his legs. Lil gazed after him affectionately.

"He's such a clown. A lovable one though." She looked at me. "You seem different today, Abby. I've been trying to figure it out all morning. Are you doing your hair in a new style?"

"Um. No."

"You have a glow about you. Perhaps that's a new top you're wearing—the pale blue is lovely."

I patted my cheeks. "It's only from the sun."

Lil laughed. "What's his name, love?"

"There's no one," I said hastily, brushing at my jeans, unable to meet her eyes. "I guess I've been getting outdoors a little more than usual, that's all."

"I see."

I tried not to think of my steamy moment with Tom under the gum tree, but heat flooded my face. My boot caught on a tree root and I tripped. Lil steadied me with her hand and raised an eyebrow.

I blew out a breath. "You're right, there is someone. But I'm no good at relationships, Lil. Not like you and Joe. The minute things get serious, I retreat. As if getting too close is ... dangerous."

"Dangerous for who?"

I hesitated, fearing I'd said too much. But Lil had shared so much of her secret self with me. She had trusted me enough to talk about her past, even though it pained her. It seemed only fair that I open my secret self to her, too.

I huffed a little nervous laugh. "I wore glasses as a kid. Such a dorky girl, so unsure of myself. I yearned for acceptance, but always seemed to try too hard. Doing homework for the popular girls, trying to emulate their style—which never quite worked in my second-hand clothes. Then I made a friend who liked me just as I was—" My throat tightened and I stopped.

Lil looked over. "In the hospital with Joe that day, you said you lost someone. A childhood friend. You blamed yourself for her death?"

I nodded. "That was her. Alice. She was one of the Deepwater girls. We both were, I suppose. Only I got away."

Lil stopped walking and searched my face. "Oh, my dear girl. I didn't know. But Abby, you weren't to blame for what happened to Alice. I'm sure you had enough on your plate dealing with your own trauma." Tears shone in her eyes, trembling on her lashes. She drew me into a hug and I melted against her, grateful for her kindness. If anyone could understand, it would be Lil. In the speckled sunlight, in the warmth, I desperately wanted her words to be true. *You weren't to blame for what happened.* But she didn't know all of it, the worse of it.

She let me go and patted my arm, and we walked on.

"You know, Abby. I used to think relationships were dangerous, too."

I shaded my eyes to look at her. "But you and Joe are so devoted. So brilliant together."

"We weren't always. At first, I was terrified. What if loving him broke down all my barricades and opened me to the sort of pain I couldn't bear? After my father died, my mother used to say that loving him made her weak. She blamed my father's death for all her problems. And I'd seen the way love had ruined —well, other people's lives. But when I met Joe, he taught me something very important."

"What's that?"

"It's not love that makes a person weak, but fear. Love is the one thing in life that can truly make you strong, Abby. If you allow it to."

"That's quite profound."

She laughed. "Joe has his moments."

My skin warmed at the memory of Tom's stolen kiss under the tree. "Maybe there's hope for me after all."

Lil patted my arm. "Anything's possible, love. If you want it badly enough."

TEN MINUTES LATER, I was sitting at Lil's kitchen table. I dug in my bag for Frankie's diary pages and unfolded them, then propped them against a jam jar filled with pink dahlias. Lil bustled about making tea and arranging the shortbread on a plate. Finally, she settled opposite me.

"Where did we leave off last time?" she asked.

"You and Frankie were happy at Ravensong."

"Ah, yes."

"I'm guessing things didn't stay that way?"

Lil adjusted the jar, making the dahlias nod in the listless air, then she tucked her fingers out of sight beneath the table edge. "Frankie formed an attachment with the young serviceman."

"Attachment?"

"She fell in love with him."

"Oh." I pressed back in my chair. "Did he love her back?"

"Yes, he did. Intensely. Obsessively, you might even say. On Frankie's fifteenth birthday he asked her to marry him. Frankie had always been a romantic girl. She wanted to have adventures and fall in love. See the faraway places she'd read about in books —India, China, and even the wilds of Africa. They planned to marry when Frankie turned sixteen. He had enough money for them to leave the country because of his inheritance. I would return to our mother in Sydney. So in January 1953, we packed up the truck and left Ravensong forever. They dropped me in Gundara with money for the train, and we said our goodbyes."

"You never saw her again?"

"No."

"Oh Lil, why ever not?"

"She made me promise not to look for her."

"Why didn't you talk about what happened?"

Lil rubbed her cheeks. "Can you imagine if I had? The authorities would have tracked them down. After what he did, they would go to jail. Or worse. They still hanged people in those days. Frankie was my sister, and my best friend. I couldn't betray her that way."

"Did you ever try to trace her?"

Lil plucked a dahlia petal and crushed it between her fingers. "No, never."

"She might still be alive."

"Even if she was, I'd never find her. She's probably changed her name. Left the country. She's gone, Abby. I've accepted that, and so should you."

She was probably right. Over sixty years had passed since Lil had seen her sister. A lifetime. But I couldn't give up hope. Not yet.

I picked up the diary pages and passed them across to her. "Thanks for being honest with me, Lil. I can't imagine how hard this all must be for you."

Lil folded the pieces of paper in half, and then in half again. She kept folding until they were too small to fold any more. Then she tucked them into her skirt pocket and got to her feet.

"I'd best clear those rose cuttings. If I wait till tomorrow, the possums will scatter them all over the yard and we'll be picking thorns out of our shoes for days."

I collected our tea things and took them to the sink. "Earlier you said that anything's possible if you want it badly enough. Do you really believe that?"

Lil put away the shortbread and joined me at the sink. "Yes, I do."

"Would you like to see Frankie again?"

She dropped her gaze. "With all my heart."

"What if I said there might be a way?"

41
LIL

Lil hung the tea towel to dry and returned to the table, sinking into her chair. She watched the younger woman from beneath her lashes. She liked Abby, but she wished the girl would leave. All this talk about finding Frankie was making her head hurt.

Abby sat opposite. Reaching into her bag, she took out a sheet of paper and passed it across the table.

"It's an excerpt from a memoir by Mary Quaile. She was a local midwife."

Lil took the paper, feeling the first stirrings of panic. "You think it's a link to Frankie?"

"Could be. Mary was born at the turn of the century, and lived in Gundara all her life. Apparently she was quite a character, had her finger in everyone's pies. And, as you'll see, she had an extraordinary memory."

Lil smoothed the memoir on the table and blinked to clear her vision.

In 1942 my brother came home on furlough and we spent two glorious weeks exploring some of his old haunts. Childhood polio had made him unfit for combat so, to his eternal chagrin, they sent him to a war office in Darwin. "A hellhole of heat and mosquitoes," he called it, and was mighty glad to be home.

In early November he took me out to see old Lars Gilbertsen's house, Ravensong, the stately wilderness mansion the Gilbertsens had built in the 1920s. Lars and his wife Inge had emigrated from Norway in the early 1900s. Lars was a recluse and his wife a raging socialite. Luckily they were also stupendously rich. According to my brother, Lars and Inge were once famous for their lavish garden parties. People would travel miles for the honour of attending. I didn't believe it until I saw the house.

It was a splendid big place, surrounded by perfectly manicured gardens—the Gilbertsens were one of the few families in the district who could still afford hired help. I got my hopes up about being invited to one of their famous parties, but Lars was ill when I met him, all hollow eyes and sunken cheeks, barely more than a shadow. And his famed parties had stopped several years before.

A sullen dark-haired boy of about fifteen greeted us. He was Lars's grandson, Ennis. Once inside, a large-boned teenage girl offered us cups of watery tea and stale Christmas cake. This was Ennis's sister, Violet. She was a shifty lass, about seventeen, clearly uneasy with company. Judging by her lank hair and dowdy attire, her spotty face, she wasn't getting the right care out here in the bush with her brother and grandfather. I felt sorry for her, and wished we could be friends, but she ignored my overtures.

Perhaps it was grief. They lost their parents when they were young. Then in 1940, two years before I met them, their grandmother Inge had died. Soon after, one of Lars's business ventures crumbled when an employee died on the job and Lars had insufficient insurance. By the time I met Lars he was sixty-five and bankrupt. For a while he lived off his assets, then eked a diminished income providing firewood around the region. A year after our visit to Ravensong, I heard Lars had died. My brother never knew what happened to Ennis and his sister. There was a rumour that Ennis enlisted, though surely he was underage. I assumed they were still living at the house, but by war's end they both seemed to have vanished.

Lil sat still. Many decades ago, she had been good at hiding her feelings. Despite the turmoil and guilt raging inside her, she always kept her face pleasant and her hands steady. Until now. The sheet of paper trembled as she passed it back to Abby. The girl was watching her expectantly. Lil pulled her hands into her lap again and took a deep breath.

"I don't see how that relates to Frankie."

"The serviceman's name was Ennis Gilbertsen, wasn't it? Which means you could locate him through army records. He might have received a service pension, or be traceable through the RSL. If you found him, you might also find Frankie."

Lil's fingers knotted in her lap. "I don't want to find them, Abby."

"Are you worried about discovering that Frankie has died?"

Lil sighed. "I'm afraid I wasn't truthful with you before."

"Oh?"

"There's a reason Frankie doesn't care to be found. The day we left Ravensong, we had a terrible row. We said things. Unforgivable things."

"What was the row about?"

"It was about him. Ennis. I was jealous, I suppose."

"You had feelings for him too?"

Lil scoffed. "Not the sort of romantic feelings Frankie had. But he was kind to us. You remember that our mother never had time for us? And because of all the days we skipped school —to look after our mother or just play truant for the hell of it —the teachers considered us a lost cause. But Ennis gave us what we craved most. What every child craves. Attention. Approval. Love."

"He locked you in a room for five years, Lil. How is that love?"

Lil got to her feet and wandered over to the window.

A sullen dark-haired boy of fifteen, Mary Quaile had written. *Lars's grandson, Ennis.* It had shocked her to see his name printed there in black and white. Shocked her to think Ennis had a life before she knew him at Ravensong. That he'd once been a young boy with a family of his own. She'd heard his stories, of course. Known about his heartbreak and sorrows— losing his parents, and then his beloved sister dying so young. But seeing it written on paper all these years later, brought such an ache to her chest she couldn't breathe. *After the war*, he used to say, *I never expected to be happy again. But you girls are my salvation. I thought I was saving you by taking you away from your horrible life in Sydney, but in the end you're the ones who've saved me—*

"Lil?"

She jerked around.

Abby looked worried. "Are you all right?"

Lil picked up the tea towel, but the drying rack was empty. She twisted the cloth between her hands. Spots of shadow swirled before her eyes. She needed a tablet.

"Actually, dear. I'm a little peaky."

Abby wilted. "It's been another big day. I'm sorry I pushed you about finding Frankie. I understand why you don't want to find her." She collected her bag then hugged Lil, placing a gentle kiss on her cheek. At the door, she looked back. "I'm glad you found your happy ending, Lil. Even if it didn't include Frankie."

Lil stood at the window watching Abby's little car zoom off down the driveway. Then, when the dust of the girl's departure had settled, Lil dropped her tea towel by the sink and marched out to the sewing room. It was time.

42
ABBY

"So that's it?" Tom paused on the brick path and squinted back at me through the late afternoon glare. "Frankie eloped with Ennis and they disappeared into the sunset together?"

I nodded. "And Lilly returned to Sydney and kept her sister's secret."

"They never saw each other again?"

"No."

"Do you believe her?"

"Yeah, I do."

Tom stopped beside a wooden arch overrun with clematis. The white flowers had long since fallen and turned to mush in the grass, but the vine was still green.

"That's quite a story, isn't it?"

"It really is."

I plucked a clematis leaf and tore it to bits. For an autumn day, it was warm. My cardigan felt hot and prickly. I started stripping it off, then realised my cardigan wasn't the problem.

"I really admire Lil for how well she survived her childhood ordeal. She created the perfect life with Joe and enjoyed a fascinating career and now she does volunteer work. She's strong and fit in her seventies. The way she chops all that firewood and tends the garden, grows her veggies and mows the lawn—I'm in awe of her." I paused, unable to voice the sudden ache I was feeling.

Tom stretched his back. "But you're worried that underneath it all she's unhappy?"

I was grateful that he understood. "Not so much unhappy as haunted."

"You care about them, don't you? Not just because of the diary. You've found a bit of a soulmate in Lil."

I smiled. Trust Tom to notice. Right from the start, Lil had seen behind my thick outer shell to the insecure mess I was inside. She hadn't judged, just acknowledged, and even encouraged me to open up about things I'd normally suppress. In return, she had trusted me with her own private self, the self she kept hidden from most people.

"We seem to understand each other."

Tom brushed my arm with his fingers. "So now that Frankie's sorted, where does that leave us?"

I hugged my cardigan around me. "I've finished the interview. The only thing it needs now is your tick of approval."

43
TOM

TOM SWITCHED on the lamp and climbed into bed. He poured himself a half-glass of brandy, then replaced the bottle on the bedside table and uncapped the lucky red marker he used for all his own editing. Then he settled back against the pillow to read Abby's interview.

It began with a portrait of Tom as a young man, struggling after his father's death, and later riding his Harley into the wilderness to fulfil his dad's bucket list. Tom poised his red pen over the first paragraph, intending to strike it out—it was far too personal—but something kept him reading and before he knew it, he had devoured the entire interview without having made a single red mark.

"Bloody hell."

He shuffled back to a favourite bit.

Gabriel is a formidable man, not just in stature—he's a glorious six foot three, with a wild mane of reddish-blond hair and river-green eyes—but also in talent. He can literally turn straw into gold. He bases his novels on the grimmest, most wretched crimes imaginable—abductions, murder, revenge killings—and transforms the tale into a story that's both beautiful and compelling in its portrayal of humanity overcoming the bleakest of odds.

"A glorious six foot three," he marvelled. "How does she even know that?" He had no idea how tall he was, and certainly not to the inch.

He went back through the pages, reading other favourite sections—there were plenty—then he returned to the beginning and started over. An hour later, the brandy bottle was empty and Tom's eyes stung—he'd been awake since five in the morning, and it was now past eleven—but he was too wired to sleep. Damn, the woman could write. He had known she was good. He had read her *New York Times* articles, each one riveting and amusing in its own way. But this was a masterpiece. She must have honed her skills since being back on home turf, because this story had a certain glow about it. It was deeply personal and revealed intimate insights, yet Tom didn't feel violated. Quite the opposite.

"She's turned me into a freaking superhero."

He laughed to himself, finishing the dregs of his brandy. *A glorious six foot three.* Hmm. Could there be another reason the story glowed—a more personal reason? Was she up there now, nibbling her fingernails, wondering if he was still awake? Her brow wrinkling as she pondered the idea of creeping down the stairs in the dark. To him.

"Christ." There was a thought. He studied his closed bedroom door. Not very welcoming for a night visitor. He swung out of bed and hobbled over. Opened the door a crack and peered along the hallway. Just the darkness, but it crackled with possibility. A rush of heat raced over his skin, and the blood pumped hard through his veins. He went back to bed breathless, but not from walking without his crutches.

He slipped off his pyjama shirt, flung it onto a nearby chair, and then settled back against the pillow. To wait.

44
ABBY

From where I sat on the windowsill in my tiny bedroom, the garden stretched away below me, a sea of night-time shadows. The white blur of an owl swept past, vanishing in a blink, and tree shapes crouched in the murky blackness. I leaned out and looked towards the orchard. Somewhere in the dark, Tom's little vintage caravan slumbered among the overgrown trees. Its roof arched like the spine of a hibernating animal, its insides foggy with the breath of something old and long dead.

Let it go. You were wrong. About all of it. Wrong about Frankie, and probably Shayla, too.

Stars blazed in the velvet sky, and watching them made it easier to forget the fearful stories I had been telling myself these past weeks. Easier to imagine happier outcomes. Frankie as an eccentric elderly woman. Her dark hair flowing as she strode about her elegant bohemian house, reconciled with her child-hood ordeal, surrounded by adoring cats. And Shayla on the coast with her dad, the two of them eating takeaway, Shayla rolling her eyes over her father's dad jokes, and then giggling because they really were funny, after all. She wore her mother's glittery Kmart jacket, and her dark hair was clean and brushed and pulled back in a scrunchie. There were no head wound or scratches. No bruises. They all belonged in the nightmare memories of another girl's past. Alice's past. My past.

Time to let it go.

I inhaled the chilly night air. Soon, perhaps as soon as tomorrow if Tom was happy with my interview, I'd be leaving Ravensong. Returning to my cottage in town. Writing my Deepwater feature for the *Express* and getting on with my solitary life. I breathed deep, trying to fill the sudden hollowness in my chest by savouring the individual layers of scent I could taste on the air. Earth and mouldering leaf litter, eucalyptus and peppery bush flowers. And was that—

"Smoke?"

I cracked open my door. The smell intensified. Something was on fire. I tore down the stairs then along the downstairs hall. Smoke was billowing from Tom's bedroom.

I burst in, met by a whoosh of flame as one curtain caught alight, then a roar as the other drape burned. Tom sprawled on the bed, probably knocked out by his meds. I shouted his name and shook him, and he woke, groggy at first. Then he registered the fire and hauled himself out of bed, grabbing my arms.

"Are you all right?"

I nodded. "Where's your extinguisher?"

Coughing, he dragged the woollen blanket off his bed. "Under the sink."

I ran along the hallway and grabbed the fire extinguisher from the kitchen. Then I rushed back to Tom's room, choking on the thick smoke. As I grappled with the extinguisher key, Tom worked on the worst of the flames at the wall near his bedside table, beating at the fire with his blanket. Flames shot along the windowsill, sending out another spray of embers. The dry wood of the old house reacted like tinder, catching alight and burning fiercely. Below the window, the Indian rug started smouldering. Tom grabbed the extinguisher from my hands and broke the seal, and aimed a stream of white powder at the flames. He doused the wall, and the ruined curtains, and finally the rug. As the last flame puffed up its dying smoke cloud, I ran to the window and pushed it wide open.

Eyes streaming, my throat raw, I turned to Tom. Soot streaked his face and arms, his bare chest black in places and for a wild, horrible moment I thought his shirt had burned off and scorched him. I flung myself against him, registering the heat of his skin as I held him tight, my face on his chest.

He steered me into the hallway where the smoke was less intense. Then he held me at arm's length and searched my face in the hallway light.

"Are you hurt?"

I shook my head. "You?"

"I'm okay." He dropped his hands and stepped away, coughing. "So much for my fancy new smoke alarm and rewiring."

"How did it start?"

Tom returned to his room. The fire had singed his beautiful Indian rug. It had destroyed the curtains and blackened the windowsill. The culprit lay on the floor beside Tom's bed. A classic old Art déco lamp had shattered, revealing a charred lump of electrical cord.

He nodded at the lamp. "There's the culprit. It was in such good shape I never thought to restore it." Without his crutches, he crossed the room awkwardly and pushed the window further open. I switched on the overhead fan.

"Why didn't the lamp short the power?"

"I plugged it into a self-sacrificing power board. Pity it didn't stop the old cable catching alight, too." He moved towards me, and hooked a lock of hair from my face, tucking it behind my ear. "You're trembling. Are you sure you're okay?"

"Yeah, fine." I pulled away from him and ducked through the doorway. "Though I'd be glad of some fresh air."

45
TOM

He watched her in the moonlight. Or rather, he watched the cocoon of quilts she had disappeared under several hours before. They had set up camp under the magnolia tree, away from the smoky air of the house, piling blankets and quilts from one of the spare rooms onto the grass. Far above their makeshift nest, the slender crescent moon cast a frail light, while the Milky Way blazed like diamond dust on black velvet.

In the silvery light he could make out a dark coil of Abby's hair on the whiteness of her pillow. A mound of quilts covered the rest of her. He pictured her hatching in there, like a colourful butterfly. Morphing into her old self again, eager to fly back to her cottage in Gundara. Now that she had her interview, and his tick of approval, what other reason did she have to stay?

46

ABBY

THE OUTDOORSY SCENT of damp grass permeated my dream, and I stirred. Was something burning? No, it was just the blistering sun overhead, the crackling afternoon air. Alice stood beside me at the school gates, our faces and arms dappled with tree shadows.

"We'll find it," Alice insisted, stamping her heels on the footpath. "Tomorrow we'll ride our bikes out there, just you and me. We can retrace your steps along the track and find the cave. Then everyone'll believe you."

I stared down at my shoes. "I don't know, Alice. Dad says we can't go there anymore."

"Come on, Abby." She nudged my arm. "If we find it, you'll stop being sad."

I shuffled my feet. "I'm scared, Alice. What if *he's* there?"

Alice wrapped her arms around me and rested her forehead against mine.

"You won't be alone this time, Abs. I'll be with you, and I'll make sure nothing happens to you. Cross my heart!" She grabbed my hand and found my index finger, held hers up beside it. The pinpricks we made a few days ago had faded, tiny red dots on our fingertips. "Blood sisters, remember?"

We touched our fingertips and said goodbye, promising to meet early the following morning behind the school bus shelter. But when morning arrived, I dawdled. Sweating and trembling as I ate my cereal, heart racing as I walked my bike towards the schoolyard. When I got there, I hid behind a hickory bush. Alice was pacing in front of the shelter, hands on hips, kicking her shoes on the gutter as she searched up and down the road, her ponytail lashing like a thin black tail.

My body turned sweaty and cold. My throat went dry. Tremors started in my chest and by the time they reached my feet I was shivering so violently I could hardly stand. Turning my bike around, I rode home. Alice would understand. She would wait another twenty minutes, then realise I had bailed and return to the little house on Green Street where she lived with her mother.

"Abby—"

Alice didn't come to school on Monday. At lunchtime, I rode my bike over with some comic books, thinking she was sick. No one answered the door. I returned the following day, but it wasn't till Friday that I saw her face again. In a colour photograph that the police brought when they came to question me—

"Abby!"

I startled awake.

Tom shook me again, his hand warm on my shoulder. "Abby, you were dreaming." He slumped beside me, his face rumpled and his brows drawn.

I sat up, pushing hair off my damp face and rubbing my eyes. I inhaled the cold air, hoping it would chase away my dream, but it only filled my lungs with the dankness of leaves and earth, and the image of poor Alice in her shallow grave. Fresh tears leaked out, and I dashed them away.

Tom drew me against him, wrapping his arms around my shoulders and holding me close. "Do you want to tell me?"

I leaned into him, breathing in the scent of his warm skin. "It won't help."

"How do you know?"

"Nothing helps."

"Try me. I'm a good listener."

I wriggled out of his arms and looked at him. I hadn't spoken about Alice, not since the investigation into her death. Not to Dad, not even to Duncan. A little to Lil recently, but not all of it.

But as I searched Tom's eyes in the shadowy garden, something in me loosened.

"I was dreaming about my friend, Alice. My best friend when I was twelve. She started at my school mid-year, when she and her mum moved up from Sydney. She was bright and hilarious, and everyone wanted to be her bestie. I don't know why she picked me. The weirdo everyone else avoided. I wore a hand-me-down uniform and outdated glasses, and I'd recently been through—well, a rough patch. But the minute I met Alice, all that changed. The old stuff didn't matter anymore. If we wanted to be duchesses dripping in jewels, then that's where we'd go in our minds, and it would seem utterly real." I held up my finger. "One day in sewing class, we pricked our fingers and became blood sisters. We crossed our hearts and declared we'd always be friends."

"You stayed in touch, right?"

"Alice died five months later." My breath hitched and more tears spilled out of me. The dream was so fresh, and the events of the past few weeks—finding Shayla, and coming here to Ravensong and learning about the Wigmore sisters, and then hearing Lil's story—had reopened old wounds. Silly how events from twenty years ago could still hurt me. My hands came up to cover my eyes, but Tom caught my fingers and pressed them against his lips.

"How did she die?"

A ragged noise erupted from me. I tried to tug my hands away, but Tom held firm.

"It's okay, Abby. I'm listening."

"It was my fault."

"I'm sure that's not true."

A knot jammed in my throat as the images tore through my mind. Alice alone, riding her bike out to the reserve. My funny, kind Alice trapped in the dark, smashing her small knuckles on a door that would not yield. Alice crying in the blackness as she grew weaker, as hunger consumed her thin body. Alice lying silently in the forest under a pile of earth and leaves.

"Abby, what happened to her?"

"Deepwater."

Tom frowned, and then his forehead rumpled. He linked his fingers in mine and squeezed my hand. "The local girl they found in the forest was your friend?"

"Yeah."

"I'm so sorry. You must have gone through hell. That's why you've been so worried about Shayla. But why do you blame yourself for Alice?"

"She was alone at the reserve. We were supposed to ride our bikes out together, but I changed my mind. So she went without me."

"Ah, poor kid. No wonder you still have nightmares. But you can't blame yourself."

There was more, but I'd already said enough. My bones had liquefied, my eyelids grown heavy. My Alice dreams always knocked me out. I meant to sigh but my whole body shuddered.

Tom released my hand and pulled me against his chest. His pyjama shirt smelled of smoke. In my sleepy state, I wilted against him. Snug where our bodies made contact. If only I had the courage to reach up and pull his face close to mine, to taste the salty warmth of his skin against my lips. To bury my face in his hair, breathe in his smoky fragrance. But how could I break down my barricades if I was unable to forget the past?

We sat there for a long time. Finally, Tom eased himself down onto the blanket and drew me beside him. I yawned and settled into his embrace, melting against the warm solidness of his chest.

Sometime later, I woke. Tom was asleep, his arms holding me loosely, his body heat warming me. He looked so peaceful in the starlight, sleepy and rumpled, his tawny eyelashes dark against the pallor of his skin, his lips slightly parted. I brushed a lock of hair away from his brow, the silky strands tickling my fingers. Good thing he was a deep sleeper. I inched closer until I could feel the soft beat of his breath on my skin, his body warm against mine. A flush of longing burned through me.

Tomorrow, I'd be gone. Out of his life, probably forever. There was no reason for me to stay after finishing the interview. Besides, Tom would be glad to return to his solitude and focus on his book. I inched closer. What was one kiss? It would only be fleeting. The brush of butterfly wings on skin, there for an instant then gone.

Tilting my face upwards, I touched my lips against his mouth. And melted. He was so sweet and warm. I wanted to linger, savour him a moment longer. I leaned nearer, my blood beginning to smoulder as I tasted him more deeply. *That's enough*, warned a tiny voice, *what if he wakes up?* I shifted closer. Tom stirred and rolled fractionally towards me. I held still, my silent breaths matching his, our lips still touching. Then he growled, a soft rumble in the back of his throat, and shivered into wakefulness. My heart punched against my ribs. Tom drew back and blinked down at me, and I stopped breathing. His hand slid up to cradle the back of my head, his fingers tangling in my hair, and with another murmur he crushed his mouth against mine.

As the cold starlight touched my bare skin, I forgot about my dream. I forgot the girls in the hidden room, and I forgot about leaving Ravensong. Forgot everything except Tom and me under the sky, and this smouldering thing between us. I forgot to breathe as I roamed my mouth along his whiskery cheek and then back to his lips, and pressed myself so close that his heartbeat raced mine through the thin cotton of his pyjama shirt.

I fumbled with the buttons. "This really has to go."

He laughed, a delicious husky rumble, and struggled out of the shirt, then flung it into the grass.

47
SHAYLA

"SOMEONE, PLEASE." Shayla's voice cracked in the darkness. "Please find me."

As if they'd hear *that*. She had screamed her throat raw. Hammered the walls till her hands throbbed. Dug her fingernails along the door seam until they turned pulpy and bleeding, all for nothing. Someone had built this place from steel. She knew it was steel because her fingers slid across it, but what did that matter? She was still trapped.

Her legs sagged beneath her like noodles, and she slumped on the floor. She opened her mouth and tried to squeeze out a few more tears, but it was useless. She had dried up inside like one of the old dishrags her mother tossed into the yard. Her stomach rumbled. Time for the food. The crumbs they threw her. She was beyond hungry. Her stomach had been grumbling forever, every boringly horrible endless moment gnawing at her like a giant rat.

She shut her eyes and curled on her side. She'd give anything for a pizza. Normally she went for thin crust, but from now on she would go for thick. The kind with cheese in it, so the bread squelched and filled your mouth with salty mozzarella. She'd get the meatlover's too. Let the juices drip down her chin, and chew and chew. She might be a wreck, but at least she still had her teeth—

She sat up. Tucking her throbbing hands in her armpits to warm them, she stared wide-eyed into the blackness. She remembered lashing out at someone. Before she came to this dark place. She had lashed out and heard them grunt in pain. She had taken off, lurching and stumbling through the trees, desperate to get away.

"Just another dream, you idiot. It never happened."

Her teeth. She had bitten them, hadn't she? Sunk in her teeth and chomped down hard. That was how she'd escaped into the trees. She probed her memory banks for more, but a door slammed down on that part of her brain.

What did it matter, anyway? She was trapped in a steel box, a million miles from anyone who cared. From anyone who'd even bother to listen.

48
JOE

JOE STARTLED AWAKE. He felt Lil roll away from him and climb from the bed. He checked the clock. It was just after three. He watched her move towards the bedroom door.

"All right, old girl?"

"Fine, Joe. Go back to sleep."

He settled back, but his eyes stayed wide. He often woke in the early hours, trapped in the grey purgatory between midnight and dawn. These wee hours were long, and yet the days—the bright beautiful days he spent with Lil on the verandah, enjoying lunch or a cup of tea, perhaps a slice of her fruitcake, watching the clouds move across the sky, or enjoying the shimmer of sunlight in the trees—those days were alarmingly short, whipping by too quickly. And then the gloomy predawn again. Dragging, dragging, as if nothing else existed and never would again.

Tonight it seemed worse.

He was restless, and his bones ached. His body felt heavy. Like knives were poking around inside his chest, making his eyes water. Since Lil disappeared into the reserve the other night, a shadow had claimed him. The angina was bad. He used the spray more frequently than usual. Worse though, were his fears for Lil. If something happened to him, how would she cope alone?

A soft bang came from the other end of the house, and he flinched.

Was that the back door?

"Go to sleep, you old fool. She'll be back in a tick."

His nerves were bad after the war. Loud noises bothered him. Chaos tormented him. He craved order and quietness. Not just craved it, relied upon it to keep him sane. The others had felt the same, his surviving mates. Needing order and harmony. Over the years they'd gone, dying one by one. He was the last, now. The keeper of the flame. The only one who remembered.

Without warning, his bladder ached. Wonderful. Now he'd have to piss, too.

He swung his feet out of bed and into his slippers. The crunch of footsteps outside drew him to the window. Was that someone in the yard? It was just the barest shadow. Was it even real? Figments came and went sometimes. The ghosts of his friends, the mates he'd lost in the war. They drifted in occasionally to say g'day, but he never minded. He had learned in the trenches that the membrane separating life and death was heartbreakingly thin.

He bent closer to the windowpane, focusing on the shadow. That was no figment. That was Lil. What was she doing out in the dark?

49

LIL

Lil navigated the dark garden, clutching the parcel to her chest. She had wrapped the diary—and its restored pages—inside an old cotton tote, and bound it with string.

She had guarded her sister's secrets for a lifetime. Kept them hidden from the world, from the people she loved. From Joe. It was time to let them go.

When the house disappeared behind her, she switched on the torch and made her way along the wallaby track. Ten minutes later she reached a tall tree with a thick white trunk and branches that clawed the night sky.

She used the gardening trowel she'd brought from the house, to scrape a hole between the gnarled roots and kept scraping until the hole was two feet deep. Then she reached for the parcel.

Her knees throbbed. Her back started twinging. Poor excuses, but she stopped and settled onto her bottom, sitting on the dirt, trying to catch her breath. Letting go had never been her strong point. Especially with Frankie.

She examined the string-tied parcel. Maybe she could read it one more time. Not the whole diary, but a page. Or two. Just to say goodbye.

50
FRANKIE'S DIARY

SUNDAY, 12TH AUGUST 1951

Since it's my birthday, Ennis took me for a walk in the garden. He showed me the caravan his grandfather had built, and the fruit trees his grandmother had planted around it. Then he took me to see the big iron birdcage. It was full of rust and ivy choked the bars, and when I asked about the birds that had once lived inside it—the green and yellow finches and the family of blue wrens—he said they'd all flown away before the war.

Still, it was heavenly to be outdoors.

The air tasted fresh. Sweet. I drank it in, relishing every breath. The air glowed yellow from the late winter sun, and the smell of the garden filled my head, making me giddy.

Ennis held my hand the whole time, saying it was romantic,

but his fingers grew damp and his grip stayed firm. Probably terrified I'd try to run away.

It crossed my mind. But where would I go? Once you get beyond the garden, the bush stretches for miles. Getting lost would be worse than being trapped in our room. So I concentrated on the two of us walking together. On the sunlight toasting my face. On the rough caress of Ennis's fingers. The friendly way our shoulders bumped as we walked.

"I've been thinking," Ennis said.

"Oh?"

"Ever since Jean Lee."

I bit my lips. I'd warned him about Lilly's nightmares. If only he had never brought us the stupid clipping.

Every night Lilly wakes up crying. Saying Jean Lee is standing over us, or hanging from the window bars, or waiting in the shadows like a ghoul. I try to tell her Jean Lee was just a poor woman whose life went horribly wrong and that she should pity her rather than be afraid. But then I'll catch Lilly crouched in front of the Warmray with the door open. Tilting her head as if listening. As if Jean Lee's voice is drifting from the ashes, recounting the grim tale of her death.

Ennis tugged me nearer. "It's time for us to leave."

"What?"

"Don't you want to be a proper family? Do the things regular people do?"

My pulse raced. "What do you mean?"

He gestured around the garden. "We'll leave all this behind us, Frankie. Start over. Find a little cottage by the sea. We'll have milking goats and chickens for eggs, and a garden brimming not just with vegies but with sunflowers and roses. Think of it, love. The three of us living together on the outskirts of some pretty town. What a fine life we'd have."

I stumbled along beside him, my ears buzzing. It sounded like a fly in a jar. Reminding me how Ennis's stories and promises had led me astray before, had lured me and Lilly away from Stanley Street that March morning three and a half years ago.

But Ennis spoke so earnestly. His face bright with pleasure, his eyes aglow. I quickly fell under his spell again, eager to daydream with him. To let his wild cheerfulness sweep me away. Because what if it was true? What if we could live a normal life and be a family?

Despite the garden with its sunbeams and leafy buds on bare branches, I could actually see our little beachside cottage. Longing coiled around me like a hungry vine and took root in my soul.

"What would we do for money?"

"I've always dreamed of being a carpenter." Ennis squeezed my hand. "I could get a proper job. Buy you and Lilly pretty new dresses. Lilly could go to school, take singing lessons. She's got talent, hasn't she? And you could do whatever you fancied." He furrowed his brow. "You'd like that, wouldn't you?"

I squeezed his fingers. "You know I would, Ennis."

"You're fifteen now, Frankie. Next year you'll be old enough to get married."

A furious blush crept up my neck. "I'm old enough now."

Ennis stopped walking and turned to look at me.

"We can't rush things, love. There's so much to plan. I'll have to sell Ravensong, so we have money to buy our cottage. It won't be easy to find a buyer so far from town. I have to repair things, tidy up the yard—" He gazed about, his eyes shining. Then he looked back at me. "There is something you need to do."

I stared up at him, mesmerised. The sun had pinked his

cheeks. He had raked his hair about so it caught the light like tufts of black fire.

"What's that, Ennis?"

He grimaced. "It's your sister."

I tore my hand free. Ennis tensed. He didn't follow me, but he swayed forward as if nervous of the space between us. I tugged at my sleeves, trying to cover my wrist bones. My body seemed in such a hurry to outgrow my clothes. I wasn't as tall as Lilly, despite her being younger, but I was awkward as a newborn colt.

"What about her?"

Ennis took my hand again. "I'm worried she'll ruin it for us, Frankie. She doesn't understand things the way you do. Would you talk to her? Tell her what we're planning and see if you can bring her round?"

FRIDAY, 2ND NOVEMBER 1951

She's such a stubborn mule. I've been trying to win her over for three months. But whenever I mention the cottage and the sunflowers, even the singing lessons, she slaps her hands over her ears like the child she is and refuses to listen.

"You idiot, Frankie. There won't be a cottage by the sea. Ennis is a criminal, have you forgotten? He stole us and kept us against our will for nearly four years. Do you think that will change?"

"He loves us, Lilly."

"If you believe that, you're stupider than I thought."

That night after dinner, Lilly sulked off to bed with her dolls. Ennis lit the Warmray. We huddled on a blanket in front of it, sipping hot cocoa and, later, a glass of sherry each. Ennis grew flushed from the wine and started rambling about our future. How we'd live by the ocean and swim at the beach whenever we pleased. Lilly called him a criminal, but she's wrong.

Ennis is a dreamer and since our talk on my birthday three months ago, his dreams had become my own. I itch with excitement when I think about our seaside cottage. The tidy garden, the goats and chickens and sunflowers. The long lazy days on the beach.

Yet part of me aches to see our mum again. Sloshed and foolish as she was, she's still our mum. And I want to see our red brick house on Stanley Street with its creaky roof and windows that stick when it rains. I want to see our favourite teacher, Mr Burg, and our school friends, even if only just to reassure them we're alive.

Ennis nudged me with his shoulder. "Do you love me, Frankie?"

"Of course I do, Ennis."

He watched me in the firelight. Flames danced in his eyes and I fell into a dreamy trance, unable to tear away my gaze. I admired his dusky eyelashes, the fierce wings of his brows, his sculpted cheeks and nose and chin. The faint freckles and whiskers and little scar nicks I had memorised.

He pulled me near. "Then you'll stay with me. Whatever happens?"

The past melted away. There was just the crackling fire and the raw neediness in Ennis's face. In that moment I'd never seen anyone more beautiful. Eagerly I nodded, my fingers curling tightly around his, my lips moving as the words leaped off my tongue in a whisper that left me breathless.

"I promise, Ennis. Whatever happens, I'll stay by your side. Always."

51
LIL

Lil flipped through the diary, saying goodbye. It was all so familiar, a part of her. The faint mustiness of the paper, the pages whispering as she turned them. The comforting slant of Frankie's distinctive writing. Escaping into the diary had eased her through some tough times. But it was also a wound she could never heal. By removing it from her life, she could stand taller, be able to face her remaining years with a light heart. Finally be free.

Be strong, Lil. It's time to let go.

But she kept flipping. When she reached the end, she trailed her fingers over the remaining pages—the ones that held Frankie's last entries. With a sharp inhale, she tore them out and stuffed them into her dressing gown pocket.

"Just once more," she promised. "And then I'll burn them."

She wrapped the diary up again and placed it in the hole. She filled the hole and dragged a rock over it, then scattered leaves and twigs to conceal the disturbed soil.

Her torch beam lingered on the disturbed ground.

Soon the wind and rain would cover her footsteps, erode all evidence that she had been here. That anything lay beneath those gnarly tree roots. She imagined the tree sending its tiny feeders through the pages, drinking up Frankie's writing. Devouring the paper, digesting her story into nothingness.

Finally setting Lil's spirit free to find the peace she had always craved.

52
ABBY

AT DUSK ON FRIDAY NIGHT, we stood at the tall entry gates to Gundara's memorial park, Tom's fingers linked in mine. The lantern parade, kicking off the Autumn Fest, made its way down the main street, the big, colourful lanterns glowing in the fading daylight. Huge bamboo-and-tissue-paper constructions bobbed over everyone's heads—animals and flowers, fish and birds, some so large they needed two pairs of hands to hold them aloft. A glowing possum sailed past, followed by a sulphur-crested cockatoo and then a huge red fox. Streams of school kids held smaller offerings, flowers and stars they'd made in community workshops. It was a dazzling spectacle of colour and light, and the mood of fun was infectious.

The parade entered through the park gates where it broke formation, the lantern-bearers merging with the crowds and heading across the bridge to the bandstand where later there'd be live music. We walked down to the blazing fire pit, finding a space between some goth-looking uni students and an older hipster couple. A girl with pink hair and nose rings adjusted the baby on her hip, and when her big gumnut lantern bopped Tom on the shoulder, she eyed his crutches and apologised. Tom laughed and tickled the baby, and the girl drifted off, smiling.

He caught my look. "What?"

"You old charmer." I slipped my hand behind his head and leaned close, claiming a kiss. "Never picked you as a baby guy."

"I'm full of surprises."

"What else have you got up your sleeve?"

"You'll have to wait till we're under that magnolia tree again to find out."

His laugh was absurdly lewd, and it started me giggling like a tipsy teenager. He grabbed my hand again and drew me against him, but didn't kiss me, just held me there and smiled into my eyes.

"You look ridiculously beautiful tonight."

I disentangled myself and did a twirl, making my vintage Diane von Furstenberg wrap dress flare above my knees. Colourful lantern-light swirled around me, and when Tom pretended to swoon, my heart soared. Was life supposed to feel this way? Loose-limbed and free, deliciously giddy, the night full of glowing flowers and birds, and beautiful men who tickled babies and made me laugh?

I linked my arm in Tom's. "I love the parade. It's my favourite thing all year."

"You look happy."

"Yeah, you too."

Tom's gaze broke from mine, and he nodded over my shoulder. "Do you know that woman? She keeps looking over here. I think she's trying to get your attention."

I twisted around. Coral Pitney stood beside the mulled wine stall, a crying child clinging to one hand and a rumpled sheet of paper in the other. She was staring right at me.

53
TOM

HE WAS IN TROUBLE. Serious trouble. As he watched Abby weave between the partygoers, the sight of her transfixed him. The swish of her bright, body-hugging dress and the glimpse it provided of her long, sexy legs. This went way beyond admiration. He had convinced her to stay a few more days, even though she'd delivered her interview on Wednesday. While tradies drifted in and out repairing the fire damage in his room, he and Abby had set up a makeshift camp under the magnolia tree. Abby said it was romantic, and Tom couldn't argue with that. He enjoyed seeing this side of her. The funny, tender-hearted person she was behind her no-nonsense façade. Slowly, she was opening up to him. And even more miraculous, he found himself opening up to her, too.

He smiled, biting his lip. He was in trouble, all right—

"Tom Gabriel?" A blonde woman with a diamond nose-stud grinned up at him. "I'm Kendra Nixon-Jones. Abby's boss at the *Express*. Enjoying the parade?"

"Yeah. It's amazing."

"Smashing interview, by the way. Abby made you sound like a star. And that picture with your gran? It's a real show-stopper."

Tom forced a smile, but something in the woman's tone raised his hackles. "Abby's a terrific writer. The *Express* is lucky to have someone of her calibre."

"It'll be in tomorrow's paper, if you're interested. We're doing a bigger print run to cater for festival visitors, and it'll be online too. Exciting, eh?"

"Hmm."

Kendra smiled, darting her tongue over her bright red bottom lip. "Do you get out much, Tom?"

"Not anymore."

She eased closer. "Pity. Why's that?"

"Guess I've lost touch with that part of my life."

"Oh?" Her eyes widened, lips parting again. "How did that happen?"

Tom's jaw clenched. She made it sound like catching a cold. But an introvert like him found it easier to hammer out dialogue on a typewriter than hold an actual conversation with another human. Not a great recipe for socialising. Admitting that would make him look weak, so he chose a more straightfor-ward answer.

"Divorce."

Kendra leaned against his arm, offering an eyeful of her ample cleavage. "Let's go out one Saturday, then. Make a night of it, just the two of us. Get you back in circulation, eh?"

The perfume wafting off her skin made Tom's eyes burn. He shifted, reclaiming his personal space. There was something predatory about this woman. Did Abby really get along with her? He glanced over at the mulled wine stall. Abby was talking to the pregnant woman with bottle-bleached hair. Beside the woman a small girl slouched, bopping her rumpled fish-lantern on the ground. The woman's voice was shrill, drawing glances from passers-by. Tom couldn't make out what she was saying. Abby didn't look happy. She was frowning at a sheet of paper and nodding her head. Should he check out what was happening? Too late. The woman gave Abby an awkward hug and moved away, dragging her scruffy child with her.

Abby returned to the fireside. She passed Tom a paper cup and smiled stiffly at Kendra. If she was pleased to see her boss, she didn't show it.

"I see you've met Tom."

Kendra made a cuddling motion against Tom's arm. "A real dish, isn't he? I can see why you sang his praises in your article."

Tom untangled himself and gulped the warm spicy wine, not taking his eyes off Abby. The firelight caught the gold in her hair, flushing her cheeks pink, but her sunny smile from before had vanished. "You okay?" he asked.

She glanced back at the stall. "That was Coral Pitney. Shayla hasn't come home."

Kendra made a scoffing noise. "There's always drama with that family."

"Not this time," Abby said. "Shayla left a note to say she'd gone to visit her dad on the coast. Coral spoke to the father today. He hasn't seen Shayla. No one's heard from her in three weeks."

Tom frowned. "And the mother's only getting worried now?"

Abby bit her lips together and shrugged. "Apparently Shayla runs off a lot. She always comes home, or the cops drag her back. When she didn't show, Coral assumed she was with the dad."

"Seriously." Kendra shook her head dismissively. "The kid'll come rushing back the minute she runs out of cash. Same old, same old."

"Has Coral gone to the police?" Tom asked.

Abby drained her drink. "Yeah, she's been at the station all afternoon, answering questions and filling out forms. They said they'd put the word out for Shayla, which means entering her details into national databases and posting on social media."

Tom frowned. "You don't sound too hopeful."

"What good are databases and social networks if she's stuck out in the bush somewhere?"

Kendra sniffed and looked at Tom. "The local cops have had a gutful of Coral Pitney. She's a real dirtbag, always up to some scam or another. Not to mention she's with a different man every week. Each of her five kids has a different father, and she's taken out more restraining orders than you can poke a stick at. Believe me, Coral Pitney draws trouble like a fly to shit. And her eldest daughter's no different."

Abby's eyes flashed angrily. "How can you say that? Shayla's just a kid. I had a feeling it was her in the campground, and Coral just showed me her photo. It was Shayla all right, and now something's happened to her. I feel responsible." She looked across at Tom, her eyes bright and wild. "The sooner I write that Deepwater story, the better. So that girls like Shayla wake up and stop taking unnecessary risks with their lives."

Kendra's cheeks shone red in the firelight. "Abby, I know you're on some weird crusade because of what happened to you as a kid. But I have to consider my sponsors. I'm not running the Deepwater story."

Abby crumpled her paper cup. "What?"

"It's old news, Abby. Ancient history."

"What about Shayla?"

Kendra sneered, light flaring off her nose stud. "The Pitneys of this world aren't newsworthy, Abby. No one wants to read about people like them. They're a burden on the system and are better off ignored."

"That's bullshit." Tom glared at her. "A kid goes missing for three weeks and you shovel dirt on the mother? Have you any idea why disadvantaged people attract trouble, Kendra? It's because people like you believe they're not worth the effort. Not worth educating, not worth listening to. Not even worth a moment of kindness. And," he added, gripping his crutches and hauling himself away, "you can quote me on that in your damn paper."

54
ABBY

"WHAT DID SHE MEAN, you're on a crusade?"

We had driven back to Ravensong in silence. Me gripping the wheel and brooding over Kendra's broken promise, Tom slumped in the passenger seat, glaring through the windscreen, lost in his own private world. It wasn't until we pulled up outside the house that he finally asked.

"She wasn't talking about Alice, was she?"

I switched off the ignition. "No."

"Is it related to why you blame yourself for her death?"

"Yeah, I suppose."

"Are you going to make me sit here all night playing guessing games?" He reached across and gently touched my cheek. "Because I will if I have to."

"Why do you even care?" I moved out of reach, my words booming in the stillness. "No one else seems to!"

"I care because it's important to you."

I flung open the door and got out, gripping my keys so hard my knuckles popped. "Murder, Tom. Three girls murdered and

God knows how many more they never found. And now, another girl goes missing and her own mother takes three weeks to even show concern." I slammed the door, and stalked away through the darkness, veering onto the path and around the side of the house. I stomped up the back steps and flopped onto a redwood chair, glaring out at the dark garden.

My heart was breaking. I kept seeing Shayla in that dark place, the cave or whatever it was, huddled in the cold. Hungry. Covered in bruised and scrapes, where she had flung herself at the rigid door, trying to claw her way out.

"I haven't forgotten you," I whispered. "Hang in there, Shayla. Everyone else might have given up on you, but I won't. I promise."

The kitchen light went on. Tom rattled around, glasses clinking, a cupboard door whispering open and closed. He came outside and placed a brandy bottle and two glasses on the table.

"Drink?"

I ignored him. A small pathetic moon clung in the night sky like a dead leaf. Out in the garden, a family of bats cried shrilly as their shadow-shapes raced over the treetops.

Tom sank into his seat and filled both glasses. He threw back his brandy and poured another. I picked up my glass and gulped the liquor as Tom had done. It burned all the way down like hell flames. I gagged and wiped my watering eyes.

"How did you do that?"

"Years of practice." His lips twitched as he uncorked the bottle. "Another?"

"No thanks," I croaked, slumping on my elbows.

"I'm a good listener if you want to offload."

"So you keep saying."

"I mean it, Abby. You'll feel better if you get it off your chest."

I exhaled slowly. Digging up the past was like exhuming a rotted old corpse, or extracting teeth. Was this how Lil had felt talking about Frankie? Of course it was. The shadows around her eyes and her ashen cheeks gave away her distress, despite her attempts to hide it. Yet she'd been brave and confronted it, and I could too.

"Remember how I said that a few months before I met Alice, I went through a rough patch?"

Tom nodded.

I fiddled with my empty glass. "One rainy April day in 1996, I walked out to the reserve alone. I got lost and this man found me ... he was holding an axe, and when he spoke to me I got scared and ran away. I must have tripped and hit my head, because I don't remember what happened next, just that I woke up in a cave. I'm not so sure now. Maybe it was a vehicle."

"That's why the caravan spooked you?"

I nodded. "Three days passed and somehow I escaped, don't ask me how. Some hikers found me wandering near Pilliga's Lookout, but when I told everyone what happened, no one believed me. Kept prisoner for three days in a cave? It sounded absurd. I returned to school and got on with it. Then I met Alice, and we were soon like sisters. So I confided in her what had happened."

"And she wanted to find the cave?"

I took a deep breath and nodded. "We picked a day, but I couldn't go through with it. Returning there, seeing the place again—" A shiver passed over my skin. Tom filled my glass, and I sipped the brandy this time, savouring the slow burn. "So Alice rode out by herself. And never came back."

Tom splashed more golden liquid into his own glass. "What about the guy with the axe?"

"When they found Alice's body a month later, shockwaves rocked the community. Suddenly, everyone was interested in the man I'd seen at the gorge. They arrested Jasper Horton a couple of months later in the reserve. He said he'd been collecting firewood. Winter was coming, and the family business was entering its busiest time of year. He remembered seeing me that day, said he tried to help me but I ran away. It turned out that Jasper had previous form. At sixteen, he accosted two schoolgirls. Touching inappropriately, exposing himself."

"Charming."

I looked at Tom. "It doesn't mean he's a killer."

"Makes you wonder though, doesn't it?"

"Jasper never confessed to killing Alice. His dad never gave up on him, and still insists Jasper was innocent. Roy told me his son was hopeless around people. Out of his depth. An oddball, I guess. People who knew Jasper said he didn't have it in him to kill."

"How did they convict him?"

"When they searched his house they found an axe, ropes . . . and a yellow hair ribbon. Jasper said he found it at the campground. Alice's mother swore it was her daughter's."

"He's looking pretty guilty from where I sit."

"Jasper was a simple guy. A loner, and uncomfortable around women his own age. He fitted the profile of an unstable predator. Besides, the town was eager to put the nightmare to bed. They had found the monster. Justice was done and everyone could sleep peacefully again."

"But not you."

"At first I believed it. Jasper was definitely the scruffy young guy I saw in the forest that day. I gave my statement, convinced it was Jasper who abducted me. It made sense because he was the last person I remembered seeing before waking in the cave. So I told them it was him and said I was absolutely sure. But I wasn't, not really. And then after—"

Tom waited, then frowned across at me. "After?"

"After Alice." I examined the golden liquor at the bottom of my glass. "I wanted someone to blame for what had happened to her. Someone other than myself."

LATER IN BED, I snuggled against Tom's back, breathing the warm scent of his skin. How did he sleep so deeply, while my eyes refused to shut and my thoughts raced like greyhounds round an endless loop?

Shayla had been missing for three weeks—twenty-one days, unseen by her family or friends, calls going unanswered, texts not replied to—and her mother had only gone to the police this afternoon. Where was Shayla now? Holed up with friends, punishing the world with her silence? Lying dead in a gully somewhere? Or was she trapped in the belly of a dirty, dank prison, growing hungrier and weaker and more terrified with every passing hour, believing that everyone had forgotten her?

I couldn't forget. Not when part of me was trapped with her.

I snuggled closer to Tom and slid my arm around his middle. He gripped my fingers and drew them to his furry chest, settling them over his heart. He murmured something I didn't catch, then his body relaxed back into sleep. I tried to follow him into oblivion, but it skittered out of reach. My blood thrummed. Kendra's voice echoed in my ears. *The Pitneys of this world aren't newsworthy, Abby. No one wants to read about people like them. They're a burden on the system and are better off ignored—*

I disentangled myself and swung out of bed. No point trying to sleep in this state. I threw on my jeans and cardi and crept upstairs to retrieve my map. Then I wandered out to the kitchen and made a pot of Darjeeling. On the verandah, I lit a lantern and sat on the redwood bench beneath it, smoothing the map on my knees.

The day of my escape from the cave, I ran and ran. Away from the hole that had trapped me. I raced like the wind, bounding over rocks and sliding down gullies, pushing through branches that clawed my face and arms. I was a fit girl, accustomed to trekking through the bush with my family, but I was only twelve. The distance I travelled that day—scrambling and stumbling, shrieking at shadows—had to be less than twenty kilometres.

I pencilled a circle around the places where they found the girls' remains, and another around Pilliga's Lookout where the hikers found me. I always thought my cave was within the radius of those areas. But what if I was wrong?

I studied the dotted lines of old trails that might once have accessed mines or logging pockets. They riddled the north end of the reserve. There was also a travelling stock route that cut through the forest southwest of Ravensong. But my map, an old one of Dad's, dated back to the 1930s. The stock route would be decommissioned, and the old trails grown over and forgotten.

If Shayla was out there, any hope of finding her was practically nil.

Tom emerged from inside the house, rumpled and heavy-eyed. "Can't sleep?"

I wriggled along the bench, making room. "I feel so helpless. People don't just disappear into thin air."

Tom tucked a crocheted blanket around my shoulders and snuggled in beside me. I leaned against him, relishing his warmth and solidness. For a moment I drifted in my thoughts, but as dawn started lightening the horizon, I shivered.

He glanced at me but said nothing.

I frowned. "What?"

"I don't want to say it."

My shoulders wilted. "Yeah, I know. After three weeks, the likelihood of her still being alive is slim. Maybe even non-existent."

"I'm sorry, Abby."

"I can't give up on her, Tom. Even if it's too late to save her, I just can't give up. I've been running those trails along the gorge for two years, half-hoping to find that cave. Half praying I won't. But what if she's there, Tom? What if she's in my cave or caravan or whatever it is, and I'm the only one with any chance of finding her?"

"How can I help?"

"I don't know if you can."

"Abby, if anyone can find that place, it's you. Whatever you need to do it, I'm your guy."

I smiled and looked at him. "You have a lot of faith in someone you've only known a few weeks."

"It feels like I've known you forever."

His hair stood up from sleep, and a tiny white feather had caught in the sandy strands near his temple, probably from his eiderdown. His mismatched pyjamas were seriously rumpled, and the sight of him—outside in the dawn cold, draped in a crocheted granny rug, helping me despite his fears that my quest might be pointless—touched a tender place in my heart. Smiling, I reached over and unhooked the little feather from his hair and blew it off my finger, setting it free to drift away on the morning air.

Tom's eyes darkened. He leaned up close and claimed my lips with his mouth. Then he pulled away. "I've a sudden yearning to evaluate the condition of the grass under the magnolia tree. Care to join me?"

I knotted my fingers in his hair. "That's possibly the sexiest idea I've ever heard."

55

TOM

After breakfast, Tom retired to the library to research the Second World War. He had ramped up the Frankie and Ennis romance, but decided on a more bittersweet ending. Having Frankie waltz off into the sunset with her kidnapper seemed wrong. And as he approached the end of his novel, he wanted to do his two heroines justice.

He booted the laptop and then leaned back in his chair. Outside, he glimpsed Abby through the trees, taking off on one of her runs. Soon—in a couple of months, he hoped—he'd be joining her. His pulse spiked as he pictured her under the magnolia that morning, writhing naked in his arms on their crocheted rug, the soft morning shadows caressing her skin, the breeze teasing her nipples. Tom had trailed his mouth across the cool smoothness of her curves—

"Whoa, steady boy."

How was he supposed to focus on the muddy trenches of France while images of Abby held prime real estate in his brain? He clicked a link to the Australian War Memorial, one of his favourite resources. But not this morning. Maybe a quick diversion? He typed in the URL for the *Gundara Express*. Perhaps if he re-read some of Abby's article—most notably, the 'glorious six foot three'—he'd be able to get his mind back on his work?

Clicking another link, he found the article. His smile withered. It was Abby's byline, and her photo—of all things, wearing the moss cardigan—but where were the words she'd written that Tom knew by heart?

> *Mega-selling true crime writer Tom Gabriel is a recluse for good reason. He detests people and people avoid him. "Tom is a womanising drunk," his ex-wife told the Express. "He's sickeningly full of his own importance and loves nothing more than to rubbish his fellow writers. He might be a hotshot in publishing, but in real life he resembles the criminal characters he so enjoys writing about. Bull-headed and arrogant, and, in his own words, emotionally stunted."*

Tom scrubbed his hands over his face. That was just the start of it. There was unflattering coverage of his divorce, speculation over his income, even gossip that he was currently dating a nineteen-year-old starlet from Adelaide. Where the hell had that come from? Oh, and a detailed account of the news camera he had smashed in a fit of public anger eight years ago.

By the time he reached the theory about him using a ghostwriter, he was ready to find a tall building to jump off. And not in a superhero way. His gut was in knots, and his jaw clenched so hard his face hurt, but worst of all was the jackhammer thump of his heart as it died in his chest. Had Abby been planning to screw him over all along?

He jabbed the print button and glared at the papers

spewing out. Abby's face, now in grainy black and white, seemed to mock him. *See, loser? Not so big and tough, after all.*

Eight years ago, he had read a different article by the first woman he ever loved. Different but somehow the same. His disbelief and anger, the horrible vertigo of having everything he'd known and trusted ripped from under him. His memories of how the press had swarmed like meat-hungry ants, trying to strip away his dignity. He had let himself trust again, but now the nightmare was back. He'd been wrong about Abby. She was no different to the others. She had prised out his inner secrets only to splash them across the front page of the *Gundara Express*. How soon before other media caught on and ran the story too?

He scraped the article from the printer and crumpled it in his fist. Let them bring it on. This time he wouldn't retreat into his shell and hide from the world. He was going to fight back.

56

ABBY

"IF YOU DIDN'T WRITE IT," Tom said tightly, "then who did, your evil twin?"

Sunlight drifted through the windows, making the lounge room appear ethereal, otherworldly. As if I was dreaming.

"I'm guessing it was Kendra." My fingers shook as I passed the article back to Tom, my stomach in knots. I had made him a promise, and failed to keep it. So why did it feel like I was the one who'd been betrayed?

"How could she research and write a feature in a few hours?"

"I don't know."

Tom rattled the pages in his fist. "But it's your byline, Abby. Half these quotes—or rather, misquotes—are from things I've said since you've been here. How would Kendra know all that?"

I shrugged miserably, lost for words.

Tom sank onto the sofa and screwed the pages into a wad. "I trusted you. Told you things I never told anyone else. And now all this crap about me is back on the front page. Seriously Abby, how could you do this?"

The room tunnelled around me. Tom was right to be angry. I was angry too. I wanted him to believe that I wasn't to blame for the article. For the lies and slander. But something niggled. If only I could remember what it was.

"Tom, why would I write all that stuff?"

"You said yourself that your readers want dirt. Scandal, divorce, gossip. You said they read about my messy life to feel better about their own. Well, you've done your job. They'll be congratulating themselves that they're not total losers like that Gabriel arsehole."

"I'd never say that about you."

"And yet there it is in black-and-white. The online article has already gone viral. I mean, 'sickeningly full of his own importance'? Is that what you really think?"

"No!"

"You did in the beginning."

He was right. Everything in the article echoed my own thoughts about him—before we met. But even then I'd never have written such a slanderous article.

"I thought that at first. But not anymore."

Tom's face was ashen, his eyes wary. "This puts you right up there in her league."

"Your ex-wife?"

"You're ambitious, clever. Much bloody cleverer than me. Telling me I'd get to approve what went to print. I thought you were different, Abby. But you're not, are you? You're just one more journalist exploiting others for your own gain."

Heat rushed to my face. I stood to attention and glared at him. "What about the Wigmore story? Your ticket back into the limelight, is it? Hello, *New York Times*, isn't that what you said?

You guard your own privacy with the ferocity of a wounded bear, but you seem unconcerned about exposing someone else's. You've made a fortune from other people's tragedy. If anyone's exploiting others for their own gain, Tom, it's you."

The atmosphere grew thick and oppressive, like the air in a hothouse. The clock ticked. Overhead, the rafters creaked. And then from deep in the house, Poe gave a long and eerie yowl that sent goose bumps over my arms and broke the spell of silence.

Tom wilted back into the lounge. "Fair call. You're right. I'm sorry, Abby. I asked for that." He looked across and offered a thin-lipped smile, crumpling the article in his fist. "I feel as if I'm reliving a nightmare I left behind in the past. Just when my life gets back on track, whammo. It's hit me kinda hard."

I sat beside him. "Do you really think I'd submit this rubbish? I care about you, Tom. And I care about my reputation. This is slander, and I'm the last person who'd risk losing everything by getting sued."

He gave a shaky laugh. "Not your style at all."

"No."

The silence drifted back. Dust motes glittered in the stillness and the wind murmured in the trees outside. Tom's fingers were still clenched around the ball of papers, his knuckles bloodless, and that told me all I needed to know. The damage was done. Not only to Tom's reputation, but to his trust in me. We might never heal this rift, no matter what we said.

Tom threw the wadded article across the room and into the shadows. "Jeez, Abby. I'm sorry for doubting you." He rubbed his eyes and then peered into my face. "Can you forgive me?"

"Nothing to forgive, Tom. You're right to be pissed off."

"But not with you. Hey, let's have a drink and forget the whole deal, okay? Stuff Kendra and her poison pen."

I got to my feet. "I'll head home today. Things to do. See to the cottage and all that."

Upstairs I packed my belongings, my heart so heavy I could barely breathe. I had wounded Tom. He tried to shrug it off, but I could see the truth in his eyes. He was deeply hurt. And that hurt was my doing. Whoever wrote the article—probably Kendra—had mimicked my style, but worse, she had known things Tom had told me in private. What a mess. I needed time to straighten it out, clear my mind. I couldn't do that if I was staying here with Tom.

When I returned to the lounge room, he was at the window.

I leaned against him and kissed his cheek. "See you, Tom."

His pupils were huge, his eyes shadowed by violet half-moons that hadn't been there this morning under the magnolia tree. He caught my fingers.

"Stay, Abby. We'll work this out. Please don't let this come between us. It's a glitch, that's all."

"A glitch?" I let go of his hand. "Tom, I'm the one who convinced you to do the interview. I'm the one who gate-crashed your privacy, and now, as you said, you're reliving your old nightmare. It's up to me to put it right."

Before he could argue further, I hurried outside and down the steps. The garden blurred as I blinked back tears. Tom might forgive, but he wouldn't forget. Not when the media fallout started. I knew how quickly resentment could eat a person's heart. My mother had resented my father for finding solace in a bottle instead of with her. My father's resentment after she left had swallowed him alive. I was no different. After I married Rowan, it took less than a year for my insecurities to kick in and send me running. Just as I was now, from Tom.

Wasn't it better to call it quits before we got in too deep? Avoid the heartache I knew was coming?

"WHAT DO YOU CALL THIS?" I slammed the latest edition of the *Gundara Express* onto Kendra's desk. "Whatever it is, I sure as heck didn't write it."

She leaned back in her chair, her cherry-red lips curling. "I call it the sensational front-page feature I asked for. The one you so dismally failed to deliver."

"It's a bunch of lies, that's what it is. I gave you a perfectly good article, with Tom's approval. How could you do this?"

She scratched delicately at her neck, her amber eyes glinting. "How could I not? Especially after the way you both spoke to me at the parade. I stayed up all night rewriting your puff-piece. Calling in favours to make the morning news. Busting my arse." She leaned on the desk and sighed. "I asked for juicy details, Abby. Instead, you give me an arty-farty piece about inspiration. Nobody wants to read that."

"What you did is unethical. Probably illegal."

"It's a small-town newspaper. A storm in a teacup. Gabriel's a big boy, I'm sure he deals with critical reviews all the time."

"It's more than a critical review, Kendra. It's a personal attack."

"He'll get over it. And if he sues, it won't be my neck on the chopping block."

"What?"

She gave a breathy laugh. "Why do you think I used your

byline? I just thank God you left all the *interesting* research on the flash drive, alongside your drivel."

I scrubbed my hands over my face. I hadn't slept, hadn't eaten, and couldn't remember if I'd even brushed my hair. But a single image burst across my mind in full technicolour. The research on my flash drive and all the notes I had dictated to my catch-all file—how could I have forgotten about them? Everything I'd learned about Tom was in that file. The personal things I'd sworn nobody else would see. My transcript of our interview. Conversations we'd had, and Tom's entire history— all on the drive I handed in with my article.

How could I face Tom now? Tell him that the whole mess was my doing, after all? How could I expose what Kendra had done when I was equally at fault?

Kendra gripped the edge of her desk and leaned forward. "You were getting too big for your boots, Abby. All your talk about Deepwater, and about warning people—you needed bringing down a peg. So the next time I say leave something alone, then bloody well leave it."

I walked to the door. "There won't be a next time, Kendra. You can stick your bloody newspaper. I quit."

AFTER THE CAVERNOUS rooms I'd grown to love at Ravensong, my cottage seemed impossibly cramped. The air was musty, the ceiling too low, and the corners too dark. My collection of small paintings resembled postage stamps after the huge abstracts adorning the walls of Tom's house. The orchid Duncan had given me last birthday had withered, its bulb wrinkled with stress, some leaves turning black. I doused it with water. It was going to die, too, wasn't it? I gave the poor thing a splash of liquid seaweed and put it in a sheltered spot outside.

At Ravensong, everyday chores were an adventure. I had loved dusting all those interesting surfaces. Polishing the cupboards in the library and browsing the bookshelves. Flicking cobwebs off the chandelier, admiring the beautiful garden views. Finding an empty room to stand in and dream.

My cottage was a shell, crammed with relics of my old life. "I'm here because I want to be," I announced to the ceiling. "This is my home. It's where I belong." It was full of my history, of everything that made me who I was. My crazy collections, my dusty old romance novels, my reminders of the past. All the constructs I'd built around me to keep myself safe. Protected.

Maybe that was the problem?

The phone rang constantly the first few days after I got home. Tom left messages on my machine, which I deleted without listening to. After a few days, his calls stopped. I slid back into my familiar grooves. I sent some articles off to the national papers, but my heart wasn't in any of them. A couple of emails came regarding the *Express*—not Kendra, but a woman from the regional network—urging me to call them back. Flack for the article, no doubt. I deleted those too.

Every day I jogged to the reserve. Some days I drove out beyond the perimeters of my previous search areas, other times I ran along old familiar tracks. One day I went up to Pilliga's Lookout. I walked north, and when the sun was at its highest point, I unfolded my map and examined my surrounds. All around me stretched a sea of tall eucalypts and areas covered in sparse undergrowth, broken only by granite boulders pushing through the earth. There was no sign of any loggers' trails, no evidence of felled old-growth trees. Not even the stock route.

I followed my compass east to the river and then returned home. Then this morning I travelled west from Pilliga's, taking notes as I ducked under low-hanging branches and trekked along the riverbank, even climbing a little way down the steep bank into the gorge.

Back at my cottage, deflated after another pointless run, I boiled the kettle. A strong hit of caffeine would perk me up. I reached for the tea canister and found the framed photo Duncan had given me the morning I found Shayla. I picked it up and traced my fingers over the four of us. Me, Duncan and Dad—and my mother. *Mum ran off and left us, but Dad's the one you blame for what happened to you at the reserve. That's pretty messed up, sis.*

He was right, my wise baby brother. It was messed up. But how could I blame my mother when I knew how bad it felt to be trapped somewhere you didn't want to be? Besides, all my memories of her were happy ones. Her fits of giggling when Dad tickled her, trying helplessly to bat him away, peeping from under her curtain of dark hair, her plump cheeks glowing pink. Her cosy cuddles, her obsession with Vegemite on toast. Where was she now? Did she sometimes think of us? Did she even know that our father was gone?

I studied Dad's big square face with its frame of wispy hair and lopsided mad-scientist smile. When I told Lil about him that day in the hospital, I had flushed with pride. *He loved his job. Loved talking about the environment and conservation. He inspired my interest in it. After Mum left, he lost his spark. Withdrew from my brother and me. From everyone.*

I took the photo into the lounge room and propped it on the mantle. Found a smile for my father.

"At least you had a good reason for withdrawing from the people you loved. Mum broke your heart, but what's my excuse? I just drive everyone away because I'm scared. Scared if they get too close, they'll discover what a terrible person I am." My mother, Alice, even Dad. The people I had lost. The people I had pushed away. I'd been blaming them for my unhappiness, but I was blaming ghosts. I had clung to them too tightly, expected too much. And now I was turning into the sort of empty, bitter person I'd always pitied. I gazed around. Four weeks ago the cottage had shone. Nothing out of place, not a speck of dust. Now there were unwashed dishes in the sink. Unopened mail cluttering the sideboard. Roses drooping in a big blue vase, their cast-off petals littering the floor. How was it possible that I'd made so much mess in such a short time? Not just of my house, but of everything?

57
ABBY

As I trod along the dim hallway, the floral carpet muffled the thud of my boots. I entered my father's bedroom and stood a moment, breathing the dry air. The last time I'd been here, Dad and I had argued. I didn't remember what it was about, just that three days later he was gone, leaving me nursing a heart that was too bruised to admit I'd been wrong.

I opened the wardrobe. Inside was a rack of neatly hung clothes—unworn for half a year, a thin haze of dust clinging to them. Each one of Dad's shirts was a memory. The yellow one he'd worn that last Christmas. His favourite green flannel with the ragged cuffs. The pale blue stripe he kept for good. Once they were gone, would we lose the memories too?

The front door clattered open. "Abby?"

"In here." I swiped at my cheeks.

"Jeez, sis! I can't believe you've finally—" He froze in the doorway.

I glanced over at him and shoved my hands in my pockets. I

attempted a bright smile, but my lips were quivering, my eyes bleary, and tear trails stinging my cheeks.

Duncan's sandy brows knotted. He took a step towards me.

"I'm all right," I said, waving him away.

"No, you're not." He pulled me against him, soothing my hair and murmuring. A faint clean whiff of soap and something sweet—caramels and sugar—wafted from his T-shirt, and I flashed back to the little mother hen he'd once been, his skinny body wrapped in one of Mum's old aprons as he fussed over the people he loved. "It's okay, Abby. Wherever Dad is now, you can bet he's happy. Hey, they probably have polluted sediment in heaven."

I wiped my eyes. "Probably more pollution in hell, wouldn't you think? I bet the old coot's down there, sifting away to his heart's delight." It wasn't much of a joke, but at least we were smiling. "Anyway, Dunc. I wasn't crying about Dad. I've cried about him so much over the years. Wishing things could have been different between us. The silences shorter, the postcards more frequent. Our visits less awkward."

"Yeah, sis. Dad was a goose sometimes, but he did his best."

"I'd forgotten that the frowning man nursing a beer bottle in front of the television was the same guy who had, a long time ago when I was twelve, threatened the police with hell and high water."

"Dad threatened everyone with hell and high water."

"I really miss him, Dunc."

"Me too. It doesn't seem to get easier like people say."

I gazed about Dad's room. "What if it never gets easier? I regret so much. How do you get past that?"

"You know what I always say."

"Shag anything with a pulse?"

"Besides that."

"Forget the past and enjoy the now."

Duncan reached over and gently brushed his thumb under one of my eyes and then the other. "Come on, I'll show you where Dad kept the rubbish bags."

We grabbed a bunch of bags from under the sink and returned to Dad's room. We cleared the wardrobe first, cramming Dad's clothes and shoes and belts into the bags and propping them by the door like lumpy sentinels. On Dad's dressing table I found a pair of cufflinks, Dad's wedding ring and his old-mannish glasses. Next to them sat a dish containing a river stone.

"Hey, Dunc. Check this out." I picked up the stone. Turned it over and read what Dad had written there a lifetime ago.

Bev, Abby, Duncan and Col.
Best Day Ever, January 1993.

I placed the stone in Duncan's hand. "Do you remember? We walked for miles into the reserve along one of the remoter tracks. Had a picnic on the edge of an ancient beech forest— chicken sandwiches and leftover Christmas cake, a flask of frozen lemonade—it was heavenly. The wind sighing high above us in the casuarinas, the river murmuring below."

Duncan laughed softly, trailed his fingers over the inscribed letters. "I remember. How old was I, seven?"

"Six. You were the star of the day, racing around looking for trees to climb, the higher the better. You were such a little nutter. Your antics had us all in stitches." A warm feeling engulfed me and I felt lighter. "It was one of our best days, wasn't it?"

"Yeah, it was." Duncan took my hand and placed the stone on my palm, then closed my fingers around it. "Keep it, sis. A little piece of heaven to remind you how good things can be."

A PACKAGE WAS WAITING for me when I got back to the cottage. It was a document-sized envelope addressed to me in Tom's handwriting. I took it inside and propped it on the coffee table, then switched on all the lights and perched on the edge of my sofa, trying to fathom what it was. Tom's novel about the Wigmore sisters, finished already? It was too thin to be a novel. A love letter then? Unlikely. It was probably hate-mail. Or worse—and this had me sinking back into the cushions, cradling the sudden queasiness in my stomach—what if he sued the paper, after all? Sued me?

I sat there for an hour, brooding and sweating as dusk turned to night. My mouth was dry, but my limbs too rigid and tense to force into motion and get myself a drink of water. Finally, hands shaking like wind-rattled leaves, I tore the envelope in half in my haste to get it open, and drew out some photocopied pages.

Tom had attached a note.

I was determined to drive into town and see you, plaster cast or not, so I got in my ute. I sat there for ages, then gave up and returned inside. Whatever your reasons for staying away, I have to respect them. If you need me, I'm here. Love, Tom. PS: I've enclosed an article that will interest you.

I set the note aside and looked at the document. A slip of paper clipped to the top bore the logo of the New South Wales Government State Archives and Records, and a handwritten memo. *Tom, colour copies of the documents, as requested.* The document header read: Gundara Police Station Record of Occurrences Feb–Nov 1953. I settled back into the cushions and tilted the pages to the light.

Tuesday, 2nd June 1953
At 10 am I left the station and patrolled Main Street. I returned at 10.30 am. The rest of the day was quiet. Then at 5 pm Harry Horton, a woodcutter aged 41 of Downey Street, entered the station. He had a girl with him. She was filthy, hands and knees cut and ingrained with dirt. Mr Horton seemed agitated and sweaty, casting nervous looks at the girl.

He stated: "I was driving back from the reserve after cutting wood with my son Roy, who's ten. My permit's in order if you care to see it. Anyhow, halfway back to town I pass this young lass wandering along the reserve road. I pull over to ask if she needs help, but can't get a word of sense from her. With all them bruises, here's me thinking she's hurt. So I coax her into the truck. Consider getting her to hospital but she seems well enough, aside from the bruises. Reckoned you lot had better see her first. She's clearly a runaway."

Harry Horton signed the above statement and departed the station. I telephoned the hospital, who sent over a nurse, one Sadie Emerson, aged 29, to check the girl. At first the girl resisted being touched and grew upset when Nurse Emerson tried to remove the satchel the girl wore across her chest. Finally, after a brief inspection, Nurse Emerson stated: "Poor little thing has nasty grazes on her hands and knees. She has black bruising around her throat, which seems to have affected her ability to speak. She is otherwise in a healthy condition, although a little thin and obviously traumatised."

After some time the nurse could elicit the girl's name as Lilly Bird, aged fourteen. She stated she lived with her mother and sister in Sydney.

Lilly Bird stated: "Mum works in the hospital. She'll be worried about me. I want to go home." She couldn't say why she was on the reserve road. When asked about the bruising on her throat, she clammed up. Nurse Emerson offered to billet her for the night. Before I shut the station, I arranged for the child to be transferred to Central Sydney police first thing in the morning.

WEDNESDAY, 3RD JUNE 1953
When I arrived on duty at 8 am, Nurse Emerson was waiting outside the station in an agitated state. She reported that the young runaway, Lilly Bird, had fled in the night, taking a small amount of cash. Enquiries at the railway confirmed that a young girl of Lilly Bird's description had bought a one-way ticket to Central Railway Station in Sydney.

For a long time I sat there, wilting into my sofa cushions, staring at the report. Had Lilly given the wrong name intentionally, hoping to give Frankie and Ennis a head start? Or was there another reason?

Lil hadn't mentioned the black bruises on her throat. She had fought with Frankie, but otherwise her departure from Ravensong had been uneventful. At least, that was what she claimed. Did the row with her sister get physical? Was Frankie responsible for her sister's bruising?

I reread the line about Harry Horton casting nervous looks at the girl. Nervous? Had the duty officer misinterpreted his body language? Harry could have been upset about Lilly's situation. But then why didn't he stay around to make sure she was okay?

I flopped back on the sofa. Someone was lying. Lil, or old Harry Horton.

Perhaps they both had something to hide.

58

JOE

HIS SATURDAY MORNING check-up took forever. Doc Worland slid the cold disc of her stethoscope over his bony chest, getting him to cough and wheeze until tears sprang into his eyes. The doctor frowned as she entered notes on her computer, then sat back in her squeaky leather chair. *I'm sorry, Joe. It's not looking good.* She prescribed an increase in medication and explained how, as the end got nearer, he would need more intensive care. *You know what this means, don't you, Joe? You and Lil will have to move into town.*

Joe nodded and smiled in agreement. He took the script and folded it into his pocket, promising to come back next week for another check.

"You're late," Lil said as he trundled into the kitchen.

He placed his shopping bag on the table. "Just in at the clinic, love."

"Everything all right?"

"Top of the pops."

"Doc Worland's happy with your progress, then?" Her eyes were wide with hope, her smile trembling at the corners.

Joe kissed her on the cheek. "All good, pet. Now, look here. I bought a loaf of that sourdough you love." He held aloft a tiny bottle of capers. "And a special treat for tonight's pasta."

Lil snatched the bottle from his fingers. "How many times must I tell you? You're sodium reduced, remember?"

Joe swallowed. Salt be blowed, he wanted to tell her, and fatty foods and sugary treats, too. No amount of healthy eating was going to help him. Not now. Let's live a little. Feast on the things we love. Cakes and ice cream, butter-fried mushrooms and bacon on toast. Scones with clotted cream and jam, Camembert toasties. Because of his condition, Lil had been dieting too—aside from the caramel slice she still made for drama group, and lately the jam tarts for Abby. Not that it mattered anymore. Why deny themselves?

Lil frowned and touched his arm. "Love, what is it?"

Joe didn't know what else to do, so he started coughing.

"All right there, Joe?"

"Something stuck in my neck."

"Need a pat?"

He shook his head. "I'll be right, Lil."

She smiled at him, and her eyes sparkled with something he hadn't seen in a while. The old warmth, the spark he'd thought lost.

Tears sprang to his eyes. He had to look away, make a show of thumping his chest. But there was nothing stuck down there, at least nothing tangible. Just a feeling. A prickly feeling that said something wasn't right. The more he tried to shrug it away, the deeper it burrowed, sharp as a rose thorn, stabbing into the pulpy core of his heart. The heart that was running out of time.

59
LIL

LATE AGAIN FOR DRAMA GROUP, what was wrong with her? She bustled about the kitchen gathering her things, her glasses and purse, and the caramel slice from the fridge. The phone rang as she was about to leave. It was Doc Worland.

"Sorry to bother you on a Saturday, Lil. Is Joe around?"

"You just missed him. He's gone fishing."

"Would you remind him to increase his dose? He seemed a little flustered this morning, and I'm worried he might forget. Will you tell him?"

"What do you mean, increase his dose?"

There was a pause. Doc Worland cleared her throat. "His condition has worsened."

Lil's fingers shot to her throat. "No, pet. You've mixed things up. Joe said you gave him the all-clear."

Another pause. "Lil, I'm sorry. He might have been intending to break it to you in his own time. But it's time you don't have, I'm afraid."

"What are you talking about?"

294

"Joe's not a well man. We spoke about the two of you moving back to town. Preparing yourselves for the inevitable."

Lil swallowed. Inevitable? The doctor's words inflamed her mind like an infection, their poison spreading through every pore, every cell of her body. The worst had happened. She blinked to clear her eyes. Her Joe. Her dearest friend, the man she loved more than life itself, was leaving her and there was nothing she could do to stop him.

"Lil, are you there? You're welcome to come in for a chat anytime. We can talk about your options."

"Options?" Lil murmured.

"Gundara has some wonderful aged-care facilities, Lil. I think you'll be pleasantly surprised."

Lil thanked the doctor for calling and hung up. Her scalp was tight. She could already feel the blood retreating from her face. Inside the back of her skull, a balloon of darkness began to expand and grow. It took shape, and despite Lil's attempts to push it down, it continued to enlarge. Eclipsing her. Finding another form. A shadow.

A girl-shaped shadow.

She made herself a strong black coffee and drank the bitter brew standing at the sink. *Oh Joe. The thing we most feared is here. How will I go on without you?* She swallowed a Xanax and took deep, calming breaths, gazing through the window and up into the pine trees where sunlight glinted through in shards. Once the dark shapes in her mind had recoiled, she boxed up her slice, grabbed her car keys and headed for the door.

An hour later she was unlocking the guide hall, when Dianne bustled up beside her.

"Oh Lil. I'm afraid we've had some bad news."

Lil wilted. More bad news? The sun shone and the sky glowed clear blue, a dream of a day, but it was fast turning into a nightmare. She dragged off her hat and sunglasses, trailing Diane inside.

"Bad news?"

"Claire was in a car accident, but don't panic. She's all right. Just a couple of broken ribs and a black eye."

"Broken ribs? Oh, poor Claire. Where is she now?"

"At home, recovering. But Lil, you know what this means, don't you?"

"Hmm." Lil was already planning flowers and a cake, or perhaps a plate of that salted caramel slice Claire was partial to. Poor Claire, of all people. When would she get a break?

The other women arrived and took their seats. Diane broke the news about Claire and they murmured among themselves for a while. Then someone broached the question on all their minds.

"Who'll sing the lead now?"

The women exchanged glances. Jenny raised her hand and Lil's heart sank. Of all the girls, Jenny was the least confident. She was still finding her way after years of domestic abuse. She hadn't even volunteered for the chorus.

Lil tried to smile. "Yes, love?"

"What about you, Lil?"

Lil pretended fascination with her clipboard. "Oh no. I don't sing."

"Wish you would though, Lil," Fiona chimed in. "It's true, you've got an awesome voice. When you taught me those vocal warm-ups last year, I got the tingles. You'd be brilliant as Madame Valjean."

A bead of sweat trickled down Lil's spine. At least she hoped it was sweat. It felt more like a cockroach. "I've no intention of taking the lead, Fiona."

Isa put up her hand. "Please, Lil. You're pitch perfect. Couldn't you at least do Fantine?"

Lil made a choking sound. "Good Lord, a seventy-seven-year-old Fantine? They'd laugh me off the stage."

"No, they wouldn't," Isa insisted. "Your voice would blow everyone away."

Diane stood up. "You can beg all you want, but I don't like your chances. I've badgered the woman enough over the years. I'll give you this, though. If any of you can convince Lil Corbin to sing in our musical, even just a walk-on part, I'll take the entire troupe for a celebratory dinner at Colletti's, my treat."

Lil made a scoffing noise. "For heaven's sake, Diane."

Diane raised her brows. "Feeling tempted?"

Lil rewarded her friend with an eye roll. When would Diane learn? Lil did not sing. She could not sing. At least not tunefully. Not anymore, not since . . . well, a lifetime ago.

"Isa, what about you?" Lil waved a sheaf of papers, eager to move on. "Interested in seeing the libretto?"

Isa nodded uncertainly, but headed over.

Diane looked at Lil. "Colletti's do a lovely chicken parmigiana, have I mentioned that?"

Lil passed the sheets of paper around. "Yes, Diane. Several times."

Diane huffed again, then wandered off to see about morning tea.

Later, Lil stood at the sink in the tiny guide hall kitchen, hands plunged in sudsy water as she rinsed cups and plates. Doc Worland's words echoed at the edges of her mind, making her heart race. *Joe's not a well man. It's time you don't have.*

She glanced through the serving hatch. The women sat around the long table in the hall, reading her amended libretto. Lil loved the sound of their chatter, punctuated by excited voices or a burst of laughter. Diane had enlisted her young nieces to play Cosette and Éponine as children, and the girls were racing around in a game of tag. Lil bit her lips together. One girl was fair-haired, the other dark, just as Victor Hugo had described. Lil gazed after them with a thin smile.

She and Joe weren't able to have children. There'd been a stream of foster kids when they first married. They were still in touch with one of their fosters—Nora, with lots of long heartfelt letters and the occasional phone call. Sporadic visits. But aside from Joe, Lil's true family were the shelter women. The good eggs and the bad, they all deserved kindness and love. All deserved a second chance. In return they had given her their trust and devotion, and that was reward enough.

It was bittersweet, the way they asked her to sing. Sweet because they were a good bunch and Lil enjoyed their enthusiasm. Bitter because many years ago it had been her dearest dream. She used to sing all the time at Stanley Street. Tapped her feet when singing wasn't possible, and hummed ditties in all the gaps between. *You're magic*, Frankie used to say. *You've got something marvellous inside you.* Her mother boasted once that Lilly had melodies running in her veins instead of blood.

Not anymore.

Lil rubbed the fluttery tightness in her chest. Even the idea of standing on stage gave her the willies. Of course, a snatch of melody burst out now and again, almost of its own accord—usually when she was teaching the women their vocal warm-ups. But for Lil to stand in front of an actual audience, sing an entire song? Decades ago she had tried singing an old favourite in the shower, expanding her lungs in that familiar way, opening her mouth wide and reaching for a note, but nothing came out. Not even a squeak. There was just the rush of hot water on her chilled skin—and the cold deadness as shadowy fingers closed around her throat.

Lil shook off the memory and bustled around, gathering the damp tea towels and wiping crumbs off the counter. She checked the clock. It was only ten thirty. She'd pop over to see Claire, pick up the groceries, and then hurry home to Joe—

A shriek came from the hall. Lil rushed over to the doorway. One of Diane's nieces had tripped and fallen. The girl was clutching her knee and crying, her leg trickling blood. Lil hesitated. She had mopped her fair share of skinned knees in her time, but the sight of the girl's twisted, tear-streaked face froze her on the spot.

First Joe. Then Claire. Now, the blood.

She collected her hat and handbag and retrieved the Tupperware containers from the fridge, then slipped out the back door. Diane was good with blood and tears. Lil had other worries right now. Unlocking her car, she dumped her things in the boot and flopped into the driver's seat.

You could do it, Lil. You've got an awesome voice.

She stroked the soft skin of her throat. Even after sixty-plus years, she could still feel the bruises. Still see the swollen black welts, the fingermarks mottling her windpipe.

When she was sixteen, Mrs O'Grady had taken her to a specialist. The kindly old doctor had examined her throat at length, and in the end proclaimed her vocal cords healthy— there was no physical reason Lilly could not find her beautiful singing voice. He suggested Lilly visit a psychiatrist, but Mrs O'Grady did not push her. Lilly didn't need anymore prodding and poking. She didn't need to remember.

She blew out a breath. How she hated getting old. Memories came so vividly. Why was that? They should fade with age, grow ever more distant. Instead, they rushed at her with the force of a gale wind. The scent of crushed eucalypt leaves, and the whispering crackling forest at night. The sigh of water racing in the gorge. And her sister's weight in her arms. The sticky heat of blood on her hands.

She buckled forward.

How could events from a lifetime ago still cripple her like this? She hadn't always been so weak. With her sister by her side, she'd been strong and hearty. Invincible. Despite their differences, she and Frankie had been a formidable team. If Lilly ever sank into despair over some jibe or insult, Frankie would elbow her and wink. *Devil take the lot of them, Lilly-bird. It's you and me against the whole rotten damn world.*

After Frankie went, it was just Lilly. Alone. And without her sister beside her, Lilly never felt quite so brave ever again.

60

FRANKIE'S DIARY

FRIDAY, 7TH MARCH 1952

I sat beside Lilly on the bed and we watched the shadows deepen around us as the sun drifted behind distant hills. For the millionth time, I tried to paint her a picture of our future happiness—"Singing lessons, Lilly, won't that be wonderful? And a tiny cottage by the sea, can you imagine?"—but she sat sullenly, staring at the floor. Her shoulders hunched, her eyes bright with anger, nibbling the tips of her long hair.

"Lilly," I said at length. "It's what we've always dreamed."

"What you've dreamed."

"Wouldn't you like to live by the sea?"

"Not with him."

"It's been four years. Everyone else has forgotten us. He's all we have."

"I hate him," she spat. "You and him, the way you're always mooning over each other. It makes me sick. I'd rather go back to Stanley Street."

"Then you're a fool. Don't you see? He's given us a better life than what we had. Mum ignoring us while her latest boyfriend eyed us behind her back? You might not remember how bad it was, but I do."

"You're the fool," she said scornfully. "Maybe it was hard at home, but we had our freedom. Mum was all right. She was sozzled half the time, but at least she never locked us up like animals."

"He wouldn't lock you up if you were kinder to him. Your sharp tongue ruins everything. If only you'd cross your heart not to run away, he'd let you play outside in the garden. All he wants is for us to be a family."

Lilly sprang away from me, perching on the far end of the bed, screwing up her face. "Are you mad, Frankie? He'll never let us out of this room. All his talk about living a normal life, being a carpenter, buying us dresses. It's a trick."

"No, Lilly. He means every word."

She crossed her arms, glaring at me from under her mop of wild hair. "Suit yourself, Frankie. You go off with him."

"What about you?"

She shrugged. "I'll go home to Mum."

We sat in silence for a long time, me on the edge of the saggy mattress, Lilly perched on the pillow. The sun withdrew its rays and shadows crawled around us. Soon it was night. One by one the stars came out, then the moon crept into view.

"Take one last look at the moon, Lilly-bird."

I waited for Lilly to say her part. Waited and waited. Finally,

I looked at her. She had wilted against the wrought iron bedhead, her face buried in her arms, silently crying.

TUESDAY, 20TH JANUARY 1953

It's stinking hot today, which is probably why our tempers flared. Or maybe it's my time of the month that made me cranky. I hate the rags. I hate feeling bloated and pimply, and it's always worse in the heat. Whatever the reason, there's now a shiny red handprint on Lilly's face. And a sting in my palm that hurts more than my guilt.

Lately Ennis has been talking about leaving Ravensong. Making lists and timetables, claiming that once the weather cools down, we'll leave. He even showed me a map of Australia where he'd circled a tiny town in Queensland. A town where no one will know us.

This morning when he left the room, I broke the news to Lilly. "Just think, Lilly-pill. We could be gone by autumn. On our way to a new life."

She narrowed her eyes. "Queensland's a long way from Sydney."

"That's the idea, silly."

"Don't you want to see Mum?"

"Once we're settled in the cottage, we can visit her on the train. You'll see. Things will change when Ennis and I are married."

She turned on me like a viper. "Married?"

I jutted up my chin. "He asked me and I said yes."

Lilly made a strangled sound. "I'll tell everyone what he's done."

"No, you bloody won't."

"You can't stop me."

I sank my head over my plate and counted toast crumbs, but jam smears swam before me and instead I saw my dreams—the cottage with its cool ocean breeze and goats grazing the yellow sunflowers—all cracking apart.

"He'll hang," Lilly whispered. "Just like Jean Lee. Ennis is a criminal and they'll string him up from the gallows. He'll swing, my word he will. Just like poor old Jean."

I lurched to my feet. My plate upended and smashed on the floor. Before I could stop myself, I shot out my hand and struck my sister, my palm hitting her chubby cheek with a loud smack. She recoiled and tears sprang to her eyes, but she didn't cry. She just glared at me with her big watery eyes, and then a little smile touched her lips.

"You'll swing too."

The blood drained from my head. My skin went cold as ice. Because somewhere deep in my heart, I feared she was right.

61

ABBY

Roy Horton opened his door and sighed. He stepped aside for me to enter, and I followed him along the hall, weaving between the boxes and broken bike, past the empty bedrooms. In the kitchen, he crossed to the sink and filled the kettle. A dismantled Winchester sat on the table, with a can of gun oil and a ratty, grease-stained tea towel.

"Don't mind the mess." Roy lifted the kettle onto the stovetop. "Tea? I'm having some."

"No thanks."

"So how can I help you, Miss Radley? Are you interested in hearing more about my boy?"

I leaned my hip against a chair back. "It's about your father. His name was Harry, wasn't it?"

Roy's head jerked up. "Pop? He died a long time ago. Did you know him?"

"Not me, but Dad remembered him. He used to deliver our firewood."

"Fancy that."

"I've recently read his name in an old police report. Back in 1953, you and your dad found a girl wandering out at the reserve road. Do you remember her?"

The kettle shrieked. Roy poured himself a mug of tea, then stood gazing down at the dismantled rifle.

"That was a long time ago. I'm seventy-three come July. My memory's a fickle mistress nowadays. Not as sharp as she once was."

"It was sharp enough when you talked about Jasper the other week."

Roy set aside his mug. He picked up the rifle and ran a cleaning rod down to the breech. "I was just a bean sprout when Pop found the girl. It's all pretty hazy from where I stand now."

"Let me freshen your memory. You and your dad were cutting firewood at the reserve. When you saw the girl on the roadside, you were heading back to town. She was covered in cuts and scratches, with black bruises on her throat."

The cleaning rod clattered onto the floor. Roy stooped to pick it up. "What's it got to do with my boy?"

"I don't know if it's related to Jasper, but something doesn't add up. In the report, the duty officer mentioned your father was looking at the girl as if she made him nervous."

"Pop didn't want trouble, that's all."

"Trouble?"

"We didn't find the girl on the road. We found her inside the reserve, up on the ridge overlooking the gorge. Pop and me had camped overnight in an old logger's hut. Pop sent me off to collect fallen branches for kindling. We sold bundles for a ha'penny, which Pop let me keep. Anyhow, that was when I saw her."

"The girl?"

He nodded. "A short hike from the hut. She was sitting on a rock, crying. In a right old state. Covered in dirt and leaves, hands filthy. But the biggest shock was her face." He picked up the gun barrel again and started polishing it with his tea towel.

"Her face?"

He inhaled noisily. "A wild thing she was, Miss Radley. A big tall girl with eyes like black holes punched in bread dough. She scared me. I started backing away, and that's when I saw—" He scrubbed the side of his head with the tea towel, which skewed his glasses and left a black smudge on his temple. "I'm not sure what it was. A pile of dirt and rubble. But I got it in my head that it was a grave. With a pale little foot poking out of it."

"A body?"

He glanced towards the door, nodding. "It knocked the stuffing out of me, so it did. Sent me tearing back to Pop, yammering in fright. Pop grabbed my shoulders and tried to shake some sense into me. Then he went off at a trot. He was gone for an age. Finally he returned with the girl. She still had that blank-eyed look, even after Pop gave her a drink of grog from his flask. He shook her by the arms till her teeth clattered. 'We don't want no trouble now, hear?' But she didn't reply. Just stared with those dead eyes."

"What did your dad mean by trouble?"

"Pop had an illegal whiskey distiller at the farm. Times were tough. We made a living from firewood in the winter, but come summer we'd have starved if it hadn't been for Pop's whiskey. They busted him a few times during the Depression. He didn't want the boys in blue sniffing around again."

"Did you tell your dad about the body?"

Roy placed the barrel on the table and cleaned his hands on the tea towel. "Later, I told him about the foot, or whatever it was. Pop said I was mistaken, he reckoned it was nothing. Just a bundle of dirty old clothes. He made me promise not to tell anyone about the girl. He said she was trouble. I'd forgotten about her until now."

"What became of her?"

Roy's shoulders twitched. "I guess she went back to wherever she ran away from. And good riddance to her. She scared the daylights out of me, and Pop too. We never returned to our old logging spot near the hut. Pop found better places on the other side of the reserve."

"Did Jasper know about the hut?"

Roy shook his head.

I took out my map and laid it over an empty section of the table. "Do you think you could locate the hut on this map?"

He shook his head. "Must be sixty-odd years since I was there."

"It was a fair drive from town if you and your dad stayed overnight. Did you take the coast highway going east, or did you travel north?"

Roy looked at the map. His finger hovered over the roads I'd mentioned. "I don't recall. The coast, maybe. I'd have sworn it was hours from town, but it can't have been. We drove along this tiny track, forever it seemed. I wanted to stop and go behind a tree, but Pop ignored me and kept driving. The track was bumpy as an old dill pickle. Torture for a kid who needs to piss. The sun made my head ache. By the time we arrived and organised ourselves, it'd be night."

"The sun? So the track went west? But if the coast road travels east, the trail would have been heading back toward town."

Roy studied the map, shaking his head. Lank strands of hair wafted around his face. His fingers traced northwards along the forest road, and it trembled a little. It drew my attention to something peeping from under the frayed cuff of his shirt. Two deep grazes, pink with new scar tissue.

Like scratch marks.

Roy caught me looking and withdrew his hand. "Damn dog plays rough sometimes."

"Oh."

He must have sensed the shift in me. The sudden tension in my shoulders, the careful way I breathed. My gaze now wide and unflinching. He stood to full height and regarded me with eyes that were, though faded, still as blue as a kingfisher's wing feather. "Sixty years is a long time to remember places. I'm sorry, Miss Radley. I'm afraid I can't help you."

"LIL? ARE YOU THERE?"

I hammered the back door, but no one answered. There was washing on the line, but Lil's Forester was gone. Wasn't Saturday her drama day? Joe was probably off fishing.

I walked along the path, past Lil's veggie patch, and dodged behind Joe's big barn-like shed. Those scratches on Roy's arm. Of course, they might be what he claimed they were—marks made by his dog. And he might have been cleaning the rifle as part of his usual routine. Lots of people hunted in Gundara. Nothing remarkable about that. But his story about finding young Lilly in the forest was bothering the hell out of me.

I pushed through the wrought-iron gate into the paddock and hurried down to the billabong, following the shriek of cicada song.

When Roy Horton was a boy, out cutting wood with his

father, he thought he saw a body. Or at least part of one emerging from a rubbly grave. Later, his father would convince him it was just a pile of old clothes, but the memory haunted him. Poor Lilly. Slumped in the bush, her eyes vacant with shock. Had Ennis murdered Frankie and dumped Lilly with her sister's body in the reserve? Was that where Lil went during one of her turns, in search of the place she had buried Frankie?

The billabong was empty, its muddy edges receded, the swans gone. Nothing to see here. I walked back up to the garden and checked for Lil's car, but she still hadn't returned. The midday sun was high, the sky clear blue. A breeze ruffled the leaves as I wandered between Joe's fruit trees.

My memory's a fickle mistress, Roy had said. *Not as sharp as she once was.* He thought the track he went along with his father was along the coast road. But Ravensong was north, and Lilly would have had to pass through town to reach the coast road. Besides, the night Lil had her turn, she had driven north and wandered into the bush along the Old Forest Road. I needed to talk to her. It was a long shot, but I needed to find that old logger's hut.

Halfway along the boundary fence, I noticed footprints on the other side. I slipped through the wire and followed the trail into the trees. It led me to a tall gum tree with a white trunk. At the base of the tree was a newly dug, cat-sized grave. Someone had piled leaves on it, and under the leaves I found a stone. I kicked the stone away and picked up a stick. Kneeling beside the mound, I dug the stick into the crumbly soil. It was slow going, but then my stick struck something hard. I prised up a parcel wrapped in canvas. Inside was a book.

A diary.

I sat heavily in the dirt. A wasp buzzed past my ear, and dry leaves fluttered down. I opened the diary and flipped through it.

Lil had taped the loose pages I gave her back into place, but torn out more pages at the end. Frankie's tiny, familiar scrawl covered every page. Deeper into the book, the writing got more chaotic, as if reflecting her growing agitation. Inky fingerprints and splatters covered the last few pages, making the writing almost indecipherable. Almost. I went back to the front of the book and started reading.

62

FRANKIE'S DIARY

SUNDAY, 8TH MARCH 1953

Lilly hasn't spoken to me since the slap.

Almost two months, the ninny.

When I offer her food or cups of tea or cordial, she ignores me. If I try to comfort or touch her, she kicks out at me. Last night she fell off the trunk while spying on Ennis out the window and skinned her elbow. When I tried to clean it, she hissed like an animal and twisted away.

Part of me feels sorry for her. The other part—well, let's just say I'm ticked off. She said horrible things about Ennis, when all he wants to do is help. Poor Ennis is a wreck. He's at his wit's end. Lilly has ruined everything and I don't know if I'll ever forgive her.

. . .

THURSDAY, 21ST MAY 1953

The day finally arrived. We packed our bags and crammed them into the old truck. The truck is bulging with baskets of produce and blankets, all Ennis's best tools—anything we might need on the trip. Ennis is excited to be leaving. He even let me wear the ring. It belonged to his mother, who died when he was little, before he came to live at Ravensong with his grandfather. The ring is thin with wear, but he buffed the surface till it shone. It's rose gold, and it fits like a dream. The perfect start to our new life.

Until Lilly saw the ring on my finger and got all wild again.

"Take it off," she demanded. When I refused, she started ranting again. "The minute we're outside these walls, I'll jump out of the truck and run. Tell everyone how awful you both are. They'll find you and hang the pair of you. And I'll be glad!"

Ennis came up then and overheard. He was wretched. I tried to calm him, but he'd have none of it. He pushed me away and rushed out the door, slamming it behind him. The lock clicked. A while later, a ruckus of clattering and banging drifted up from the yard. What was he doing? I climbed on the trunk and peered out, but couldn't see.

I nudged Lilly with my foot. "Stupid girl. See what you've done?"

"I hate you, Frankie. I wish you were dead."

"Thanks to your rot, we'll both probably end up in a ditch."

She glared up at me. "You and him were in the garden yesterday, whispering and giggling. Holding hands. He thinks I'm going home without you—"

"Hush." Kneeling beside her, I took her grubby hand and

bent near her ear to whisper. "Don't you remember our plan, Lilly-bird? Win his trust so we can escape?"

She shoved me away. "Liar! You love him and you're going to marry him. You'll forget all about me. All you care about is him."

"That's not true, Lilly-pill."

"He's a criminal. He said he'd chop off my feet if I tried to run away. How can you love him, you make me sick!"

"It isn't like that."

"I won't go home without you. We made a promise, remember?"

Again I glanced over my shoulder. "Calm down."

"I'd rather be dead in a ditch."

"Lilly, please."

"I'd rather kill you myself than let you go with him!" She kicked out and her foot caught me in the stomach. I staggered backwards and fell onto my bottom, and it knocked the wind out of me. When I could speak again, I crawled over to her and stood up, pushing my face into hers.

"I will marry Ennis, and there's nothing you can do about it. We're going to disappear, Lilly. No one will ever find us. Now, you can keep your trap shut and come with us. Or you can—"

The key turned in the lock. The door sprang open. Ennis stormed over and dragged me into the bright room, kicking the door shut. He had piled Lilly's things on the table. The tiny suitcase she had packed her meagre belongings in, the sunhat Ennis bought her a few weeks ago especially for our trip. And the small knitted bag holding her cut-out dolls and other treasures. They had been in the truck. I packed them myself.

I tore free of Ennis's grip. "Why's all her stuff back here?"

His eyes were wild, his hair ragged around his shoulders, the skin on his lips chewed raw. He hooked his fingers around my arm and drew me over to the fireplace.

"She's not coming with us."

"But you promised!"

"No," he said in a dead voice. "We're leaving without her."

"Then we'll drop her near a town. Let her find her own way home."

Ennis shook his head. "She'll tell the cops what I did. Send them after us. She's right, Frankie. I'll hang."

"Oh, Ennis. Lilly won't say anything. She blurts out a load of rubbish sometimes, but don't listen to her. You know what she's like. She'd never hurt me like that."

"She'd hurt me."

"No, she wouldn't." I smiled up at him. "Once she gets home to Mum, she'll forget all about us. She won't say a word, I promise."

"Here." Ennis slipped a cold object into my hand. "Careful. It's sharp."

My lips parted as I registered the knife, but I couldn't drag my eyes away from Ennis. Despite his ragged appearance, he was calm, speaking rationally. No sign of the wild raving boy he sometimes became. No fire, no fury. His eyes were hard as stones.

"You do it, Frankie. She trusts you. It'll be easy. Look, I'll show you."

I blinked, trying to clear the grey haze. Trying to hear through the sudden roar in my ears. When his slim fingers tightened around mine, I flinched. He didn't notice, too intent on positioning my grip around the knife handle.

"Like this, see?"

He raised the knife to his neck, placed the tip beneath his ear and tilted the blade forward. "Rest it here lightly, in this little valley under the jaw. Then a downward push, this way, towards the front of the body." He spoke matter-of-factly, as though explaining how to skin a rabbit. "Make sure it goes deep, you don't need to thrust very hard. Up to the hilt is best."

Recoiling, I dropped the knife. It clattered onto the floor. I backed away from it, my insides churning. My mouth quivered, so I jammed my fingers over my lips. Had I heard right, had I understood?

Ennis trailed after me. "She won't even realise what you've done. Won't cause a fuss or struggle. She'll just drift off to sleep." He smiled and cupped the side of my face. "You can even hold her if you like. Hold her close to you, like a little lamb."

I backed away, pressing against the wall.

All our beautiful dreams, our magical plan. Walking hand in hand on the beach. Learning how to milk the goat so we could make our own cheese. And our cosy cottage, and us living our dream life, the three of us a family at last.

All I had were those dreams.

Ever since that hungry vine claimed my soul, I had gone to sleep with those dreams tucked around me like a downy quilt. Had woken with them shining in my eyes like starlight. My dreams kept me going through the dreary days as I trudged through the hours. My chores, my confinement. The patching of clothes, the mending of socks and pillowcases and shirts. Our boring room with its tiny, stupid window. The world beyond the bars that had forgotten us. As I lived a life I didn't want, my dreams made it all bearable.

"They could be real," Ennis whispered. "Our dreams could be real. But Lilly stands in our way."

I lowered my fingers. My trembling stopped. The haze was clearing. I stumbled over and collected the knife. Then I linked my fingers in his and gave them a squeeze. "She won't suffer?"

He shook his head.

"She'll go quickly?"

"Like a candle winking out."

"Oh, Lilly." I shut my eyes, reminding myself of all I would lose. The cosy cottage with its sea view, the milking goats, the roses and sunflowers—building a normal life with Ennis, being part of a proper family. Knowing how it felt to be loved. Truly loved.

Everything that Lilly was threatening to destroy.

I blinked, looking back at Ennis. The haze cleared, and I slipped the knife into my pocket.

63

ABBY

A CAR MOTOR rumbled in the distance, bringing me back to the present. As it got louder, I silently prayed that the vehicle would keep going, speed past and continue travelling along the road and away. But the rumbling increased as the car slowed and turned into the Corbins' driveway. Moments later a door slammed.

I got to my feet. I could see Lil in my mind's eye, tall and graceful, striding in that confident way she had, climbing the verandah stairs and rattling her key in the lock, pushing open the back door, calling Joe's name. And then I saw the young girl Roy Horton had described, bruised and vacant-eyed, weeping in the dirt beside her sister's grave.

"Oh, Lil," I whispered, hugging the diary against me. "What happened to you?"

She was near the house when I found her, collecting washing off the line, bundling it under her arm. She looked over and waved. Her soft pink dress flattered her figure, and the hint

318

of lipstick and powder she wore made her seem pretty and youthful.

"Abby, darling. I saw your car and wondered where you were. It's Saturday, what are you—" She dragged off her sunglasses and squinted. She must have seen the book in my hands, or noticed the wooden-legged way I walked towards her, because her smile faltered. The clean clothes tumbled to the ground. "Oh no, Abby. No."

My legs were stiff from sitting on the ground for so long, and as I approached her, I stumbled. I was still clutching the diary against my chest, my thoughts reeling from what I had read. The threat Lilly had posed to her sister and Ennis—and the terrible danger it put her in.

"You told me that Frankie and Ennis dropped you at Gundara and then drove off together. But that's not true, is it? Frankie never left with Ennis, did she? She ended up at the reserve. With you."

Lil reached for the diary. "Give it to me, Abby. You had no right to read it."

I sidestepped her. "Ennis killed her, didn't he? He killed Frankie. Why didn't you inform the police? You might have helped them catch him, made him pay for what he did to you both. For what he did to Frankie."

"I've told you already. Ennis loved my sister. He would never hurt her. He and Frankie packed up and left Ravensong to start a new life together. They dropped me in Gundara and then continued on their way. Whatever it is you think you've discovered about me, you're mistaken."

"Lil, do you remember the day Harry Horton took you to Gundara police station? You were distressed, weren't you? Do you remember why?"

The pine trees whispered overhead as a breeze ruffled the branches. Lil shivered.

"Frankie and Ennis left me on the roadside and drove away."

"No, Lil. Harry Horton told the duty officer he found you wandering along the reserve road. But that wasn't true, was it? You were in the forest when he found you. Filthy and distressed, your neck so badly bruised you could hardly talk. Something happened in the reserve that day. To your sister."

Lil squeezed her eyes shut and massaged her forehead. "No more. Please, no more."

I took a step towards her. "Did Frankie attack you? Did you fight back, is that how she died?"

Lil looked away across the yard.

"My sister couldn't bring herself to do what Ennis asked. Ennis should have known that Frankie would never hurt me. But he wasn't the most rational person on the planet. His faith in my sister was strong. They were both dreamers, and sometimes their dreams were absurd. The pair of them, peas in a deluded little pod. I suppose that's how we ended up at Ravensong in the first place—Frankie and her wild romantic dreams."

"What happened to her, Lil?"

A long pause. Then she sighed. "My friendship with Frankie died long before she pocketed Ennis's knife. Long before she decided to solve the problem I'd become. So many betrayals, so much resentment between us during our years at Ravensong. Ennis played mind games and pitted us against one another, but Frankie and I were partly to blame as well. Five years in forced proximity will test any relationship, no matter how strong. It will find the tiniest of cracks and turn them into ravines. But we were still sisters. Nobody could break that bond."

"Frankie changed her mind?"

"Ennis unlocked the door for her so she could come downstairs afterwards. But Frankie didn't want to hurt me. She distracted Ennis while I crept out of the house. I ran away into the bush. I ran and ran. When I couldn't run anymore, I crumpled and slept where I'd fallen. When I woke, I ran some more. Days passed, then I fell and cut my knee. A man found me. He and his boy were cutting wood nearby, their truck parked on an old service road. The truck was full of fresh-cut logs and reeked of pine sap. The man, I don't remember his name, dropped me at the police station. Next morning I got on the Sydney train. Found my way to Stanley Street. A policewoman found me, and—" She scraped a fingernail over the back of her hand. "They said my mother had died. I went to stay with Mrs O'Grady. Her husband was a carpenter. He let me watch him build things. Pencil boxes, a tea tray, nothing too fancy. He taught me how to work with wood. Not very ladylike, I know." She glanced up. The skin around her eyes was white, but the tips of her ears glowed scarlet. "Mrs O'Grady encouraged me to keep busy. She said working with my hands would help me untangle the knots in my mind."

"Did it help?"

"I suppose so."

"And Frankie?"

Her eye twitched, and she rubbed it with her thumb. "I never saw her again."

Cicadas shrilled in the distance, probably at the billabong where, almost two weeks ago, we had laughed at Joe's antics with the swans. Lil glanced down the hill. Was she remembering too?

"Lil, do you know a girl called Shayla Pitney?"

Lil took out a hanky and dabbed her face. "Should I know her?"

"Shayla disappeared four weeks ago. Do you think you could help me find her?"

"How could I do that?"

"When you have your turns, you return to the place where Harry Horton found you."

"Oh, Abby." She folded her hanky and tucked it back in her pocket. "Why would I go back there?"

"Because that's where you buried Frankie."

Lil shook her head and seemed to wither into herself, her shoulders bowed, her body slumped. She clamped her fingers over her lips, her wedding band gleaming gold against her freckled skin, her smile replaced by a frown as she stared back with blank, glassy eyes.

A deadweight settled over me. I had pushed her too far. She looked so frail and lost, so unlike her usual self. Was she having a turn? I slipped the diary into my bag and took a step towards her.

"The grave is near an old logger's hut. The Hortons used to go there. Shayla could be inside. I think you can find it."

Lil shut her eyes, and when she finally looked back at me, her lips trembled, and her pupils were huge and black. "Is it connected to my nightmares?"

"Yeah, Lil. I think it is."

"I don't know where that place is."

"A map might jog your memory?"

"I don't think so."

"Then we'll go for a drive, you might see something you recognise."

"No."

"I think Shayla is in danger. You can help me find her."

"Danger?"

"I'm worried someone has trapped her in the hut. She could die there."

Lil clamped her fingers over her mouth. "Oh, Abby. You're too late. The shadows—"

"Too late? Lil, what do you mean?"

"Oh, dear. My pills." She patted her hips then twisted around and looked at the house. A tremor went through her, and she took a step but faltered and then just stood there, blinking rapidly, her chest rising and falling as if she was struggling to breathe. "I'm afraid I'm unwell. My pills. Would you get them for me?"

"Where do you keep them?"

The colour had drained from her face, leaving her skin doughy and pale. She squinted, as if against a bright glare, her eyes small and dark. "In the kitchen. The white cabinet behind the door. Hurry, please."

I ran up the stairs into the kitchen and found the cabinet. On the top shelf was an array of packets and pill bottles. I scanned the labels and chose two, then hurried back outside. Lil was no longer in the yard. Had she come inside after all? I walked along the hallway where the bedrooms were.

"Lil?"

A car motor roared outside. I ran into the lounge room and crossed to the window. Out on the road, a glimmer of metallic green flashed past, barely visible between the trees. My heart started pounding, my pulse exploding in my ears. Where was she going? And why had she left without her pills, saying nothing to me—?

I went utterly still.

Picturing her face as she stood under the trees outside just now, the blank emptiness in her eyes. Then another image came to me—a long dirt track meandering through the forest, and the afternoon sun glaring between the trees. At the end of the track, hidden among the bracken and overhanging branches, was a horrible dark cavelike place where a scared teenager huddled in the shadows.

TWENTY MINUTES LATER, I pulled onto the roadside near the turnoff where we'd found Lil's car the night she disappeared into the forest. I walked a little way into the bush, calling to her. There was no sign of her or her Forester, so I went back to my car and took out my map, spreading it across the wheel.

Roy Horton couldn't remember if his father had driven east towards the coast, or north along the reserve road where I now sat, otherwise known as the New Forest Road. He did recall travelling west along a narrow track. *We drove forever it seemed. It was bumpy as an old dill pickle, torture for a kid who needed to piss.*

I trailed my finger northwards over the map. At the furthest point of the kidney-shaped forested area, tucked into a bend in the river, was Ravensong. I found a pen in the glovebox and marked its location with a blue cross. Then I examined the area surrounding it.

I ran and ran, Lil had said. *And when I couldn't run anymore, I crumpled and slept where I'd fallen.* How far had Lilly Wigmore travelled? For days she had trekked through dense bushland, over hostile and unfamiliar territory. Lilly was a city girl. She'd spent the past five years trapped in an attic. Not used to the physical exertion needed to navigate the harsh terrain. She couldn't have travelled far. Ten kilometres a day, fifteen at most? So in two days, she might have travelled thirty. I drew a thirty-kilometre radius around Ravensong, but it still left a sizeable gap between the likely position of the loggers' hut, and the spot where the hikers had found me.

I drew a straight line between Ravensong and Pilliga's Lookout.

At the midpoint, a vehicle track crossed the line at right angles. The track curved westwards, but not from the reserve road. There was another road, perhaps part of the now-defunct travelling stock route. This secondary road ran southwest off the New Forest Road but then petered out at a creek, reappearing a few kilometres later, where it intersected with the west-running trail. It was some distance from Ravensong. Lilly would have taken more than a few days to walk it. It was worth a look, though.

Back on the road, I sped north. Bushland crowded both sides of the roadway, but on my left was the Deepwater Gorge Reserve. Narrow dirt trails cut into the scrub at intervals—most of them overgrown with grass and weeds—probably old forestry trails or forgotten driveways. Then I passed one where the grass lay flat and brown under fresh tyre tracks.

I did a U-turn and pulled onto it. Was I wasting precious time I didn't have, or would it lead me to Lil?

It made sense that she'd return to the place Harry Horton had found her. A frightened young girl covered in dirt and badly bruised, crying beside the grave she had dug for her sister. Called back there now by her nightmares. Perhaps to an old logging hut nearby that held a caged nightingale of its own.

64

SHAYLA

SHE COULD HEAR A MEWLING SOUND. At first she thought it was Mrs Bilby. One night, when Mrs Bilby was small, Shayla had sneaked the rabbit under the covers and cuddled her to sleep, only to wake in the night when Mrs Bilby clawed her and started making a horrible squeaking noise, squashed beneath Shayla's arm.

But it wasn't Mrs Bilby making the noise now.

Was it *her*?

Shayla rolled in a ball and jammed her knees against her chest. Lately she'd been hearing voices—her mum, or Jesse her best friend, or sometimes even Mrs Cartwright, her favourite teacher—but one voice she didn't recognise. It was louder than the others, nearby but muffled, saying something about kissing the stars and moon, of all things. She tried to ignore it, but the words rolled around inside her head like marbles in a jar, making her dizzy.

She crossed her arms, burying her face in the sleeves of her denim jacket. The jacket wasn't really hers. And it wasn't

Mum's glittery red one, because there were no scratchy sequins. Where had it come from? She liked the way it had smelled. Sweet and flowery. Faintly of honey. It didn't smell that way anymore. Now it was like the rest of her, horrible and funky.

Her stomach gurgled. She'd gone beyond hungry. Now she was just numb. Not sleeping but not awake either. She tried to think of something lovely to soothe herself, but the marbles kept rolling and the shadows kept slipping and sliding, and the voice kept rasping somewhere in the dark—

The door rattled.

Shayla jerked in fright, her limbs shooting out, her head jolting back, bumping the wall. The air turned solid in her lungs. She brought her knees up under her chin, and hot tears —the tears she thought she'd run out of—spilled over and scalded her face.

The door shrieked open. Light erupted so bright it hurt her eyes. Someone stood in the doorway. They spoke to her, their words sharp and urgent, but Shayla didn't want to hear, she didn't want to know what the person was saying. She clamped her hands tightly over her ears and shut her eyes.

65

ABBY

THE FIESTA BUMPED along the rocky track, rattling over potholes and diving into washouts so deep that the car's underbelly squealed as it struck half-buried boulders and stones. I was about to turn back when I saw a familiar car. Lil's green Forester. I pulled over beside it and got out.

"Lil, where are you?"

I walked further down the track until it ended at a bank of blackthorn. And there, cutting between the spiky branches, was a narrow trail. I ran along it, searching the surrounding trees. Huge stumps pushed out of the ground, and nearby were the fallen crowns, remnants of once-magnificent trees felled for timber. This narrow track may once have been another vehicle road, one that gave logging trucks access deeper into the forest. Now it was barely wide enough for a person. The trees became denser and more tangled, and soon I was ducking under limbs and shoving aside leafy boughs. Then the track widened and I burst out into a clearing.

On the other side of the clearing, the track grew narrower and continued on. It led to a cluster of tall granite boulders like oversized, lopsided marbles. Bushes crowded around the boulders, almost but not quite hiding a dark patch at their base. Maybe a cave entrance. Or a small dwelling.

I walked towards it, the blood roaring in my ears. Was that netting? Blackish-green camouflage netting snarled up in the undergrowth, like flotsam washed up on a riverbank after a flood, with leaves and branches snared in the mesh. I stopped, sensing eyes boring into my back from the surrounding woodland.

"Lil—?"

The breeze moaned through the casuarinas, creaking the branches. I glanced over my shoulder. Why didn't I tell anyone where I was going? A pulse thumped at the base of my throat. My skin was suddenly damp. Slowly I picked my way closer to the boulders. As I approached, the dark patch morphed into a dwelling. I could make out a narrow door. Other elements emerged from the tangled mess of netting and vines—heavy plank walls and the low curve of a roof line.

The loggers hut.

I approached it as silently as I could. The door was rusty and discoloured, and stood ajar. Nearby on the ground lay an open padlock with the key still in it. Lil must have been here. Had she taken Shayla somewhere else, knowing I would follow her here? I shoved my shoulder against the door. Metal shrieked against metal as it lurched all the way open and I staggered inside.

The black cavity breathed out a bellyful of rank moist air, and it folded around me, filling my lungs and dragging me backwards in time. I was twelve again, shivering in the dark, my teeth clattering as I curled into a ball on the smelly mattress, my ears alert for the crunch of footfall outside.

Breathe, Abby. Just try to breathe.

I stepped deeper into the dark. "Shayla?"

My voice echoed off the walls. Slowly, my eyes adjusted. The single-room dwelling was the size of a smallish caravan. A bucket sat near the door and a grimy mattress festered in the shadows. Sheets of galvanised tin lined the ceiling and walls and floor, riveted along the joins. Black streaks coursed down the walls from years of water seepage, but otherwise the metallic lining remained hard and unyielding, a surface that no amount of scratching or scraping by small fingers could penetrate.

A muffled sob broke the stillness. I whirled to face the far corner. At first she was just a denser patch of shadow huddled against the wall. Legs drawn tight against her chest, her face buried in her arms. I let out a ragged breath.

"Shayla?" I went over and crouched beside her, pressing my hand to her shoulder. "Thank God, you're alive."

A skinny arm came out and slapped me away. "Get off!"

"I'm here to take you home. Can you walk?"

She shrank closer to the wall. "Who are you?"

"My name's Abby. Your mum's worried. I promised her I'd find you."

She peered up at me with enormous eyes. For a heartbeat I was staring at a younger version of myself—the mop of brown hair, the round, pale face. She even wore my old denim jacket with roses embroidered down the front, the one I had tucked around her in the campground all those weeks ago.

Shayla glanced to the door. "Is Mum out there?"

"No, but you'll see her soon."

"I was so mad at her. I wanted to go to my dad's, so I tried to hitch a lift to the coast. This car stopped, and I got in. The lady was nice, she gave me a drink of water. She wanted to bring me back to Mum's, but then . . ."

"You woke up in here?"

Her forehead wrinkled, and she glanced back at the hut. "No, I ... yeah, I guess."

"Come on. We'd better go." I held out my hand, and she grasped it and got to her feet. Her legs wobbled so violently that I put my arm around her shoulders, guiding her across the hut and through the doorway. As she stepped into the late afternoon light, she cringed away from the brightness and her eyes started streaming. I fished out my sunnies and let her slide them on. She peered at me.

"Ray Bans," she remarked. "Can I keep em?"

"Sure."

"Got any food?"

"A Mars Bar in the car." I grabbed a roll of mints from my pocket. "This'll have to do until then. They're sugar free."

"Shit," she murmured huskily, grabbing the roll and shoving the mints in her mouth. "What's the point of sugar free? Are you some kinda health freak?"

"Not really." I tried to smile, but we weren't out of the woods yet. Despite the girl's bravado, she looked terrible. The cut over her ear looked inflamed and a pink stain discoloured her cheek. Purple hollows ringed her eyes, and her skin was an unhealthy, pasty grey. "Let's get going. You need to see a doctor."

But she hovered, shuffling her bare feet in the dirt. She squashed the empty mint wrapper in her fist, then jammed it in her pocket, looking down at herself. She stuck out her filthy foot and tilted it from side to side. Dried blood crusted her big toe, and it looked like the nail was gone. She stared at it for ages. Then she twisted around to gaze into the murky hole of the hut doorway. Her lips trembled, and she softly moaned. She bit her lips, trying not to cry.

"It's okay." I grasped her arm. "You're gonna be okay."

It was a lie. She would jump at noises, avoid the back seat of cars, sweat in cramped spaces and sleep with the light on. She would start crying for no apparent reason, and the smallest things would set her off. Worst of all, no one would understand why her behaviour was so erratic. I groped around in my mind, wishing I knew how to reassure her. To help her grasp that she was safe, and that she could stop being scared. At least until the nightmares began.

But then she barrelled into me and flung her arms around my neck, her skinny body convulsing with sobs. Suddenly we were both crying, her tears scalding my neck and mine soaking into her matted hair. We clung like that for a long time, shivering in the dying sunlight, holding each other so tightly I didn't think we'd ever be able to let go.

"THAT'S THE CAR—" Shayla stopped dead on the deserted track, eyeing Lil's Forester. "The one I got into." She took a step back and started gulping sharp little breaths.

"This one's mine," I said quickly, pulling out my keys and unlocking the Fiesta. The hazard lights blinked in friendly greeting, but Shayla stared around wide-eyed at the trees.

"We're not alone, are we?"

I searched the surrounding bushland. Was Lil out there now, watching us? Not the Lil I had grown to trust. The other Lil. The cold-eyed one I had met in the bush that night. Prickles raced over my skin, my senses in overdrive. Would she try to stop us?

I pulled open the passenger door.

"Hop in, kiddo. Let's get out of here."

Shayla climbed in and a heartbeat later I was reversing away from the Forester and bumping along the potholed track. When Lil's car vanished behind us, the tension finally wilted out of me in a long sigh. Shayla drained my water bottle and practically inhaled the Mars Bar, and then hung her head forward over her knees.

"Feeling better?"

"Like a pig's arse."

"You wanna lie on the back seat and try to sleep?"

She glanced at me with panicked eyes. "I'm fine here. With you."

"You sure? It's over an hour back to town."

She crossed her arms and glared through the windscreen. "You're just like Mum, trying to get rid of me."

"Is that why you ran away?"

"Yeah."

"You don't get along?"

"Nah. We argue all the time."

The Fiesta rattled along the potholed track, scraping its belly over stones, its wheels skidding on the loose gravel. We turned onto the weedy stock route, and then nearly forty minutes after leaving the hut, we were back on the New Forest Road. Shayla slumped forward and started sobbing into her hands. I spoke quietly to her, though nothing I said brought her comfort. But as we entered the town outskirts, she perked up and started singing to herself, her forehead resting on the passenger window as she watched the passing scenery fade into twilight with wide, tear-bright eyes.

"Hey," I said. "Next time you feel like running off, do me a favour?"

"What?"

"Come and stay at my place. Or just pop in for a visit."

"Really?"

I nodded. "We can go and see your dad if you want to."

She frowned. "You'd do that for me?"

"Course I would."

"Why?"

"Hitching to the coast by yourself is pretty messed-up, right?"

"Tell me about it."

At Gundara Hospital, I found a park in the visitors' emergency bay. As we made our way to Admissions, I rang Coral Pitney and explained where her daughter was. Then I waited with Shayla while they checked her over and filled out forms. When they wheeled her upstairs to the ward, I walked beside her. Had anyone called the police yet? I hoped not. It might be better if they didn't arrive until after I'd made myself scarce.

I glanced at the exit. It would take me an hour to get to Lil's. But once there, what would I say? Would Lil remember what she'd done, would she even believe me?

A nurse tightened a blood-pressure cuff around Shayla's arm, but Shayla pulled away from him and grabbed my sleeve. "Stay with me, Abby."

"You'll be fine, sweetie. You're safe now."

"You promised not to leave. To take me to the coast. Now you're fobbing me off on these jerks?" She glowered over her shoulder at the nurse checking the heart monitor, then leaned nearer to me and took my hand. "Please, Abby. I'm scared."

"I'll stay till your mum gets here." I lowered my voice so the nurse wouldn't hear. "But I have something to do, and then I'll come back."

"Promise?"

"You bet."

She sagged, nodding, and kept her eyes on me.

She looked so small and vulnerable in the bed, with her grubby feet and grazed knuckles, and her pale, wide-eyed face. Her mother said she was trouble. A problem best ignored, according to Kendra. Instead I saw a smart, brave kid who needed love and acceptance. Someone to teach her how to create healthy boundaries. *We learn so much from others*, Lil had said. *But if our role models display unhealthy behaviour, how are we supposed to know what's right?*

I settled on the bed beside Shayla and slipped my arm around her, remembering the moment I'd seen her in the hut, struck by her resemblance to a younger version of me.

"Hanging in there, kiddo?"

"Hmm." She buried her face in my shoulder. "Did you mean what you said? About me coming to visit?"

"Sure thing."

"Mrs Bilby ran away, but if I get another rabbit can they come too?"

"The more the merrier."

"Mum says I'm trouble."

"My dad said the same about me."

We fell into silence. I wandered over to the doorway. Where was Coral? Her daughter needed her. Didn't she want to see that Shayla was all right, give her the reassurance she desperately needed? Soft shoes whispered on the lino. Hushed voices, the discreet beep of monitors, the clang of a steel trolley. But still no Coral.

I glanced back.

The nurse was attending Shayla's head wound, applying a wad of sterile dressing. He must have pressed too hard for her liking, because she swore loudly and elbowed him in the ribs.

I bit my lips together and tried not to smile. After what she'd been through, that tiny act of defiance gave me hope. I didn't care what Coral or Kendra or anyone else said. Shayla Pitney would get along in life just fine.

66

JOE

While the oven was heating, Joe stood at the kitchen table and cut up six green apples. He tossed them in lemon juice, then measured cinnamon and nutmeg into a cup of brown sugar, humming along to the record he'd put on earlier, Ella Swings Lightly, an old favourite from way back. He followed directions for the pastry, frowning as he rubbed cold butter into the flour. Quite a job. Hats off to Lil, who always made it look so easy.

The recipe Joe was using was one of Lil's favourites, given to her by his mother, who'd adored Lil. Lil drolly referred to it as Nan's Apple Pud, but the pie itself was nothing like a pudding. The pastry was buttery and crisp, the filling richly sweet. Typical Lil, always having her little jokes.

He glanced at the window, alert for sounds of her car, and saw himself mirrored in the glass. A hunched little old man in an apron, holding a rolling pin. A ghost. He stared at the reflection and wished a part of himself could linger there in the window after he'd gone. To watch over Lil.

It broke his heart to leave her, but what other choice did he have?

Once, many years ago, during one of their deep and meaningfuls, Lil had confessed her greatest fear. *Let's not move back to town, Joe. I like it out here. I feel free.* He had reminded her, gently because he understood the topic was sensitive, that one day they would be too frail to cope with maintaining the garden and cutting the firewood, not to mention all the other daily tasks of living independently. But Lil dug in her heels. *I don't want to live in an old people's home, Joe. I don't want to feel trapped. If anything happened to you, I couldn't go on alone. Do you understand what I'm saying, Joe?*

He reassured her nothing would happen to him, but that was years ago. He hated to admit it, but time was running out. Hence the apple pie. His way of saying sorry for the bad news he was about to deliver.

"Don't worry, Lil," he said, eyeing the man in the window. "I'll watch over you."

When the pastry was done, he wrangled it into Lil's good pie dish and scooped in the filling. He draped lattice strips of pastry over it and sprinkled the lot with sugar. Standing back, he frowned. The pie was wonky, but Lil wouldn't mind.

He'd serve it with that old bottle of Tokay he'd been saving. The wine's rich honey and orange-rind flavours would wash the apples down nicely. The Tokay had become another favourite since serving it—a lifetime ago—at their wedding. They'd saved this bottle for another landmark occasion, but decades had passed and it was still gathering dust. Joe was tired of putting things aside for later. For him, later would never come. There was only now. Today. He'd make the most of whatever time remained.

He heard Lil's car and went to the window. She was never this late. Probably held up at drama group, or running errands. But when she parked askew in the driveway, he knew something was wrong.

She stumbled along the path, her lovely hair windblown, her face twisted in a frown. Joe opened the door, and she sagged into his arms.

"Oh, Joe."

"Love, what is it?"

"I'm so afraid, Joe."

He studied her face a moment, then kissed her damp forehead and smoothed her hair. As he held her close, his eyes stung with sudden wetness.

"It's time, isn't it?"

"Yes, pet. It's time."

"I've made Nan's Apple Pud."

She perked up. "It smells wonderful. And I see you've brought out the Tokay." She gazed into his eyes, resting her palm against his wrinkled cheek. "What a feast we'll have, eh? And then, my darling, we can lie down and enjoy a nice long sleep together."

His old ticker beat joyfully. He wouldn't have to leave part of himself behind. He wouldn't have to worry himself sick about saying goodbye. They would still be together. In a sudden flush of love, he took her face in his hands and kissed her.

"You're my girl, Lil."

"Always."

While Joe set the table with their best glasses and plates, Lil went over to the cupboard where they kept their tablets. She collected Joe's prescriptions then her own and carried the little bottles over to the chopping board. And as Ella Fitzgerald's sweet voice drifted through the house, Lil crushed the tablets under her wooden rolling pin.

67

LIL

A vase of roses sat on the bedside table, their perfume drifting in the air. Joe removed his socks, wriggled his toes to air them, and then climbed under the covers.

Lil settled on the bed beside him.

The pie had been a treat. They ate the whole thing and finished the Tokay. Lil had assembled some of the missing puzzle pieces for Joe. Her nightmares, her long disappearances into the bush. Vague flashes of a young girl on the roadside, climbing into Lil's car . . . she was thirsty and Lil offered her a drink. She probably put something in the water, Xanax maybe. Had they argued? Had the girl nodded off, oblivious as Lil half-carried, half-dragged her along the bushy trail to a place she had visited many times before? It was all so vague. Lil couldn't remember what was real and what was a dream.

Only that she was to blame.

Joe had listened in silence, reaching for her hand. At first he had not believed, but Lil persevered, recounting dates and even pulling out the rumpled pages she'd torn from Frankie's diary.

I'm a monster, Joe. I've done horrible things, unspeakable things. How can I keep going, knowing what I am?

With tears in his eyes, Joe had nodded understanding. He gave her fingers a reassuring squeeze. *The Lil I know isn't a monster, love. The person who committed those crimes was trying to fix something. She's part of you, Lil. But not* all *of you.*

She had wept bitterly, and Joe had wept too. His words meant everything to her, but they couldn't soothe her pain. Those young lives cut short. Lil had wanted to help young women like them, give them a chance in the world. Help them be their best selves. Understanding what she had done crushed her soul. But surely she *had* been trying to save them, hadn't she? She must have intended to set them free, the way she had once longed for someone to set her and Frankie free—but life got in the way. Had she really forgotten the poor things, left them there to die? In the dark. In that horrible place. The place she had trapped them in.

"Sing me a song, Lil?"

Wiping her eyes, she looked across the bed. "Oh, Joe. I can't."

Joe started humming. Dear fool that he was, he started swaying his fingers in the air as if conducting an orchestra. Trying to cheer her. "Come on, love. Help me out here."

She climbed under the covers beside him. "I haven't sung in donkey's years."

He stopped conducting. Taking off his glasses, he placed them on the nightstand, on top of the book he'd been reading. Lil noticed his bookmark was only a few pages from the end.

"How can you bear not to finish it?"

Joe smiled. "I've read it before. I know how it ends."

Lil smiled back, more for his benefit than her own, because her lips quavered and she wasn't sure they'd be able to stop.

Something in the sad way Joe had spoken touched a nerve in her. She didn't know what that nerve was, just that it bothered her. Like a spot on her vision, small yet distracting.

She blinked, but the spot grew darker.

Other flashes of memory came back. Hiding in the trees, watching Abby approach the logger's hut and shove open the door, save that poor girl. And later, when Abby and the girl were out of sight, Lil, the shadow-Lil, had stumbled along the narrow trail and watched them from behind a big tree stump. She waited till they'd gone and then drove home. Still fighting the shadows. But by then it was too late.

Lil swallowed her panic and snuggled under the covers beside Joe. She wanted to yawn, but her lungs were heavy, the air in them treacly and thick. She blinked, and her sister appeared before her. Not flushed and frightened as she'd been at the end, but lean and pretty with freckles dotting her nose, and eyes that danced with mischief.

If only they'd never met the young soldier. Never listened to the stories of his grandfather's magical house with its chandeliers and shadows. Its wrought-iron birdcage filled with green and yellow finches, scarlet parrots, willie wagtails, and teeny blue fairy wrens—

"Lil?"

She startled back to the present. Joe was watching her. For a moment she felt wide open, exposed. As though by catching her in an unguarded moment, he had glimpsed her memories. Perhaps even seen the woman she sometimes became, the one in her nightmares. Recognised her at last for the monster she was.

He kissed her brow. "Feeling all right?"

She examined his face, finding comfort in his familiar features. In the tenderness shining from his eyes. She touched his cheek. "You're a good man, Joe. The best."

He caught her fingers, the way he used to, and gave them a nibble. "You're my girl, Lil. You know that, don't you?"

"Always."

Melting against him, she savoured his warmth and tried to ignore the descending heaviness. Tried to pretend it was just another of the afternoon naps they'd taken together over the years.

"Lil?"

"What's that, love?"

"Will you sing me to sleep?"

Her heart dissolved. How could she refuse him this one last request? She linked her fingers in his and started humming. Shakily at first, then the words flowed. It was Fantine's song of broken dreams, the one the women had urged her to perform in their production. It was a beautiful song, but the frail, quivering notes that left her throat were full of rust. Her voice was part of another life, a life she had buried deep in the earthy black shadows beneath a gum tree. Buried and tried to forget.

Closing her eyes, she let the words of the song eclipse her thoughts. And then something magical happened. She felt it in her chest. The strands of her voice unravelling, the kinks smoothing out, the snarls and tangles gone.

"Beautiful," Joe murmured.

His words strengthened her. She settled back and allowed her voice to soar, sweet and strong as it lifted them up and carried them both away.

68

ABBY

Lil's car sat in her driveway at an angle, the driver's door open and the keys still in the ignition. She had arrived home in a hurry, but where was she now? I bounded up the verandah steps and hammered on the back door. It swung open.

"Lil?"

A clean tablecloth lay over the table, decorated with a vase of roses. Teacups and wineglasses and a large cake plate sat in the drying rack on the sink. The air smelled sweet, of apples and pastry and sugar.

"Lil, are you around?"

A frail voice drifted along the hallway. Someone was singing, could it be Lil? I knocked on the bedroom door. The singing stopped and Lil called my name. She and Joe were tucked up together in bed. Joe was asleep, his head resting against Lil's arm.

Lil blinked at me, and then beckoned me closer. "Abby?"

"Yeah, Lil. It's me."

"I'm so sorry. For everything." Her words slurred, her eyelids drooping.

Beside her Joe lay still, his face grey. His chest rose and fell with every shallow, laboured breath.

"God, Lil. What've you done?"

"We'll be asleep soon." She dabbed beneath her eye with the back of her hand. "I won't hurt anyone ever again."

Numbly I stood there. "Asleep?"

"My blackouts," she murmured. "My memory lapses. Those turns I've been having since I was a girl. I didn't know where I went. What I did while I was gone. And sometimes I had nightmares. Terrible nightmares, but I didn't think for a moment they could be true."

"Lil, have you taken something?"

She pressed trembling fingers against her cheeks. "I told Joe about our talk under the trees this afternoon. After you found the diary. He thinks the shock of you reading the diary dislodged something in my brain. I started remembering. Just glimpses, but they made me realise that perhaps my nightmares were real." Her head dropped forward and her body shook as she sobbed. "Is it true, Abby? Did I hurt those girls? Did I ... hurt you?"

"Oh, Lil."

The pills. All those pills they kept in the kitchen cabinet. Lil might have been taking a sedative for her turns or for anxiety. Joe, for his heart. Mixing meds together or with alcohol could be fatal.

I ran down the hallway to the lounge room and picked up the phone. Dialled triple-zero and then waited, trembling. Why didn't anyone answer? My pulse boomed in my ears, but the phone stayed silent. No dial tone. I checked under the table. Someone had cut the cord.

I gazed around frantically. The farmhouse was an hour from town. I could bundle them both into my car and race back to the mobile signal at the turnoff. Call an ambulance and meet them halfway.

"Can you stand, Lil?"

She shook her head. "It's too late, Abby."

"Let me help you, then. I'll bring the car closer to the house, then Joe doesn't have to walk so far."

"Abby, let us go."

"Lil, you can't just—"

"There isn't much time left. Please." She gestured at the chair under the window. "Sit beside me a moment."

I pulled up the chair and sat. Lil took a rumpled wad of pages from her pocket.

"Read them. Please, Abby. Afterwards, you can show the police and explain what happened. You'll have enough evidence against me, I'm sure. But for now just read what my sister wrote. Perhaps it will help you understand."

I took the pages from her fingers and smoothed them on my lap.

69
FRANKIE'S DIARY

My head hurts. I want to sleep because it's after midnight, but I can't. Lilly's not here. After she bandaged my head, she ran out and I haven't seen her since.

Everything is a jumble. I keep crying, which isn't helping this horrid headache. I have to stop writing to wipe the blood leaking down my cheek. Lilly says I need stitches. She ran and got a needle and thread, offered to do it herself, but I shoved her away. I can't bear her touching me. Not now. Not after what she did. What we both did.

"Ennis?"

He doesn't answer. He's lying on our bed with his eyes closed. Sleeping, sleeping. That's what I keep telling myself. If I say it enough maybe it'll be true? I try not to look at the blood soaking the bandage around his neck. Soaking the pillow and sheets beneath him. I pulled the covers up, but it quickly drenched them as well.

There's a noise outside. Louder than the sizzling candle on the floor next to the bed. Louder than the snuffling of my tears. It's a hacking noise. Whomp, it goes. Whomp. Then I realise. Lilly is digging a hole.

That was a lifetime ago. Now, my tears have dried. I've become numb to the horrible sound. Resigned. I wish Ennis hadn't given me the knife. I wish instead he'd taken my hand and lead me down the stairs to the truck, calming me with his words. Let's leave her here, Frankie. By the time anyone comes, we'll be long gone. It won't matter if she tells, because by then we'll be halfway to our dream life.

It replays in my mind, haunting me.

The knife. The knife in my pocket.

Lilly sat on the floor in our room, knitting by candlelight. How many times have I warned her she'd ruin her eyes? I sat down beside her, pulled the knitting from her fingers, and held her hands.

"Listen, Lilly. The truck's packed. Ennis is fetching a drum of water from the tank. He won't be away long, ten minutes at most. If you slip out now, he won't even—"

"No," she said stubbornly. "Not without you."

I touched my pocket and glanced over my shoulder at the door. "If you don't go now, you won't leave at all. Please, Lilly. This is serious. After all the trouble you've caused, you're not safe. You must go—"

The door burst open. We twisted around.

Ennis loomed in the doorway, frowning at us. He started towards Lilly. I ran up to him but he shoved me out of the way.

He grabbed Lilly by the arm and dragged her towards the bed, but she raised her fist and punched him right in the face.

"You'll hang for what you've done to us," she cried. "They'll tie a rope around your neck and string you up, and I'll be in the front row, cheering."

Ennis's ears turned scarlet. He rubbed his cheek, then studied the smear of blood on his fingers.

"I'll tell them what you've done." Lilly's voice raised to a shriek. "You'll swing!"

"Damn you, Lilly. You've ruined everything."

"You're the one who's damned, Ennis. You're the one they'll string up, not me."

She'd gone too far. Ennis changed from the boy I'd grown to love into someone else—the damaged boy who emerged sometimes, the one who ranted and raved and bellowed about the horrors he saw in the war. He gripped her by the throat, roaring into her face. His words made no sense, they were just a string of nonsense spilling from his mouth, and they came in such a torrent that my blood went cold.

I sprang across the room, grabbing his arm. He swung back his elbow and clipped me across the chest and I stumbled. My head struck the corner of our trunk. I swam in blackness, my ears ringing. I could hear a dull thumping. Blood pounding my ears, I thought at first. But it was Lilly, still in Ennis's grip. She was banging her fist on the wall, her eyes bulging, her mouth gaping like a goldfish.

Ennis was killing her.

I scrambled up and ran over, digging my nails into his knuckles, trying to tear apart his fingers. Lilly's lips were turning blue, her eyes rolling. I shrieked at Ennis, hammering him with my fists. His body was so tense that his arms were like steel, immune to my blows.

My legs turned rubbery. My arms flopped by my sides. Sticky heat dripped into my eyes, and when I wiped them, my hand came away red with blood.

Lilly was gagging. I ran to her, but again Ennis shoved me away. My vision blurred. The room shrank around me. Black sparks swarmed across my eyes and I swayed on my feet. I thrust my hands into my pockets.

Something pricked my palm. A sharp sting, and it cleared my head. I drew out the knife Ennis had given me.

Hours ago he had closed his fingers around mine and shown me how easy it was to force the blade into flesh. I gripped it now and with a cry, plunged it into him, but it wasn't easy. The blade jammed. Ennis didn't flinch, so I put my weight behind my hands and shoved myself hard against him.

He grunted and lurched away from Lilly, slapping his hand over his neck. Blood leaked between his fingers and ran over his hand. He turned and looked at me, the whites of his eyes engulfing his pupils. As he fell to his knees, he croaked out my name.

Lilly dropped to the floor beside him, gagging. She coughed, hacking the air out of her lungs, then gave a long, shuddering moan as she tried to draw it back in. Ennis collapsed face down. Blood pooled around him, soaking into his white shirt. I knelt beside him.

"Lilly, help me get him into bed. He's hurt."

Lilly just looked at me, her eyes wide and streaming, her face shiny with tears. She didn't seem to understand. Her chest heaved as she gulped the air back into her lungs.

I dragged Ennis to the bed. He was so heavy. I cried out again for Lilly to help me get him up on the mattress, but she was gone.

. . .

MONDAY, 25TH MAY 1953

For two days Ennis lingered. I left his side only to use the privy or rinse his dressings. Otherwise I just sat there, not even writing in my diary. Just staring into the shadows, trying to wish myself away to anywhere else but here.

Then late in the afternoon, as the shadows in the corners blackened, I noticed the stillness.

"Ennis?"

I shook him. When he didn't move, I pressed my ear against his chest and listened. I felt his neck for a pulse, thinking he must be asleep. His skin was cool, so I laid down next to him on the bed, trying to warm him. I draped my arm across his chest and rested my face on his.

The next morning, Lilly returned. She had slept downstairs on fresh sheets in a bed she'd made up herself. She stepped into the room and wrinkled her nose.

"What's that smell?"

Lilly's words were a whispery rasp. Her throat was black and blue, and one of her eyes looked bigger than the other, a purple half-moon blooming beneath it. She'd bitten her lips raw and had a vacant look about her, like a sleepwalker. I barely recognised her as my sister. She had changed so much overnight, become a shell. Escaped into herself to a place where even I couldn't reach her.

"Go away," I whispered.

She turned away, casting a dead-eyed glance over her shoulder at me before disappearing through the doorway into the bright room.

TUESDAY, 26TH MAY 1953

We buried him in the garden in the hole that Lilly had dug.

I helped her carry him from the house. He was heavy, and it took us forever. Getting him down the stairs was the worst. Then along the hallway, through the kitchen and outside onto the verandah. I almost wept when we got to the steps leading to the garden. Lilly said we should roll him down to save ourselves the effort. How could she be so heartless? My fist shot out of its own accord and struck her ear. She yelped and started bawling.

"Bury him yourself, then!" she cried in her hoarse whisper. "I'll just run away, shall I? Leave you here with a corpse. Have fun rotting in hell together!"

We continued in silence after that. She got her way at the hole and simply rolled him in. He hit the bottom with a horrible wet sound, and I heard something crack. I sank to my knees in the dirt at the edge. My mouth opened, but no sound came out. I wanted to throw myself into the hole with Ennis, but I couldn't move.

Lilly left me alone. Sometime later I woke to a thumping, rasping sound. It was Lilly's shovel. I must've been asleep for hours, because it was afternoon and she'd filled in the grave.

I sat there till the sun sank, staring at shadows. I asked Lilly to fashion a memorial with the date and his name, but she refused.

When night came, it got cold. We trudged back inside and Lilly lit the Warmray. She wound a fresh bandage around my head and then peered into my eyes. Her stiff fingers chafed my cheeks. She squeezed my hands, trying to warm them like Mum used to do when we got sick, but they stayed like ice.

WEDNESDAY, 27TH MAY 1953

At dawn, I wrote for a while by candlelight. Writing makes me tired, but my head is jumbled and I can't think straight unless I put it down on paper. All around me, the world is blurry. Sun shines into the bright room, but a grey haze hangs over it. Over me. Lilly packed a bag with our supplies. She thinks if we walk long enough, we'll find a town.

"Why don't we take Ennis's truck? Driving can't be all that hard."

"It'll link us to him. To this place. What if someone comes here? They'll see the grave and figure out what happened. We killed him, Frankie. We'll be hanged like Jean."

You killed him, Lilly. I might've plunged in the knife, but only to save you. You provoked him. You riled him up and sent him over the brink. Of course I never said it aloud, though I wanted to. Afternoon arrived and Lilly came up close and peered into my face, her brows knotted in that worried way she has.

"You need a doctor," she told me sternly. "That gash on your head needs stitching. And you're pale. Not yourself. To be honest, Frankie, I'm scared."

SATURDAY, 30TH MAY 1953

At least, I think it's Saturday. Sunday at the latest. It's early in the morning. I'm huddled on the cold ground in a patch of watery sunlight. My feet are ice blocks, but at least today I can move my fingers.

For three days we walked along the road. With every step I grew more tired, began dragging my legs. The food we brought is gone, and we're fighting over the last of the water. After it runs out, what then?

At dusk, we came to a dirt track that snaked into the bush. No cars had passed by, and I feared we were still miles from town. Lilly was keen to press on, but I said we should turn back.

While we dithered on the roadside, the sky turned dark and rain started belting down. Thunder roared overhead and Lilly screamed. Lightning struck a nearby tree. It came crashing onto the road ahead of us and exploded. We ran along the track into the trees and took shelter near a big rock.

By morning the storm had passed. We wandered back the way we came, trying to find the main road again. Trudging around boulders and skirting prickle bushes and weaving between the trees like two ants along an invisible bread trail. When we reached a deep gorge, I knew we were lost. Lilly wanted to forge ahead, but the wind was bitter and my fingers and feet were numb. My legs gave out, and I crumpled to the ground. Lilly flopped beside me. She was trying not to cry, but tears made lines down her dusty face.

"Frankie, we're going to die and it's all his fault."

"Don't be ridiculous," I mumbled. "No one's going to die."

Lilly tilted back her head and rasped at the sky. "I hope you're happy, you rotten bastard!"

If only she'd shut up. Her voice gives me a headache. I've put up with her whingeing and whining and carrying on for the last twelve months and I'm sick of it. Sometimes I wish I'd plunged the knife into her stupid neck, instead of poor Ennis's.

MONDAY, 1ST JUNE 1953

I can barely write, I'm so cold. My teeth chatter and my fingers are as stiff as the twigs that poked into my ribs last night and kept me awake.

Lilly made a campfire, but it fizzled out. We huddled together for warmth, but still froze half to death. I want to go back to Ravensong. Our bed was cosy, and there was a load of firewood for the Warmray. Veggies in the garden and eggs from the hens. At least we'd be warm and fed. Lilly says no. If we return, the authorities will find us and hang us for murder.

"We lived there for five years," I reminded her, not bothering to hide my irritation. "No one found us. Why are things any different now?"

She didn't answer. Just tipped back her head and glowered silently up at the midnight sky.

70

ABBY

Folding the pages, I looked across at Lil. My heart ached for her, for the young girl she had once been. All that trauma and fear. Living under lock and key in the attic, and her sister's betrayal—no wonder her young mind had fragmented itself as she struggled to cope with everything that happened. I was trying my best to understand. But mostly I was struggling with the horror of what she'd done. To those other girls. Almost to me. Most of all, to Alice. How had someone who cared deeply about the welfare of women fallen so far?

Lil was watching me with tiny eyes, her face chalk-white.

"When I woke next morning, Frankie lay still. I tried to rouse her, but she was gone. Whatever finally took her—the head injury or the bitter cold—I'll never know. I sat with her all day. Talking to her. A slipstream of words that barely made sense. You can be with Ennis, if he makes you happy. I won't say anything, Frankie. I won't tell. Of course I won't, I never intended to anyway. I just wanted you to return home with me so I wouldn't have to face our mother alone. Once upon a time,

357

we'd been friends. The very best of friends. We shared all our secrets and dreams, our plans for the future. Somewhere along the way, we turned against one another."

"You buried her there."

She shifted on the bed and nodded.

I leaned forward. "Where Roy Horton found you."

Lil glanced over, lines creasing her brow. "The boy ran away. A man came back. He found some heavy rocks and put them on Frankie's grave. He said that way, the animals would leave her alone."

"Oh, Lil."

"Sometimes I hear her voice. When the moon is high and the stars shine bright, she speaks to me."

"What does she say?"

"She says the person it's always hardest to forgive is yourself. But Abby—" She exhaled softly. "I don't think it's possible to forgive what I've done."

Lil once told me that anything was possible if you wanted it badly enough. My lips parted to remind her of this, but the words jammed in my throat. An image of Shayla flew into my mind. The way she'd been standing outside the logger's hut, inspecting her blood-caked toenail. Her gaze had drifted back to the doorway, and she shuddered. My heart broke for her. I knew what she was thinking right then, because I'd been thinking it too. Part of her stayed trapped inside that dark place and always would.

Lil was right. Some things you could never forgive.

"Another girl got away," Lil murmured. "At least I'm thankful for that."

"Another girl?" Did she mean Shayla—or someone else?

Oh, it's you. All grown up.

A flash came to me. I was twelve again, locked in the dark

cavelike place where three days had already passed in a terrifying blur. The door shrieked open, and I cowered as a painful brightness blinded me. Someone called into the darkness, their voice barking harshly like a bird's cry. Or had I only imagined it? I ran out into the sunlight, my eyes streaming as I stumbled away into the trees.

"It was me, Lil. You opened the door for me. Same as you opened the door for Shayla today."

Lil searched my face, tears spilling down her cheeks. "I'm sorry, my dear. So deeply sorry."

My chest constricted, and I slid back into the darkness. As a kid, I had hidden behind a hickory bush and let my best friend go to the reserve alone. Shayla's mother, bitter and downtrodden by life, had almost let her daughter slip away. Ennis and Frankie, so desperate to build the family they never had, had destroyed themselves. Did fate exist, a giant cog in the wheel of life leading us towards the inevitable? Or could we control our own destinies by simply making better choices?

Lil crept her hand across the quilt towards me. "Abby?"

"What, Lil?"

"Will you sit with us? Until—"

A lump wedged in my throat. I didn't answer, just took her hand. As the silence settled, I whispered goodbye to my friend. The woman who had taken me under her wing and shown me the love and acceptance I'd always craved, yet whose actions—known to her or not—had caused such devastation.

The person it's always hardest to forgive is yourself.

Somewhere, a clock ticked. My tears turned cold on my cheeks. I sat frozen among the shadows, not wanting to move. Vaguely I noticed the distant rumbling of a car motor, but just as quickly dismissed it. The room was dark, almost cavelike.

My gaze drifted over to the door. It was open. There was

nothing keeping me here now. I should go. Call someone, explain what happened. I tried to stand, but my body wouldn't move. My limbs felt small and fragile, my bones brittle as a bird's. Or a child's.

I shut my eyes.

If I listened carefully in my mind, I could still hear her singing. Her voice was frail and rusty, hauntingly beautiful as it echoed through the night. It wove a spell around me and kept me here in the dark, where it felt strangely safe. Her voice, the voice of my captor, leaving a ghostly trail around me in the stillness.

71
TOM

"Abby?" Tom limped along the path towards the house. The place was in darkness, but Abby's car sat in the driveway behind Lil's Forester, so they were here. At least he hoped they were.

"Abby, it's me. Everything okay?" He hauled himself up the back steps and across the verandah. It felt good to move without his crutches and brace, despite the pain. He was his old self again, the one who'd slept under the stars and wrangled snakes and tasted true freedom. The one who'd do anything to protect the woman he loved. "Abby?"

The back door was open. He knocked, and then ventured into the darkness, breathing the sweet scent of custard and apples.

On the drive out here, he had told himself she was all right. Abby was capable and strong. She could handle anything. But Duncan had sounded so worried on the phone earlier. Almost panicked. *She left the hospital a few hours ago, Tom. Is she with you, is she okay?* Abby's brother had just started night shift when another nurse mentioned an injured teenage girl. Duncan

361

went to see Shayla who told him Abby rushed off in a hurry as soon as her mum arrived. Tom knew she'd come out here. Finding Shayla would have triggered her old fears. It made sense she'd come to Lil and Joe's, to find comfort with the people who loved her. If only it didn't sting so much that she hadn't come to him.

"Lil?" His voice echoed in the stillness. "It's Tom Gabriel, are you about?"

He found the light switch and blinked in the sudden brightness. Dishes sat neatly in the drying rack. Roses on the table, everything in order. He tried to ease the kink out of his shoulders. Tried to tell himself it was probably nothing. But the silence was eerie, unsettling. Not even a TV going or radio, no quiet murmur of voices. Nothing. So why couldn't they hear him calling?

"Joe, mate? It's me, Tom. Are you here?"

He reached the hallway. There was a glow at the end.

He made his way towards it.

The door was open.

Lil and Joe were in bed, bathed in soft lamplight. He eased out a sigh. They'd fallen asleep with the light on, that was all. He went to close the door, when a third figure caught his eye. She sat like a statue at the bedside, staring down at her hands. If she'd heard him calling before, she made no sign.

"Abby?" His whisper echoed softly in the stillness. When she didn't reply, he took a step into the room. "Hey, it's me. You okay?"

What was wrong with her? Surely she wasn't still mad at him about those stupid things he'd said about the botched article? He glanced at the bed again. Lil and Joe were too still. A prickle of musty air swirled around him and he shivered. He moved to Joe's side of the bed and gently patted the old man's shoulder.

"Joe?" There was no response, no rise and fall of breath. Beside him, Lil looked just as peaceful. Just as still.

Abby looked up, the lamp glow touching her face.

Tom cursed softly and rounded the bed in a few strides, kneeling in front of her, gathering her icy fingers into his hands. Grime and tears streaked her cheeks, and she'd bitten her lips raw. Her eyes were red-rimmed, huge and shining as she finally looked at him.

"Tom?"

He had no words to offer, just an urgency to wrap her up, hold her safe. He got to his feet, feeling his leg bones grind, and dragged her into his arms. She sank against him, as if the strength had drained from her body.

"They're gone, Tom."

"What happened, were you with them?" He looked at the bed, and something in him softened. "Both of them together. What are the odds, eh?"

"It wasn't an accident, Tom. They ... Lil, I mean. She—"

Abby's knees buckled, and Tom caught her. He lifted her into his arms and carried her out of the room, down along the hallway and through the brightly lit kitchen. When the cool outside air hit them, Abby pressed her face into his shirt and clung to him.

He got her down the stairs, but when he started along the pathway to the cars, she wriggled out of his arms and stood facing him. Her eyes blazed, as if the cold air had woken her from a terrifying dream.

She frowned. "Why are you here, Tom?"

"Your brother rang me from the hospital. He was worried. The police want to talk to you about Shayla. I tried to call but your mobile was out of range. I rang Lil, thinking you might have come here, but the line was out. So I drove over."

"Drove?" She looked down at his legs. "Where's your brace?"

"Devil of a thing to drive in. It's back at the house."

"But your legs ..."

"Abby, forget my legs. I can see you're not okay. How can I help?"

She glanced up at the house, then her face crumpled. She didn't cry, but grasped his hand and led him to the steps.

"Are you still a good listener?"

Tom lowered himself onto the steps, pulling her down beside him.

"The best."

She inhaled a shaky breath, and then let it all out in a rush. Frankie's diary, and her confrontation with Lil under the pine trees. How she followed Lil and finally found the logging hut and rescued Shayla. Coming back here and saying her painful last goodbyes.

"I trusted her, Tom."

"Jeez, Abby. I'm sorry."

"She couldn't remember doing any of it. At the end, she had flashes. I want to hate her. After everything she did, I really want to hate her—"

"But you can't."

"Not yet. Maybe when it all sinks in."

"She was your friend."

"She killed those girls, Tom."

"Are you absolutely sure it was her?"

"She knew where to find Shayla. She unlocked the hut door. Shayla recognised Lil's car, she remembered getting into it. It destroys me to say it, but there's no doubt in my mind it was her."

Tom blew out a breath. The pine trees creaked overhead in the darkness and he gazed up at them. "Abby, if it makes you feel any better, the Lil you knew wasn't the same Lil who committed those crimes. I'm not justifying what she did, far from it. Joe said she suffered from psychogenic amnesia. Possibly it was more than that."

"What do you mean?"

"It's like she fragmented into two distinct personalities. The gentle Lil you knew, and the hard one you encountered in the bush that night. A split usually happens when someone can't process trauma, so a second identity appears who's better equipped to cope with it." He blew out a breath. "I've researched identity disorders for my books. As far as I know, people who split don't usually re-enact their trauma on others. They're not usually violent at all. It's a popular trope in the movies, but not in real life. I just don't get it."

"She said she was sorry."

"She would have been devastated."

"She was."

He glanced over his shoulder into the house. The kitchen light still blared. The table with its cheerful cloth and vase of roses looked so peaceful and inviting, that for a moment the nightmare seemed an impossible mistake. If it hadn't been for Abby's hunched form on the step beside him, he could almost believe that none of what she'd told him tonight was real. He looked back at her, intending to draw her closer and offer comfort, but something about her had changed. She sat stiffly now, ramrod straight.

He took her hand. "Come back to Ravensong with me,

Abby. Stay in your old room, if you like. Best if you're not alone tonight, eh?"

"No, Tom. I'm going home. To the cottage."

He tried to smile. "Mind if I join you?"

She pulled her hand free and clenched it in her lap. "I'm fine, really. I just want to be alone right now."

"At least call your brother. He's worried about you. And if I can help in any way—"

"There is one thing." She got to her feet, not looking at him. Not looking at the house. Her gaze sliding away to the shadows. "I'll be pretty busy from now on. It might be best if we don't see each other anymore, Tom."

"You shouldn't be alone, Abby. Not tonight. We don't have to talk. Just let me be there for you."

Her face was stony, as if she hadn't heard him. Tear-tracks streaked the grime, her face puffy and her lips bitten raw, but the steel in her eyes was unmistakable.

"See you, Tom."

He stood and watched her walk away. Watched her climb into her car and drive out of his life.

He wasn't okay with her being alone.

He wasn't okay with any of this.

But if Abby wanted him to stay away, then he would respect her decision.

After what she'd been through today, she would need time to heal. To let the scar tissue grow over her heart. To process what had happened and make her peace with it. As much as he wanted to safeguard her and fight her demons for her—he also understood that she needed to face them on her own terms.

7²
ABBY

SIX WEEKS LATER

AS WINTER SETTLED IN, the air turned icy. I shivered outside the courthouse, my scarf wound tight under my chin. Bare branches poked the sky, and an icy breeze scuttled leaves along the deserted footpath.

I clutched the small book to my chest. Once the police had scanned the contents of Frankie's diary into their database, it had come back into my possession. A closed court hearing deliberated over the evidence, as well as testimonies from those who'd known Lil, and of course my account of her time at Ravensong. They agreed she had been suffering from prolonged PTSD, because of her kidnapping as a child and the consequent traumatic death of her sister.

On the strength of this evidence, they released Jasper Horton. Although the compensation he received would never restore the time he'd lost, Jasper, at fifty-one, was now a free man.

I left the shadows and walked into the bright sunlight. The indistinct sound of voices made me look back. Two figures emerged from the rear of the courthouse and hurried towards a battered Hilux parked on the kerb. The border collie tied in the tray began to jump and yelp at the sight of them.

Roy Horton stopped to light a cigarette, brushing ash off his grey suit. He looked up at the man beside him and patted him on the shoulder. Jasper stood taller at the contact. He looked over to where I stood and pushed up the bill of his base-ball cap, then lifted his hand in a wave, friendly and somehow uncertain. Beside him, Roy nodded over.

I unclenched my fingers from the diary and waved back.

My pulse fluttered like a damaged bird, still trapped in the cage of my old fearfulness. I had been wrong about Jasper, we all had, and it would take some time to soak in. The logic-loving hemisphere of my brain knew he wasn't responsible for my nightmares—or for Alice and Shayla, and the other girls—but the emotion hemisphere needed time to catch up.

The men climbed into their ute and sped away.

I drove home, wanting only to shower away the day and forget. But I had one last thing to do. Out in the yard, I made a pile of newspaper and kindling in my old brick barbecue and set it alight, waiting until the fire blazed up and became hot enough. Then I took out Frankie's diary.

I crouched in front of the flames, gripping the tattered book in my hands. Already in my mind I could see it burning. See the pages with their familiar handwriting curling and turning black, and then collapsing into ash and puffing out of existence. Tom's question drifted back to me. What makes a good person do bad things, and a bad person go beyond normal human experience and commit the unthinkable? I couldn't answer that, but maybe Frankie had come close. *Lilly's always been needful and intense ... without me at her side to keep her anchored, I fear she'd burrow too far into herself and disappear.*

Despite what Lil said about being happy at Ravensong, it was a dangerous sort of happiness. In the end, they had all paid a heart-breaking price for it.

A price some of us were still paying.

My brother always said remember the good times. Stop torturing yourself over the bad. One day, I would remember the swans and the riverweed and the smell of strawberry tarts. And the tall elegant woman with a smile like sunshine, twirling in the doorway wearing a hand-dyed gown she refashioned herself. One day, I would remember it all with a forgiving heart.

But that day was not today.

"Goodbye, Lil," I whispered, and threw the diary into the flames.

AT THE FLORIST I chose the biggest, most glorious bunch of flowers they had—roses and gerberas and orchids probably transported from far north Queensland, laced with leafy sprigs of white wattle. I bought a cheesecake at the bakery for good measure and then drove over to Green Street, where Alice's mother still lived alone.

"I think about her every day," I told Helen, shifting my weight on the soft cushions of her cane sofa. Rays of afternoon light glowed through her sunroom window, warming the chill that had taken hold of me earlier at the courthouse. "I'm so sorry for what happened to her."

Helen unwrapped the cheesecake and set out two plates. "Me too, Abby."

"I still dream about her. Not every night, but most." I hadn't come here seeking forgiveness, but the cosy warmth of Helen's smile loosened my tongue. "Please don't hate me, Helen. But I have to confess something horrible. It was my fault Alice was at the reserve that day. We planned to go looking for the cave, but I bailed on her. So she went alone."

Helen stopped slicing the cheesecake and lay down the knife. She came over and sat beside me, taking my hand.

"I blamed myself, too. I guess it's what we do, when we lose someone we love."

"I'm so sorry."

"Oh, love. It wasn't your fault. My Alice was loyal and funny and kind. She would have wanted to help. But she was also a stubborn little mule. I could lecture till I was blue in the face, and she'd march off regardless and do her own thing."

"But if it wasn't for me—"

"If it wasn't for you, Alice would have been miserable. Having you as her friend made her the happiest I'd ever seen her. She idolised her father, and our divorce broke her heart. Meeting you was the best thing that could have happened to her."

Tears rolled hotly down my face. How could that be true? Helen should be railing at me now, showing me to the door. Telling me never to darken her house with my presence ever again.

Instead, she slid her arm around me and rested her head against mine. "I'm glad you told me, Abby. I'm so proud to hear how much my daughter wanted to help you. And I'm proud of you for getting through such a godawful ordeal and staying a good person. That takes a lot of courage. Most of all, I'm grateful you still think about her and even dream about her sometimes. Alice would have loved that."

<h1 style="text-align:center">73</h1>
<h2 style="text-align:center">ABBY</h2>

WHEN A FIST HAMMERED my front door, I set aside my teapot and scuffled out in slippers and pyjamas to see who it was, assuming it was probably my brother. It wasn't.

Tom held a glorious bouquet—giant peachy pink chrysanthemums nodding dreamily from an assortment of fresh leaves and perky white waxflowers. I took it from him, inhaling the sweet peppery scent of the bush.

"What's the occasion?"

"Just wanted to say congrats on your feature article about Deepwater. It's a stellar piece, Abby. It really tugged the old heartstrings. Well done."

"Thanks, Tom."

He gestured at the flowers. "I was going to leave them on your doorstep, but I saw the light on and hoped maybe—" He cleared his throat and shrugged. "Well, you know."

I hid my smile in the flowers. "They're gorgeous."

He hesitated, searching my face. Was he trying to gauge my reaction to his unannounced arrival? Could he see the flush of warmth rushing into my cheeks? Hear the thump of my pulse?

He dipped his head to catch my eye. "Editor, hey? You totally deserve it. Poor old Kendra resign, did she?"

"Not exactly. The network thought the paper was becoming too sensational. Not reflecting the values of the community. So they sacked her and offered the position to me."

"Sweet."

"Yeah, it really was."

"You deserve it, Abby. The sky's the limit, eh?"

I hadn't seen him since Lil and Joe's funeral. He had held my hand during the brief service—or rather, I had clung to his —but when it was over he quietly left. I was grateful for the space. Space to think and grieve. For Lil and Joe, but also for my father. My mother, too. And for Alice. I wasn't exactly at peace, not yet. But Helen Noonan's words had touched me deeply. *Meeting you was the best thing that could have happened to her, Abby.* My dreams were getting sweeter, and the scars on my heart were healing. I was writing a feature article about the lost girls of Deepwater, the ones whose remains were never identified. The road ahead of me would be rocky. Strewn with the debris of old fears and insecurities waiting to ambush me. But for the first time in my life I felt equipped to travel it.

I hugged the flowers, breathing in the familiar bush perfume that wafted from them. A hot prickle dampened my eyes, but I blinked it away.

"They smell like Ravensong."

Tom swayed forward. "Those big leaves are from our magnolia tree. The one we camped under."

"Oh." I drew back, my skin suddenly flushing. "I'm making a cuppa. Want one?"

"Thought you'd never ask."

I gestured him in. "Welcome to my devious little corner of Hicksville."

He smiled lopsidedly as he stepped inside. He was taller than he'd been on crutches, despite the faint limp. The shadows under his eyes were gone, and he'd actually shaved.

I shut the door and hurried off in search of a vase. Tom followed me into the lounge room. I arranged the flowers on the dining table and set the kettle to boil. Then I stood, hand on hip, waiting for him to speak.

He checked his watch and gazed about, then checked his watch again.

My mood deflated. Did he have somewhere to be? Who brought a girl the most spectacular flowers of her life, only to stand around eyeing his watch? I had half a mind to kick him out. Was I so dismal at reading the signs that I'd misinterpreted his reason for coming here? I slumped, my chin jutting. He was tying up loose ends, wasn't he? Bringing me flowers to sweeten what was coming—The Talk. *It's been nice knowing you, but now that things are all weird and awkward between us, it might be best if we parted ways. Permanently.* The exact thing I had told him outside Lil and Joe's that night. So why did it hurt so much?

Tom wandered over to the television. He switched it on and cranked up the volume, then settled on the sofa and patted the cushion next to him.

"Take a seat."

I gritted my teeth and wandered over. Really, now he wanted to watch television? Then I stopped in my tracks, staring at the screen. Was that Tom? My mouth dropped open as the camera panned back to show him sitting on a platform opposite an attractive, middle-aged female presenter. I tore my attention away and looked at him.

"What in blazes?"

Again he patted the seat. "Just sit, will you?"

I flopped onto the cushions. "Tom, what's going on?"

"Shush." He laughed, putting his finger to his lips. "You'll miss the good bit."

For the next twenty minutes, I sat in gobsmacked silence. Tom talked about his early struggles as a young writer before he got published, and how it felt to have his books adapted for film. How sudden fame pushed his limits as an introvert, which led to him abusing alcohol. His doomed marriage, his failings as a husband, and how hurt he'd been when his journalist wife had retaliated by publicly humiliating him via the media. And how recently, he had learned to move on. Life was looking up. He had finished a novel that his publisher loved, and he'd started another.

To wrap up, the interviewer leaned over and asked, somewhat flirtatiously, if Tom was seeing anyone.

"There is someone," he told her. "Someone I'm crazy about. Who I might even love. Who I *do* love," he amended. "But me being me, I said a bunch of stupid things that I deeply regret. I only wish it wasn't too late to take them back."

The interviewer asked if, given a second chance, he'd do anything differently. Tom nodded. "I'd trust her. Absolutely and completely. And I'd make sure this time I was worthy of her trust."

The show finished, and Tom switched off the TV.

I stared at him. "You just bared your soul on television."

"Yup."

"The writer most notorious for his refusal to be interviewed?"

"Uh-huh."

"On the same show that approached you years ago, and you

responded by smashing the cameraperson's very expensive equipment?"

Tom grimaced. "Not my proudest moment."

"So what changed? I mean, the Hermit of Ravensong exposes all on national TV?"

"Hermit, well, yeah. Fair enough."

"But why, Tom?"

"I knew you felt responsible for Kendra's article. And when you stayed away, I finally realised that was why. You were scared of the media making a meal of me. So I got in first and bared it all before the swarms had a chance to."

"You did it for me?"

"Abby, I never blamed you for what Kendra did."

"You should have," I mumbled. "I have a confession to make, Tom. I left all my research notes on the disk I gave her."

Why was he smiling? He should be storming to the door right about now, vowing never to see me again. And I would have totally understood.

He shrugged. "That explains how she knew so much."

"Why aren't you mad at me?"

He reached for my hand, but didn't take it. Just brushed his fingers lightly along my wrist.

"Because you're the best thing that ever happened to me, Abby. And I meant what I said just now in the interview—that I love you—and I just wish I knew how to win your trust again. Any ideas?"

"You love me?"

"Madly. And I think it started that day you climbed through the window for me. I still have the scar." He rotated his arm and tapped his elbow. "I think of you every time I see it. Which is every day."

"Romantic."

"I thought so."

"For what it's worth, Tom. I sometimes think of you, too."

He smiled crookedly and huffed. "I don't know why you bother with me, really. When we met, I was a bear with a sore head. I shut myself away from life because I feared getting hurt again. You were right about me. I was protecting my safe, lonely little world. Then, when you came along ... I fell hard and fast. For a while, everything seemed good."

"Until the article. With my byline."

"It was just a bunch of words, Abby. The first time it happened, all those years ago, I crumbled. My life fell apart. This time?" He leaned closer, searching my eyes. "I missed you so damn much I barely noticed anything else. But it wasn't just the article, was it?" He collected my fingers, his touch feather-light on my skin. "I know you're still hurting after all that's happened. Lil and Joe were your friends. Especially Lil. You loved her, and then you had to discover what she'd done. To those other girls. To Alice. And all those years ago, to you. You're still reconciling all that, I understand. So I tried to cheer you up. Distract you a little by—"

"Baring everything on TV?"

"Yeah. Did it work?"

"Absolutely."

He bit his lip and smiled. "I guess what I'm really trying to say is this. If you ever need a friend, or a sparring partner, or even just someone to annoy, then my door's always open."

He kissed me on the cheek, then rose and crossed the room to the door. At least I'd gotten one thing right in my article— my real article. He was kind of magnificent. In the doorway he looked back. He searched my face for the space of a few heartbeats, and then tipped up his chin in a last farewell and slipped out.

I sat very still.

My mind whirled with everything he'd said. During the televised interview. And then afterwards to me. *You're the best thing that ever happened to me, Abby. I love you, and I just wish I knew how to win your trust again.* Something had shifted between us, but I couldn't place it. Tom hadn't changed, not really. He was still my cranky, funny, wonderful Tom. But he had pulled down the barricades surrounding his heart and let himself come back to life.

Wasn't it time I found the courage to do the same?

In my bedroom, I pulled on my jeans and boots and dragged my overnight bag from under the bed. Tom's flowers had already filled my cottage with the scent of Ravensong, and as I packed my things I breathed it in.

You're the best thing.

I went out to the lounge room and grabbed the flowers, then ran outside, kicking the door shut behind me.

Tom was reversing out of the driveway.

I waved, squinting against the headlights as I hurried down the slope. The ute rolled to a stop on the kerb. Tom buzzed the window down and leaned over.

"Everything okay?"

"Just dandy."

I hauled open the passenger door and climbed in, settling my bunch of bush flowers in the cavity behind my seat. Then I looked over at Tom's gorgeous, mystified face.

"Lil said something the day she showed me the swans. It's not love that makes a person weak, but fear. I think I've been afraid all my life, Tom. Because of fear, I lost my best friend. And I let my dad slip away without telling him that in those dark days after my abduction, his belief in my story—in me— was the only thing that gave me courage. I married a good man and then broke his heart. All because I was afraid. Of getting trapped again, of losing myself. But that old loggers' hut didn't trap me and ruin my life. It was my fear. And now I'm ready to let it go."

Tom's eyes gleamed in the dash lights. "Sounds like a plan."

"You know, a wise man recently told me if I ever needed someone to annoy, then his door's always open."

"The offer still stands, Abby. Always will."

I slid my arm around his neck and pressed close, kissed him on the mouth. "Hey, you."

He rested his forehead against mine. "Yup?"

"You're the best thing that's happened to me too, Tom. Besides, I'm missing Ravensong like crazy. You wanna get out of here?"

He looked at me for the longest time and then smiled. "That's possibly the greatest idea I've ever heard."

DEAR READER

Thank you so much for reading UNDER THE MIDNIGHT SKY—I hope you enjoyed it! If you did, please consider telling your friends and family, and leaving a quick review on the store where you bought it. I'd be very grateful, as reviews help get the attention of other readers.

If you'd like to learn more about me and my other books, check out my website at annaromer.com

Happy Reading!

ACKNOWLEDGMENTS

This book was first published in 2019 by Simon & Schuster (Australia). Since then I've given it a facelift—inside and out—and would like to acknowledge the people who helped and encouraged me along the way.

A big thank you to Selwa Anthony who put a lot of thought and work into the first edition, and who has been a wonderful inspiration to me for many years. This book is for you, Selwa. Thanks as well to my awesome team at Simon & Schuster.

Russell Taylor for always believing in my dreams even when I forgot how to. My sister Sarah for all her behind-the-scenes work to keep me afloat. Honestly sis, you have my back in so many ways, I appreciate you beyond words! My sister Katie for being hilarious and inspiring, often at the same time.

My niece Hailey for her ingenious insights and editorial help. My nephew Luke for reminding us how fun it is to kick off our shoes at dusk and fly around on the maypole spinner.

A special thank you to my mum, Jeanette, for her wisdom and strength, which helped me through some rocky patches the year I wrote this. And also for her assistance with some tricky research questions, among them: "Mum, what did you use for toilet paper in the 1940s?" (You'll have to read Frankie's diary for the answer!)

And finally, a heartfelt thank you to my readers. Your encouragement and kind words touch me more than you know, and keep me striving to become a better writer with each book. My love and thanks to you all.
Anna, April 2023

ABOUT THE AUTHOR

Anna Romer is an internationally bestselling Australian author who writes mystery and romance, both historical and contemporary, with elements of paranormal woven in—ghosts, haunted houses, and fairytales.

She lives on the coast of North Eastern Australia and when she's not writing she's a keen gardener, knitter, bushwalker and conservationist.

You can learn more about Anna's books by visiting her website at annaromer.com

ALSO BY ANNA ROMER

The Outlaw's Daughter

Maeve & the Wolf

The Ghost of Briar Rose

Lyrebird Hill

Thornwood House

Beyond the Orchard